MW00416150

BAD FAE RISING

THE PARANORMAL PI FILES - BOOK THREE

JENNA WOLFHART

This book was produced in the UK using British English, and the setting is London. Some spelling and word usage may differ from US English.

Bad Fae Rising

Book Three in The Paranormal PI Files

Cover Design by Covers by Juan

Copyright © 2019 by Jenna Wolfhart

All rights reserved.

No part of this book may be reproduced in any form or by any electronic or mechanical means, including information storage and retrieval systems, without written permission from the author, except for the use of brief quotations in a book review.

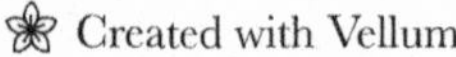

ALSO BY JENNA WOLFHART

The Paranormal PI Files

Live Fae or Die Trying

Dead Fae Walking

Bad Fae Rising

One Fae in the Grave

The Bone Coven Chronicles

Witch's Curse

Witch's Storm

Witch's Blade

Witch's Fury

Protectors of Magic

Wings of Stone

Carved in Stone

Bound by Stone

Shadows of Stone

Order of the Fallen

Ruinous

Nebulous

Ravenous

Otherworld Academy

A Dance with Darkness

A Song of Shadows

A Touch of Starlight

Dark Fae Academy

A Cage of Moonlight

A Heart of Midnight

A Throne of Illusions (Coming Soon!)

1

Lurking in the bushes of the Crimson Court's gardens, I watched the vampire. He lounged on the bench that had been named after Balor Beimnech's father, basking in the moonlight. If Balor knew the inky-haired vamp was here, he'd probably want to burn the intruder to a crisp. Hell, he'd probably want to do the same to me. I was on guard duty tonight—my very first actual guard rotation—and I'd let a vamp drift onto the grounds unseen.

I took a moment to size up the intruder as my legs groaned beneath me. I wasn't really used to squatting like some kind of overgrown frog for longer than a second, if even that. My thighs burned. He was tall, like most vamps, his raven hair long and drifting across his pointy shoulders like a curtain of pure silk. One leg was crossed over the other, and his hands were neatly tucked into a posh black overcoat, the kind that was popular with rich humans who lived in the countryside.

Vampire society was strange. Half of them were dirt poor while the other half lived in luxurious style.

Finally, I stood and rested my hand on the cool golden hilt of my sword. I didn't really want to fight a vamp, not when Balor's alliances were so important now. But I would if I had to.

He didn't even turn to face me as I approached. Instead, he continued to stare forward, his eyes locked on the ancient stone statue of the Morrigan—the powerful female fae who was reincarnated every time she died until her final untimely death nearly a century ago. Not a single muscle in the vampire's body clenched as my footsteps echoed around us. He'd been expecting me, it seemed.

"It's impolite to sneak into someone else's home," I said, striding to stand before him and block his view of the Morrigan.

He shifted his gaze to me, his black eyes rimmed in red. I tried not to look nervous about that fact. Red-rimmed eyes meant he was hungry. Of course, he couldn't really drink from me. With my half-shifter heritage, my blood would be poison in his mouth. Hopefully, he could smell it on me.

"Hello, Clark." He laced his hands behind his head and leaned back against the bench.

I stiffened, and my heart flickered a little in my chest. Huh. Maybe he could more than smell it on me then. "How do you know my name?"

"I know more than just the name you present to the world."

That was...ominous.

My mouth went dry. I flicked my eyes around the courtyard to make sure no one else was around. But it was the middle of the night. Except for two other guards patrolling the grounds, the fae of the Crimson Court were asleep. The courtyard sat in the center of the property, each wing of the building rising high around us. Most of the windows were dark. Only a few lit lamps shot up through the maze of bushes and trees and paved pathways, barely illuminating the shadowy courtyard.

We were alone.

"Look, I'm going to have to ask you to leave." I pushed back the bottom of my coat to reveal the sword hilt underneath, hoping that would have the effect I wanted.

He lifted an eyebrow. "You would risk the alliance by fighting me when I have done nothing but sit here and have a conversation with you?"

"You're trespassing, and you know it."

His thin lips twitched as he stood from the wrought-iron bench—despite the urban legends, fae were not allergic to iron at all. Sucking in a sharp breath, I dropped my head back to look up at him. He was a hell of a lot taller than I'd realised. Over six feet. His inky hair fluttered in the cool breeze.

"No need to worry." He shot me a glittering smile. "I will leave without the need for a fight."

Despite myself, relief shuddered through me as air whooshed from my lungs. I had improved a lot when it came to fighting skills, but I had a long way to go. And this vamp? I could tell just by looking at him that he was strong, powerful, and deadly.

"I just need to deliver my message first."

I narrowed my eyes. "Fine. What's the message?"

"I know who you are." A slow smile spread across

his lips. "I know your true surname is not Cavanaugh, and I know why you have hidden it from your new Court. I cannot imagine Balor Beimnech, Prince of the Crimson Court, would be pleased to know the truth."

My heart raced as my biggest fear took shape before me. "You're lying."

His eyebrows winged upward. "Am I?"

This couldn't be happening. Chest tight and palms slick, I stared hard at the vampire. His face was impassive, his body relaxed. He looked like this was nothing more than some calm, everyday discussion. Just another midnight chat that meant nothing at all. Like he wasn't holding my worst fear directly over my head.

I sucked in a deep breath and plunged my mind forward, desperate to know the truth. Maybe he was lying. Maybe he was just trying to get a rise out of me. Maybe he'd heard about the new initiate into Balor's House, and he wanted to see if he could ferret out some information about me.

Maybe Balor had sent him.

It was easy enough to get inside the vamp's mind. There were no walls, no boundaries to keep intruders out. I slipped inside and listened.

She's done well to hide it for so long. It's a shame that I have to hold it over her now. Cedric and Molly would be very proud—

I jerked out of his head and stumbled back, blood rushing through my ears. His words echoed over and over and over in my mind.

Cedric and Molly. Cedric and Molly. Cedric and Molly.

No.

No, no, no.

"Please, don't," I whispered to him, tears flooding my eyes. "Please don't tell anyone."

"You've found a home here," he said with a nod, his eyes flicking to my steel. "They've welcomed you into their Court. An interloper, unbeknownst to them. You've found purpose here. It would be a shame for you to lose it, for your Prince to cast you away from here."

I ground my teeth together. "What is it that you want?"

Because that was the only explanation for this. The vampire wanted something from me, and he knew I would give anything to him if that meant keeping my past a secret.

Basically, he was blackmailing me.

He took a step closer. "There is a dangerous, murderous rogue vampire on the loose in London. I need you to find him and kill him."

Say what now?

"What makes you think that I can—"

"I know what your power is, and your history as a private investigator." His red-rimmed eyes flicked down at the sword again. "You've become a good guard, but I know where your strengths lie. Finding missing things."

"Okay," I said slowly. "But don't think I didn't notice the whole killing part of the equation. That's not really my forte."

Since joining the Court, I'd been in my fair share of fights. I'd even killed a vamp, one who had been transformed into a member of the walking dead. That didn't mean I was going to become some kind of violent assassin though. I was good at ferreting out information, at discovering hidden truths. I could protect myself—sometimes—if that was necessary, but this was something else entirely.

It was murder.

"Well, Clark. You're going to have to make it your forte. Because if you don't, I will reveal who you are to every single fae of the Crimson Court. And then your new life will be over. You have until the end of the week."

He shoved a photograph into my hands, turned sharply on his heels, and began to walk away. A moment later, shadows enshrouded his tall form, and he was gone, leaving me alone with nothing else but the errant beating of my heart.

~

It took more than a moment for me to gather my wits. I'd just had a load of shite dropped onto my head, and I had no idea how in seven hells I was going to deal with it.

This much I knew: a mysterious vampire who could walk through shadows knew my secret. He was going to tell the world who I was if I didn't do exactly what he wanted. And, what he wanted was for me to kill someone.

My heart roared. I sat hard on the bench where I'd found the vamp, my gaze hazy as I stared numbly ahead at the statue of one of the Morrigan reincarnations. I didn't really know my fae history well, though I had started trying to learn. This Morrigan, with her cracked smile and hair down to her waist, was probably Alana, the second to last Morrigan to ever live.

Back in the 'olden days' there was always a Morrigan alive. When one died, another was born, but there hadn't been one for almost a century.

I glanced away, realising that I was trying to distract myself from the overwhelming urge to flee. It had been so long since I'd let myself think about what had happened all those years ago. I didn't want to think about it now, let alone let a arsehole vampire blow the whistle on me.

I had made a life here in the Crimson Court. At first, I'd wanted nothing more than to get the hell out, but it had begun to feel like home. I had a purpose. I had friends.

I had Balor.

Never in my life had I felt like I belong somewhere. But I belonged here.

I didn't want to leave.

Dammit. Tears poured down my cheeks as I stared down at the photograph. Curling my hands into fists, I knew I had no other choice. I was going to have to find the damn vampire and take him out of the equation. At least he was a murderer himself. At least I would be doing London a favour. And it was the only way to hold onto my life. It was the only way to keep Balor from banishing me away from his side forever.

Bloody vampires.

~

I drifted back into the building, eyes glazed. That was how I found myself smashed up against a very large, very muscular chest. Pain lanced through my skull as I knocked hard against him. Blinking, I stumbled back and found myself face-to-face with Balor. His scent washed over me: jasmine blossoms, oak moss, and patchouli. His visible red eye swept across me, surprise evident in his expression. And then he frowned.

"Must I remind you that on-duty guards should be focused and aware at all times?" His low voice rumbled from his chest, sending a wave of shivers across my skin.

Balor and I had a...complicated relationship. I wanted him, and he wanted me, but there was a pesky prophecy in the way of us ever consummating our desires. I mean, it could potentially end up causing his death and all.

Still, I couldn't just brush the desire away that easily. It wasn't something I could just turn off, even if he could.

"I was focused, thank you very much. Maybe you and your chest full of muscles shouldn't just appear out of nowhere."

His lips twitched. "Chest full of muscles, eh?"

"Don't act so cocky," I snapped, though I wasn't irritated in the least. Bantering with Balor made my hysteria ebb away. It made me feel as if my life wasn't spiralling out of control after all. Of course, it also reminded me of what I had to lose. Him.

"I'm glad I found you," he said, taking my elbow in his hand and steering me down the corridor. "The Circle of Night has called me in for a meeting, and I'd like you to come with me."

"The Circle of Night?" I frowned. That was the name for the wealthiest members of vampire society. I didn't have much experience with them myself. All the vamps who had hired me for PI work hadn't been lucky enough to have been turned by the rich. "Are you seriously telling me we have to go deal with more vampires?"

I realised a second too late what I'd said.

Balor shot me a frown. "What do you mean, *more* vampires?"

I stumbled over my next words. "Just that we've encountered quite a few recently. With the whole Sluagh business."

It was a weak excuse, but Balor seemed to buy it.

"Welcome to life in the Crimson Court, Clark. We have an alliance with the London vampires. That means we interact with them quite often."

So it seemed. Still, I frowned. What were the odds that a vampire sneaked into the Crimson Court to blackmail me the very same night that Balor was summoned to go speak to the Circle of Night? Seemed like pretty low odds to me. So, what the hell was going on? I'd agreed to find the vampire. I'd given in to the damn blackmail. Surely he wouldn't have ratted me out.

Right?

"Clark." Balor's deep voice broke through my thoughts. He rounded the dimly-lit corridor to stand before me, frowning. "Something is wrong. Your mind seems anywhere other than here. If you're attempting to read my thoughts again...you know that is a useless endeavour."

I gave him a weak smile and tried to find my way back to the banter. "So you say, but don't forget that I've overheard you once before."

His single eye narrowed. "Clark."

"I'm kidding. I'm not reading your mind. Just trying to figure out what the vampires could possibly want with us. Don't forget I killed that vampire Sluagh in the cemetery that night."

If they'd somehow found out...well, the alliance wouldn't be much of an alliance anymore. The deal between vamps and fae were this: we didn't murder each other. It was pretty simple, really.

"I don't think that's what this is about." Balor dropped his hand on my shoulder and squeezed. My breath stilled in my lungs as I ached to lean into his touch. "But just in case, we will take some backup. Moira and Duncan are coming with us."

That was great and all, but I didn't think it would do much good. The Circle of Night wasn't some small band of vamps that four fae could easily take down. There were hundreds of them, and they were strongest at night. Probably a good idea for me to take my sword.

2

The four of us stood on the pavement outside of the Circle of Night's headquarters. It was a tall and commanding building spiralling up into the dark, cloud-studded sky. Sections of the building jutted out overhead, rounded stainless steel bubbles that gave off a steampunk kind of vibe. Years ago, this building had been home to the global insurance markets. At some point, the vampires had taken over. No one knew how or why.

I was pretty sure it involved some blood.

Balor was dressed in an impressive black suit. It fit him perfectly, which meant that the outline of his corded muscles were more than a teensy bit visible through the expensive material. Duncan was decked out in a similar fashion. To be honest, I'd have to say Duncan looked kind of ridiculous. He looked like a tank in every day life. Now, he looked like an oversized kid playing dress up. He pulled at his collar, shifted in his shiny shoes.

Moira and I wore dark trousers and suit jackets.

Balor had tried suggesting we wear dresses, but we were pretty firmly in the "no" camp on that one. How the hell were we supposed to fight in skirts?

Vampires might be bloodsucking creatures of the night, but apparently they prized their dress code. For years, no one had ever been allowed inside the building unless they were wearing business professional attire. Something about wanting to keep the place as pristine as possible, but I was pretty sure it was just a way for them to seem wealthy and high class.

When we pushed through the front doors, it was all I could do not to gasp out loud at the magnificence of the building. Every wall of the towering central atrium was pure glass, providing a full view of the sparkling lights of the city. I'd heard about this place, but I'd never been able to imagine it until now. At night, the vampires basked in the glow of the city, and then black panels slid down over the glass at night, to protect their sensitive skin from sunlight.

In the center of the floor sat the Lutine Bell, held up by four dark columns. In front of it sat a bronze stand, with the Loss Book encased in glass. The vampires wrote every major loss in that book, each delicately written with a feather quill pen. When something good happened in the Circle of Night, the vampires would ring the bell twice. But when tragedy struck, the bell would only ring once.

I couldn't even imagine what it must feel like to hear that bell ring, and then wait, bated breath, for the other chime. And then the sinking heart when it never came.

A vampire with salt white hair smiled and strode

toward us. He, too, wore a pristine suit, only his was the colour of pearls. He was tall and slim, and every finger was decorated with golden rings that glistened underneath the sparkling lights that surrounded us.

"Balor," the vampire said with a purr in his voice, sticking out his hand at our Prince. "So nice of you to come on such short notice. And your associates."

"Matteo," Balor said, his voice sounding rough and raw next to the smooth silk of the head vamp. "I believe you've met my guards before, Moira and Duncan."

Matteo gave a slight nod and then inclined his head toward me in silent question.

"And this is Clark. She recently joined us." Balor didn't elaborate, and his voice was flat.

Matteo's red-rimmed eyes shot my way. His gaze was sharp and intense, as if he were trying to see underneath my skin. "Yes. Jonas mentioned her. We have you two to thank for his safety."

"Jonas was the vampire we found in the cellars beneath the Viaduct Tavern," Balor quickly said to me.

Ah, the good ole' Viaduct Tavern, which was currently in the process of being rebuilt. When Balor and I had gone up against a sorcerer transforming supernaturals into Sluagh, we'd found some trapped supes in the cellars beneath the pub. Balor's method of solving the situation involved burning the whole damn place down. I hadn't agreed, but Balor was Balor. Sometimes, he liked to burn things.

"Shall we head to my office? I'm afraid I have something rather important to ask of you. Your associates may join us, of course."

The vampire flashed us all a smile, one that put me a little on edge. Alliance or not, we were now in the den of the vampires. They could have easily set a trap, and we'd walked right on into it. At the moment, if they decided to attack us, the doors were right behind us. It was a quick and easy exit. Going further inside their den...

"I have to admit my interest is piqued," Balor said, falling into step beside Matteo as he led the way out of the central atrium.

We passed underneath the towering skylights and strode toward a dozen escalators that criss-crossed overhead. Matteo took us to the third one down, and we rode silently, passing clusters of vampires that shot inquisitive glances our way. Dozens more had strode toward the balconies of the floors above, watching us as we rose deeper and deeper into the heart of the Circle of Night.

I had so many questions about this place, but I bit my tongue. I'd have to ask Kyle, our resident computer whiz, later.

On the third floor, Matteo led us past a cluster of leather sofas, down a corridor, and into an expansive office with a breathtaking view of London. A pristine oak desk sat in the center of the marble-tiled floor. The rest of the room was empty, making the space feel cavernous, minimalistic, and intimidating.

"Now." Matteo laced his hands together and strode from one end of the room to the other. "We have a problem."

My heart began to beat a little harder. Had he found out about the vampire I'd killed in the cemetery? Neither Balor nor I had told a single soul, and my act of violence hadn't been witnessed by anyone else. No one else could know. Could they?

"If you have a problem, then *we* have a problem," Balor said.

Much to the annoyance of most of the fae population. Balor was one of the few Princes and Princesses to align themselves with other supernaturals. It had been the cause of more than one battle. And I was pretty sure that the past few fights were only the beginning.

Matteo stopped sharply. "One of my sons has been abducted. His name is Byron Graeme. He's the second to youngest, and he's always had a tendency to get himself into a bit of trouble. Unfortunately, it seems as though he's gotten himself into more than a bit this time. He's been missing since Sunday."

Balor frowned. "You believe someone would have the audacity to abduct one of the sons of the Circle of Night?"

"I wouldn't have believed it, no. However, one of my other members seems to be witness to it, though he refuses to speak of it aloud for fear my wrath will render him ceaseless."

Um. Okay then.

Balor's eye flicked my way, his expression unreadable. "What is it you wish us to do, Matteo?"

Matteo smiled. "I believe you already know, do you not? Even though you do not wish to admit it. I wouldn't either. Her power is most useful when one is not aware that it exists."

I wet my lips. Well, shit. He was talking about me.

Balor's expression did not change, but there was no mistaking the tensing of his shoulders.

"There are rumours," Matteo said by way of explanation. "Of a psychic in your midst. I assume that is why you brought her along, though I believe our alliance would ensure that she did not read my mind, Balor. Or I would be forced to retaliate."

Balor raised a single eyebrow. "Are you making a threat, Matteo?"

"I am merely saying that her presence here suggests that our alliance is not as firm as I believed it to be. However, I am willing to overlook it. If you help me find my son."

Balor nearly growled. Matteo's eyes glittered.

Two powerful supernatural leaders were facing off against each other, both vibrating with unspent energy. Balor Beimnech did not like anyone—and I do mean *anyone*—challenging his authority. But Matteo of the Circle of Night wasn't just anybody. He was the leader of the wealthy London vampires, just as strong and assertive (and probably stubborn) as Balor. He probably had secrets as deep as Balor did. Enemies who would want nothing more than to take him down.

I could see why he probably didn't like the fact that Balor had brought me along.

Clearing my throat, I lifted a hand. "If it helps, I haven't read your mind. Though it does sound like you might have something to hide if you're that worried I will."

Balor whipped toward me. "Clark."

I pressed my lips together, falling silent, but the corner of one end quirked up.

Matteo tsked. "Looks like you also need to get control of your guards."

"Clark is not wrong," Balor said with a frown.

"That said, we will help you find your son. I am going to pretend that you haven't threatened me, just this once. I have stuck my neck out, time and time again, in order to remain an ally with you. Do not make me regret that, Matteo."

Matteo's eyes glittered, and he gave a slight nod. "Very well."

The tall, suit-clad vampire strode over to his desk and pressed a button on his phone. A moment later, the door to his office cracked open. Three more vampires strode inside. Well, *strode* was probably putting it wrong. Two of them walked with purpose, but the third was hung up between them, his wrists tied to a broomstick.

His eyes were heavy-lidded, his cheeks gaunt. Bloody marks had been carved deep into his exposed stomach. I glanced away.

"He knows where my son is, but he refuses to talk," Matteo said, his voice loud and commanding. "I wish for your psychic to read his mind, and then for you to go and bring my son back here."

Sucking in a sharp breath, I glanced to Balor. His expression was grim. Balor knew how much I hated using my power as an interrogation technique. And this was definitely that. Hell, it looked liked they'd spent the past three days trying to pry this vamp's mind open. They'd clearly been torturing him. He could barely stand. For the first time since I'd heard about what Balor had done to bridge the gap between supernaturals, I wondered if this alliance was such a good thing after all.

Balor gave me a slight nod. I knew what he was

thinking, even if he was one of the only beings in the world whose mind I couldn't read.

He wanted me to do this. The alliance was at stake. With everything that had happened in the past few weeks, keeping peace with the vamps was more important than ever. Two of the Houses under Balor's rule were now without Masters, and Nemain across the pond wanted nothing more than to see his head on a spike.

As much as we wanted to avoid a war, the time would come when we would have to fight. And we needed as many on our side as possible.

Letting out a hollow sigh, I turned to Matteo. "You're going to have to question him when I get inside his mind. Otherwise, I might not hear what you need to know."

A strange smile flickered across Matteo's face. "Very well then."

I glanced at Balor one more time, then Duncan, whose expression was as unreadable as always. Finally, I met Moira's eyes. She gave me an encouraging thumbs up. She, too, knew I hated this, but sometimes, we had to make sacrifices for the Court.

I sucked in a deep breath and dove inside.

3

The vampire's mind was mush. Whatever they'd been doing to him had left him a husk of the creature he'd once been. It was easy to slip through his thoughts, though they shifted like sand through my mental fingers.

He wasn't thinking much of anything. They must have beaten the thoughts right out of his head. It wasn't until I heard the distant murmur of Matteo's silky smooth voice that bits and pieces of words began to drift through the vampire's muddled mind.

No, no, no, no, no! I don't want to talk about Byron the Bloody again.

Matteo was questioning him now. All he needed to do was steer the vamp's mind in the right direction, and it would be easy enough to get the information he wanted badly enough to threaten the alliance.

I pressed in a little deeper, waiting and listening.

He's in Leadenhall Market, but I can't tell him that. They'll kill me. They'll find out. No, no, no, no, no. I won't say. I won't say. I WON'T SAY.

His voice grew so loud that I could barely breathe around the reverberation in my skull. Sucking in a sharp breath, I yanked my mind out of his, my feet stumbling against the cool marble floor.

Matteo was staring intently at me when I raised my eyes, one perfectly-manicured eyebrow arched toward the lofted ceiling.

"That was very interesting," Matteo said coolly. "I have never seen a psychic perform until now. Your face..."

"It wasn't a performance," I said in a flat voice. The tortured vampire's inward voice had sounded scared, panicked. I couldn't help but wonder why, and a part of me didn't want to share the info with this head vamp.

Matteo's expression sobered immediately. "Tell me what you heard. Where is my son?"

I let a beat pass before I spoke. "Leadenhall Market."

"Leadenhall Market?" Matteo curled his hands into fists and snarled. "You're telling me that my son has been right around the corner this entire time? *You're telling me that*?"

This vamp was intense. Even *I* thought that, and I'd spent the past few weeks in Balor the smiter's presence. Sure, I could understand his frustration. His son was missing. But there was no need to shout at me like I was the enemy. Unless there was way more going on here than he'd shared…

"Matteo," Balor said, his tone a warning. "Do not yell at my fae."

Matteo's eyes were still fiery when he turned to my Master and my Prince, but his voice was measured and calm. "My mistake. You can understand why I might be on edge. Or would you? You have yet to sire a son, an heir. When you do, you will know what it is to feel a father's wrath."

My entire body froze, and my breath got stuck in my throat as I watched the two supernatural leaders stare each other down. Did Matteo know? He couldn't. Not unless he'd sought out Caer himself, and vampires *hated* prophecies. It was just a wild stab in the dark. Everyone knew Balor hadn't yet had an heir, and Matteo wouldn't be the first to wonder about it.

"Your anger should be directed toward the abductor, not toward me or my guards," Balor said quietly.

Tension peppered the air. For a moment, no one spoke. Finally, Matteo turned toward the guards holding his prisoner, and he flicked his fingers. They disappeared out the open door, and then shut it behind them with a click. As Matteo was turned away from us, I yearned to reach out and read his mind. Even if he was acting on father's wrath, there was something I didn't quite like about this whole thing. It was hard to trust him outright. But, I knew if I put even one pinky toe inside his head, he would know it. And then this whole thing would come crashing down, including the alliance.

Matteo turned back toward me and laced his hands behind his back. "So, my son is somewhere in Leadenhall Market. Did you happen to hear where?"

"I'm afraid not."

He turned toward Balor, arched a brow. "Perhaps you will find him sitting on the stoop of one of those shops."

"If he was abducted, that is highly unlikely," Balor

said. "Why would he be lurking around the market in the middle of the night? All the shops are closed. What would he be doing there?"

Matteo's face was an unreadable mask. "I'm afraid I haven't a clue. Perhaps you and your psychic can figure it out."

"We will need some identifying information," Balor said, voice still cold as ice. "You have a number of sons. I do not know what Byron looks like."

Matteo gave a nod, strode over to his desk, and rustled through some photos in his top drawer. After a moment, he strode back over to the group and handed the photo to Balor. My Master's eye flicked across the image, he gave a nod, and then passed it around to his guards. Duncan first, then Moira, and then me.

When I glanced down at the photograph, it took every ounce of self-control to keep my face blank and my body from falling flat on my arse. I had only just seen another photograph of this very same vampire an hour ago. With blurry eyes, I lifted the image closer to my face, just to make sure, my heart beating wildly. Yes, it was the same bloody vamp. There was no mistaking his violet eyes, his sleet gray hair.

Matteo wanted us to find and save the very same vampire that I'd been blackmailed to kill.

Balor seemed to notice the tension that was now wreaking havoc on my body. Hell, he could probably smell my sudden spike in adrenaline. I hated his power. It was sometimes even better than mine. All it took was the slightest of sniffs, and he knew exactly how I felt. "Clark, is there a problem?"

Breathing slowly, I looked up from the photo and pasted an uninterested expression on my face. I wasn't sure it was entirely believable. My heart was raging like a runaway bull, and my palms had gone slick with sweat.

"Just trying to commit him to memory, though that's not very hard," I said through clenched teeth. "I've never seen anyone with this colour hair before."

Matteo frowned and took the photo, slipping it back into the top drawer of his desk. "What is your plan here, Balor?"

Balor squared his shoulders. "My team will investigate the market. If and when we find something, we will let you know."

That seemed to satisfy the vampire. He strode over to our Prince and stuck out his hand. Balor frowned, but he took the vampire's long, slender hand in his and shook.

~

Once we were outside, Balor took the lead for our short trek from the Circle of Night's headquarters to Leadenhall Market. My head was spinning, my mind replaying everything I'd seen and heard that day. What in seven hells was going on? One vamp had come to me, demanding I kill Matteo's 'murderous' son or else he'd reveal my secret to the world. And then Matteo himself had demanded we save his 'innocent' son or else the alliance would suffer greatly.

Something strange was happening. The coincidence of the entire situation was way too much for any rational person to believe. But what exactly was it? And how the hell was I going to fix this? If I helped

Balor, the vampire would tell the Crimson Court about my past. But if I didn't help Balor, then his Court would find themselves without one of their most important allies at a time when they were on the brink of war.

I had no idea what I was going to do. Both of my choices kind of sucked. I could help myself and risk the future of the Court. Or I could help the Court and end up dead.

It was an impossible choice, and the only thing I could do was go along with the ride. I didn't have to make a decision until Matteo's son was standing right before me. For now, I'd help find the vamp. And, if we did, then I'd decide.

With a deep breath, I gave a nod to myself and continued through the streets with my fellow guards.

Moira cocked an eyebrow, falling into step beside me. "You okay? You kind of look like you've shit your pants, if I'm honest."

Moira and her ever-present bluntness turned my grim-set lips into a smile. "Something about Matteo felt off to me. He seemed like he really wanted to goad Balor, even though they're in an alliance. Plus, I wasn't a fan of the whole torturing thing he did on that vamp, even if his son is missing."

"Ah." Moira gave a nod of understanding. "Matteo is Matteo, I'm afraid. A vamp with power who loves his place in his world. He's not overly fond of Balor, even though they've made an agreement to work together against their enemies. Remember that Balor is more powerful. I think Matteo is probably threatened by that."

"So, if he's not so fond of Balor, then why did he make an alliance with him?"

"Because now he has something to hold over Balor." Moira and I passed underneath a streetlamp, the glow illuminating broken bottles and rubbish that littered the pavement. "Plus, it means the fae of London stopped fighting against him and his growing insurance market empire."

"And Balor?" I cocked my head toward our Master, still leading the way. "Why did he want to align with a vamp like that?"

Moira lifted her shoulder in a shrug. "I'm pretty sure for the reasons he's said. He doesn't want supes to be at odds anymore. He doesn't want us all fighting against each other, not when the humans are feeling so uneasy about our existence. He just wants us to survive."

We both went quiet after that. The only sound was our footsteps on the pavement, the heavy thud of boots. Over the tops of the buildings, the golden glow of the rising sun was beginning to light up the dark streets. It wouldn't be much longer before night was vanquished and a new day in London began. The streets would bustle with humans on their way to work; cars and buses would rumble by.

Vampires would have to head inside.

We turned the corner, and suddenly, we were inside the infamous Leadenhall Market. Curving beams rose high overhead, holding glistening skylights in the ornate roof. Every shop was painted the same: in vintage shades of green, maroon, and cream. Cobbled streets stretched out before us, leading to a wide variety of modern shops, restaurants, and pubs.

"We only have a few moments until full sunrise," Balor said, resting a hand on the hilt of his sword and frowning around at the very empty market. "Let's split up into twos and explore as much as we can. Meet back here when the sun is high. Clark, you're with me."

A thrill went through me, and my lips twitched with the desire to smile. Ignoring the flutter of my heart, I joined Balor as he began to move down the left-hand street. A part of me wondered if I should tell him about the vampire who was trying to blackmail me. Maybe I should just come clean. Maybe I could tell him instead of trying to hide it all. That would make this whole thing a hell of a lot easier, but...

He would demand to know what the vamp was using to blackmail me.

How could I tell him? How could I let my world get twisted upside down? How could I explain that I was the reason for all the horror he had to endure?

But how could I not?

"You seem on edge," Balor said in a low voice, his eye flicking around our surroundings for any sign of the missing vamp. "Your scent is...off."

"I don't like Matteo," I said.

I mean, it wasn't a lie. The meeting with Matteo had set me on edge, and not just because he'd ordered us to save the very vampire I also had to kill. The guy was a muppet.

"Sometimes we have to work with individuals we aren't fond of."

"I don't trust him."

Balor stopped, turning toward me. "Not every vampire in London is like Matteo. We ally ourselves with him as a way to ally ourselves with all of them. He's the leader of the Circle of Night. Until he isn't, he is who we must work with."

"I just don't want to see something happen to the Court because of him," I said in a rush of words. "I don't want him to be the reason everything falls apart."

Balor arched a brow. "Where is this coming from, Clark? Did you read something in his mind?"

My heart thumped. I didn't want to keep the truth from Balor anymore. I didn't want to hide things from him. So much had happened between us, it felt like a betrayal now.

But I didn't know how to tell him the truth.

I also didn't know how *not* to tell him.

"No, he made it pretty damn clear that I needed to stay out of his mind. Listen, I think I need to tell you something, Balor. It's something that I—"

"Wait." He held up a hand, his fiery eye zeroing in on something just behind me. I whirled on my feet, fully expecting to see the blackmailing vampire standing behind us, fangs bared.

Instead, I spotted a river of blood stretching across the cobblestone.

Balor moved around me and crouched beside the blood. He dipped his fingers into the red, and then lifted it to his nose. He frowned, and then stood.

"Supernatural blood," he said in a low voice.

"You can tell? How?"

"There's a hint of magic in it. Whether it's vampire or shifter or fae, I cannot tell." His frown deepened. "Though, after what we learned tonight, I'm guessing it is vampire."

4

After another half hour of searching Leadenhall Market, we returned to the Crimson Court empty-handed, unless you counted the dried blood on Balor's fingers. Until sundown, we wouldn't be able to make much more headway on the case, which meant that I wouldn't get much further on my issue either.

I only had a few days left before my entire world fell apart, and I still didn't have a clue what I was going to do.

We entered the expansive lobby of the renovated Battersea power station that the fae of London called their home. After the Sluagh fight and the fire, things were looking a little worse for wear, but the ever present chandeliers still sparkled like stars. The marble floors showed hints of the fire, small patches of black scattered throughout.

Elise strode up to us, her silver hair shining underneath the glow of the overhead lights. She pressed her lips together, her ever present smile now vacant for once. "I'm afraid I have some bad news."

I shot her a wry smile. "Of course you do. It wouldn't be the Crimson Court if we had some good news dropped on us after a bizarre night with some vampires."

I swore a whisper of a smile flickered across Balor's lips before his gaze turned as dark and serious as always. Always the Prince and the Master, Balor rarely smiled. "Tell me."

"Well, I hate to be the bearer of bad news." She grimaced. "Aed is here. He wants to talk to you about Fionn and Tiarnan."

"Right." Balor's shoulders tensed, and I could sense his power rippling off his body in waves. "We knew this was coming. Where is he?"

"He's in the Throne Room, with two more of the Fianna."

He gave a nod, and then began to march down the corridor in the direction of the Throne Room. "Clark, Moira, Duncan. You're with me. Elise, go find Cormac and tell him to be in the wings in case there is any trouble."

We followed Balor to the Throne Room. This was not a positive development, exactly. The Fianna were not going to be happy. In order to protect me from Fionn's death curse, Balor had burnt the Master of House Futrail to a crisp. Said Master had also been working with a sorcerer to raise an army of the dead. So, he definitely wasn't an innocent in all of this. His followers might not agree with that though.

Balor threw open the heavy doors of the Throne Room and strode down a long stretch of red carpet to his throne made of a thousand crimson skulls. Near the back of the monstrosity, I noticed a new addition. A lopsided thing in the shape of a cauldron. My lips twitched as I took up my space by his side. I'd given that skull cauldron to him, kind of as a joke. I couldn't believe he'd actually added the thing to his throne.

Aed and his two fellow warriors stood before us. The new leader of House Futrail was even larger than Fionn. He had thick shoulders and a wide waist, his trousers clinging tight to a massive pair of thighs. His hair was long and scraggly with a fuzzy beard to match. Beneath it all peered out a deep-set pair of orange eyes.

Balor had warned me about Aed. He looked powerful, yes, but not in a magical way. He just looked like a massive amount of brute strength.

Even though Aed had been the one to show up unannounced and demand an audience with Balor, he still inclined his head toward the Prince, showing the subservience always present in the Crimson Court, no matter what political manoeuvrings might be going on beneath the surface.

"Aed," Balor said, leaning back into his throne and shining his glittering eyes on the fae below him. "Tell me what I can do for you."

"I am here about what happened to Fionn." Aed's voice was deep and gravelly, his accent lilting just as Tiarnan's had. Just thinking of the fae warrior's name made my heart clench tight. He had betrayed me so horribly. I still hadn't forgiven him. I doubt I ever would. Tiarnan had pretended he'd wanted to get close to me. He'd *used* me to get information.

And then he'd turned on us all.

"It is a deep shame that Fionn has perished," Balor said slowly. "But he was a traitor to this Court and to Faerie as a whole."

Aed's eyes went sharp. "Should he not have had a trial then? Should he not have received his punishment from Faerie as a whole?"

"There was no time for that." Balor's voice was firm and even. I doubted it would stay that way for long. He was being patient with Aed for now, since he had lost a fellow warrior and a Master. He would clearly be mourning. But Balor did not like being questioned. And he certainly didn't like being challenged.

I'd kind of found that out the hard way.

"And what about our brother, Tiarnan?" Aed asked, his voice growing loud. "He has vanished without a trace. Did you condemn him to death without a trial, too?"

"Tiarnan decided to leave on his own account. I have no knowledge of where he went."

Aed went silent, scowling. After a moment, he finally spoke. "My House is not happy about what has happened. Fionn ruled us for centuries. He should have ruled us for a century more. We will not forget very easily."

And with that, Aed turned and strode out of the Throne Room, leaving the massive oak doors open after he and his two warriors had made their dramatic exit.

"Duncan," Balor said, keeping his gaze locked on the double doors. "Tell Kyle to keep an eye on them. I fear we haven't heard the end of this."

~

Balor stopped me on my way back to my room. He edged in front of me, blocking my path. "Clark. A word in my penthouse, if you don't mind."

He'd added the whole 'if you don't mind' to the end of that sentence, but he didn't mean it. This wasn't a question. It was an order. And I was too tired to argue. Sighing, I followed him up the curving staircase to his penthouse. Once inside, he poured me a gin and tonic before making a Scotch for himself. I settled in on the couch, but I couldn't relax, despite the comfort it usually provided.

Balor couldn't read my mind, but he knew me far better than anyone else. He knew something was wrong.

But instead of asking me about my strange reaction to Matteo, he surprised me by settling in beside me and turning his attention onto something else entirely. "What did you make of Aed?"

I took a soothing sip of the cool drink. "He looks like he spends a lot of time lifting heavy things."

The corners of Balor's lips tipped up. "That he does. Anything else?"

"I'm not sure." I took another sip. "He didn't stay very long before he stomped on out of there all dramatic-like."

Another slight smile. "It did seem like he rehearsed that, at least in his head."

I set down my drink and twisted toward him, doing my best to focus on the conversation rather than on the way his lips curled. Instead of the musky scent that threatened to drag me down into the depths of desire. Instead of the way his alluring power washed over me.

I cleared my throat. "He didn't bring up the fact that Fionn had temporary control over the Court. Do you think he doesn't know?"

"If he does, he's keeping the information close to his chest."

"Who gave Fionn that power anyway?" I asked with a frown. "I thought Faerie didn't have a central leader anymore."

"There is no central leader, but there is a council. They're spread far and wide these days, but they have the power to grant control of a Court to another Master, if it becomes necessary. Fionn lined everything up the way it needed to be. They just gave him the nod."

I took a deep breath, bracing myself for my next question. "Is Nemain on that council?"

I hated thinking her name. I hated saying it even more. It took me far too close to the edge of things I didn't want to discuss.

Cedric and Molly. Cedric and Molly. Cedric and Molly.

And it seemed Balor was the same. Immediately, his face clouded over.

"No. After what she did to my sister, she will never be on the council."

"She did a terrible thing," I said in a harsh whisper.

Balor's face hardened. "She did an *unspeakable* thing. And now she wants to take control of my Court, too."

I sucked in a deep breath. "Do you think she's trying to take control over *all* the Courts? She took over the Silver Court. Now, she's targeting yours. What if...what if it isn't about your alliances at all? What if her goal has always been to take control of all of Faerie?"

I expected Balor's expression to turn even darker. I expected to see the rage in his eye. Instead, he softened. He placed his hand on top of mine, traced his thumb across the delicate skin on the back of my hand. I shuddered in response, my entire body clenching tight.

"You are catching on quite quickly to the machinations of the faerie courts," he said in a low voice. "I am lucky to have you by my side, Clark."

Shivers coursed across my skin, and my heart leapt out toward his. His words only reflected everything I felt inside. I felt lucky to be by his side. I never wanted to leave it. And yet, I would have to. Unless I did the one thing that would only end up turning him against me.

Tears threatened to spill from my burning eyes. Slowly, I pulled my hand out from underneath his, even though I wanted nothing more than to curl up inside of his touch. "We can't do this."

"I know, Clark." He sighed, the weight of his role falling heavily onto his shoulders. "Trust me. I know. But sometimes, I want nothing more than to say damn the prophecy so that I can take you into my arms."

My heart thumped hard. Caer, the goddess of prophecies and dreams, was never wrong. What she foretold always came true. So, when she'd told Balor that his only son would one day be the death of him as well as the end of the Crimson Court, he'd had to listen. That meant he could never have sex again.

A fact that I was not too fond of myself.

"I will keep looking," he said softly, reaching out once more to take my hand in his. "I will never give up. Even if it takes me two hundred years, I will try to find a way to change the prophecy."

My body instinctively leaned toward him. I didn't even realise what was happening. One moment, I was staring into his eye, and the next, my arms were wrapped around his neck. Our lips crushed together. The heat of him enveloped me, and the scent of jasmine and moss flooded my senses.

Nothing else existed but Balor.

Nothing else mattered.

Not the damn blackmail. Not the damn prophecy.

All that mattered was his lips, his arms, his skin.

We pulled apart after what felt like hours, both of us clasping tightly to each other. My hands found his shirt, and I squeezed tight, dropping my forehead to his. He pulled a shuddering breath into his lungs and pulled back, his eye sparked with heat.

"Clark," he said in a low growl. "If you don't go now, I will not be able to control myself."

Slowly, I extracted myself from his arms, heart beating madly. We had to stop doing this. It wasn't good for either one of us. It only made me want him even more, it only made me get closer and closer to fully falling for him. And falling for him was too dangerous. For both of us.

"Maybe we should stop being alone together," I said in a whisper, cheeks flushed with heat. I wanted nothing of the sort, of course, but the more we kept doing this, the closer we would get to dancing across the edge of something we could never take back.

Balor closed his eye. "Maybe we should."

5

I only had a few hours of sleep before I had to fall out of bed and slip into my training clothes: loose-fitting gym trousers, a light tank top, and a pair of worn-out sneakers. Before Tiarnan had fled like the coward he was, he'd given me the name of a shifter in London who could help me get a handle on my powers.

Until recently, I'd never even come close to shifting, so I hadn't thought it was necessary to learn anything about that side of my heritage. But now, my powers came upon me unbidden, which was more than a little dangerous. I didn't know what type of creature I could transform into. For the safety of pretty much all of London, I needed to figure things out.

No one wanted a massive bear charging through the city streets, least of all me.

I slipped on a black leather jacket to keep warm in the early March air. Soon, London would begin to warm. Spring was on the horizon, and I'd have to take part in my very first Crimson Court changing of the seasons. That pretty much meant a massive party where every fae in London got drunk, and happy, and very, very frisky.

I would have to make sure to stay on the opposite side of the room from Balor.

Taking a deep breath, I pushed out of my room, jogged down the stairs, and out the front door of the building. I wasn't on duty until later, when we'd go out hunting for Matteo's son again. With everything so up in the air, and with my big decision looming, I needed something to do. I needed to keep myself active. Otherwise, I'd probably lose my damn mind.

My eyes squinted against the bright midday sun as I strode alongside the river path. Since joining the Crimson Court, I'd started rising earlier in the day, but I also spent more time out on the streets at night than I ever had before. I'd become accustomed to the way that the dark shadows fell across the buildings. The glare made me wish I'd picked up a pair of sunglasses.

After taking several turns, I found myself standing before an old warehouse of a building. Unlike the Crimson Court, this warehouse had not been renovated in the slightest. It looked old and abandoned and graffiti painted the rolling metal doors that were held shut by two padlocks the size of my head.

Frowning, I glanced at the slip of paper where I'd written down the address. This was it. My stomach dropped. If this was where the shifter lived, then did I really want to be taking lessons from him? Could I trust him?

Tiarnan had been the one to give me his name, after all...

Just as I'd begun to back up down the skinny alley, another set of metal doors began to roll up from the ground. A figure appeared, large and muscular with dark wavy hair that hit just past his shoulders. About twice as tall as I was, he looked as though he could crush a car in his bare hands.

He ducked underneath the half-rolled door and shielded his eyes with a petrol-stained hand. "You Clark?"

My stomach twisted as I contemplated turning heel and getting the hell away from here.

"Yeah. I'm guessing you're Ronan."

"You guessed right." He flicked his eyes up and down my body, and then he gestured for me to join him in the secluded warehouse. Which was very dark. And very hidden away from the rest of the world. Frankly, this whole thing seemed like a terrible idea. At least I had my sword, one he could probably break in half with his bare hands.

He stopped, cast a glance over his shoulder. "You coming or not?"

"Alright, but I want to leave the door cracked."

He chuckled underneath his breath and shook his head, not bothering to respond. Instead, he ducked underneath the metal door and disappeared into darkness. My heart thumped. Should I really trust this guy? He looked kind of wild, and he wasn't particularly forthcoming. That said, he was a shifter. It was pretty normal for them to act this way.

Squaring my shoulders, I thumbed the hilt of my sword and followed Ronan into his warehouse. Inside, I had to blink several times while my eyes adjusted to the dim lighting. There was a single lightbulb hanging in the middle of the room, barely illuminating the dingy space.

A large rusted cage sat in one corner, with a pile of blankets and pillows on the floor inside of it. On the other end of the room was a study of sorts. An old sofa, a few armchairs, and a wide-screen TV.

I arched an eyebrow and turned toward Ronan, who was watching me carefully. "You live here?"

"Don't act so surprised," he said in a grunt. "I am a wolf shifter. We like dark dens."

"Where's your pack?"

Not all shifters lived in packs, but the wolves tended to prefer that kind of lifestyle. They formed a bond, mentally and physically, that was unlike anything I'd ever experienced...until I'd joined the Crimson Court. Even then, the magic was different. They fed off of each other's powers. To find a wolf alone was more than a little odd.

"My pack was killed by fae."

I stiffened, eyes widening. "But I thought there was an alliance with the Crimson Court—"

"Balor's fae didn't do this. The Fianna did."

Suddenly, I realised exactly *how* Tiarnan knew this shifter, and a pool of dread spread through my gut. Behind Balor's back, the Fianna had broken the pact of violence, and they'd come after this shifter's pack. That meant he was probably pretty pissed off. And Tiarnan had sent me straight into his grease-soaked hands.

"Look." I took a step back. "I had nothing to do with that. Hell, I didn't even know it happened. Tiarnan never said a word to me about it. I don't want any trouble. I just came here to learn how to shift. That's all."

"Don't worry." Ronan uncrossed his arms. "Tiarnan didn't have anything to do with it either. I have no beef with him. And, as long as you aren't an arsehole, I don't have any beef with you either."

"Well, okay then."

He snorted and waved me over to the cage side of the warehouse. Just beside it sat a sparring mat much like the one in the Crimson Court. The only massive difference was the red stains that peppered this one. Definitely blood.

I followed him, shrugging off my jacket as he kicked off his shoes and strode to the center of the blue mat. He rolled back his shoulders, cracked his knuckles, and motioned for me to join him.

After I toed off my boots and joined him on the mat, he gave me a once-over again. His eyes lingered for just a second too long, causing a blush to creep up my neck.

"Tell me what we're working with. What have you done so far?"

"Not much," I admitted. "Until a couple of weeks ago, I'd never shifted in my life. So far, it's just been my eyes. They go pitch black, giving me better vision in the dark. Strangely, sometimes time seems to slow down a bit, like I'm getting super ninja powers. I don't suppose I can shift into a ninja, huh?"

He gave me a wry smile. "Doubtful. What else?"

"I mean..." I shrugged. "That's it."

"Interesting." He strode around me once, circling my body. "So, something fairly nocturnal. Have you had any cravings?"

I arched a brow. "Cravings?"

"Yes." He stopped before me. "For blood."

"Erm, no."

A strange smile spread across his face. "Then, you're likely not a wolf."

I couldn't help but shudder at that. Clearly, he was talking about himself, which ewww. Did wolf shifters really crave blood? No wonder they tended to get into fights.

"Lovely. Maybe you and the vamps have much more in common than you think."

His smile vanished. "I'll get along with the bloodsuckers when they start minding their own damn business. Fae, too. You're always sticking your noses where they don't belong, the lot of you."

I watched him walk around me once again. "Sounds like you aren't a fan of the alliance."

"I am not a fan of allying myself with anyone, if you haven't noticed." He gestured at the empty warehouse behind him. "Now, back to you. What was happening when you managed to shift your eyeballs? How were you feeling?"

"It keeps happening in the middle of fights. I guess I'm always feeling kind of angry. And scared," I decided to add, even if I should probably keep that tidbit to myself. He was probably going to find some way to use that emotion against me.

"Good. So, we just need to find your emotional pinch points, and then push against them as hard as we can."

Yep, looked like I was right. Great.

"Isn't there an easier way?" I couldn't help but ask. "You know, like deep breaths and meditation songs and whatnot? Centring the mind, focusing, or some kind of yoga thing? I think I'd prefer that."

"Unfortunately, no," he said, practically growling. Every hair on my arms stood on end. He grinned at my obvious discomfort. "If you want to be a shifter, you've got to train like a shifter. And that involves a shedload of emotion. But if you ain't up for it, there's the door."

I bit back a growl of irritation. "Fine. Get on with it then. Or are you just going to be all talk and no action?"

"You don't want to see me in action, love. Trust me." He rounded me again, taking slow and steady footsteps in a wide circle, to my left and then to my right. "And it'll take more than a whinging ginger to get my blood flowing."

I narrowed my eyes, spinning in place, tracking his every movement around me. "Tiarnan didn't mention what a wanker you are. Of course, he was busy being a massive one himself, so I could see how it might have slipped his mind."

"Nice try, love," he said with a chuckle. "But I've been called far worse than that."

"Oh yeah? So have I."

"So then why don't you keep that in mind and see how much aggression you can take out on me." He lowered his hands and then waved me forward, bending his knees into a fight stance. "Come on, ginger bird. Let's see what you've got."

I blinked at him. Was he bloody serious? "You can't honestly expect me to fight you."

He chuckled again. "I don't expect anything of the sort. But yeah, go ahead and try." His eyes flicked toward the sword still sheathed to my side. “No weapons.”

“Yeah, that’s *totally* an even fight,” I said with a roll of my eyes, but I still unhooked my weapon’s belt and let it fall to the padded floor with a thunk. Staying light on the balls of my feet, I curled my hands into fists and waited. I had no idea what he’d do next. So far, Ronan hadn’t been anything like I’d expected.

He came at me in a rush. And fast. *Too* fast. His body slammed into mine, his hands making a tight grip on my arms. He had me pinned against the mat in less than a second.

Ronan leaned over me, grinning, his wavy hair falling into his face. “Got you, fae.”

My heart thundered hard in my chest. “That wasn’t really fair. You probably weigh triple what I do. There’s no way I could have stopped that.”

“Wrong.” He let go of my arms and pushed up from the floor, motioning at me again. “And again.”

With a deep breath, I gritted my teeth. This time, when he ran at me, I managed to dodge out of his path just in time. His shoulder still slammed into mine, no doubt leaving behind a bruise the size of my head, but at least I was still on both feet.

But before I could take a deep breath and steady myself, I was flat on my back once again. He grinned down at me. “How’re you feeling? Angry and scared yet?”

“No.” I glared at him. “Just annoyed.”

“Hmm. We might have to rethink this.”

My eyes narrowed into slits as he stalked around me, his eyes lighting up with pure evil. Or, at least that was what it looked like to me. "What do you mean, we might have to rethink this?"

"Your emotions aren't being tested enough to get your blood flowing." He chuckled. "I have a better idea. Fighting isn't the only way to get your heartbeat racing."

6

Okay, *now* I was getting kind of angry. I propped my fisted hands on my hips and stared him down. "You better not be trying to shag me."

"That would bother you, would it?" Grinning, he crossed the floor until he stood just before me, towering overhead like some kind of massive oak tree. "I don't blame you. A wolf shifter like me is too much for most women to handle."

"Okay, now you're just being ridiculous." But despite how obnoxious he was being, heat flooded my cheeks.

"I could throw you over my shoulder, and you know it."

Was he being serious? No, he couldn't be serious. He was just trying to get a rise out of me, since knocking me to the ground hadn't worked.

Speaking of said ground...

With a grin, he pushed me over again. This time, when he pinned me, he didn't move away. He straddled my hips, leaning down until his hot breath whispered across my ear.

Everything within me clenched tight, my heartbeat roaring. His breath tickled my ear, my neck, my cheek. And then his lips whispered across mine, just gently enough to send a spark of heat through my core.

I shuddered.

The arsehole actually made me shudder.

A strange desire flooded through me, an animalistic heat that craved more of his touch.

And then his teeth gently bit down on my throat.

Irritation, desire, and fear tore through me all at once. A storm of emotions that crashed into each other like three charging waves. They rushed over me, making me feel as if I were drowning in it all.

My breath quickened, my body trembled. And then that strange wave of animalistic heat began to grow. When I opened my eyes, the world around me had changed. Colours were brighter, more vivid. The dim lights that had lit the room when I'd first entered had been replaced by glowing bulbs that cast everything into strange shades of yellow and red.

Ronan pushed away from the floor and sat back on his heels, smirking. "I told you there was another way to get your heartbeat racing. Turns out I was right."

"You're such a bastard," I hissed, glaring up at him. His face looked strange through my shifted eyes. But then I realised it wasn't my eyesight that had made his nose lengthen, had made his hair grow thick. He had partly shifted himself.

Which meant...I'd made his heart race, too.

I felt far more smug about that fact than I should have.

~

Balor was waiting for me when I returned to the Crimson Court just before sundown, tired, a little beat up, and a lot more confused about what I was. Tonight, I'd have to deal with the vampire situation. But first, I was in desperate need of a nap. Too bad Balor had other things in mind.

He pushed off the wall outside my bedroom door, frowning. "Where have you been?"

"Training. With that shifter I told you about." Back when Tiarnan had first given me Ronan's name, I'd told Balor about my hesitation in seeking him out. He'd seemed to approve of the idea in theory, reservedly. There were no other half-shifters in the Court to talk me through my powers, and he wanted me to learn exactly what I could do.

Little did he know that my training would involve a lot more...erm, *contact* than he'd probably imagined.

I didn't really want to tell him. Sure, Balor and I had both decided that nothing could happen between us. We didn't have a commitment, and we never would. But that didn't mean there was nothing there. That didn't mean that I wouldn't be pretty upset if Balor tumbled around on the floor with some other female.

My cheeks flushed at the memory.

Next time, I would have to make sure that Ronan stuck to the fighting side of things. Not the...whatever the hell that had been.

Balor's shoulders relaxed. "After last night, I thought you might have...well, nevermind. You're here now."

"You thought I'd gone?"

"Clark, I often think I am only moments away from losing you."

My breath caught in my throat as our gazes locked. I didn't really know what to say to that. At one point in time, his words would have been true, but not anymore. Or, at least, not until I was forced to flee because arsehole vampires wanted to ruin my life.

Balor cleared his throat, stepped back. "Did Ronan help you with the shift? Did you learn anything?"

"Kind of." I pursed my lips and glanced away, unable to meet his eyes for fear he'd see exactly how Ronan had helped me partially shift. "Though I don't really know what it means yet."

"Keep working at it," he said. "I assume you've planned another training session with him?"

I gave a nod, swallowing hard.

"Good." He took a step away and sucked in a deep breath. "Unfortunately, these new lessons can't interfere with your duties here at Court. Get yourself cleaned up and have a quick bite to eat. We'll be heading out to track down Matteo's son as soon as full dark has set in for the night." He glanced at his watch. "I imagine that gives you less than an hour."

~

I met Balor and the rest of the guard team downstairs in the command station after I'd taken a five minute shower and downed a few slices of stale pizza from two nights before. The Crimson Court had its own personal five star restaurant on the premises, but I rarely had time to eat there. Every fae on "campus" had a position, a job. Some took up more time than others, to put it mildly. And mine happened to be one of the more time-consuming, all-encompassing, twenty four seven, seven days a week kind of deal.

Not that I was complaining. I actually kind of loved it.

When I strode into the brightly-lit, buzzing base, Kyle, our resident computer whiz, tossed me a soda. I caught it in mid-air, shooting an appreciative smile his way. He'd read my mind. I was in desperate need of caffeine.

The others were clustered around a large table that sat in the center of the room. Currently, it was covered by a mound of papers. Some were print-outs. Some were photos. All of it was a bloody mess.

"What's all this then?" I cocked an eyebrow at Moira.

Moira fluttered her hand at the mess. "Research or something. Trying to see if there's been any reports in the area."

I stared down at the top papers. There were some police reports mixed in. "If the humans had found a vampire, wouldn't they have brought him to us?"

It was one of the few agreements the fae courts had with the human authorities. Whenever something supernatural came up, they usually handed it over to us to handle. Exceptions were only made if the courts couldn't handle it themselves. But a rogue vampire wandering around? The humans would have brought the issue to Balor.

Moira clucked her tongue. "The humans don't seem too keen on sharing info lately. Not after what happened when they arrested Balor."

"Plus, the whole Tower of London thing," I muttered.

After we'd fought against the sorcerer in the Tower of London, we'd gotten every supernatural Sluagh out of there. They were now hiding out in the bowels of the West Norwood Catacombs until we could find another sorcerer to undo their curse. *If* it could be done. We'd done our best to clean up the mess, but the sorcerer had killed a slew of guards before we'd shown up.

Naturally, the humans suspected we might be involved.

The days of peace were over. Unfortunately, it could only get worse from here.

Balor strode into the command station, shoulders thrown back, fiery eye hidden behind a sleek black patch. Everyone inside the room stood a little taller, a little straighter. He commanded that kind of respect, even if it kind of annoyed me at times. Even if there wasn't the magical fae bond between us, I would respect him anyway.

"Kyle," Balor said by way of greeting. "Tell me what you've found."

Kyle wasn't one for conversation, or one to have all eyes focused on his face. His cheeks were dotted with pink when we all turned toward his bank of computers. "There haven't been any reports of random vampires wandering around, but I don't think we expected that...right? I mean, if someone took him, he's not just going to be wandering the streets."

"Quite right," Balor said. "All signs point to him being taken. Perhaps as leverage against the Circle of Night."

Elise drifted over to the table, frowning. "That's a good point. The Circle of Night is infamous, and they are extremely wealthy. It could be a way to ransom them for money."

"Matteo didn't mention a ransom though. I think he would have brought that up if they'd gotten some kind of call."

Elise shrugged. "Or, he's being blackmailed. If that was the case, he might not want to tell us about it."

Blackmailed. My heart beat a little faster. Could that be what was going on here? If so, it was another indication that none of this was a coincidence. Was the same vampire going after Matteo that had come after me? If so, why? What exactly was going on here?

Nothing about it made any sense.

Balor let out a heavy sigh. "Anything else that might prove useful, Kyle?"

Kyle pushed up from his desk and strode over to join us at the table. He dropped a small stack of papers on top of the mess before taking a long gulp of his soda. "A few odd reports about some unlicensed selling going on in Leadenhall Market, mostly after hours. The police have spotted them on three separate occasions. Each time, the sellers seemingly vanished before they could be questioned."

"Okay." Balor slammed his finger down onto the papers. "We start there. Maybe Matteo's son is caught up in whatever this is."

I arched a brow. "Drugs, you think?"

"Could be." Moira pulled a sheet of paper out from under the pile of others. "There's this other report about a vampire found dead, but he wasn't staked. It happened several weeks ago, so I assumed it wasn't related to this."

"No, that can't be right." Balor shook his head. "Vamps can't overdose."

"Well, something killed him."

We all stared down at the report, dumbfounded. None of this made much sense, and every puzzle piece that came our way only seemed to complicate matters even worse. We had a missing vampire, an angry father, some supernaturals selling stuff in the night market, and another death that may or may not be unrelated.

Meanwhile, I had to figure out what the hell I was going to do when we finally did find the missing vamp.

If we found him, that is. I was starting to wonder if we would.

7

The world was quiet in Leadenhall Market. In the distance, bells tolled throughout the city as the last rays of sunlight disappeared behind steel and concrete buildings. Balor and I had come alone while the others spread the search outwards, just in case we were way off base in expecting to find Matteo's son here.

We stood on the edge of the cobblestone path, hidden in the shadows of a closed shop's doorway. So far, we had seen no sign of the unlicensed sellers, and we didn't want to tip them off if they strode by.

I blew on my cold hands and then shoved them into the pockets of my leather jacket. Even though spring was on the horizon, the London air was still as chilly as always. A heavy fog hung low on the streets, transforming the red and cream storefronts into slabs of shadowy grey. A single lamppost was lit up in the distance, barely visible through the thick fog.

Balor cocked his head, as if listening to something in the distance. His jawline rippled as his body shifted closer to mine. This was the first chance we'd really had to speak in more than rushed words all day. I'd been thinking about the vampire. About the blackmail. About the truth.

Cedric and Molly.

My mother, and my step-father.

"Balor…can I ask you about something?" My voice came out barely a croak.

He glanced down at me, his expression hidden by the shadows that were quickly closing in around us. "Of course."

I pulled the cool night air into my lungs. "Why did Faerie allow Nemain to get away with what she did?"

Balor tensed, glanced away. "She told the council that my sister had done terrible things. Murder, deceit, treachery. It was all lies, of course. I tried to tell the council that she was nothing if not good, but they believed Nemain over me. They won't allow her on the council, but they will allow her to rule."

Have you ever wondered if what Nemain said was true?

"I'm surprised they haven't done a thing, even when she's making obvious attempts against your Court, too."

"Many of the council do not approve of my recent decisions."

I blew out a hot breath and leaned against the doorframe, heart racing so fast that I could barely move. This was my chance to tell Balor what I'd been hiding from him all this time. My moment to watch the warmth in his eyes transform into hate.

"Besides," he continued. "The council did not approve of my actions in the situation either. Truth be told, I cannot blame them. I made mistakes. We all did."

I blinked at him, my blood going cold in my veins. "Your actions? Mistakes? How were you involved? Weren't you here, in London, throwing one of your seasonal balls?"

The skin between his eyes pinched tight. "How would you know that, Clark?"

I wet my lips and glanced away. Could I really tell him? Even not knowing what mistakes he was referring to? Only two seconds ago, I'd felt almost ready, but I wasn't so sure once again. If he was more involved than I'd known…

"I might not have been a member of a Court at the time, but I still heard plenty of rumours."

In fact, I'd only been fifteen. Young enough to be manipulated in the worst way possible. But old enough to know better.

Balor pushed back his shoulders, and the strong, intimidating Prince that he truly was peeked out around the edges. It had been awhile since he had demonstrated that side of himself to me. We had gotten so close, we had come to a strange understanding. He had begun to seem less like the smiter then he had when we'd first met. But I couldn't let myself forget that the reputation of the smiter hadn't come from nowhere. I had seen him burn his enemies alive. I had seen him torch entire buildings. And, here he was, clearly suspect by my words.

A part of me liked to think that he wouldn't have a problem with the truth. That because we had gotten to know each other, he would forgive anything I had done in the past. But, looking at him now, I remembered why I had kept it from him for all this time. Balor, the lover, would never harm me. But Balor the smiter? He might.

"You mentioned wanting to tell me something earlier. What is it, Clark? You've been acting odd the past few days. Is there something you need to tell me?"

I couldn't do it. Not right here. Not right now.

"No. I'm just trying to understand some things a little bit better."

Balor didn't look convinced, but he didn't argue. Probably because a slew of voices drifted toward us, the silence peppered by the shouts of male voices somewhere deep inside the market. My eyes locked with Balor's, and he gave a nod, thumbing the hilt of his sword.

"It sounds like they're around the corner," Balor said in a low voice. "If they are unlicensed sellers, like we think, they are likely hocking something illegal, dangerous, or a combination of both. Be careful. Stay behind me. And follow my lead."

Our tense conversation thankfully forgotten, Balor inched in front of me and made his way across the cobblestone street. Our footsteps echoed against the lofted ceiling of the market, despite our attempts to stay silent as we approached the voices in the distance.

As we edged around the corner, the group of males blurred into view. Balor paused in the shadows, likely waiting so that he could eye up what they were doing. There were five of them, and from the looks of their slender forms and pale faces, they were vampires. None of them were Byron, the vampire I either had to kill or save. Yeah, I was still on the fence about that, particularly now that Balor and I had that tense—and confusing—conversation.

They were all standing around a small folding table that was covered in what looked to be bags of blood. Like, hospital bags. I wrinkled my nose, fully expecting one of the vamps to bite down into the bag and begin drinking with delirious glee. I mean, that's what vampires did, right? Drink blood. But they almost acted as though they needed to give the table a wide berth. They were standing near it, but they were looking at it with slight disgust painted across their features.

I inched closer to Balor, and cocked an eyebrow. "Are they selling human blood? If so, how are they able to resist drinking it themselves?"

Before Balor could answer, all the vampires twisted our way. Whoops. I'd forgotten that their hearing was a little bit more heightened than my own, and my words had probably drifted straight into their vampy ears.

And none of them looked particularly happy to see us. One of them even growled. The others quickly blocked our view of the table. Balor growled right back, a low hum emanating from his throat. And, to give the vampires some credit, they winced and cast their eyes to the ground.

Balor stalked across the cobblestone to reach the group, and I followed close behind him. When we reached them, the leader, I was guessing, finally glanced up to meet his eyes.

"What's going on here?" Balor asked in a low, dangerous voice.

The growly vamp took a step forward in front of

the others, pushing his shoulders back as if that would make any difference at all. His eyes were more than a little rimmed in red. They had fully been taken over by the colour, his hunger so intense that his entire eyeball was pure crimson. "None of your business, fae. Best turn around and walk on out of here. We don't want any trouble with you, but this is not under your jurisdiction."

Balor snorted. "Anything in this city is under my jurisdiction. I won't give you a third chance to tell me what's going on. I will only ask once more. What are you doing?"

The vamp licked his lips and cast a nervous glance at his friends who stood behind him. "We're just selling some blood. This is our shop. That's all you need to know."

Balor took a step closer, so that he could see the table over the vamp's head. "Human blood? Because if you have harmed humans, then you'll have more than just me to answer to."

The vampire let out a low chuckle, which was probably a bad idea on his part. Balor really didn't like it when people laughed at him or showed him anything but full, undeniable respect. These vampires were not only selling what looked to be human blood, they were clearly challenging the most powerful supernatural in the city. With arched brows, I crossed my arms over my chest and waited for the inevitable blowback from my Prince.

Balor reached out and curled his hand around the vampire's shirt, jerking him up from the ground. The vamp's feet dangled over the cobblestone, and pure fear rippled through his red eyes.

"You do know who you're speaking to, yes?"

"A fae who is forced to make alliances is a fae who is not as powerful as he wants everyone to believe."

Balor's growl deepened, and he threw the vampire across the cobblestone. The creature fell with a hard smack on the ground, his head slamming against the pavement. His body went limp. Obviously, it didn't kill him, but his head had smacked hard enough against the stones to take him out of the equation temporarily.

And it seemed to have the effect Balor intended. The four other vampires were shuffling away from him, no defiance at all shown on their pale faces.

"Will one of you tell me what the hell is going on here?"

"We're just selling some blood," a small silver-haired vamp said with a trembling voice. "It's not human blood. No need to freak out. It's just shifter blood."

My eyebrows shot to the top of my head. "Why the hell are you selling shifter blood?"

The vampire looked nervously between me and Balor. Balor took the opportunity to stride forward, snatch up a bag of blood, and take a long sniff of the contents. With a growl, he nodded and threw the blood back down on the table. "He's not lying. The blood smells like the other blood we found on the cobblestones. It's tinged with magic, so it can't be human blood."

"See?" The vampire took several steps back. "It's not human blood. We haven't killed any humans. Can we go now?"

Balor sneered, his red eye flickering with anger.

"Not until you tell me why you're selling shifter blood in the middle of the damn night."

Moira and Duncan rounded the corner behind us just as the other vampires began to gather up all of their supplies by throwing them into a large cardboard box. They wanted to flee. And I couldn't blame them for that. Balor looked like he was about to explode.

Moira took one look at the scene and scowled. "What the hell is going on here? Why do they have a load of blood bags?"

"They're selling shifter blood for some reason," I said, filling her in. "But why? We don't know."

Moira pressed her lips together in a thin line. "Oh, I have an idea. It probably has to do with that dead vamp we heard about. Shifter blood is poison to vampires. What better way to kill your enemy than by poisoning them?"

We all turned toward the vampires. One was sprinting halfway across the cobblestone now. Balor didn't move. Instead, he continued to stare at them with narrowed eyes. Vampires were fast, and they knew the dark streets of the city. Still, we needed to stop them. We'd found some information, but it wasn't enough. We still didn't know how Byron fit into this or if he even did.

"Balor?" Duncan asked as the final vampire spun on his feet and began to run down the cobblestone street. "Need me to go after him?"

"No. I think it's time for me to have a chat with Matteo."

8

Balor had us gather the rest of the blood bags before heading back to the Court while he went to have a chat with Matteo. From the tone of his voice, it was clear he had a suspicion that Matteo was more involved in this black market shifter blood business than he'd let on. For one, the so-called shop was only minutes from his home and the Circle of Night's headquarters. It was difficult to believe that these vamps could be doing this without his knowledge.

Hell, even without his approval.

Matteo and the Circle of Night did not always play by the rules. They hadn't gotten wealthy because they were smart or because they were lucky. They had grown their empire because they were calculating and ruthless. Once again, I could see why some fae might not be truly pleased to be aligned with them.

Moira blew out a hot breath as she dumped the last blood bag into the leftover cardboard box. "These blood bags are disgusting. I really don't understand how anyone, supernatural or not, could drink this rubbish."

"They need it to survive," Duncan muttered. "But I sure am happy that I've never been turned into a vampire."

Vampires could be turned, just like in the legends, or they could be born. No one quite understood vampire reproduction, but no one understood the mechanics of most magic. Like the fae, a new birth wasn't something that happened particularly often. In one female's lifetime, she might birth one or two offspring. Even if that fae lived hundreds of years. We were not like humans, though shifters were. My mother, when I'd known her, had always told me that she had mated with a shifter for the single hope that she would have a son or daughter.

And so she ended up with me.

Of course, that meant there hadn't been much love from her when it came to my real father. She'd been in love with another male, a fae.

A fae I wished she had never met.

Fingers snapped in front of my eyes. "Clark? You've gone off into la la land again. You seem to be doing that a lot lately. Is there something going on that you need to talk about?"

Blinking, I turned and gave Moira a half-hearted smile. There was so much warmth in her eyes, and concern. Little did she know how much she would hate me, just like the others. How would that warmth change if she found out the truth? This warrior fae might be hard at times, and blunt as all hell, but she'd welcomed me into the Court with no questions asked. I couldn't bear the thought of her hating me.

My face must have reflected some of what I felt inside because Moira's eyes narrowed in concern. "You know you can tell me anything, right?"

I wished that were true. I wished that I could fully open up to my friends.

But I couldn't.

"Sorry, I guess I'm just distracted by everything that's been going on lately. I worry what's going to happen next time Nemain makes a move against us. She did whatever she could to take control of the Silver Court. She's going to keep coming after ours. It almost feels as though we're focused on the wrong thing. Finding this vamp. Dealing with this blood."

Moira gave a nod. "I know what you mean. But there's not much we can do. Besides, if she does come at us again, we're probably going to need the help of the Circle of Night. So, helping Matteo is hopefully helping us in the future when we need it."

"It's not that I don't understand that. It's that it almost feels like this is a purposeful distraction, something to take away our focus while she makes her next move."

And I wasn't lying or coming up with excuses just to satisfy her curiosity. I truly was worried. Since I had joined the Court, Nemain had made it more than clear that she was willing to go to great lengths to take down Balor. It hadn't worked the first time when she sent a spy into the middle of the Court. And it hadn't worked the second time when she had somehow gotten Fionn on her side. She had made some mistakes and she had underestimated the Crimson Court. Something told me she wouldn't make those same mistakes again.

Moira and Duncan moved down the street, disappearing around the corner while I grabbed the last two bags of blood. Just as I turned to catch up with them, a pair of strong arms wrapped around my waist and lifted me from the ground,. A shriek ripped from my throat and I kicked out my legs, squirming against my captor as hard as I could.

A familiar voice whispered into my ear. "Stop fighting. It's no use. I've got you, and if you don't make this difficult, your death will be a peaceful one."

Well, fuck that. Peaceful death, my ass.

I narrowed my eyes, still squirming and kicking my legs into the air. "You're that damn vampire, aren't you? The one selling shifter blood."

"Ding, ding, ding." I could practically hear the smile in his voice. "Lucky for us, your little Prince vanished into the darkness from whence he came, leaving you here for me to find. I smelled the shifter blood on you when we saw you earlier, and I thought you would be a lovely addition to our inventory."

Fear churned through me, even though I was a load more irritated than scared. Adrenaline spiked in my veins, causing my insides to heat up a thousand degrees. My eyes burned and my mouth went dry. A soft buzzing filled my head as my vision charged from one form to the next. Suddenly, the shadows around us lifted. I could see better, I could see further, and the colours of the market had changed into vivid shades of yellow and red.

"Hey, arsehole," I said, my tongue heavy in my mouth. "I think you picked the wrong shifter to fuck with."

Maybe. I didn't entirely believe that. For one, I still

hadn't shifted fully into whatever animal I could become. Kind of annoying, particularly when my animalistic side would certainly come in handy right about now. I knew I wasn't a wolf, and I probably wasn't a bear, but hopefully I was something with claws that could gorge this bloody vampire's eyes out.

His grip around my waist tightened, and his fangs sunk deep into the skin below my neck. I immediately stilled, my body going cold.

"That's right," he murmured softly against my skin. "I will rip out your throat if you do not stop fighting me."

Tears burned my eyes. "You wouldn't. It could kill you. You could end up ingesting some of my blood."

"Not enough to kill me." He took a long, slow sniff along my skin, sending new waves of fearful adrenaline spiking through my gut. "I can smell you, you know. You may be shifter, but you are also fae. That means the poison in your blood is watered down. I could taste a little. It might make me sick, but it wouldn't kill me."

"You don't know that." I swallowed hard and mentally crossed my fingers that he wouldn't know the truth about what I said next. "I doubt you've ever tasted blood like mine before. I've heard it's even more potent than normal shifter blood."

He let out a light laugh, his lips tickling my skin as he clenched his teeth tighter around my neck. "Nice try. I can't fault you for the attempt. But you are not the first half-shifter I have met. I know what your blood can do. And what it can't. Now, be still, and I will make this quick."

The world blurred before me, and I bit hard on

the inside of my cheek. This could be it. This could truly be the end of the road for me. Killed on a quiet, dark street in the middle of the night. Alone with nothing and no one but myself. Maybe I deserved it. Maybe this was the way that fate came for me. I'd been running from it all my life, and I'd finally slowed down long enough to let the past catch up.

It was only fitting that it would happen here and now, when I'd come so close to telling everyone the truth.

No.

A strange resolve strengthened in my gut. I didn't want to die. Certainly not here, and certainly not now.

Adrenaline coursed through my veins, and new waves of heat churned in my gut. My body began to scream, a strange new magic pulsing through me. I gritted my teeth against it, almost overwhelmed by the sheer force of it. It pushed at my limbs, dragged down my face. My legs went weak beneath me, and I struggled to stand against the grip the vampire had around my waist.

A strange gurgled cry escaped from his throat. The tension around my waist released. I fell to my knees, body pulsing and screaming. Sharp, white hot pain shot through my arm. And suddenly, it felt as if it were no longer there. My mind screaming, I twisted toward it. And I couldn't believe what I saw.

A wing.

A single black wing in place of an arm.

And then the pavement rushed up to meet my face.

~

Groaning, I opened my eyes, half-scared I was alive and half-scared I was dead. Had the vampire taken me?

A deep voice let out a rush of curse words, and a warm hand wrapped around mine as I attempted to push up. My head reeled; my body screamed. Through slitted eyes, I tried to take in where I was, but everything was blurry around me.

"Stop this," he said. *Balor.* Relief charged through me as his power washed over me. A gentle caress against my cheek. A soft flutter at the bottom of my hair. And then a firm push back onto what I assumed was one of the healing ward's beds. "Calm down and get some rest, Clark."

I leaned back and tried my best to relax, but my heart still raced. The last thing I remembered, I was two seconds away from death. And my arm had changed into a wing. Balor had been at the Circle of Night, and Moira and Duncan had been nowhere to be seen. How the hell was I okay?

"I thought I was dead." Ouch. So, talking hurt. My throat felt like sandpaper.

A beat passed without words. "What happened?"

I cracked open my eyes again. Still blurry. "What do you mean, what happened? I was hoping you could tell me."

"We found you in the market. Passed out and clutching some black feathers."

"That damn vampire attacked me," I said, frowning to myself. "His fangs were in my neck. He was two seconds away from killing me. I don't really know what happened next. I mean, I think my arm shifted, but that's the last thing I remember."

"I see." His grip on my hand tightened. "I think more than your arm shifted, Clark."

"No." My heart thumped hard. "It was just my arm. After that, I passed out."

"I don't know much about shifting, but I do know this. Those first few times involve a lot of blackouts. You won't remember that you did it, nor will you remember anything that happened while you were in your animal form. You say there was a wing? Hopefully you pecked that vampire's bloody eyes out."

Balor sounded amused, but all I could feel was pure dread forming in my gut. "I could have killed someone and not remember it?"

That was pretty much my worst nightmare, second only to Balor finding out the truth about my past. It had always been what I feared when I thought of my shifter side. Losing control. Having no idea what I'd done. But I couldn't ignore the fact that it had happened. And I couldn't help but wonder how long it would be before I did it again.

9

"Surprise!" Elise's musical voice drifted into my ears. I cracked open my still puffy eyes and turned toward the doorway to see my silver-haired friend beaming at me from across the room. She held a birthday cake in her hands, decorated with elaborate frosting. I sat a little higher, ignoring the wave of nausea that rolled through me.

"I come bearing gifts." She smiled and kicked the door shut behind her. "And by gifts, I mean one gift. A cake."

"I knew there was a reason I liked you." I grinned back. "Thanks, Elise. I hope you brought a knife or else I'm eating the whole damn thing at once."

"Way ahead of you." Elise plopped the cake down on the table and extracted some utensils from her purse. After making a sharp cut through the center of the cake, she made quick work on the rest of it. A moment later, she handed me a slice so big it was practically a fourth of the cake, not that I was complaining. The more, the merrier as far as I was concerned. The shift—if I'd really done it—had left me starving.

"For some reason, I have a feeling this isn't healing ward approved." Still, I sunk my teeth into the gooey frosting and moaned in pure pleasure. Around a mouthful of food, I said, "Oh my god, this is amazing."

She perched on the edge of the bed, taking a much smaller slice into her hands. "I thought you might need some cheering up. Sounds like you had quite the night last night."

Last night. Inwardly, I groaned and tried to keep the panic at bay. If another night was over, that meant that I was that much closer to the end of the blackmailing vampire's deadline. Not ideal, especially since I was temporarily bedridden.

Yay.

"Apparently, I shifted. Not that I can remember it." Sighing, I took another bite of the cake. "The last thing I saw was a wing. So…I guess I'm a bird."

Elise set down her cake. "You don't sound even remotely chuffed about that. Were you hoping for something else?"

"No. I mean, I don't know." A pause. "I'm glad I'm not a wolf or a bear or anything like that. I've always been afraid of being dangerous, of being some kind of violent predator. On the other hand…I guess I never imagined I'd be something so….useless."

Elise pursed her lips. "You fought off that vampire in your bird form. Doesn't sound harmless to me."

"*Maybe* I fought him off. I don't actually remember what happened. He could have just hightailed it out of there when he realised that he probably couldn't trap a bird without a cage."

"Maybe. Or maybe not." She shrugged. "Those ravens at the Tower of London weren't useless either, if you remember. They saved us."

A strange sensation churned through my gut. I'd almost forgotten about those ravens. When we'd been trapped by a sociopathic sorcerer without any hope of an escape, the birds had somehow come to save us. It had been one of the more bizarre things I'd ever seen in my life, and I'd seen plenty of bizarre things by now. Balor had thought perhaps the ravens were supernatural themselves, sworn to protect the tower at all costs.

I arched a brow. "You think those ravens are shifters?"

"I'm not sure. They're *something*. But, useless? They're not that. And, as far as I'm concerned, you aren't either."

~

After a few more hours of rest, I felt up to heading back to my room. The fae who ran the ward were skilled in healing, and while they couldn't completely clear my head, they eased the pain in my bones to nothing more than aches. On the way back upstairs, I couldn't help but notice that night had already fallen. Shadows caressed the windows. Unease thumped through my gut. I'd spent far too long recovering from my shift. Time I didn't have to waste.

A tapping sounded on the window, and the blackmailing vampire's face appeared on the other side of the glass. My stomach dropped. I glanced behind me, fearing that Elise or Moira or Balor would catch me. But the corridors were empty. It was starting to get late. Most fae would be in their rooms by now, and the guards were likely in the command station making preparations for the next mission.

I had the night off, but I could already tell that it would not be a quiet one.

I crossed the floor, threw open the door, and shut it quickly behind me. "What the hell are you doing here?"

The vampire laced his hands behind his back, peering at me through his curtain of raven hair. "Your progress has been much slower than I anticipated."

"You said you were giving me until the end of the week."

"And yet it looks as though you have spent the majority of your first day in bed."

I sucked a sharp breath in through my nose. "Yes. Because I got wounded trying to find your rogue fae. Who, by the way, I learned is named Byron the Bloody, son of Matteo, the leader of the Circle of Night. Didn't think to mention that to me when you decided to blackmail me?"

He smiled. "I assumed it wouldn't take you very long to discover those details."

"What do you want?" I asked, glancing back behind me. "You can't just keep showing up here like this and expect no one to find it odd. If anyone catches us, you won't get what you want."

"You're right." He steepled his hands beneath his chin. "However, I need an update. Have you made any progress at all?"

I blew out a hot breath. "A little. Byron was last seen in Leadenhall Market, where some vamps are selling shifter blood on the black market. There's no sign he's involved in that, but that doesn't mean he isn't. Those vamps seemed willing enough to kill anyone who got in their way."

The vampire arched his brows. "You think him dead? Unlikely. He's far too much of a roach for that."

"Well, I don't know what to tell you. That's all I've got."

"And what do you intend to do next to find him? I assume the guards will be heading out into the city this evening for another look?"

"I'm off duty tonight," I said dryly. "Like I said before, I got wounded."

He inched forward, his eyes flashing. "Well, you best get back on duty. You have until Saturday at midnight, fae. Wounded or not, I intend to make good on my promise."

A shiver slipped down my spine, and I narrowed my eyes. "Why do you want him dead? He's Matteo's son, one he's insistent is innocent in all of this. I wouldn't be inclined to believe him normally, but he's not the one blackmailing me into killing someone."

"I am no innocent, but neither is Matteo. Read my mind if you do not believe me."

I blinked at him. That was probably the first time I'd ever had someone practically *ask* me to enter their mind and read their thoughts. It caught me off guard, unmoored me, but my shock sure as hell wasn't going to stop me from going through with it. With a deep breath, I plunged my mind into his.

Matteo isn't innocent. Neither is his son.

That was it. The only thought that echoed in the vampire's head. With a frown, I pulled myself back into my own mind.

"You can control your thoughts," I said with a frown.

"Perhaps."

"Well, that's hardly going to get me to believe you, is it?"

He leaned in and smiled. "You don't need to believe me, Clark. You just need to kill Byron before I reveal your secret to your Court."

10

"So, what's the plan?" I asked as I strode into the command station in a fresh set of guard clothes. After the vamp had shown up to give me a second course of threats and blackmails, I'd decided that I couldn't afford for the guard team to head out on a mission without me.

Balor, who was bracing his hands on the center table, frowned. "You need to rest. Go back to your room."

I sucked in a deep breath. "Look, I'm fine. I rested. The ward healed me. I can't just sit in my room all night and not help."

"Clark," he said, his voice a warning.

"I'm not trying to challenge you," I said quickly. "But I've had an idea. Remember the shifter who has been training me? He might know something about this black market blood. Plus, if we gave him a visit, it would give me a chance to ask him about what happened to me last night."

It was fifty, fifty, whether or not Balor would go

along with this. He'd given me an order, and he didn't like to back down. Not to mention that I couldn't blame him for wanting to protect me. Still, I'd brought a pretty tempting proposal his way. If shifters were being attacked, word was probably spreading in the community. Ronan might know something useful.

Finally, Balor gave me a nod. "Alright. We'll go and speak to your friend, but you'll come straight back here if there's any trouble."

~

Balor decided that just the two of us would visit Ronan instead of the group as a whole. For one, Ronan had given me more than an indication that he was a bit of a loner. He wasn't particularly fond of visitors. Showing up with a whole posse probably wouldn't endear him to us, or get him to talk. Two…well, two was what worried me. Balor had Kyle going through CCTV for any sign of the black market vamps, and he'd sent Duncan and Cormac out to patrol through the market again.

As much as I didn't want my team to fail, I couldn't help but hope they wouldn't find anything.

When we reached Ronan's warehouse, he was outside, leaning against a metal pole and waiting for us. His massive form shifted out of the shadows, his long wavy hair cutting across his thick shoulders. He wore a faded pair of black jeans, a black tank, and a leather jacket. It was hard not to stare.

"Clark." He gave a nod. "I appreciate the warning text, but you didn't give me a chance to respond."

"If I'd asked, you might have said no."

"I *would* have said no." He pushed away from the pole and motioned for us to follow. His back was tense. So was Balor's. A part of me had wondered if bringing Balor along was such a good idea. After all, Ronan's methods of training were a bit…unconventional. I hoped he wouldn't bring it up. Otherwise, Balor might just burn his entire warehouse to the ground.

Not that Balor had any right to be mad about my training. We weren't a couple. We weren't even close to being in a relationship. I worked for him, and I served him, and that was it. Past that…we were kind of friends? Nothing more. Besides, it wasn't like Ronan and I had even done anything beyond training. Just some pushing around and some straddling. Harmless stuff. Right?

Still, I was pretty sure my cheeks were blazing red.

We ducked into Ronan's warehouse, and it was just as dimly-lit as it had been the last time I'd been here. Ronan pushed the door down behind us, crossed the room, and pulled three beers out of his mini fridge. He handed one to me, one to Balor, and then took a chug of his own. After a deep gulp, he wiped his lips with the back of his arm, and narrowed his eyes.

"What's all this about then? I don't appreciate a visit from the Prince of the Crimson Court." He shot me a quick glance. "Wasn't part of our deal, tiny bird."

I winced. His nickname for me had started out as a way to insult me, a way to get my blood boiling. Truth was, I didn't mind it at all, but I could tell by the look on Balor's face that he wasn't too fond of some other male calling me anything but Clark.

"It's important," I said around the strange lump in my throat. "I wouldn't have brought him here if it wasn't."

He arched a brow and leaned back against the wall. "Important to the Crimson Court? I don't tend to like to get involved in fae business."

"I think you'll find that this affects you, too," Balor said, voice deep. "We've recently discovered an issue involving shifters of this city."

Ronan's face remained impassive. "If you've got a shifter problem, you're talking to the wrong guy and you know it. I don't get involved in shifter business. I keep to myself. You need to go talk to the Pack."

The Pack was much like the Circle of Night, minus the wealth. They were the governing body of the shifter population, run by wolves. Their leader had been the one to make the alliance with Balor's Court, as well as the Circle of Night. So, Ronan wasn't really wrong, in theory. If Balor had a shifter problem, he usually took it to the Pack. Just not tonight.

"I think you'll understand why we came to you instead of going to them," Balor said. He flicked his eyes toward me. "Clark?"

My cheeks warmed as Ronan's dark gaze turned my way. I knew what he was thinking, even if I hadn't yet made an attempt to dig around inside of his brain. The reason I'd brought a fae Prince into his home better be good. He'd trusted me, and he'd given me a chance. And now I was dropping supernatural messes right into his lap.

I took a deep breath and plowed forward. "We've

recently discovered that there's a black market for shifter blood."

Ronan's eyes flickered. "Well, that's certainly odd. Wonder who would want to buy shifter blood."

His tone was sarcastic. Ronan knew exactly who would want the poison.

"So, you've heard about this before?" I asked.

"No." He gave a quick shake of his head. "Can't say it surprises me though. Vamps will do anything to get ahead." His gaze shifted back toward Balor. "Sometimes, fae do, too."

A low growl rumbled from Balor's throat. I decided to ignore it.

"They've been selling it at night in Leadenhall Market. We stumbled across them last night. They had a lot of it. They must be getting it from somewhere."

"If you're asking me how vampires are getting shifter blood, then you aren't as smart as I thought you were, tiny bird."

I rolled my eyes. "I mean, obviously, they are taking it from shifters but—"

"*Killing* shifters," he said, cutting in. "So they can make some extra cash. And you wonder why I don't want anything to do with vamps."

"Have you heard of any shifters missing?" Balor asked.

"Like I said, I'm not involved in the community," Ronan replied, narrowing his eyes at Balor. "After fae killed my entire pack, I decided I'd stick to myself. I have no desire to get involved in all this shit. If you want to know why, then look at what you're right in the middle of. You can make all the alliances you want, but there will always be those who skirt the rules. It's one big bloody mess out there, and I want nothing to do with it."

Balor's single red eye glittered as he took a step toward Ronan. "Only cowards run from danger."

"Only arseholes demand fealty." Ronan's impassive expression turned hard. "And I know why you're asking me about this instead of the Pack. You're afraid if they find out what's been going on that they'll break the alliance. They'll separate themselves from you, or they'll demand you choose between them and the vamps. You can't have that, can you? No, the fae Prince of the Crimson Court must rule us all."

I rolled my eyes and stepped between them. "You're both being really annoying right now. There are some vamps out there killing shifters so that they can sell their blood. Blood that is then used to kill other vampires. Let's try to focus on the real issue here. Lots of people are dying."

Balor let out a low growl, one that was matched by Ronan. A part of me just wanted to walk out of the warehouse and leave them to testosterone at each other, but time was running out. Not just for all the innocent shifters out there but for my chance to find Byron.

"Look. Balor, I know you just want everyone to be happy about the triple alliance between fae, shifters, and vamps, but there are deep wounds that go way back. For Ronan, it's a lot more recent than that. He's not trying to end the alliance. He's not trying to take over the Pack, or the Circle, or the Court. He's just sticking to himself, so give him some slack for that, okay?" I turned to the shifter. "And Ronan, I know you've been through a lot of shit, but don't be heartless. These are your fellow shifters. Is there anything at all you can tell us that might help us find out who has been targeted? Have you heard anything at all?"

For a moment, neither male spoke. I stood sandwiched between them, charged tension peppering the air like sharp bullets of magic. They were both stubborn. Neither one of them wanted to back down. But finally, Ronan rolled his eyes and stepped back.

"I've heard some mutterings, but I don't know how much of it is true." He shook his head and crossed his arms over his chest. "Most of the time I don't pay attention to gossip and rumours."

"What have you heard?" I asked, twisting toward him.

"Not much. Just a little chatter about some shifters gone missing. I really don't know much more than that. But, if I were you, I'd check out Gordon's Wine Bar. That's where a lot of shifters like to party. Maybe someone there has heard something more. They can be pretty discreet, given the right price."

I glanced at Balor, who gave a nod. "Thank you for your cooperation."

"Yeah, I'm not doing it for you though." Ronan jerked a thumb my way. "I'm doing it for the tiny bird."

Speaking of birds…

I couldn't help but frown. "Can I meet you outside, Balor? I want to ask Ronan about my shift."

Balor hesitated. He clearly didn't want to leave me alone in here with Ronan, and I couldn't really blame him. The whole exchange between them had been charged as hell, and even though Ronan had given us some information, I knew he'd done so as grudgingly as possible. He didn't trust Balor. Balor didn't trust him. Just another fun night in the supernatural underbelly of London.

Still, Balor gave me a questioning look, as if considering it. When I nodded, he strode over to the metal doors, pushed them up, and disappeared into the night.

When I turned back toward Ronan, he was watching me carefully. "You two sleeping together or something?"

"What?" Heat rushed into my cheeks. "No. Of course not. He's my Master and my Prince, and I—"

"I've never been fond of the whole Master thing or the magic that bonds you all together. Sometimes, I think the supernatural world would be a better place if the Courts dissolved altogether."

"Pack magic isn't much different," I bit back. "Not with your alphas and that mind-melding thing you all do."

"I'm not in a pack anymore. Anyway, something happen with your shift?"

"Kind of? Maybe?" I filled him in on what had happened the night before. The shifting wing, the passing out, all of it. I decided not to mention that everyone suspected I'd pecked the vamp's eyes out, mainly because…just, eww. No need to go there.

Ronan gave a nod when I finished. "That's going to happen the first few times you shift. That's why it's important that you do it in a safe location, like here." He gestured toward his cage. "I'm guessing your *Master* won't let you train tonight?"

"Unlikely," I said. "We have murderous vamps to catch."

"That's what I expected you to say." He cocked a grin. "Just get back here as soon as you can, so I can take you through the steps enough times that it becomes second nature. In the meantime, let's just hope you don't shift in public again."

Unease churned in my gut. "You really think a bird is that dangerous?"

"Not a bird," he said. "You're a raven."

11

Ronan's words echoed in my ears as I pushed the warehouse door down behind me. Balor moved in to my side, searching my face for... well, I didn't know what. I knew he could sniff out some aspect of my emotions, but I wasn't feeling anything other than confused right now.

A *raven*. What were the odds?

"Is something wrong?" Balor demanded. "What did he tell you?"

"He thinks I'm a raven." I blinked at Balor. "You know, like the ones we encountered at the Tower of London."

He was silent for a moment, his lips pressed tightly together. "You mean the ones who saved us."

"Yeah." I cocked my head. "You don't think...?"

"What are you asking, Clark?"

"Do you think they sensed I was there?" It sounded daft out loud, so I shook my head just as soon as the words had popped out. "Nah. That's total rubbish. It's just a coincidence. That's all."

But it didn't feel like a coincidence. It felt very much connected, as weird as that would be. I'd never heard of normal animals reacting that way to shifters, especially not when they weren't in their animal forms. For a conspiracy of ravens to sense me from across the tower…well, it didn't make any sense.

To compound my confusion and unease, I looked up to see Balor watching me with a strange expression on his face. "Who did you say your parents were, Clark?"

My heart jolted in my chest. "I didn't say."

Cedric and Molly.

"Now might be the time to share that information," he said.

"I haven't said because I don't know." Eyes burning hot, I pushed past him and strode toward the pavement that would take me away from this conversation. Why was he asking me this? What the hell did it have to do with me being a raven? Did it have something to do with my mother? Surely, it couldn't. She hadn't been the shifter, and neither had my stepfather.

Balor caught up to me and fell into step by my side. "I understand this is a sore issue for you, but this could be important, Clark."

Frustrated, I stopped short, but I couldn't bring myself to look into his eye for fear he'd see exactly why it was such a difficult thing for me to discuss. "I've never met my father, okay? I thought I made that clear before. He was never in my life, so I don't know who he is or what he could shift into."

I stared hard at the pavement before me, my eyes blurring with tears. If only my mother had let me meet him. If only he'd been the parent in my life instead of her. Everything might have gone differently.

"I'm sorry, Clark," Balor said softly, taking my arms gently in his hands and turning me so that I faced him. Through my burning tears, I stared hard at his chest, at the arms that had held me so close to him before. His scent settled over me, tempting me to draw closer still. All I wanted was to curl into him, to lose myself in the powerful strength of him. "We'll talk about this some other time. I know how hard it is to think about the ones we have lost."

My heart jolted again. He meant his sister, the last Princess of the Silver Court. The fae Nemain had killed.

Slowly, I extracted myself from his arms. "I feel like I should be the one to apologise. I just..."

"I know. I understand." He smiled and slipped his finger beneath my chin. "We do need to talk about it, but now is not the time. Let's go find some murderous vamps."

~

Gordon's Wine Bar was busy. Humans and shifters were packed into the underground space in the heart of London. Built years ago, the space had been transformed into a popular, thriving pub for happy hour drinks and late night bar crawls. We stepped inside, pushing through the thick crowd of bodies. Up ahead, a small bar was surrounded by a throng of impatient customers. Over to our left stretched the tunnel that dug deep into the earth. The walls curved overhead, creating dirt-packed caves full of shadows. Candles flickered on the walls, casting an eerie ambiance over the place.

Balor's hand touched my elbow, a comforting reminder that he was there. He leaned closer, his lips brushing against my ear. "Keep an eye out but try not to look as though you're searching for anything. We can blend in here."

A shiver coursed down my spine, but for once, it wasn't from unease. It was almost a thrill, the excitement that Balor and I were practically unseen in the midst of so many tipsy people. Smiling, I turned to face him, pressing my hands against his chest. "You mean, like this?"

His lips quirked, and his eye sparked with heat. "I won't argue with that approach."

"Good." I slid my fingers up his muscular chest and laced my hands around his neck. "Because I think this is the perfect way to blend in."

Balor reached down, wrapped his arms around my hips, and jerked me closer to his chest. Pressed up against him, I could feel the wild beat of his heart. Distantly, I could hear my mind hammering at me hard, demanding to know exactly what the hell I thought I was doing. We were here on a mission, to find that missing vamp. I was days away from being exposed, days away from being banished, or worse. And yet here I was throwing myself at the one male I could never have.

A wicked smile curving across his lips, Balor leaned down again. I pressed into him, enjoying the way my core clenched tight, relishing in the way his lips whispered across my earlobe. "I think I've spotted something. Just behind you. Don't turn your head too quickly when you look."

Disappointment sunk deep into my bones as he pulled back and shot me a wink. For a moment there, I'd thought he was being affectionate because he wanted me. To hell with the ruse. I just wanted to be wrapped up in his arms. Biting back my disappointed sigh, I slowly shifted to the left, just far enough for my gaze to drag across the caves.

"It's too dark," I whispered back. "Let's go closer."

I took Balor's hand in mine, and we weaved through the crowd to the subterranean section of the bar. Candlelight flickered all around us, casting strange shapes on the dirt-packed walls. The tables were full, groups of humans gathered together, animatedly talking about their lives and their days.

In the back corner, though, things were going a little bit differently.

Three shifters sat at the small table. Three vampires stood by said table, gesturing wildly at where Balor and I stood, right smack dab in the middle of the exit of the caves. Slowly, I eased further into the bar, sinking into the shadows by one of the tables.

The vamps kept gesturing at where we'd just stood, as if they were trying to get the shifters to leave. One female and two males, all wearing black. They were varying shades of pale, but none of them looked as if they'd seen sun in years. Probably because they hadn't. The shifters, all males, were red-faced and glassy eyed. Clearly, they'd been at the bar for more than one drink. I couldn't tell what kind of animals they were, but from their rugged beards and messy hair, I was guessing they were some kind of wolf.

I pushed up onto my toes and whispered into Balor's ear. "What do you think is going on?"

"I'm not sure," he replied. "But the humans are starting to take notice."

He wasn't wrong. The humans at the next table over had stopped their conversation and were now turned in the direction of the supes. Their eyes were pinched together; frowns pulled down their lips. With the current atmosphere of London, this wasn't a good thing. Any public supernatural fight needed to be squashed as quickly as possible. We didn't need any more ammunition for humans to hate us.

"Maybe we should step in," I said when one of the shifters pushed back his chair and stormed to his feet. The chair toppled to the ground, the wood cracking from the force of it. The humans who had been watching let out gasps of shock and scrambled away from the shifters.

Balor pressed his lips together. "You might be right about that. Time for you to go back to the Court."

I blinked at him. "Excuse me?"

He didn't even bother glancing my way as he inched toward the supes. "I told you before we left that you would have to return to Court if there was any trouble. Well, this is trouble. You're still recovering from your shift. Go home, Clark."

Home.

The word hurt my heart.

"No, I'm not going to leave you here to deal with this on your own," I argued.

Power rippled off Balor's body in waves. "Go back to Court. That is an order, Clark. Don't make me use the bond to control you."

"I'm not going home," I said through clenched teeth.

One, I really wasn't going to leave him here. And two…well, Byron was involved in this somehow. I wasn't going to risk Balor finding him without me and delivering him right back into Matteo's waiting arms. Then, I'd never get a chance to do what I needed to do.

I still hadn't decided if I would. But I couldn't let that choice be taken from me. Not when it meant the end of everything.

Balor's strength began to build. He closed his eyes, curling his hands into fists. Power rippled across my body. Less a caress this time and more like an unstoppable force. The bond between us snapped tight, curling me toward him, making my body feel as though it could do nothing more than turn around and walk right out of this bar.

Gritting my teeth, I yanked myself back. The power fizzled into nothing between us.

Balor's eyes narrowed. "How did you do that?"

But before I could answer him, a fist slammed into his face.

12

Balor stumbled back. Rounding on his attacker, dark red flickered in his eye. I sucked in a breath, my heart hammering hard. One of the vamps stood before us, wringing his hand by his side. Clearly he hadn't expected the Prince to be as hard as a rock. His mistake.

Balor's lips curled up into a wicked smile. "You're going to regret doing that."

Before I could stop him, he'd flown into the fight. The vampire hurled his fist at Balor, but my Prince was too fast. He ducked out of the way, but the vampire didn't stop there. They moved through the bar at an impossible speed, limbs flying, tables crashing to the floor. The humans screamed, jumping up from their chairs and pushing their way out of the bar. In the corner, the other supes stood watching, mouths open wide.

Another one of the vamps spotted me, and then charged across the room.

"Get out of here," I yelled at the shifters. "They want your blood. They're trying to kill you."

I managed to get out the words just before the vampire's body crashed into mine. I hit the floor hard, my breath whooshing out of my lungs. Stars danced in my eyes, the vamp crushing me against the stone. I reached down, wrapped my hand around my sword, and yanked as hard as I could.

Steel sliced through the air as I brought my blade right up against the back of the vampire's neck.

He stilled, fangs poking out between his lips.

"Most things don't kill vampires," I hissed into his face. "But you can be staked. You can be burned. And your heads can be chopped off. Lucky for me—and unlucky for you—my sword is one swipe away from ending this fight right here and now."

Balor appeared at the edge of my vision, done with the vamp who had attacked him. I didn't dare look his way or move even the slightest of inches. I knew that if I did, the vamp would get the advantage again.

Not that it would last long. Balor unsheathed his own sword and pointed it right at the back of the vamp's head.

The vamp's red eyes widened even more. "What are you even doing here? This bar is for shifters."

I lifted my brows, angling my blade even closer to his neck. "One might wonder why *you're* here then, unless it's precisely because you knew you'd find some shifters here."

He wet his lips.

"Yeah." I grinned. "That's what I thought."

~

We left behind a mess at Gordon's Wine Bar, a fact that did not go over very well with the human owners. They came out to inspect the damage while we bound up our new prisoner with rope the humans had found in their stock room. They didn't ask a lot of questions, but I guessed they didn't need to. I was pretty sure they got the gist of the incident.

Vamps threatened shifters. Fae threatened said vamps. Fight ensued.

"Listen, ah," the human, a male named Raoul, said just before we exited the caves. "This is usually one of my busiest nights, and all my customers got the hell out of here when you guys decided to fight."

Balor caught the implication. "I'll make sure you're compensated for the trouble."

Raoul lifted his hand, gave a nod.

The trek back to the Court was fairly quiet and uneventful. Balor and I were silent, not wanting to speak for fear of giving something away to the vampire. I was desperate to ask him about Byron, but I bit my tongue. If I rushed into this with guns blazing, it would only make Balor suspicious. And I'd already made him suspicious enough.

Once back at the Court, we took him down into the dungeons beneath the building. After the recent attacks, half of the cells had been blown to bits, but Balor had been quick in getting a wall rebuilt between the surviving tunnels and the damage. Along one wall sat a row of cells, each manned by thick steel bars.

There were no windows. Only darkness and shadows and flickering torches that hung on the walls.

The vampire finally decided to speak. "You can't possibly expect me to stay down here. I require blood to survive."

Balor kicked open the nearest cell and pushed the vamp inside. "You'll have your blood. For your sake, I hope it isn't the black market shifter kind."

Even though he was pale as salt, I swore all the blood drained from the vamp's face. "I don't know what you're talking about."

"Of course you don't," Balor replied, locking the cell door behind him. "Unfortunately, I won't be able to let you out of here until you come up with some information. For your sake, I hope you just forgot. Luckily, we have a way to find out."

The vampire narrowed his eyes. "You can't do this to me. I'm a member of the Circle of Night. Matteo will have your head on a spike if he finds out you held one of his vampires hostage. Not only will your alliance be dead but so will you."

I raised my eyebrows and turned to Balor. That was…interesting.

Balor pressed himself up against the bars. "Matteo and I have already spoken. He knew I planned on taking you prisoner, and he approved. You won't be getting out of here until I get some information."

The vampire's eyes flashed, and he cursed underneath his breath. "I don't know anything. Besides, the sun has almost risen. I'll be unconscious within minutes."

"We'll see." Balor pushed away and stormed down the corridor. I followed quickly behind him, having zero desire to stay underground with a vampire who looked as though he wanted nothing more than to rip us both to shreds with his sharp fangs.

I waited until we were back above ground before I asked the question that was bubbling beneath the surface. "Did Matteo really give you the go ahead to lock that vamp behind bars?"

"Of course not," Balor said, his tone clipped. "Matteo would not allow anything of the sort. I imagine he will not want to believe that his own vampires are behind his son's abduction, and if I present it to him without evidence, I am certain that he will not react very well."

"You sure about that?" I cocked an eyebrow and followed him into his office. "Looked like he was pretty okay with torturing his own vampires if that meant finding out what happened to his son."

"Matteo operates by his own rules, just as I do. I would not be pleased if he took one of my fae captive without consulting me. He would feel as if he had every right to lock the vamp up, but that *we* don't."

"So, why aren't we going straight to him to talk about this?"

Balor sighed, dragged a hand down his tired face, and crossed the office to his bar. He was quiet as he poured himself a drink and tipped the contents down his throat. After a moment, he poured himself another glass, and then made me a gin and tonic.

"The situation is becoming trickier and trickier to handle."

I took the drink and leaned back against the leather seat. "Because you're worried what the Pack will do if they find out."

"The Pack. The Circle. The Courts." He sighed. "Hell, all of Faerie. The situation is not good, Clark. Vampires are killing shifters. They're then selling the blood to other vamps. I daresay they're also selling the blood to humans and shifters, too. I wouldn't even be surprised if some fae have bought into it, though I hope no one inside my own damn House has gone anywhere near it."

I gripped my drink tighter in my hand. "Surely, a Crimson Court fae wouldn't buy black market shifter blood."

"A House Beimnech fae wouldn't," he corrected me. "But, as I have learned, not every fae in this Court is loyal to me."

Well, shit. He had a point. I mean, Aed and some of the other Fianna had only just stormed into this House days ago, demanding some kind of justice for what had happened to Fionn. Would they go so far as to buy shifter blood, as a way to cause problems?

"On top of that," he continued, "the vamp we captured is part of the Circle of Night. The vampires selling the blood were found in Leadenhall Market, only a few streets away from the Circle's headquarters. I find it difficult to believe that Matteo is not aware of this."

A fact that had crossed my mind more than once. I was glad Balor and I were on the same page, for once.

"So, let me get this straight. If the shifters find out what's been going on, they'll get pissed off and retaliate against the vampires," I said, pausing when Balor gave a solemn nod. "And then, if the Circle finds out, they could potentially retaliate because they were involved from the start." Another nod. "And then if the other Houses and Courts find out…this would be ammunition against the alliance. Another reason to revolt against you."

Balor let out a long sigh and closed his eyes, tipping back the remnants of his amber drink. "Basically, Clark, I don't see a way out of this that doesn't end in war."

~

Balor and I had three more glasses each. Or, maybe, I had three more, and Balor had about six. He was clearly on edge and exhausted, and I couldn't help but feel for my fae Prince. As I'd quickly learned over the past few weeks, Balor had one goal and one goal only. That was to keep his people safe. He would do anything for them, including aligning himself with supernaturals that didn't deserve his support.

And now it seemed like that alliance would be his very undoing.

A little light-headed, I pushed up from the chair and tiptoed over to the bar. Balor, who had taken up his place behind his desk, watched me with dark eyes. A small smile spread across his lips.

"I think you've had enough, Clark," he said as I clumsily poured a shot of gin into my empty glass. "We don't want you to have a hangover tomorrow. Not when you have a vamp's mind to break down."

Over the past couple of hours, as the sun strode purposefully into the morning sky, we'd come up with a plan. When the vamp woke back up at sundown, I would use my power to find out everything he knew about the black market blood business. That included whether or not Matteo was involved, as well as the location of Byron the Bloody. If Matteo was involved, well, then Balor would be forced to confront him about it. But if he wasn't? Then, we'd return his son and take down the black market vamps with his blessing.

That was obviously the ideal endgame. It would keep everyone happy, except maybe the other Courts. But hopefully, they would never have to find out about it.

Of course, that meant that I couldn't kill Byron. The whole plan hinged on being able to return him to his blameless—hopefully—father. If I did what I had to do in order to keep myself safe, then everything Balor had worked for, everything he'd sacrificed, would be for nothing.

And I didn't think I had it in me to take that from him.

13

"I think maybe you were right," I said when I downed the contents of my gin and tonic. My head felt more than a bit fuzzy now. I was full-on tipsy. Laughing, I plopped the drink down on Balor's desk. "That was one too many for me. Whoops."

Balor let out a low chuckle, a sound that sent shivers across my skin. I so rarely heard him laugh. It was a nice sound. One I wanted to memorise, one I hoped I could never forget. I wanted to take it with me when I finally had to leave this place.

My smile slipped from my face.

Balor pushed up from his chair and crossed the room. "Tell me what's wrong."

I blew out a hot breath, glanced away. "Just worried about the Court. Everything seems so crazy right now. It's made me so…exhausted."

My bones felt so weary; my eyelids were so heavy. Sighing, I leaned back into the chair and tried my best to keep my eyes open. But it was no use. They wanted to shut, so they did.

Balor chuckled again, sending new waves of warmth through my core. "Let's get you to bed."

A delicious thrill went through me, and I ached to push up onto my toes and wrap myself tight around his powerful body. But it was as if my mind and my eyelids were at war. Instead of doing anything of the sort, I merely smiled.

Strong arms wrapped around me and lifted me from the chair. My head nestled into his shoulder, the scent of him enveloping me as we left his office behind. I wasn't sure what happened next. All I could do was fall deep into Balor's arms.

~

When I woke up, he was beside me. I was curled up in my bed, tucked tightly beneath my soft duvet, head nestled into the soft pillows. He'd taken me back to my room, just like he'd said, but he hadn't left me to go back to his.

I could feel the heat of him radiating against my back, and one strong arm had been slung across my body.

Heart clenching tight, I twisted toward him. His eyes were closed. Both of them. His eyepatch had been pushed up onto his forehead, leaving behind a pair of long, dark lashes. Sucking in a sharp breath, I lifted my hand and traced the shape of his eye, in awe of how he looked like this. Naked. Vulnerable. Less like a Prince and more like a man.

A slight smile curled on his lips. He reached up

and clasped tightly to my hand. "Careful. I would hate for your finger to get burned."

"Your eyes are shut," I breathed. "You won't burn me."

"Not on purpose." He pulled his hand down to his lips, and then kissed my palm. Sparks shot through my core. "Don't act so surprised. You've seen my face without the patch before."

"I mean, not really, Balor," I said. "Only when you were burning things, and it's kind of hard to look at your eye when there is fire shooting out of it."

His smile widened. "I want to look at you."

My heart thumped.

Slowly, I pulled my hand away from his lips and reached up to his eye patch. The material was soft against my fingers as I pulled it down over his fiery eye. Once it was firmly in place, Balor flicked his other eye open, warmth shooting through every inch of his red iris.

"Sleep well?" he asked, his dark voice curling around me.

"I think so," I replied. "But I have to admit that I'm surprised to see you here. In my bed."

"Disappointed?"

"No."

"Good." He tucked a finger underneath my chin, pulling my face closer to his. "I thought you might need some tending to when you woke up with your hangover."

I wet my lips. "Well, there you're wrong. I don't have a hangover at all."

Or, if I did, his presence in my bed had fully cured it. There was no headache. No dizziness. Well, no dizziness from the previous night's drinks. There sure as hell was dizziness though, the kind that was a direct result of his mouth being only inches away from mine.

"Ah. Too bad." He pulled back, causing a disappointed gasp to pop from my throat. "I suppose I should return to my own bed then."

"No, wait," I said in a strangled voice. "I actually think I might have a headache coming on."

A wicked smile lit his lips. "Is that so?"

"Yes. Is there something you can do to fix it? Heal me, maybe?"

Balor had many talents. He could sniff out emotions. He could burn things with his eye. And he could heal himself. I was pretty sure the last talent didn't extend to healing others, but I was also pretty sure that what he had planned had nothing to do with any of that.

My heart raced in my chest as his head dropped closer to mine. Surely he wasn't going to take this any further. Surely we were just dancing around the edges of what we could and couldn't do again. He'd made it more than clear, on multiple occasions, that we couldn't cross that line. Hell, I didn't want to cross it either.

I mean, I wanted to, but the risk was far too great.

Still, it was impossible for me to pull away. I was drawn to him, and it went far beyond whatever supernatural bond we shared. This was something more. Something almost primal.

"Oh, I can certainly heal you, Clark." And that was when I knew exactly what he had in mind.

Balor pushed me back onto the bed and shifted his body on top of mine. My breath came out of my throat in hurried gasps, every cell in my body sparking with an intense desire I'd never felt before, not even with him. My body arched toward him, instinctively.

He pressed his lips to my throat, his mouth dropping hot kisses along my skin. His power rippled off his body in waves, a deep darkness that curled across my skin like a dangerous caress. I shuddered against him. Despite every logical thought in my brain telling me to pull back and run away, I couldn't bring myself to do it.

I needed him. More than I'd ever needed anything in my life. My bond with Balor was more than magic. It was more than lust. Something deep within me responded to him in a way that made my heart shake like a leaf in my chest.

"You are the most beautiful creature I have ever seen in my life." He lowered himself down the front of my body, lips dragging across my exposed skin. When he reached the top of my jeans, he slowly unbuckled them and pulled down the material.

I shuddered at the sudden feel of cool air on my skin, but the chill didn't last long at all. Balor Beimnech licked his lips and lowered himself between my thighs.

~

When I awoke again, I felt dazed. Delicious warmth had flooded my body, and every single cell felt relaxed, satisfied, but also ready for more. I turned toward my Prince, eyeing up the slope of his nose, the strong line of his jaw. His lips twitched.

"Don't tell me you're ready for more already," he murmured. "It's only been five minutes."

"Isn't there something that you want?" I asked softly.

"Oh, there is," he said, turning toward me. "But today is not about me. It's about you, Clark. I want to please you as many times as I can. We only have a few hours left until we have to leave this room, and I want to make the most of it."

There was a sincerity in his eye I'd never seen before, and it made my breath catch in my throat. Whatever walls had been between us were gone now. His Princely mask had been discarded on the floor along with my clothes. He'd opened himself up to me, finally. This was what I'd wanted. It was everything I could have imagined.

But there was a dark cloud hanging over us, one I couldn't ignore.

"Aren't you worried that we're just ignoring the inevitable?"

His smile dimmed. "The inevitable?"

"Nothing has changed, Balor, as much as I want it to." I swallowed hard and glanced away. "The prophecy is still the prophecy. Your life is still at risk. I thought we had agreed we weren't going to tempt fate."

"Pleasing you doesn't tempt fate, Clark. I won't get you pregnant with my tongue."

Heat rushed into my neck. "You said before that you were worried about being able to control yourself if we let ourselves give in like this."

"The alcohol helps," he said with a slight smile.

"Much like it helps fae resist their Master's bonds. Perhaps we should both stay drunk all the time."

"You don't mean that," I whispered.

His expression darkened. "No, I don't, but why are you bringing this up now? I can see that you want this as much as I do. Maybe I was wrong before. Maybe we should try our hardest to make it work. Yes, it may prove to be impossible, but what is life if we don't try?"

His words made my heart ache. I wanted nothing more than to say yes, than to give the bond between us a shot. He was worth it, even if we found out that we couldn't make it work. But there was something clanging in the back of my mind, a truth that was growing louder and louder with each moment that passed us by.

I was hiding something terrible from him. I was going behind his back, going after the one vamp he needed to protect in order to keep his alliances alive. How could I stay here, like this, knowing that? It wasn't right, and it wasn't fair.

Balor deserved far more than that.

14

To say things got awkward after that would be the understatement of the year. Hell, I'd pretty much kicked the fittest fae in the entire world out of my bed, right after he'd pleasured me like I'd never been pleasured before. I had no idea how I was going to look myself in the mirror after that.

He was brutally silent when he slipped out the door, and I had to jump into the shower just to wash his scent from my skin. It was too much of a reminder of what we'd done. If I didn't scrub it away, it would keep sneaking into my nose for the rest of my day, tempting me to throw myself back into his arms.

Not that he'd have me now.

After my shower and a fresh change of clothes, I slipped into my boots and padded through the bustling corridors of the Crimson Court. I found Moira, Elise, and Ondine in the command station. Ondine wasn't one of the guards, but she stopped by from time to time, usually bearing some form of plant life to cheer things up in the steel-encased room.

"Clark," she said, face brightening beneath her pixie cut hair. Since getting captured by Lesley, Ondine had decided to chop off her signature brunette locks in favour of something a little different. It worked on her.

"Looks like you've brought Kyle another plant," I said, biting back a smile at the cactus Ondine had plopped next to Kyle's mound of soda cans.

"The ones I've brought him so far keep dying," she said with a wave of her hand. "I figured he probably couldn't kill a cactus."

"Watch me," Kyle said with a slight smile. Ondine grinned back.

Moira and I turned to each other and raised our eyebrows.

"Anyway, I hope this keeps things a bit cheerier in here for you, Kyle. I know it must be gloomy when you spend fifteen hours a day sitting in front of a computer."

Kyle glanced up, peering at her through his mess of ginger hair. "I don't mind it, but…thanks, Ondine."

Ondine beamed, and then she turned on her heels and strode out of the command station without another word. I turned to Kyle, biting back a grin as I perched on the edge of his desk.

"Well, that was certainly nice of her, don't you think?" I asked.

"Hmm," he said, tapping away on his keyboard.

"I wonder." I lifted my eyebrows and grinned at Moira, who was watching the exchange with eager eyes. "Maybe it would be nice to repay the gesture. Kind of as a thank you."

Kyle paused in his key-tapping. “You think she’d like that?”

“Yep,” I chirped. “I certainly do.”

“Last time I checked, she’s a fan of chocolate,” Moira added.

For a moment, Kyle didn’t say a word. Then, he nodded, grabbed a can of soda, and popped the tab. He was back to work within seconds, eyes and mind focused on the screen before him. But I knew he’d filed the suggestion away somewhere within the card catalog that was his brain. Hopefully, he’d listen.

“Speaking of…gestures,” Moira said, tugging on my arm as we strode over to the center table where maps and reports were still spread across the surface in a crazy jumble. “I heard a rumour.”

My cheeks flushed. “Oh god. Do I even want to know?”

“From the tone of your voice, sounds like it’s more than just a rumour.” She dropped her voice into a whisper. “Did Balor really go back to your room this morning?”

I gritted my teeth, pawing through the reports as a way to keep my hands occupied with something else. Otherwise, I might need to go punch a wall or something. “Yes. But it’s not what you think. Okay, so maybe it kind of is, but it also isn’t.”

“You’re babbling nonsense, Clark.” She leaned closer. “Is he that good that he knocked your sense right out of you?”

“Shh,” I hissed at her when Duncan strode by.

She waved her hand. “He’s heard far worse from us.”

She wasn’t wrong about that.

"So, tell me what the deal is," she said. "Did you two finally consummate your relationship?"

"Not exactly," I said. "We can't be together. It's just…not an option."

"Right," she said slowly. "And why is that?"

Balor didn't want anyone to know about the prophecy. The fact that he couldn't have an heir meant that he was vulnerable if the wrong person found out. It brought the line of succession into question. Someone like Nemain would be delighted to take advantage of that. I knew we could trust Moira. She'd never tell a soul. But still, it wasn't my secret to tell.

"Master. Guard. You know the drill. It could make our jobs complicated."

It was the excuse we'd come up with, but it sounded hollow to my ears.

Moira shook her head. "You two are idiots."

"Oh yeah?" I arched a brow. "And when was the last time you went on a date?"

"Erm," Moira said.

"Exactly."

"None of the fae in this House really do it for me," she said, glancing at Cormac, Duncan, Kyle. "They're all like brothers to me."

"Clark," Balor said as he strode into the command station with his shoulders thrown back. He expertly avoided my gaze, instead glaring hard at Moira. "Enough gossiping. Come with me. Now."

~

Balor was broodier than normal, and that was saying something. All the softness he'd held in his eyes hours before was totally gone now. It was like he'd flipped a switch on his emotions, shuttering them behind his Princely mask. His jaw clenched tight; his gaze was dark. So, yeah. This was going to be a fun night.

He pushed opened the door of the dungeons and motioned for me to go before him. Sighing, I strode down the dimly-lit corridor, to the cell where our prisoner sat waiting. He was on the floor, legs crossed beneath him, a dull, bored expression on his pale face.

"I thought maybe you'd forgotten about me," he said. "I need some blood."

"You'll get some blood when you tell us what we need to know," Balor said in a low growl.

"What's his problem?" The vampire jerked his thumb toward the Prince.

"You're a large part of it," I replied. "You should probably be glad that you're in there instead of out here, to be honest."

The vampire's face paled even more. "Look, I know you think I have something to do with some shifter blood or something, but I really have no idea about any of that."

"I mean, I hope you're telling the truth. Otherwise, Mr. Scowly over here is going to get even angrier."

"Clark," Balor said. With a scowl.

"Ask the other two vamps who were at the bar if you need to. They'll vouch for me."

"Forgive me if I don't find your word, or theirs,

particularly believable. Not only did your so-called friend attack me, but you launched yourself at Clark. Why did you do that if you have nothing to hide?"

The vampire licked his lips. "Vamps get nervous when fae Princes lurk in the shadows. I was merely protecting myself."

I rolled my eyes. "Nice try."

"Look, if you're not going to believe me, why are you wasting your time asking me questions?"

"Oh, we haven't even gotten started yet," I said with a smile. "Have we, Balor?"

Balor grunted.

"What are you going to do? Torture me?" The vamp let out a hollow laugh. "Good luck with that. Matteo might forgive your capture of me, but he would never let you get away with harming one of his."

"Torture would take too long," Balor said with narrowed eyes. "Instead, you've got to deal with Clark."

Once again, I'd found myself in the position of interrogating an enemy. When Balor and I had made the plan the night before, I'd been half-drunk on gin and half-drunk on lust. It had seemed like a good idea at the time, but so had jumping into bed with my Prince. In the harsh light of day—well, night, actually—none of that seemed like a particularly great plan anymore.

"Clark," Balor said, his harsh voice cutting through my thoughts.

It wasn't difficult to read between the lines. We'd made a plan. It was time for me to follow through. It was an order, and he wouldn't hesitate to use the bond between us to force me to obey. Not that it would work. The last time he'd tried to use the bond on me, I'd been able to break free. I was pretty sure it had something to do with my half-shifter blood, but I also wasn't entirely sure how much control I had over it.

Besides, I wasn't in the mood to make Balor angry.

Er, *angrier*, that is.

"Fine," I said. "Be sure to ask him where Matteo's son is."

Taking a deep breath, I plunged myself forward into the vampire's mind. He seemed to sense what was coming, and hastily tried to throw up a barrier between us. I easily pushed it aside. Most supernaturals didn't have the strength of mind to hide their thoughts from me. So far, only fae had ever stood a chance against my power. And then, only the strongest of the Court. With practice, a vampire might have the power to push me aside, but this vamp wasn't trained at all.

His thoughts flittered around me. Angry images stained by red. Words poured over me, whispers of conversations that had happened decades past. Even though he was no match for my power, I could tell by his frantic thoughts that he was still trying to resist me. And he wasn't doing a terrible job. If I didn't have Balor with me to direct the vamp's thoughts, I probably wouldn't learn much at all.

In the distance, I heard the familiar rumble of Balor's deep voice.

If I think about the black market shifter blood, will the ginger bird know I was involved? Shit. I just thought about it. How can I not think about it? Don't think about it. Don't think about it. Don't think about it.

Another rumble in the distance.

Maybe if I just sit here still like this for long enough then she'll bugger on out of my head. Can she hear this now? Oh my god, I bet she can. Don't think about the black market shifter blood. Don't think about the killings. Don't think about them. Don't think about it. Don't think about it.

Okay, this guy was getting annoying now.

He's going to ask me about Byron next, isn't he? Bloody hell, he just did. Are these fae really working for Matteo? They must be. He's going to kill us when he finds out that we took Byron to the warehouse.

Quickly, I pulled out of the vampire's head and whispered at Balor, "Ask him the address of the warehouse."

"Shit," the vampire said before I had a chance to reenter his mind. "You really can read me, can't you?"

"I mean, yeah. What the hell did you think I was doing?"

"Bluffing? Hoping your weird vacant gaze would freak me out enough that I'd talk?" he asked, eyes wide.

"Well." I crossed my arms over my chest. "Did it work? Matteo might be more forgiving if he finds out you gave up the info willingly than by having it extracted out of your head."

The vampire swore under his breath.

"You have five seconds," I said. "After that, I'm right back in your head again, and I'll find out exactly where your warehouse is."

With a deep breath, the vampire spilled his secrets.

15

The warehouse, as we learned, was an old abandoned location at the edge of the city. Our prisoner didn't know much about the logistics of it all, but he managed to spill that it was where the black market runners were bottling and bagging the blood, and where they were keeping the shifter prisoners that they later killed for said blood.

Of course, that only meant one thing. Balor and I were going to have to go and check the place out.

We grabbed our swords, got into one of Balor's many cars, and sped down the street toward the warehouse. Silence peppered the air between us, an ever-present reminder of the tension that had thickened like impenetrable gunk. It was as if we'd travelled into the past, back to my first days at the Crimson Court when neither of us had been certain of the other.

Back before we'd let ourselves care.

Being back to this hurt far more than I wanted to admit.

"Balor," I said after far too many quiet moments. "Silence isn't the answer."

"Then, what is the answer, Clark?" He turned toward me. "I suggested we keep ourselves apart. You agreed but then spoke as though you wanted more. I gave you more, and then you wanted to put space between us once again. Now, I'm giving you space. Are you telling me again that's not what you want? You're starting to give me whiplash."

I stared at him, at his hard face, his cold eyes. "Can't there be some sort of middle ground?"

"Perhaps when you tell me what it is you're hiding from me, then I will consider this 'middle ground' you're suggesting."

All the blood drained from my face. Sucking in a sharp breath, I turned away from Balor to stare out at the city streets that blurred by. Now that we were back to his cold, harsh ways, he was focusing on my past and my secrets. From the moment we'd met, Balor had known I was hiding something. He wasn't stupid. At first, he'd demanded I tell him everything I could about my past, but he'd let it go over time.

Looked like he wasn't letting it go anymore.

"I know there's more about your past than you're telling me, Clark. You didn't come from nowhere. You had a family. You had a home." His voice was grim as I kept my gaze locked on the window. "The longer you refuse to share even a hint about your past, the more I wonder exactly how bad it could be."

"Do you think we'll find Matteo's son in this warehouse?"

Balor was silent for a long moment, no doubt noting that I had completely avoided responding in any way whatsoever to his questions. I knew my actions would only lead him to ask more questions in his mind, but I didn't have the heart to come up with a lie. He wanted to know about my mother and father. Well, he knew about them alright. As soon as I said their names, he would know exactly who I was.

"Unless the vampire knew how to manipulate your power, then yes. Byron should be in that warehouse, which means this will all be over very soon."

Those words did not comfort me. In fact, they did the opposite. The sooner I came face to face with Matteo's son, the sooner I'd have to make my choice.

"Your scent is still off, Clark," Balor said. "It has been since the meeting we had with Matteo at the Circle of Night. If this was your first mission, I'd chalk it up to nerves. But you've faced far worse than this and more than survived. There's something different about this mission for you. Something about you has changed."

"You know, your power really is creepy sometimes."

"I am not the mind reader, Clark."

"You might as well be."

~

We pulled up outside of the warehouse half an hour later. Gravel crunched underneath the tires, and the moon hung low behind the square steel building. The place had seen better days, to put it mildly. Steel panels drooped along the side of the building, rust curling around the edges.

The roof looked as though it had half caved in, leaving behind nothing but exposed metal beams.

There were a few cars parked right by the entrance. Through the single window, yellow and orange lights flickered from inside.

"The vampires really picked a posh location for their big business idea," I said dryly.

"Yes, the rust gives it an elaborate street feel that is certain to draw in customers."

I bit the inside of my cheek, not daring to let myself smile. "Wonder if they'll be on Grand Designs. The architecture of the dilapidated roof has a certain charm."

"It is so intricate that it must have taken them years to get this right."

"Okay," I said, doing my best not to laugh. "What's our move here?"

"Get in and get out, hopefully with Byron in tow. Avoid killing anyone. Bonus points for getting the names of the arseholes running this show. We'll put a stop to them, but we'll have to fill in Matteo about our movements…as long as he isn't involved."

Sounded dreadfully easy. Which meant…it wouldn't be.

Balor and I crossed the parking lot to the soundtrack of crunching rocks, moonlight shooting an eerie glow across the exposed beams of the warehouse. There were no guards or warning bells, which meant these vamps weren't expecting visitors. A fairly reasonable supposition. This place was in the middle of nowhere, and we never would have found them without my power.

When we reached the door, Balor gave a polite

knock. I thumbed the hilt of my sword, ready to make my move if it came to that. Shuffling echoed through the thin wood. Long moments passed by as we waited. They were clearly eyeing us up, and most likely making some plan of attack. Still, we waited.

The door finally cracked open, and yellow light spilled onto the ground around our feet. A skinny vampire stood just on the other side, long scraggly hair hanging down into her bony face. "Yeah?"

"We're going to need to come inside," Balor said. "Best if you just allow it to happen."

She narrowed her eyes. "I ain't no fan of faeries, no matter if you're the bloody Prince or not."

"That's fine with me," he said in a low drawl. "I can't say I am a fan of murderous vampires myself."

She swore under her breath and started to slam the door in our faces. Balor's fist shot out. His arm reached through the gap just in time, preventing the door from shutting completely. The wood slammed into his skin, but he didn't even flinch. He merely smiled.

"Like I said, we're going to need to come inside."

"If I were you, I'd just go along with whatever he wants," I said, craning my head around his massive body to look up at the vamp. "He can get pretty crabby when he gets turned down."

A low grumble grew in his throat. The vamp's eyes widened, face paling. Little did she know the growl wasn't directed at her at all, but at me. Still, it had the effect I'd hoped for. She stepped back and opened the door, shuffling away as the two of us strode inside the dingy warehouse.

I glanced around.

The warehouse was mostly empty. Steel beams criss-crossed overhead, the open ceiling providing a perfect view of the glittering city lights in the distance. The sky was dark and full of clouds, but moonlight washed the warehouse floor. In the far corner of the expansive, empty space sat four cages large enough to hold an oversized dog. But instead of mangy mutts, I found myself looking into the angry eyes of four shifters and a single vampire.

A vampire with sleet gray hair.

"Looks like we found where they're keeping the shifters they plan to murder," I said, narrowing my eyes at the female vampire, who had slowly begun to back away from me and Balor as we took in our surroundings.

She held up her hands, shook her head. "Look, I don't want any trouble. I'm not even involved in all this mess. I'm just here to keep an eye on things, to feed the shifters until the others come back."

I arched a brow and turned to Balor. "You believe her?"

"Not in the least," Balor said in a dry voice. "Seems like a booming business that could rake in some serious cash. I'm sure she wants her cut."

"You can take my cut," she said in a rush. "I don't need it. Just let me go, and you can have whatever they were going to pay me."

"So, you're a member of the Circle of Night, too then?" I asked, flicking my gaze down at her clothes. She was practically wearing rags, holes pockmarking a cream shirt that looked as though it might have once been yellow. I didn't like to judge. Hell, I'd worn something similar once upon a time, when I'd still been on the run and penniless. But members of the Circle liked to show off their wealth. Clothing, to them, was a status symbol.

"Oh, no." She shook her head. "I wish. I thought helping them feed their prisoners might get me an edge in, but I don't need that." She took another step back. "I've been on the streets for a long time. I can handle it. You don't need to kill me. Just let me go."

I let out a sigh. "We're not here to kill you. We just want to release the prisoners, including Byron over there."

My heart raced as I jerked my thumb in the direction of the cages. I'd taken one look at the vamp when I'd first come in and had known within a millisecond that he was the vamp I'd been sent to save. Or kill. His sleet gray hair was unlike anything I'd ever seen, his violet eyes rimmed in a deep crimson that suggested it had been a long-ass time since he'd fed.

He was watching us carefully, as were the shifters. None of them had said a word.

"Byron the Bloody?" Her eyes widened. "You don't want to release him. Or the shifters. They'll kill you."

"They can certainly try," Balor said, voice low. "Tell us where the keys are, and we'll let you go."

The vamp pressed down the front of her yellowish shirt, eyes wide and face pale. She was clearly terrified that we were going to rip her head off, but she almost seemed more scared of helping us, like the vampires she served could hold a candle to Balor's powers. Maybe, if she'd been living on the streets, she had no idea what Balor could do. As unlikely as that was, it wasn't a total impossibility.

"This is Balor Beimnech," I said to her. "The Prince of the Crimson Court. Also sometimes known as Balor the smiter. Because of his flaming eye."

"I know who he is," she whispered before turning to meet my gaze. "And I know who you are, too."

I stiffened, flicking my gaze toward Byron. How could she know? How had she found out? Did she know the vampire who was trying to blackmail me? Or was this information flittering through the vampire community at a terrifying speed? If that was the case then—

"You're Clark, the new psychic in the Court." She licked her lips. "If I don't give you what you want, are you going to read my mind?"

I blew out a breath of relief. Clark, the psychic. That made a hell of a lot more sense. Of course she would have heard about the new addition to the Crimson Court, one who could read minds, especially now that I was formally helping out the leader of the Circle of Night. I'd panicked for no reason. Jumped to a ridiculous conclusion.

But still, that didn't change the fact that one vampire had discovered the truth. What was to stop it from happening again?

But before I could give her an answer, the door of the warehouse burst off its hinges and careened across the floor toward my boots.

16

"Ack!" I jumped back from the shattered door as if it were a coil of unruly snakes. Several familiar faces streamed into the warehouse, shouting and growling as if they were in the middle of some kind of wrestling game on TV. The new arrivals on the scene were the shifters from the night before, the ones we'd encountered in Gordon's Wine Bar.

The vamp's red eyes widened, and she began to sprint across the floor. One of the shifters jogged sideways, blocking her path of escape.

"Not so fast, vamp." He wrapped his massive hand around her skinny arm. "You're not getting out of this that easily."

"What is going on here?" Balor asked, his bellowing voice echoing in the empty space.

The shifters all turned his way.

"I could ask you the same thing," said the shifter, who was still holding tightly to the vamp. He had curly dark hair and a thick beard to match. His biceps strained against his black shirt, a camouflage green that matched his boots. "It shouldn't surprise me that I would find the fae Prince in the middle of a pow wow with some vampires killing our kind, but it does. I can't believe we all fell for your lies about unity and alliances and everyone getting along singing shite songs around campfires."

Balor shifted back his shoulders and strode toward the group of shifters. They were carrying daggers, but they'd kept them sheathed and strapped to their thighs. None of them had changed into their animal forms, but I had no doubt they would if they truly felt threatened.

"Be careful when you make accusations," my Prince said, narrowing his eyes. "Particularly when they are unfounded."

"You're saying you're not working with these vamps?" the shifter asked. "Then, why the hell are you here?"

"Anderson's right," one of the smaller shifters, with pitch black, pointy hair, added. "Why are you here if you ain't stealing our blood?"

"I'm guessing we're here for the same reason you are. To free the shifters." And the vamp. Maybe. "Did you not notice that we warned you in the bar? Or did you conveniently forget that when you decided to accuse us of being involved?"

Anderson exchanged a glance with his two friends. "Sure, we remember. But we also couldn't help but wonder how you had that info in the first place. Only someone involved would know what the vamps were planning to do."

"This is ridiculous," I said, stalking toward the

shifter and his new prisoner before sticking out my hand at the vamp. "Give me the keys."

She shook her head. "If I do, they'll kill me."

"Let her go," Balor said. "She has the keys to the cages."

Anderson looked as though he were considering the option. But then he frowned, twisting the vamp's head with a sharp snap. The female vampire's eyes widened, and then went vacant, before her body fell with a hard smack on the floor. My heart thundered in my ears, horror churning through me.

"What the hell did you do that for?" I said in a harsh whisper. "She was going to help us."

"She was helping *them*," the shifter said with a snarl. "The vamps who have been killing our kind. She got what she deserved."

I just stared at him as he knelt on the floor and began to dig around inside the vampire's yellowish pockets. I'd known that shifters could be brutal, but I'd never seen it with my own eyes. When they got angry, they got *really* angry, and nothing but blood on the ground could satisfy their animalistic need for violence.

"You shouldn't have done that," Balor said quietly from behind me. "This could threaten the alliance."

The shifter scoffed, pulling a set of keys out of the dead vamp's pockets. "Are you really acting like I should give two shits about the alliance when vampires have been killing shifters for their blood?"

"Obviously, that's an issue," Balor said in as even of a voice as he could. "But adding more bodies to the pile is only going to exacerbate the issue."

"Exacerbate smacerbate," Anderson replied,

jingling the keys as he stood. "As far as I'm concerned, the alliance was fucking broken the second a single vamp put his fangs in one of mine."

So, this was going well. Not that I was particularly surprised. The shifter wasn't wrong. Vampires had kind of taken the alliance, stomped all over it, and then spit right into its face. Still, we needed to put a stop to all this bloodshed. We were all toeing far too close to breaking a line that could never be put back together again.

"Listen," I said, snatching the keys out of the shifter's hands. "I'm not going to pretend like this whole thing isn't pretty horrific, but you have to look at the bigger picture. The black market blood business is run by a few rogue vampires. *A few*. No need to undo all the progress supernatural London has made because of them. Hell, that would probably make them happy, to be honest. There are always going to be those who want to screw things up for everyone else."

These were Ronan's words, only I'd tried to present them in a more optimistic way than he had. Instead of giving up, it just meant that we needed to fight that much harder.

The shifter merely crossed his arms over his beefy chest. "Nice try, but we're not going to be convinced by flowery words."

With a frustrated sigh, I glanced back at Balor.

"What will convince you to keep the peace?" he asked.

"No more of all this nice shit," the shifter replied, ripping the keys out of my hands. "Right now, no one in the Pack knows about all this but us, but it's not going to stay that way for long. Unless, you bring us their heads."

My eyebrows shot to the top of my head. "Excuse me?"

Anderson flashed me a grin. "Not literally. If you only brought us their heads, I'd be sorely disappointed that we didn't get to take out judgement on them ourselves."

"Explain," Balor replied.

"The vamps running this show have killed our kin," the shifter answered. "If you want to keep the alliance solid between the Pack and your Court, those vamps need to pay for what they did. But *we* get to decide their punishment. Find them, and bring them to us. Do that, and I won't take this issue to anyone else in the Pack. And we won't go after any other vampires."

Balor let out a heavy sigh.

"As long as," the shifter said, twisting on his feet toward the cages, "my brothers here are okay with that?"

The shifters in the cages all murmured their agreement, and Anderson turned back our way with a wide smile. "So, it's settled then. Bring us the murderers, and we'll stay aligned with your Court."

It took Balor a moment to answer. In theory, the shifter's proposition wasn't a terrible idea, but I understood the Prince's hesitation. Matteo wasn't here to agree to it, and he would likely want to punish his own vampires the way he saw fit. What he had in mind would no doubt be far different than whatever the shifters had planned.

It wasn't really our place to agree. But we also didn't have much of a choice.

Balor finally gave a slow, solemn nod. "Agreed. We will find the killers and bring them to you."

My heart beat hard in my chest as the shifter stepped forward and dropped the keys into Balor's open palm, a display of the new agreement they had formed between them. I watched my Prince make this new pact, somehow calming the anger and the frustration of the shifters, anger that had been very much earned. He was good at this. I could see why he'd gotten the Pack and the Circle to agree to join him as allies. There was something about him that exuded strength and power that was impossible to ignore.

The keys jangled as he turned from the shifters and strode across the floor to the cages. I trailed behind him, my heart so torn in two that I could barely breathe. Any second now, Byron the Bloody would be out of that cage and standing before me. The impossible choice I'd been avoiding could no longer be pushed aside. I had to decide. I couldn't keep going back and forth. I could either do my part and help the Court or I could save myself.

"Balor," I called out behind him. He paused just as he was about to put the keys in the lock. He twisted to glance over his shoulder at where I stood wringing my hands in the middle of the warehouse floor. "Maybe we should call Matteo first, let him know what's going on."

I had no idea why I'd said that. It was a terrible idea. But calling Matteo meant stalling things.

Balor's eyes pinched together. "I think it's best if we handle one thing at a time."

“What does Matteo have to do with this?” Anderson barked out as he strode over to Balor’s side.

“See?” Balor raised his eyebrows at me, and then turned to the shifter. “This is Matteo’s son, who was captured along with your friends.”

“Byron the Bloody,” the vampire hissed as he wrapped his hands around the cage bars and leaned forward to glare at the shifter. “So, keep your paws to yourself, mutt.”

The shifter growled.

“And this is why I want to deal with one faction at a time, Clark,” Balor said in a tired voice. “Now, everyone, calm yourselves down, so we can get you out of here.”

“Why did they capture you anyway?” I asked the vamp, but everyone ignored me as Balor unlocked Byron’s cage door and then the doors of the shifters. All the prisoners spilled out onto the floor, hackles raised. Byron glared at the shifters. The shifters glared at Byron. Balor stood in the middle of it all, looking calm and in control but also kind of exasperated.

And then Byron turned to look at me.

A strange expression flickered across his face as I glanced from his shiny shoes to the top of his sleet gray hair. There was something odd about him, though I couldn’t put my finger on what it was. Not his eyes, though they were such a deep shade of violet that it was hard not to stare. There was something about him that felt a bit more rough around the edges than the other vampires of the Circle of Night. Something raw. Maybe it was because he’d spent the past few days locked up in a cage.

I wet my lips. Here I finally was. Facing my saviour or my doom.

"Clark," Balor said. "Stay here with Byron while I walk the shifters out of the warehouse. I'll be back for you two in a moment, and we'll take him straight back home."

I understood what Balor was doing. There was too much tension peppering the air, and Balor wanted to make sure the shifters went on their own merry way instead of following us back to the city. They'd made a pact, sure, but now that their friends were free, there wasn't much to stop them from breaking it. Except honour. And I wasn't sure how much honour these shifters had.

I gave a nod, keeping my gaze locked on Byron's face, heart thumping hard.

When the door of the warehouse slammed shut, I reached for the hilt of my sword.

"I know why you're here," Byron said just as my palm curled around the steel. His voice was somehow smooth and rough at the same time. "You've been sent to kill me, haven't you?"

My eyes began to burn. "What makes you say that?"

"I know there are some vamps that have it out for me," he said quietly, eyes flicking to the sword where my hand rested, tensely. "Maybe you've figured it out. I'm half-shifter." He sniffed. "Like you."

Realisation dawned, and I could kick myself for not noticing it before. Of course. That made sense. I'd wondered why the black market vamps would have abducted another vamp. They'd done it because he wasn't a full vampire at all.

"So, your mother?" I arched a brow.

"Shifter," he said. "It's only because I'm my father's son that I've survived this long, but it doesn't stop a lot of vamps for wanting me out of the equation."

A tense beat passed before I spoke again. "I was told that you're dangerous. A murderer."

"Ah." His eyes drooped in the corners, and he smiled. "And do you believe that?"

I stared into his violet eyes, clear and bright. Red rimmed the edges, but there was nothing uncontrollable about his hunger.

"Why do they call you Byron the Bloody?" I asked.

He let out a low chuckle. "They don't. I came up with that name myself, hoping to convince the vampires that I was one of them instead of something else. I don't think it worked. Do you?"

Shit. I blinked at him, the moments stretching out like elastic bands that might snap tight at any moment. The past hung over my head like a sharp sword. All I had to do was plunge my own blade right into his heart, and I could avoid getting sliced myself.

All the breath left my lungs. My eyes closed.

I couldn't do it.

17

My hand drifted from my sword hilt. Byron's violet eyes followed my movement, his breath catching so loud that it echoed in the cavernous space. "You aren't going to do it?"

"No," I said quietly. "I'm not an assassin, and you don't deserve to be killed because of where you've come from. You just have to promise me one thing."

"What's that?"

"Please don't tell Balor that I was sent here to kill you. He can't know. Okay?"

The vampire pursed his lips, but he gave a solemn nod. "I can do that in exchange for you sparing my life."

He reached out a hand, a slight smile playing on his lips. With a sigh, I took it and shook. His grip was strong and certain, and nowhere near as cold as a vamp's touch normally was. How could I ever thought I could do this? How did I even consider it for a moment? Letting him go meant the worst possible future for me, but I'd figure something out. I would leave London. I would get the hell out of here. I'd planned on leaving before. No big deal.

But it felt like the biggest deal in the world.

The door cracked open, and Balor's head popped into the warehouse. "Come. It's time we get you back home."

~

Matteo was waiting in the lobby for us when we returned to the Circle of Night. The sky had begun to lighten, but we'd made it back in time for the leader of the vampires to wrap his arms tight around his son. Tears filled my eyes, burning them. I couldn't believe I'd been so close to ending this male's life.

"Thank you," Matteo said, lifting his eyes to give Balor a nod. "You have fulfilled your end of the bargain, therefore I will fulfil mine. The alliance is safe."

For now, I thought, hearing the unspoken words drifting toward me from his mind. We might have settled things for now, but there would no doubt come another time when the bonds between fae and vampires were shaken.

Speaking of…

"Matteo, a word?" Balor asked with a raised eyebrow.

The four of us trailed up the escalators and into Matteo's office. Just outside the door, Matteo sent his son on his way, suggesting a soothing bath and a rest in bed before the sun fully rose in the sky. Before he left, Byron gave me one last look full of meaning, and then disappeared down the corridor.

"He looks terrible," Matteo said, stalking over to his desk and slamming a fist hard onto the wooden surface. "Tell me who did this to him."

"Vampires," Balor said quietly, pursing his lips. "It seems they wanted him for his blood."

Matteo's face paled. "For that black market blood business? You cannot be serious."

"I'm afraid so," Balor said, regarding Matteo carefully. I knew that he still suspected that the leader of the Circle of Night had been more than aware of the dealings going on just down the street from him. To be honest, I suspected him myself, and I was dying to slip inside his mind to see if we were right.

Of course, it didn't make much sense. Matteo had been clearly distressed that his son had gone missing, and he looked as though he wanted to string up the culprit and watch them die a slow and horrible death. So, if Matteo was involved in the black market, had he not known that they'd taken his son? And who would be idiot enough to go against the most powerful vamp in the city?

"I am going to find them and kill them," Matteo said in a low growl.

"Before you do that," I said, raising my hand, "we have another suggestion for you."

"Less a suggestion and more of a command," Balor added.

Matteo shrugged back his shoulders and narrowed his eyes. "A *command*? I am not one of your fealty-giving fae, Balor Beimnech. We may be allies, but you do not command me, and I'm offended that you would even try."

"Regardless," Balor said, voice firm and steady. "Vampires of this city have banded together to create a black market for shifter blood. Many shifters have been killed in this process, and the Pack is out for blood. Not that I can blame them."

Matteo pressed his lips firmly together. "What are you suggesting?"

"I'm suggesting that if we don't do something to rectify this, then the days of peace in London will be over."

Matteo clucked his tongue, braced his hands on his desk, and leaned forward. "You talk of peace when my son was abducted right on these very streets."

"Abducted by other vampires. Not shifters. As far as I can tell, they're blameless in this."

"And those vampires will be dealt with," Matteo said in a low voice.

"Yes," Balor said, striding forward. "They will. By the Court and by the Pack. It's the only way for the shifters to get the justice they feel they deserve."

Matteo narrowed his eyes. "You're suggesting that I allow you to hand my own vampires over to the Pack? You cannot be serious, Balor."

"Oh, I am more than serious. It will happen whether you like it or not. And, if you make any attempt to stop us, consider the alliance done."

I blew out a hot breath as Balor and I drove back to the Court. "So, yeah. That was something. I had no idea you were going to stand up to him like that."

"I did what had to be done." He gripped the wheel tight in his hands.

"You do realise that you effectively chose the shifters over the vampires. He's not going to like that very much."

"Matteo needs this alliance just as much as I do or he wouldn't have agreed to it." Balor twisted the wheel to the right, the car rumbling down the clogged London road. "When his son was missing, he tried to use it to his advantage to get what he wanted, but he always knew I'd do anything to find Byron. So now, I'm calling his bluff."

"Well, let's hope he doesn't call your bluff right back," I muttered underneath my breath.

"The shifters are what we have to worry about right now," he replied. "They're the ones who have been truly wronged in all this. As long as we can prove that we will police the criminals among us, then they will stick by our side."

I sighed and leaned back in the seat, watching the flickering lights pass us by. "Do you ever just have the urge to, I don't know...give up and run away? Go somewhere that no one knows who you are, where no one knows the complicated power struggles that we have to deal with every damn day?"

"Of course," Balor said quietly. "But as the Prince of the Crimson Court, I do not live my life for me. I live it for the fae. And they need me to do whatever it takes to keep them safe. If that means dealing with complicated power struggles every damn day, then so be it. Their lives are worth my pain."

I twisted toward him, smiling sadly. Balor's devotion to his Court was one of the things I loved about him. I'd witnessed it first-hand time and time again, a devotion that I'd rarely seen in anyone else. He wanted what was best for them, and he gave up so much to keep them safe.

When we returned to Court, dawn was breaking through the sky. It had been another sleepless night, and I was beginning to feel a bit like a vampire myself. Wake with the dark, sleep with the light. My body ached, and my eyes felt like a pair of puffy clouds. I was so tired that I could probably fall asleep standing up.

Balor took my elbow in his hand and steered me toward the stairs, leading me toward the upper floor and my room. I swallowed hard. This was the first time he'd touched me since the…incident. It brought back a flood of memories I'd tried so hard to block out. The feel of his lips on my skin. His smile as he lowered himself between my legs.

A lump formed in my throat. Was this how Balor felt every time he gave something up for the Court? Because it felt terrible. As soon as my time ran out and the blackmailing vampire realised that I hadn't killed Byron the Bloody, my truth would be revealed to the world. That included Balor and everyone in this Court.

I'd done what I could to save the alliance, but now that meant I had to save myself.

Before the end of the week, I would be gone.

"You're very quiet, Clark," Balor said, his voice rumbling in his chest. "I have to say, that's unlike you."

"Well, I feel like a pile of rubbish so that's probably why."

"You seemed on edge in the warehouse. Was it Byron?"

"Byron?" I blinked at him. Had my face given away that much?

"His heritage. You said you hadn't met many half-shifters before, and you'd been attacked by the very same vamps that took him prisoner. I know your past is a sore issue for you. I thought seeing him might have brought back some memories you'd rather not face right now."

"Balor." We came to a stop outside my door, and I sunk against the frame. "I know you want to know about my past, but I am far too tired to get into that right now. Don't worry. You'll know soon enough."

A strange expression flickered across his face. "What in the bloody hell is that supposed to mean?"

I gave him a weak smile. "It just means I won't be hiding it from you for much longer."

I wouldn't be hiding it because I wouldn't be in London. When he found out, I'd be as far away from him as I could get. I just had to hope he could never find me.

18

I only slept a few hours before I was out of my bed once again. It wasn't like I could really sleep anyway, knowing what was hanging over my head. There was a lot I needed to get sorted, including a one-way ticket straight out of London town. Despite my attempt to leave the Court without being seen, Moira intercepted me on my way out the front door.

She was looking as bright-eyed and bushy-tailed as she usually did. I was mildly jealous. What I would give to have a normal life instead of this twisted up thing I couldn't escape. "Heard you caught yourself a missing vamp."

"Yeah. Turns out those wankers who tried to take me went after the only other half-shifter in the city."

"It's odd that they would even bother. No offence." She shrugged. "Didn't they say that your blood was less potent?"

"They did, but I don't think we should expect sociopathic vampires to make logical decisions."

"Hmm." She flicked her golden eyes up and down my all-black ensemble. "Where are you off to this early? I figured you'd be asleep until noon."

"I need to go see a man about a dog."

She scrunched up her face in confusion.

"It's an expression," I said with a smile. "I'm going to train with Ronan again."

"Ronan, eh?" She lifted her eyebrows. "I heard Balor talking about him the other day. Well, he wasn't *talking*, really. More like ranting. I don't think he's too fond of that guy. I'm surprised he's approved you to go back there, honestly."

My cheeks flushed. "I didn't ask him."

Moira snorted. "Gotcha. I'll cover for you, if I can. What's my excuse? You've gone shopping?"

"I don't think Balor is going to believe that I decided to go hunting for shoes and mascara after the past few days that I've had."

"Hey." She held up her hands and grinned. "Don't knock the shopping. There's nothing quite like retail therapy. Or at least that's what Elise always says."

"I'll keep that in mind," I said with a laugh before turning toward the door, casting a glance over my shoulder at my friend. "Thanks, Moira."

"No problem." She gave me a mock salute and watched me leave, giving me a grin. But when I turned to give her one last look before the door shut behind me, a strange, unsettled expression had taken shape on her face. And then she was gone.

~

My knuckles rapped on Ronan's metal door. An irritated grunt punctuated the silence. After a moment, heavy footsteps thudded toward me. The door rattled up, revealing a half-naked Ronan wincing into the sunlight. He took one glance at me, rolled his eyes, and walked away. Luckily, he left the door open for me.

I ducked underneath it and strode inside. Ronan now leaned against the wall, stirring a stick in a coffee mug. He didn't even glance my way as the door slammed hard behind me, plunging us back into the dimly-lit darkness he liked so much.

"You do realise that it is *seven in the bloody morning*."

"Up late?" I glanced at the beer cans scattered around an overflowing bin. "Don't tell me you have some company."

"I might." He chuckled. "Jealous?"

I drank in the muscles of his chest, at the way the ridges of his abs formed strong peaks along his stomach. His skin was smooth and dark, yet gloriously rugged at the same damn time. He looked like the kind of guy to star in a superhero film, throwing tridents at his greatest enemies. It was really hard not to stare.

"Yeah right. You wish."

Yeah right? You wish? Ugh, Clark. Come on. You sound like an idiot.

"Er, maybe I should go," I said when he didn't reply.

He cracked a smile. "I'm kidding. Last night's party was a party of one. It's not often that I have guests."

"Oh." I pulled on the edge of my leather jacket. "I mean, I don't care. I just didn't want to intrude."

He set down his coffee mug. "Why are you here at seven in the bloody morning, Clark? You look like you haven't slept in days. More shifting trouble?"

"Actually, no." I shrugged off my leather jacket and tossed it onto the sofa. "But it's going to happen again, and I need it to happen under my control. Can you train me today?"

He pursed his lips. "You really aren't very good at advanced notice, are you?"

"Do you have anything better to do today?"

He let out a grunt of amusement. "Alright. I'll train you today. On one condition."

I arched a brow. "Oh yeah? What's that?"

"Tell me what's the rush. What's got you so spooked?" He held up a hand when I opened my mouth. "And don't tell me you're not flapping your wings all worried like. I don't need to be a mind reader like you to read your face."

I stared at him for a long moment. Despite how willing he'd been to help me, I wasn't entirely sure that Ronan was trustworthy. He didn't exactly play by society's rules, supernatural or otherwise. He'd holed himself up in here, and I had to wonder how often he even saw the light of day. Plus, he clearly held a grudge against those who had wronged him.

That said, if he'd wanted to harm me, he'd had plenty of chances to do it by now.

"I'm going to leave London," I finally said, wincing at the way the words sounded out loud. So far, it had only been a thought, a plan in my head. Now, it felt far more real.

"Huh." He shook his head and grabbed his coffee again. "Can't say I expected that. Mind telling me why?"

"I don't belong in the Crimson Court," I said. "I should have left the day Balor inducted me into his House. There are things from my past. Things I'm not going to talk about. Anyway, they're going to come to light in a couple of days. I need to be gone when they do."

"Well, that certainly sounds ominous." He kept his joking grin, but there was a hint of concern in his eyes.

"Before I go, I thought it might be a good idea to get a handle on my shift. That way, it won't happen in the middle of a village square or something."

Realisation dawned in his eyes. "You're going to fly out of London, aren't you?"

I didn't answer, heart thumping hard.

"You're worried that Balor will be able to track you if you leave any other way. With all the CCTV on the streets, on the trains, it would only take one hack into the system for his tech guy to track you down." Ronan pushed away from the wall and strode toward me. "One might wonder what Balor would learn that would make him go to that much trouble to find you."

I sucked in a breath, took a step back. "You're going to tell him about this, aren't you?"

He regarded me for a long moment, his dark eyes flickering across my face. After a moment, he smiled. "No, I don't think I will."

Could I trust him? I'd blurted out far more than I should have, all because my antsiness to get the hell out of here had made me careless. It wouldn't be the first time that I'd trusted the wrong male. Tiarnan had betrayed me. Would Ronan betray me, too?

Closing my eyes, I reached timidly toward his mind. There was strength around the edges of it, a solid power that was difficult to push past. After several moments of trying, I managed to get through his strength, dipping deep into the very heart of him. There was a roughness to his thoughts, and anger. Not at me but at the world. Ronan was carrying a grudge on his shoulders, an ever-present reminder of who he'd once been and how he'd been wronged.

She's an irritating little thing, but her secret is safe with me. I never really liked Balor anyway.

With a relieved sigh, I pulled back into myself, opening my eyes to see Ronan had strode even closer to me. Now, he was only an inch away, so close that our chests almost brushed against each other.

"Why do you look so worried? I told you I wouldn't tell Balor. Your secret is safe with me, even though you haven't given me a damn clue what it is."

"Thank you, Ronan." I reached up and wrapped my hand around his, squeezing tight. It was all I could do to keep the tears at bay. Everything was falling apart, and soon I'd lose everyone I'd come to care about. And the city I'd called home these past ten years. It made me more grateful for Ronan than I could ever explain.

"Whoa now." He chuckled. "Let's not get all mushy. I'm just helping you learn how to shift. No big deal."

"Right." I sucked in a sharp breath through my nose and pulled my hand away, averting my gaze from his rippling abs. "Time to work on my shift."

~

Three hours later, I was toast. And by toast, I mean that I didn't transform into a raven again. Ronan had spent hour after hour, talking me through the things I needed to do in order to stay in control of the change. There was a lot of pushing me to the ground and a lot more shouting at me. None of it seemed to work. It had only succeeded in giving me some seriously nasty bruises on my bum.

"You realise the problem with our approach is that you aren't afraid of me." He strode over to his mini fridge, found a beer, and popped the tab. "I should be offended, but…"

"But what?" I blew at my wet hair and leaned against the wall behind the sparring mat.

"Well, there are other ways. You said you don't want to try those, but we'll never make any progress if you don't get riled up."

Heat flushed my neck. "Surely there has to be a better way."

He shrugged and downed his beer. "Like I said, you're not afraid of me. No matter how many times I push you, it's not going to change your gut reaction to me."

"I really am not in the mood for your games."

With a slight smile, he grabbed a glass, strode over to a little metal sink, and filled it with water. He crossed the room, lifting the drink my way. But when I reached out to grab it, he poured it down the front of his chest.

Rivulets of water dripped down his skin, curling around the ridges of his abs. Adrenaline spiked in my gut, causing a new wave of heat to rush through me. His lips quirked, and he knelt before me.

"Face it, Clark. There's only one way for me to get your shift going. I'm more than happy to oblige, but only if that's what you want. Your choice."

I wet my lips and stared into his dark eyes. Something deep within me was crying out for me to say yes, a primal part I'd long ago buried deep inside my gut. The shifter side of me wanted to curl toward Ronan, to let him tease me as a way to start my shift.

Nibbling on my bottom lip, I gave a nod. "Okay, but we need some boundaries."

"Boundaries do not make for a good shift, Clark." With his chest dripping wet, he leaned toward me, coming so close that I had no choice but to place my hands on his skin.

He was hot. Blazing hot. His skin pulsed underneath my fingertips, slick and warm and thumping in time with the beat of his heart. I shuddered, dropping my eyes to where we touched. His muscles were magnificent, perfectly sculpted and impossibly strong. He could probably hurl me into the air with a single arm.

And a part of me wanted him to do it.

His dark eyes sparked with heat as he dragged his tongue across his lips. "May I?"

My heart thumped hard. "May you what?"

"Make you shift. It will be worth it. I swear."

"Okay," I breathed.

19

I wasn't sure what I expected him to do, but when he leaned forward and placed his hot mouth on mine, I couldn't help but gasp. Heat poured from his body into mine, strong sparks that made every single cell in my body turn to flames.

I tried to keep control. I tried to think around the pure fire that shot through my veins, but I couldn't. Despite it all, I let out a moan. A low growl erupted from Ronan's throat in response, a deep, guttural, animalistic sound that sent wave upon wave of goosebumps over my skin. His mouth was rough and hard, his tongue dancing between my parted lips.

My fingernails dug deep into his skin as I clung on tight, opening my mouth wider and giving in to the kiss. His arms wrapped around my back and pulled me close. I lost myself in the moment, forgetting all the pain and fear of the past few weeks. The prophecy no longer mattered. The blackmail was gone from my mind. All that was left was the heat and power that radiated between us.

His growl growing louder, Ronan dipped his hands beneath my shirt. Breath ragged, I pulled away from him, wordlessly shaking my head. Desire pounded through my body like a storm. As much as a part of me wanted this, and even though I would be gone from this place within days, I couldn't bring myself to cross that line.

I couldn't bring myself to forget Balor.

Still, the heat of our kiss had done the trick. Pain lanced through my body as my bones began to crack. Arms trembling, I gritted my teeth, crying out when a new wave of pain tore through me. Every single part of me shook. Every bone cracked. All the pleasure of the kiss was replaced by the worst form of torture I'd ever felt.

And then all was black.

~

When I awoke, I was fully clothed in an extra pair of jeans I'd brought along with me. I was also not a single bit feathery. One of those was a good thing. The other, not so much. Other than that, everything hurt, much like last time.

Groaning, I twisted my face sideways to see Ronan sitting on the armchair across from his sofa—where he'd placed me, apparently—staring at me. His eyes were dark and full of an intense emotion I couldn't read.

"Well?" I arched my brow. "I guess that worked?"

"Oh, it worked," he said in a flat voice. "It also brought a storm of ravens pecking at my door."

I pushed up from the sofa, momentarily forgetting the pain. "Say what now?"

"You heard me." He crossed his arms over his chest and leaned back in his chair. "After you shifted, I put you in the cage just to make sure you didn't hurt yourself flapping around in the rafters. You were screeching like mad, and a bunch of ravens came flying to help you."

I stared at him, heart thumping hard. This couldn't be a coincidence. Ravens had helped us at the Tower of London, and now they'd come calling again. But what did that mean?

"Is that normal?" I asked. "Do wolves respond to you when you howl?"

"When wolves hear us howl, they run. In the opposite direction. Animals don't like shifters. Except for you."

~

After I'd rested, Ronan gave me a beer and swore it would ease some of the pain I felt in my veins and in my bones. Strangely, it kind of worked. Half an hour later, I was back on my feet and headed to Court. Training wasn't over, of course. I still needed to shift a couple of more times before I stopped passing out. And, even then, I needed to figure out how to do it on my own…without Ronan's particular brand of assistance.

It wasn't like I could just take him with me.

Back at Court, I kind of hoped that I could just avoid Balor and the others for the next twenty-four hours while I prepped and packed and made a plan of escape. I was glad I had a little extra time before my deadline came and went. The last thing I wanted to do was fly out of here with no idea where to go. When I'd first gone on the run, I'd spent a lot of time sleeping on the street. I'd do it again if I had to, but if I planned this right, I could hopefully find a bed.

As if sensing my arrival, Balor was waiting for me in the lobby with his lips pulled down into a frown. He took one look at me and scowled.

"I knew Moira was lying," he said by way of greeting.

I pushed past him, keeping my eyes firmly on the ground ahead of me instead of on his face. "Excuse me. I need a shower."

"You went to see him again, didn't you?"

I stopped in my tracks, sighing. "I need to train, Balor. He's the only one who can help me get control of my shift."

"You also reek of him. His scent is all over you."

Closing my eyes, I spun in my boots to face him. "The training requires physical contact. I can't shift unless I have a spike in emotions. You know that. The only times I've ever come close to shifting before were when we were in the middle of fights."

"You don't smell like you've been fighting, Clark," he said in a low rumble. "You smell like…tell me if you slept with him."

"Balor," I said in a thick voice, flipping open my eyes to see him bearing down on me. "Please, can we not have this conversation? I don't want to fight with you, especially not right now."

He arched a brow. "Why not right now? What's different about this moment than any other?"

My heart thumped. It was different because it was one of the very last times I would be able to look into his face. I wanted to memorise every line of it, commit it to memory in a way that would last the rest of my life. But I didn't want to remember him like this. Scowling at me. Angry at me. Hatred bubbling beneath the surface.

"I am exhausted, Balor. Shifting takes a lot out of me." A pause. "And no, I didn't sleep with him. I couldn't anyway, not even if I wanted to."

His eye flashed. "Why?"

"Why do you think?"

~

I was halfway through packing my bag when a knock sounded on my door. Shoulders slumped forward, I shoved the bag into my closet before answering. My tall, powerful Prince stood in the corridor, hands slung in his pockets. He'd given me about ten minutes alone before he'd come back for more bickering.

"Balor." Sighing, I went to shut the door, but he shoved his hand through the gap before I could manage. "I don't want to fight with you right now. I just need some peace and quiet for once."

"I'm not here to fight. I'm here to talk to you about the mission."

Confusion rippled through me. "What mission?"

"We made a vow to the shifters. We need to find the vampires behind the black market blood trade and deliver them to the Pack," he said.

Oh. Right. Of course. With my mind firmly

distracted by my new plan to flee London, I'd completely forgotten that our mission hadn't truly ended. In my head, we'd delivered Byron to his father, and that was that. But we still had to take care of those arsehole vamps.

He. Them. Not we.

With a sigh, I leaned against the doorframe. "I think I'm going to sit the rest of this one out. I'm sure Moira or Duncan will be more than happy to take my place."

Balor frowned. "This isn't like you. Usually, it's next to impossible to stop you from charging out the door and into the streets. I was under the impression you liked getting out in the field, taking down our enemies."

"I do." My heart squeezed tight. More than anything. "But I'm not like you, Balor, remember? I'm half-shifter, which means I'm weaker than you. I don't have a battery inside of me that never runs out. Sometimes, I need charging. Now is one of those times."

His gaze never faltered. "Is this about what's happened between us? If that's the case, I can assign one of the other guards to act as your partner from now on. Once we finish this mission."

"That's not it. I swear I'm just tired."

He reached out, took my hand in his, and squeezed. I couldn't help but think that very same hand had only hours ago been pressed up against Ronan's slick chest. I glanced away.

"I know, Clark, and I'm sorry. But I need you for this. All we have to do is find these vamps. Hopefully, it will all be over tonight. And after that? Hell, I'll give you three full days off from guard duty. To rest, repair, and work on shifting with Ronan, as much as I hate that idea. Moira said you wanted to go shopping. You can do that, too, if you'd like."

My heart pulsed. He was being so nice to me. Too nice. It reminded me of the podcast set-up he'd done for me after my first week in the Court. I'd barely had time to even think about recording since then, too caught up in guard duties. But it was the thought that mattered. Just like now.

"Why is it so important to you that I finish out this mission?"

"I'm going to need your power to make sure we've tracked down the right vamps." He gave me an apologetic smile. "And I thought the shifters might be more inclined to deal favourably with us if you were involved. You bridge that gap, Clark. That could prove important, and we need all the advantages we can get if we want to ensure the alliance survives."

Damn it. Damn him. Damn the bloody vampires. Damn it all. Balor needed me. The Court did, too. He had never pleaded this way with me before. Hell, I'd never seen him plead with anyone. This was important to him, and I couldn't ignore that. Not only that, it would be my last chance to help him before I had to run.

At least I had one more day. That was enough time to help the Court, and then get the hell out.

~

Everyone stood in the command station, waiting for us. The crew surrounded the central table while Kyle squatted behind the bank of computers in the corner. I couldn't help but note that his cactus was still alive and well. Ondine would no doubt be pleased.

"Clark," Moira said quietly as I took up my spot beside her. She dropped her voice to a low whisper. "Sorry. I tried my best to distract him with talk of shoes, but he could sense something was up."

"Him and his bloody power," I muttered.

"Right." Balor strode over to us, placed his hands on the table, and leaned forward to meet each of our gazes in turn. "This will be the last time we have to deal with this issue or any like it. After this, I demand life in Court goes back to normal."

Everyone murmured their agreement. I couldn't help but wonder, what the hell was normal in the Crimson Court? I was pretty sure we were living in it.

Duncan cleared his throat and dropped a few printed-out photographs on the table before us. They showed several hazy figures darting through the streets and then standing around a small table in an alley. It was impossible to see much more than that, though I understood exactly what he was trying to point out.

"You found the vamps," I said with a nod.

"Kyle found them," Duncan corrected.

In the back corner, Kyle cleared his throat. "For once, it wasn't that hard. They've made no attempt to be stealthy about what they're doing. All they did was go straight back to their corner in Leadenhall Market. From what I was able to see, they have a regular chain of customers. Probably two an hour, from about ten at night until four in the morning."

I frowned. That meant that these vamps sold

twelve poisonous blood bags every single night they put up shop. That was a lot.

"How many blood bags does one shifter provide, anyway?" I couldn't help but ask.

"About eight," Kyle replied. "Could be twelve if he's a particularly large shifter."

"So, they're basically draining the blood of a shifter every single night." I shook my head and met Balor's hard gaze. "And then setting up the future deaths of twelve vamps."

"That is a lot of bodies," Moira said.

"We have to stop them," I said, a new resolution forming in my gut. All this time, I'd been so distracted by my bloody secret that I hadn't fully come to terms with what was going on in the London streets. These black market blood traders were killing so many innocent supernaturals. All for a bit of extra cash.

A ghost of a smile flickered across Balor's lips. "There's my girl."

My heart thumped hard as I caught the look. The wicked flicker of amusement, the heat in his eye. That was the one I wanted. The one I needed to memorise forever. Because it might be the last time I ever saw it.

20

Four of us headed to the market to take down the vampires. Balor was insistent he come along. He'd started this mission with me, and he intended to finish it out. Duncan and Moira had joined us as well, while Kyle sat on the other end of a walkie talkie strapped to Moira's belt. He had managed to tap into the CCTV live feed, so that he could direct us toward the vampires.

"Turn right now." His scratchy voice broke through the silence. "They're at the end of that street. It looks like there are three of them, so you have a major advantage."

I poked my head around the corner, heart hammering hard in my chest. Kyle was right. At the end of the road, just on the outskirts of the red-and-cream market, the vampires stood around their disgusting blood bag table. Three of them. Different ones than we'd seen the last time we'd been here, and none of them were the vamp who tried to abduct me.

Sucking in a sharp breath, I pulled away from the

corner and shook my head at Balor, who was two seconds away from charging right into their midst. I pointed at the opposite end of the street, motioning for them to follow me away from the vamps.

When we were finally a safe distance away, Balor's impassive face transformed into irritation. "What are you doing, Clark? We don't have time to pussyfoot around."

"Those aren't the same vamps," I whispered.

The skin between his eyes pinched tight. "What do you mean? They're selling black market blood. Of course they're the same vampires."

"They might be involved in that group, but they aren't the same ones we ran into the other night. Which means, there's a lot of them. Taking these guys out will only put a bandaid on the situation. A very weak bandaid, especially if none of them are the leader of the business."

Duncan crossed his arms over his chest. "What do you propose we do? The longer we wait to take them down, the more lives are lost."

"Well." I sucked the cool night air into my lungs. "I have an idea."

~

When the human rounded the corner with her newly-purchased blood in hand, it only took one silent punch from Moira to take her down. Duncan grabbed her limp body as it fell, holding her up as a way to keep her from crashing to the ground. I grabbed the blood bag from her fingers, wrinkling my nose. Then, I tossed it to Balor, who cracked it open and poured the liquid all over the ground.

We'd done this same move five times already, and the cobblestones were now a gory shade of red. I had a feeling it was a stain that would never come out.

Duncan lifted the human into his arms and carried her away from the carnage. He'd deposit her in a doorframe several blocks away. By the time she woke up, the vampires would be long gone, along with her opportunity to purchase more poison.

I was pretty surprised by how many humans we'd encountered. A couple of vamps had shown up, but it appeared that humans were the most interested in these blood bags. Another sign that relations between the human side of the city and the supernatural side were quickly disintegrating. But what I truly couldn't believe was that the vampires were selling humans so much poison. Poison that could kill their own kind.

It boggled the mind.

"It's almost daylight," Balor said quietly when Duncan rejoined us. "That should be the last of it."

"Thank god," Moira muttered. "As much as I enjoy punching things, I am not a fan of that thing over there."

She pointed at the blood puddle.

"That makes two of us," I said.

I poked my head around the corner again and eyed up the vamps. Judging by the yellow streaks in the sky, they only had about half an hour before they would need to be safe inside from the sunlight. They had begun to gather up their supplies, dropping everything into a cardboard box. After they'd cleared the table, one of the vamps folded it up and stuck it under his arm. One of the others grabbed the box, and they hurried out of the market.

"Okay, it's go time," I whispered to my fellow guards.

Quietly, we hurried down the street after the vampires. With their enhanced hearing, we had to be careful to keep our footsteps light and stay far enough back that they wouldn't spot us trailing them. It would kind of defeat the purpose if we were caught.

Their path was a maze. We ducked into thin alleys, pushed past junky old cars, and scrambled across wide empty streets. After what felt like years, we finally came to a stop outside a tube station.

The vampires darted underground with their folding table and cardboard box in tow.

"I hope everyone has an Oyster Card," Moira muttered, pulling the purple card out of her back pocket.

We headed underground, hurrying through the barriers. Our attempt at silence and stealth had gone right out of the window the second the vamps had headed for the tube. They were ahead of us, and if we didn't rush, we would likely lose sight of them before they boarded their train.

We reached the platform just as the train rattled into the station. Halfway down the platform, I spotted the vamps. They still hadn't looked our way, too focused on the opening doors before them.

When the doors opened, the four of us slid inside, covering the hilts of our swords with the bottoms of our jackets. Even at the strange hour, humans were piling into the train. As we began to rumble away from the platform, I craned my head, keeping a firm eye on the vamps.

They got off twenty minutes later, hurriedly rushing up the stairs to the street. The sky was almost yellow now, and the top curve of the sun poked above the horizon. One of them shouted, and then broke out into a run, clearly distressed about the rapidly-approaching sunlight. All we could do was follow suit.

"Where the hell are we?" I whisper-shouted through laboured breaths as we raced down a residential, tree-lined street. It was pretty much the opposite of what I imagined when I conjured up ideas of what a vampire's lair might look like. There were no gloomy gothic castles. No flickering torches lining the street. Not even any bats, either.

Very disappointing.

Instead, it looked like any old human subdivision. There was even a playground across the street.

"Chislehurst Caves," Moira panted, shooting me a thumbs up.

"How the hell do you know that?"

She pointed at the walkie talkie. "Kyle. He's following us on his map app. They're just up ahead. There have been rumours going around for years that vamps live there, but no one has ever found firm evidence. I thought it was just another old legend, like all the others."

Chislehurst Caves. The manmade tunnels were located on the southern outskirts of London, spanning what was rumoured to be twenty-two miles. Once used as mines, and then mushroom cultivation, and then a shelter during wars, it was now merely used as a tourist attraction, much like most old things in

London. According to legend, it was easy to get lost in the caves, and the guided tour side of things only spanned so far before the darkness took over.

There had been many stories over the years of humans vanishing off of tours, never to be seen again, which was where the vampire rumours had come from.

So, yeah. This was going to be fun.

The four of us followed the wide stone stairs deep into the earth. The gates that were normally locked against visitors had been left open, wide wrought-iron doors with peeling black paint. As we followed the path marked with signs and plaques that gave details about the caves, our footsteps echoed all around us, adding to a kaleidoscope of sounds. Dripping water, eerie screams, and the rush of wings.

Frowning, I glanced at Balor. He was tense, on edge, with his sword drawn as he led our group deep into the caves. Moira noted his stance, pulling her own sword up before her. I opened my mouth to ask Balor exactly how many vamps could possibly be down here, but he shook his head and held a finger to his lips.

I widened my eyes in understanding. Every single sound was echoing across the walls. If we spoke, there was no telling if our words might drift straight into a vampire's ears. Right now, we still had the element of surprise. It needed to stay that way.

21

The wide walls of the caves narrowed before us, branching off into two separate tunnels that led away from the main entrance. We slowed to a stop just before a junction, glancing around for any sign of which direction the vampires might have gone. Duncan held up his glowing hand of light, gesturing toward one tunnel and then the next.

They both looked identical to me. Dark stone walls that sloped low overhead, carved into tunnels by chalk in centuries past. As I peered into the darkness, I couldn't help but think the tunnels looked as though they went on forever. There was no end in sight. Only shadows.

I pressed my lips together, and pulled my sword from my sheath. The steel was heavy in my hands, but comforting, familiar.

Balor cocked his head and listened. I followed suit, even though my hearing was nowhere near as good as his. In the distance, I could hear the distinct echo of scuttling against stone. Laughter. A few more shrieks. Glass clinking against glass.

Narrowing my eyes, I shifted toward the left tunnel, suddenly certain that was where we'd find the vamps. I pointed the way, cocked an eyebrow at Balor. A strange expression crossed his face, and then he nodded.

Silently, we made our way down the pathway. As we approached the curve in the end, Duncan doused the glow of his power, plunging the four of us back into infinite darkness. I wrinkled my nose at the pungent smell that surrounded us: paraffin and sedimentary rock.

We rounded the corner, coming to a stop on the edges of a cavern that opened up before us. Inside, about a dozen vampires were lounging around as if they owned the place. Maybe they did. A small fire burned in the center of their party, several folding chairs scattered around. They had bottles of champagne and beer sitting on the very same folding table I'd seen them carry down here.

Looked like they were celebrating another successful day in the black market blood trade.

I moved to take a step forward, but Balor shot out a hand to hold me back. He inclined his head toward the left, and I followed his gaze. There in the shadows of the far wall sat two humans, heads drooping forward, eyes glassy.

My heart began to race in my chest. They were clearly alive but barely. Small holes dotted their necks, the edges of their wounds stained in red. The vampires were feeding on these humans, and from the looks of it, they were doing very little to ensure they survived.

Vampires rarely drank straight from the vein these days. It was far too easy for them to lose control and end up snapping a human's neck, their animalistic need taking control of their mind and their body.

We needed to put a stop to this.

"Eh!" one of the vampires shouted as she stood from a folding chair by the fire. Her blazing red eyes were aimed right on our little group in the shadows, her fingers lifting to drag across the sharp point of her fangs. "We've got visitors."

Slowly, the group of vampires turned to face us. Out of the corner of my eye, I swore I could see the glassy gazes of the humans lift and stare.

Swallowing hard, I tightened my grip on my sword and bent my knees. My fellow guards did the same around me. Balor did nothing of the sort. Instead, he lowered his sword and strode out of the shadows, glancing around at the party raging on.

"Celebrating something?" Balor asked, disdain dripping from his voice.

The female vampire strode forward, coming to a stop only inches away from Balor's muscular chest. She dropped back her head to look up at him, peering through a curtain of purple-streaked hair. Sniffing, she narrowed her eyes.

"You weren't invited, fae," she said through clenched teeth. "Take your little underlings and get the hell out of here."

"I'm afraid that will not be happening," he said, voice even and calm. "Unless you can somehow convince me that you aren't involved with the black market blood trade."

Surprise flickered across her pale face, and she glanced to one of the three males we'd tracked down here. "Good going, idiots. Did you not happen to notice that the fae Prince was following you?"

"That's her," another vampire said, blurring out of the shadows. His face was covered in scars that hadn't yet healed, a face that I would never forget. It was the vampire who had attacked me. And, if his wounds were any indication, I'd attacked him right back.

Well, my raven had.

The female raised her eyebrows. "The little one?"

I narrowed my eyes. "I'd rethink calling me the little one when you know exactly what I'm capable of."

I mean, I was talking shite, of course, but they didn't know that. No sooner did I know how to force myself to shift than I knew how to control anything I did in my bird form. Not only that, but I wasn't too fond of the idea of pecking people's faces off, murderous vamp or not.

The female vampire snorted, and crossed her arms over her chest. "Go on then. Transform into your little bird and attack. See how long you survive in a cave full of vamps."

"Enough," Balor said, striding forward and blocking my view of the vamps. "Who is the leader here?"

"You're talking to her," the female said dryly.

"Good. Come with me, and none of your friends here will be harmed."

"You sound like a guy who is used to having his

orders followed, no questions asked." She glanced over her shoulder and whistled at the rest of the vamps. "But you're on my turf down here. We far outnumber you. I'll give you one more chance to get the hell out of here before we're forced to attack."

Balor drew his sword. The female's eyes went hard.

"Very well," she said.

Chaos broke out in the cave. As the vampires swarmed Balor, I tightened my grip on my sword and let out a shout of pure rage. I stormed toward them, weapon raised high, Duncan and Moira by my side. We crashed into our enemies, Balor already spinning through the cave with a grace and speed that was unrivalled by anyone else.

Claws hurtled toward my face. I swung my blade to parry, and the sharp end sunk deep into the vampire's arm. He screamed, falling to his knees. I pulled my weapon back, panting hard as adrenaline rushed through me. Before I could catch my breath, another vampire ran at me. The one from the street. The one who had tried to take me.

I held up my sword and waited, but he slowed to a stop just out of my weapon's reach. His eyes glittered as he stared me down, his red irises so bright that they practically glowed in the darkness.

"I've been wanting a second chance with you," he hissed. "Now, I have it."

"I mean, good luck with that." I inclined my head toward my blade. "I have a sword. I also have Balor Beimnech."

It was a bit of a bluff. We were supposed to deliver the vampires, as many as we could, to the Pack.

Anderson had made it more than clear that he wanted them with their heads attached, which probably also covered the whole burning to a crisp thing. If Balor set free his impossibly brutal power, none of the vampires would survive.

We needed to wound them. Not kill them.

But this vampire didn't know that.

He danced to the side, fangs bared and claws held high. I couldn't help but notice that he looked ridiculous, frankly. Less like a dangerous, feral beast and more like a cat who had been cornered by a mountain lion. Every time he moved, I followed suit, keeping my eyes locked on his face. His eyes flicked just over my shoulder. Sucking in a deep breath, I whirled.

But I wasn't fast enough. A pair of arms wrapped around me, sharp claws digging deep into my skin. I tried to whip away, but the vampire was strong. His sharp fangs sung deep into my shoulder, biting so hard that it felt as though he would take a chunk of my skin along with him. Pain lanced through my body; stars dotted my eyes.

I screamed.

And then the entire cave went brutally silent.

The vampire's mouth stilled on my skin. I panted hard, trying my best to block out the pain.

"Let her go," Balor growled from somewhere behind me. "Let her go or I will open my eye and burn you all."

Shit. My heart thumped hard in my chest. "No. Don't do it."

"If you burn us all, you'll only end up burning her, too," the female leader's voice drifted into my ear.

"You speak as though I have no control over my

power." Footsteps echoed across the floor with the unmistakable gravity that only Balor had. "I've spent my entire life harnessing my flames. I can direct the fire right at your friend's body. Clark will feel the heat of it, but she won't get burnt."

I honestly had no idea if Balor was bluffing. I'd seen his power in action, and he'd never given any indication that he could control the flames to that extent. But it did make sense. When he'd been forced to retaliate against Fionn, the Fianna had been the only one to burn. And when the Sluagh had swarmed into our Court, he'd directed his power right at them.

On the other hand, that could have just been luck.

My heart thumped hard as the tension in the caves ramped up another notch. Moments stretched out into what felt like hours, as silence curled around me, suffocating me.

Finally, the vampire released his grip around my waist. He took a step back, shaking his head.

"Sorry, mate," he said to the raven-pecked vamp. "I'm not in the mood to be fried today."

Flames soared through the caves. They surrounded the vampire, curling around his body. His guttural scream shot through the night, joining the roar of the building fire. Balor flipped his patch back over his eye and turned to face the other vampires, who were now staring at him with open mouths.

I dropped my gaze to the floor, gritting my teeth against the orange flames that completely consumed the vampire. There was nothing worse than seeing someone burned alive…even if seconds ago he had been trying to kill me.

"Now, you can see that I am not bluffing," Balor

said, striding forward to hold up a pair of chains, dangling them before the leader's eyes. "It's time for you to come with me."

She ground her teeth together, glaring up at the Prince. "Where are you taking me?"

"You'll find out." He touched the bottom edge of his eye patch. "Or I can leave you here to burn."

22

"Sometimes, Balor's power terrifies me," I muttered to Moira as we trailed behind our leader out of the caves. After liberating the humans, each of us had taken our own vampire prisoner. Mine just so happened to be the vampire whose eyes I'd pecked out in bird form. We'd tried to bring along the ones who seemed most deeply entrenched in the business, leaving behind stern warnings for the rest. We didn't have enough hands to take them all with us, and they would no doubt be gone by the time we returned.

Moira cocked an eyebrow. "Only sometimes?"

"Okay, most of the time," I conceded. "At least when he uses it. In normal daily life, I almost forget about it."

"You're an idiot if you forget for even one second that your leader can burn you to ash any time he wants," my prisoner said.

Rolling my eyes, I jerked on the chain, forcing the vamp to shuffle faster down the street.

Cormac and Elise were waiting for us at the curb

with two of Balor's cars. We piled all the vamps into one, while we got in the other. It was a tight fit, elbows and knees jostling together. I'd somehow managed to get sandwiched right between Balor and Moira, my body effectively mashed into the Prince. It was all I could do to keep my mind focused on the task at hand, and what lay beyond it. We'd captured the vampires. Once we'd delivered them to the Pack, this whole thing would finally be over.

And then I'd be gone.

Half an hour later, we pulled up outside of Ronan's warehouse. For some bizarre reason, Balor had decided this was the best place in all of the city to do the handover. When I'd called Ronan to fill him in on our impending arrival, a string of curse words had been his only answer.

The lone shifter male who hated company was about to get a shedload of it.

As always, he was waiting for us outside. Anderson, and two fellow shifters, were also there. None of them spoke aloud. Instead, they watched the procession of fae and chained vampires climb out of the cars and head toward the warehouse. Wordlessly, Ronan opened the door, waiting with one strong arm propping up the metal, as we all filed inside.

I expertly avoided his gaze, though I could feel his eyes hot on my face. As he rolled down the door behind us, I turned to shoot him a quiet whisper. "It wasn't my idea, okay?"

"No, I can't imagine it would be," he said, voice full of meaning. "I can't say I ever thought you'd be bringing your fae Prince back here again."

There was double meaning to his words. Ronan

and I had not only come far too close to crossing a line, but he also knew I planned to get the hell out of dodge in only a few hours.

"Don't worry," he said, slamming the door down hard behind us. "My lips are sealed, even if you did bring this insanity to my doorstep."

"Sorry." I gave him an apologetic smile. "Balor seemed to think this was a good neutral ground. I'm sorry I accidentally got you involved."

He grunted. "The Prince doesn't think this is neutral ground at all. I'm pretty damn sure he wanted to get a good look at me again."

I wanted to tell him he was wrong, but I wasn't entirely sure he was. Balor was glowering in the corner. His face was impassive, just as it always was when he was taking care of business, but I could read the look in his eye. He still wasn't a fan of Ronan.

"Right." Anderson clapped his hands and sized up our prisoners. "Is this it then?"

"These three have been highly involved in the business from the start," Balor said, motioning to the three males we'd captured. His gaze landed on my attacker's last. "This one seems to be in charge of the actual abductions, as witnessed first-hand by Clark."

"I have a name, you know," the vampire growled in response.

"Not anymore, you don't," Anderson grunted before turning to the female. "And her?"

"She's the leader. She runs the whole thing."

A smile spread across Anderson's face. "Well then. I have to say I'm surprised, Balor. You made quick work of this. To be honest, I wasn't entirely sure you'd pull through."

"I made a promise," Balor replied. "The blood trade vampires in exchange for a confirmation of our alliance."

Anderson nodded. "This all of them?"

Balor was silent for a moment before he answered. "We came across a den of them in the Chislehurst Caves. As I'm sure you can understand, we couldn't bring all of them with us, though I can guarantee they won't be an issue anymore."

Anderson's smile dimmed. "How many did you leave behind?"

"About six."

"Balor," the shifter said. "Our agreement was that you'd bring the vampires to me. All of them."

Uh oh. I'd been worried this might happen.

"I understand your concern," Balor said. "However, I have brought you the vampires most responsible for what happened to your kind. The others were involved in a low level way. Sellers on the street and nothing more. Were they blameless? Of course not. If we could have brought every single one of them with us, we would have. You thirst for justice. These were the vampires running the trade. Here is your justice."

Anderson tapped his chin, and then let out a heavy sigh. "You talk a good game, Balor. No wonder you've made it as far as you have. Alright. It's agreed. I'm happy to remain in alliance with you, though I'm not at all happy that it means we're at peace with the vamps. If they do anything else against us…"

"Understood." Balor gave a nod.

Relief whooshed from my lungs as Anderson and his fellow shifters took the chains and led the vampires out of the warehouse. Balor trailed just behind him, helping him get the prisoners into the cars. Ronan stood in the far corner, back against the wall, where he hadn't moved during the entire exchange.

I found myself walking over to him and leaned against the wall by his side. "So."

"So." He kept his gaze forward.

"That was fun, huh?"

"And you wonder why I like to keep to myself."

"Come on, that wasn't so bad, was it?" I elbowed him in his side. "Just a little friendly exchange of some murderous prisoners. No big."

"Pretty damn morbid when you really think about it."

I cocked an eyebrow. "Morbid?"

"You're sending those vamps to their deaths," he said with a shrug. "Hard to get much more morbid than that."

I stared at him. Of course he was right. "I hadn't really thought of it that way."

"Shifters can be brutal," he replied. "Those vamps are not up for a fun time."

"Well, I mean, they did kill dozens of shifters, and they made a bunch of poison that will kill a lot of vampires." I shifted to face him. "They aren't exactly blameless in all of this."

"You're right. They're not." He gave me a strange smile. "But it's still morbid, and a little bit fucked up."

"I mean, you're just describing the supernatural world as a whole, really."

"Speaking of…" His voice dropped to a low whisper. "I really was surprised to see you show up here with your Court posse tonight. Have you changed your mind?"

I flicked my eyes toward Moira, Duncan, and Balor. They were all outside the open warehouse door, saying their goodbyes to the shifters. "I haven't changed my mind, no."

"Then, why are you all wrapped up in this? Shouldn't you be getting ready to…well, you know."

I gave him a weak smile. "They needed me. I had to finish out my last case. Tomorrow before sundown. That's when I have to…you know."

"You should practice your shift again," he said. "You're nowhere near ready to do it on your own."

"Tomorrow after lunch?"

Balor would no doubt come calling on Ronan when he realised I'd left the Court. It would be one of the first places he would look, along with my old flat. I couldn't be here after the deadline, but if I made a swift exit early in the day, I'd have enough time to practice my shift with Ronan before I had to fly.

He gave a nod. "Tomorrow after lunch. Do you need some money?"

"I can't ask that of you."

"Can't ask what?" Balor said as he strode toward us, hangs slung into his pockets as if he didn't have a care in the world. He looked calm, relaxed, but I knew him well enough to know that it was an act he put on like a glove.

"Just talking about my training," I said quietly.

Balor's eye twitched, but he didn't say a word. Instead, he wrapped an arm around my waist and leaned down to murmur in my ear. "Come on. Let's get you to bed."

23

When we got back to Court, Balor sent me to my room. Alone. Not that I'd expected anything else. That little moment in front of Ronan had only been a way for him to show off his testosterone to another male who he felt might be infringing on his "territory" or whatever. At least, that was what I was guessing.

I didn't pretend to understand the male brain.

When I pushed open my door, I almost screamed when I saw who sat on my bed waiting for me. My blackmailing vampire with raven hair smiled as I hurriedly shut the door behind me, heart hammering hard. He was wearing an actual cloak this time, the dark material curtained around his face and hiding his entire body from view.

"What are you doing here?" I asked, my fisted hands trembling by my sides. Frowning, I crossed the floor to the window to peek outside. The sun had popped up in the sky, new beams of daylight streaming across the tops of the buildings. "How the hell are you here? I thought vampires went unconscious with the sun."

"A few of us have found ways to deal with that," he said in a calm and measured drawl. "This cloak is one of them."

That was unsettling. For so long, the entire supernatural world had revolved around certain rules, certain conventions. A vampire's inability to walk around the world during daylight hours was one of them. To hear that some of them had somehow found a way around that unnerved me, particularly after the events of the past week.

"Lovely. I'm sure that's not going to end up causing problems *at all.*" Crossing my arms, I dropped the curtain back over the window. "You didn't answer my other question."

"I didn't need to. You know why I am here, Clark Cavanaugh. Or, should I say *McMann.*"

My heart thumped hard, mouth growing dry. "Look, you've already proved that you know who I am so there's no need to rub it in. I get it, okay?"

"If you 'get it' then why is Byron still alive?" he asked, his voice turning icy. "Why is he back at the Circle of Night with his father?"

"Byron is still alive because it's a lot more complicated than taking him out just anywhere and anytime, okay?"

"You had a chance," he said. "You and Balor rescued him from the black market blood trade. But instead of fulfilling our bargain, you delivered him right back into the waiting arms of his father."

"Balor was with me," I argued. "I couldn't just take him out right then and there. Besides, we don't exactly have a *bargain*, do we? You're blackmailing me into killing him. That's a massive difference."

His lips twisted into a smirk. "One might think you don't plan to kill him at all. Tell me, how do you plan to infiltrate the Circle of Night?"

A beat passed as a flush filled my neck. It was a good question. One I didn't have the answer for, particularly since I'd never considered I'd need a cover story for the vampire. I had assumed I'd be long gone by then.

"You leave that part to me," was all I could manage to come up with on the spot. "It will be taken care of by Saturday night. Okay?"

The vampire regarded me for a long, brutally silent moment before he stood and brushed off his dark cloak. "You have less than a day, Clark. Get inside the Circle of Night and kill Byron the Bloody or else I'll reveal to the world exactly who you are. The daughter of Cedric and Molly McCann, the fae Nemain hired to murder Balor Beimnech's sister."

~

I sat on the edge of my bed, breathing hard through my nose, for a long while after the vampire left. He'd spoken the words out loud, words that I had refused to allow myself to even think until now. I'd buried them down deep inside of me, covering them up as best I could so that no one, not even the best psychic in the world, could drag them out of me.

And yet there they were, bouncing around the room with horrible abandon. Now that they were out there, it was all I could think about. It was as if it had only just happened, days ago instead of years. My parents had killed Balor's sister. The only family he'd had left.

And I had helped them.

Hastily, I jumped to my feet and grabbed my half-packed bag from the closet. I shoved in as many clothes as I could, wondering exactly how much I could carry with a pair of raven claws. I wouldn't be able to manage my sword. That much was certain. But I couldn't go without a weapon, so I threw in a small dagger, hoping that would be enough if I ran into any trouble.

I zipped up the bag and tossed it back into the closet, staring at it for a long while before shutting the door. With a deep breath, I crossed the room a few times to gather my thoughts. I pushed down the reminder of my past, at the memory of what my parents had done. I wouldn't be able to focus if I had those thoughts blaring around inside of my head.

As much as I wanted to run now, I needed to do this right. The vampire had only just left. He might be lurking outside, waiting to see if I'd run. I couldn't give him any reason to spill my secret early. Instead, I spent the next few hours pacing the length of my room, waiting until the clock chimed noon.

Leaving behind my bag, I slid out of my room and padded down the corridor to Moira's room. When she cracked open the door, I smiled. "Have a minute?"

"Sure?" She opened the door wider and ushered me into her room. She was in a pair of spotted pajamas, her golden hair bunched up in a messy bun on top of her head. Her curtains were shut tight against the sunlight; her covers were rumpled as if she'd literally just rolled out of bed.

"Sorry to wake you," I said, twisting my hands together.

"Clark?" She lifted a brow. "You're kind of scaring me here. What's going on?"

"I'm going to need you to cover for me again."

A beat passed before she answered. "I got a good look at Ronan last night. I can see why you have a thing for him."

"No." I shook my head, closing my eyes as the tears threatened to spill down my cheeks. "This isn't about Ronan. It's about me."

"What are you talking about?"

"Moira." I strode forward, took her hand in mine, and squeezed. She looked so alarmed by the action that it would have made me laugh under normal circumstances. Moira wasn't much of a hugger, or the kind of fae to hold someone's hand. She didn't pull away though. "I need to go do something. I'll be gone for…awhile. Can you keep Balor from coming to look for me?"

"Of course." Her eyes searched my face. "Where are you going?"

"I'm going to train with Ronan."

"Ah, so it *is* about him."

"No." I shook my head hard. "Listen, there's something that you're going to find out about me soon, and I just want you to know that it's not as bad as it sounds. Okay, so that's wrong. It *is* as bad as it sounds, but I'm not that girl. Okay? That's not me. If I could go back in time and take it back, I would. Just remember that."

Her eyes widened, ever so slightly. "I know who you are, Clark. I've always known."

"What?" I sucked in a sharp breath and stepped back, taking my hand along with me. Confusion and fear pounded through me, making my breath ragged in my throat. "What do you mean?"

"I know what your parents did."

A long beat passed between us. "How is that even possible?"

"Caer told me. A long time ago," she added at my widening eyes. "I only just put it together the other day, but I know now that you're the one she was telling me about."

"I don't understand," I breathed.

"You aren't the only person who has visited Caer for help," she said with a sad smile. "She didn't give me what I wanted, but she did give me a message about you. The daughter of two killers, a friend like I've never known, an enemy of the Crimson Court."

Sorrow poured through me. "I'm not your enemy, Moira. You have to believe me."

"I know. Caer said as much. And she also said that one day you would need my help. Besides, you're not the only one with secrets."

My heart squeezed tight in my chest. All this time I'd been so terrified of how Moira would react when she found out the truth. But she'd known all this time. And she wasn't shouting at me to get away from her. I'd been so afraid that she would turn her back on me, that I would lose one of the only friends I'd ever had in my life.

"I don't understand why you're helping me," I told

her. "Shouldn't you be turning me in? Shouldn't you be taking me straight to Balor?"

"You said it before, Clark. All of that is in your past. It's not you." She strode forward and held out a hand, gripping tight when I wrapped mine around hers. She met my eyes and gave a nod, smiling slightly. "I'm going to miss you, you know. Now, go on. Get moving. I'll hold him off as long as I can."

24

My eyes were full of tears when I returned to my room. The last thing I'd ever expected was for Moira to accept me for who I was and who I'd once been. There had been no judgement in her eyes, no anger. Hell, she hadn't even cared that I'd kept the truth from her for so long.

She'd been understanding.

Had I been wrong about everyone else, too?

I grabbed my bag and slung it over my shoulder, pausing to stare at myself in the mirror. My eyes were puffy and red, and purple bags formed pillows on either side of my nose. Looking at my reflection, I saw no sign of the fifteen-year-old who had fled the states for fear the Courts would find her out.

I'd been so scared then. So meek. I'd let my parents convince me to help them. I had snuck into the Silver Court and had listened in to the Princess's thoughts, found out where she planned to be the next day.

At the time, I hadn't realised what my parents were up to, but I should have known.

After they had tracked her down and slit her throat, I'd gone straight to the Court to tell them what had happened. I'd turned them in. I'd given the faeries their names.

The very next day, my mother and step-father were dead, along with the rest of my family. Only my grandmother and I had survived.

Sucking in a sharp breath, I gritted my teeth and glanced away. Moira might be able to forgive me, but I didn't see how Balor could do the same. It was his sister. His family. I'd taken her from him in the worst possible way. Sure, she might not have been a good leader. I'd heard as much from her thoughts. But that didn't mean she'd deserved to be slaughtered like that.

I pushed away from the mirror and opened the door.

Balor stood on the other side of it.

He took one glance at the bag I'd slung over my shoulder and stormed inside, slamming the door hard behind him. My heart raced as he strode from one end of my room to the next, his fiery eye so fierce that I was almost afraid he might rip off his patch and burn a hole in the ground.

"I knew something was off with you, Clark. I've smelled it on you for days." He pointed at the bag. "You're leaving. Where are you going? Why?"

"Balor, please don't make this harder than it has to be," I whispered.

"I can't agree to that until I know whatever the hell this is." He threw up his hands and stalked toward me. "I know you wanted to leave the Court when I first made you join. I gave you opportunity after opportunity to leave, and yet you decided to stay. I don't know what's changed, Clark. I don't understand why you're trying to run away."

"I don't belong here, Balor."

He blinked, let out a harsh laugh, and shook his head. "That's the biggest load of rubbish I've ever heard. You've been thriving here, Clark. Don't try to tell me you haven't, because I can tell."

"That doesn't mean I belong."

He narrowed his eyes. "Is this about Ronan?"

"*No*. This is about me." I tried to push past him to the door, but he blocked my path.

"Tell me why you're leaving. Give me a reason. I'm owed that, Clark. I'm your Master, and your Prince and—"

"Not anymore." I curled my hands into fists and tried to move past him again. He stepped sideways, blocking me.

"I don't accept that," he said in a gruff voice. "You were inducted into my House. The bond between us was formed. I know you feel it there between us."

"I feel something between us, Balor, but it isn't the bond." I sucked in a deep breath. "And you can try to use that power on me, but it won't stop me from leaving the Court. I can break through the bond. You know it's true."

"Clark, please." He reached out and grabbed my hand, pulling my palm to his lips. I shivered as his mouth moved against my skin, sending sparks of pleasure shooting through my core. Tucking his thumb underneath my chin, he forced me to gaze up into his eye. "I've never met anyone like you. I don't know what I'll do with myself if you're not in my life anymore."

The earnest look in his eye hurt my heart. I didn't know what I would do without him in my life either. But I knew that all his words would only turn to dust in his mouth when he knew exactly who he was speaking to. I had helped killed his sister. He should hate me. I wouldn't even blame him when he did.

"I'm not who you think I am," I whispered hoarsely.

"You are everything I think you are and more." He gazed down at me. "I know you feel as though it's been hard to fit in here. You're different, and your powers aren't as strong. But that doesn't mean you don't belong. That doesn't mean that I can't see the strength of you. Hell, Clark, you're one of the strongest and fiercest fae I've ever met."

My heart pulsed in my chest. "That's not what I mean, Balor."

He pulled back, frowning. "Then, what do you mean?"

I closed my eyes. He would find out soon enough. At midnight, my blackmailing vampire buddy would come straight to the Court and tell him everything. I'd wanted to run before Balor discovered the truth, but he was standing before me now, begging to know everything.

Would he let me leave if I told him? Would he let me run?

Maybe it didn't matter if he did. Maybe it was time he heard the truth. From me. Not from a strange vampire. Not from someone else.

I took a deep breath and plowed forward, my

heart racing so fast that it made me feel as if I might pass out at any moment. "There's something I should tell you, Balor. Before I go."

His eye darkened, and he nodded. "I thought there might be."

The door flew open, cutting through our conversation. Moira and Elise stood in the corridor, eyes wild and cheeks dotted pink.

"Sorry we're interrupting," Moira said, casting me a wince, "but this couldn't wait."

Balor let out a heavy sigh. I stared at my friends, heart beating hard. Moira knew why I needed to leave. She'd heard the truth. She wouldn't be interrupting now unless she'd gotten some really, really bad news.

"Tell me what's happening," Balor said, resignation in his voice.

Elise pursed her lips and brushed her silver hair out of her face. "We got a call from the Circle of Night. They're…well. Moira?"

"They're fuming," Moira filled in. "They pretty much threatened to come over here and kill every single fae in this Court if we didn't listen to them."

Balor narrowed his eye. "They threatened you? Are you sure it was the Circle of Night?"

It was odd to say the least. We'd just helped Matteo find his son, and had risked our necks in order to deliver him safely home. Why would they be threatening us now? We'd done everything they wanted us to do.

"We warned him we were going to deliver those vampires to the Pack. He shouldn't be angry about this," Balor said in a low voice, dragging a hand down his tired face. "I specifically spoke to Matteo about this."

"Yeah, but he didn't seem totally convinced, to be honest," I added. "He never agreed to it, remember? He just kind of…glowered."

"This isn't about the black market shifter blood," Moira cut in. "It's about something else."

Elise's eyes flicked my way. "Byron the Bloody, the vampire you saved. He's dead now. And the Circle of Night seems to think Clark is the one who killed him."

"What?!" Balor practically roared, his voice so loud that the three of us jumped. "I will not stand for this, alliance or not. He cannot threaten me and my innocent fae for crimes they did not commit."

Moira's grimace deepened. "Unfortunately, it sounds like he has proof."

25

So much for leaving London before midnight. Balor demanded I stay at the Court, going so far as to leave Duncan in charge of watching me. As soon as night fell, the entire guard faction gathered together and drove across the city to the Circle of Night's headquarters downtown.

I'd tried several times to talk to Balor, but he'd been off making calls and plans, too busy to hear me out. I knew he didn't believe I'd killed Byron, but…he was still more on edge than I'd seen him in a long time.

"Can I talk to you about this, Balor?" I asked from where I was sandwiched between Duncan and Cormac in the car.

"No. You won't say a word, especially not when we reach the vampires."

He was under the impression that I was involved *somehow* and that it explained my strange actions—and scent—the past few days, even if I hadn't killed Byron myself. And he refused to hear it. If he didn't know about it, he'd argued, then it didn't happen, and he wouldn't have to lie to the Circle.

I was pretty sure it wasn't going to be as easy as that, no matter that I hadn't done it.

Matteo and two of his fellow vampires stood in their pristine suits just outside the front doors of their steel building. They barely paid us any notice as we climbed out of our cars. Rage simmered beneath the surface, their red-rimmed eyes sparked with hate. Matteo's two friends strode over to the entrance, and opened the double doors, one handle each.

Inside, I could see hundreds of vampires. Swallowing hard, I followed the rest of the guards into the front lobby, tipping back my head at the sight. Every floor was full, the vampires crowding around the edges of the balconies to stare down at us from above. It was brutally silent inside, and dark. If a tiny droplet of blood fell to the floor, every single one of us would hear it.

Pretty unnerving, to say the least.

Matteo pulled on the ends of his white jacket and strode to the center of the floor. He stood by the Lutine Bell, levelling his eyes at our group. Without a single word, he reached over and pulled the rope. One ominous clang echoed through the quiet space.

"My son has been taken from me," he shouted, tipping back his head so that the entirety of the Circle could hear his words. His voice was magnified by some strange magic, rising up from the ground floor to those who sat above.

I swallowed hard and cast a glance at Balor. His body was tense, but his face impassive, as if Matteo's words had no effect on him at all. Long moments stretched out in the silence, Matteo's eyes zeroing in on the Prince, as if he expected him to answer.

Finally, Balor cleared his throat. "I am sorry for your loss, Matteo. We will have something sent over from our kitchen, with condolences."

"I don't want your damn condolences," Matteo snapped. "You and your faeries were involved in his death."

Balor threw back his shoulders, and frowned. "I understand that you must be experiencing a lot of grief right now, but I can assure you that none of the House Beimnech fae were involved in your son's death."

Matteo arched a single brow. "And you can vouch for that? Wholly and completely with no reservations at all?"

"Of course."

"Huh," Matteo said with a low, dangerous chuckle. "Then, you're saying that none of your fae have been acting suspiciously as of late? Sneaking out of the Court? Going off on their own without telling you where they are going?"

Balor frowned, keeping his gaze focused hard on the vampire before him, but I knew his attention had been shifted my way. More ammunition for him to believe I was involved. I had been sneaking out. I had been going off on my own. Mostly to see Ronan, but Balor had no proof of that.

"What my fae do and do not do is my concern, not yours."

"It's my concern when my son ends up dead!" His voice boomed, echoing harshly throughout the cavernous building. "You tried to be so clever about it, too, didn't you Balor? Save the kid, deliver him home, and the father would never suspect what you did."

Balor narrowed his eyes, and a soft growl emanated from his throat. He'd been as patient as he could with Matteo and his accusations, but there was always a limit to what Balor could stand. If Matteo pushed him much harder, I doubted Balor would hold himself back for much longer.

"My guards put their lives at risk to save your son," he replied, his voice low and dark. "If you continue to hurl threats and accusations at them, then I cannot promise they will be there to risk their necks again."

I wet my lips and glanced from one angry leader to the next. I hated this. We'd done so much to ensure peace in the alliance. We'd worked so hard at settling the black market blood problem in a way that didn't end in a war between the supernatural factions of the city. All of that seemed lost now. All because of me.

But it didn't make sense. I hadn't killed Byron. In fact, I'd spared him. There was no reason at all for Matteo to believe that I'd been the one to take him down. Maybe he was bluffing. Maybe, just maybe, he was an angry, grieving father who was lashing out.

Matteo's bitter chuckle echoed through the building. "You act as though I would go anywhere near accepting your help again. The time of peace is officially over, Balor. Your Court and my Circle are now enemies. When your fae killed my son, it was over. There is nothing you can do to make that up to me, even if you weren't involved yourself."

Alright. Enough of this bullshit. I'd refrained from reading Matteo's mind because I knew he would take that as a personal attack against him. If he was calling for a war, there was no reason for me to keep my mind-reading hands to myself anymore.

Something strange was going on. Before the situation escalated any more, I needed to find out what that was.

Just as I sucked in a deep breath to plunge my mind deep within the vampire's, a figure shifted in the edge of my vision. In any other circumstance, I might have just ignored it. It was probably a guard, or one of Matteo's lackeys. But there was something about his silhouette that caught my attention. Something familiar. Something that dragged my view away from Matteo's face.

The ground beneath my feet disappeared. Striding toward Matteo was a male vampire who had visited me not only in person but in my very worst nightmares. Tall and lithe with raven hair, the vampire and his smug face doused all the warmth in my body.

It was the vampire who had been blackmailing me. The one who had tried to get me to kill Matteo's son. Confusion rippled through me. It didn't make any sense. Why was he here? Why was Matteo smiling at him?

"Ah. Thaddeus. So glad you could join us. You're right on time for the reckoning of the faeries."

"There will be no reckoning," Balor growled in response.

I just continued to gape at Thaddeus. His eyes cut my way, and he smiled. Ice slipped down my spine as I took in the expression on his face, at the smugness that permeated through every single inch of him. He was up to something. He was the reason I'd been brought here. I didn't know how, and I didn't know why, but I knew without a doubt in my mind that he was behind this.

He must have gotten some other poor idiot to kill Byron. And now he was going to try and pin it on me.

"Hello, Balor," Thaddeus said politely. "Hello, Clark. I don't believe we've ever been probably acquainted. My name is Thaddeus, centuries-old member of the Circle of Night." His smile widened. "I am the Trial Master, here to ensure our enemies receive proper punishment for their crimes."

"Matteo," Balor growled. "Explain yourself. Why is your so-called Trial Master here?"

"You know why," Matteo answered, turning his attention on me. As if in unison, all the vampires in the building turned my way. "To try Clark Cavanaugh for murder."

26

My face flushed with heat, and my heart flickered in my chest. Balor had told me to keep my mouth shut, but fuck that. "This is ridiculous. I didn't kill Byron. I helped him escape the black market blood traders, so that he could come back home. Hell, I even had a second alone with him in the warehouse after we got him out of the cage. If I'd wanted to kill him, I would have done it then. Not when he was in a building full of vampires!"

My voice went sharp at the end, my words echoing through the building. No one said a word. Instead, they all turned to Matteo for confirmation. It was the truth, dammit, and I had people to vouch for me. Balor, Anderson, and his shifter friends.

Of course, the vampires probably didn't want to listen to any of them.

Thaddeus was probably the only one they'd listen to. He was clearly a high-ranking vampire with a lot of responsibility in the Circle of Night. He was also the vampire who had wanted Byron dead, so yeah.

That wasn't going to be particularly helpful. In fact, I had a horrible suspicion that I wasn't going to like anything he said.

Matteo spread his arms wide. "You've heard her voice now, yes? You'll remember what it sounds like?"

A murmur went through the crowd.

"What game are you playing at, Matteo?" Balor asked with a frown. He still hadn't glanced my way, a fact that hurt me far more than I wanted to admit. Only Moira was shooting me the occasional glance, checking to make sure that I was okay.

I really wasn't okay.

"Good." Matteo smiled and turned to Thaddeus, holding his hand palm up. "The recording please, Trial Master."

A part of me wanted to roll my eyes at the use of his title, but I was far too unnerved by his command. What recording? What could he possibly have? Some kind of video surveillance feed of me being somewhere I shouldn't be? There wasn't anything like that though. I'd truly been on my best behaviour. There was nothing I'd done but try to help the vamps.

Matteo took the cell phone in his hand, and then pressed play. My voice drifted into the silence, unmistakably me.

"Byron is still alive because it's a lot more complicated than taking him out just anywhere and anytime, okay?"

The recording clicked, and then my voice continued. *"Balor was with me. Besides, we don't exactly have a bargain, do we? You're blackmailing me into killing him. That's a massive difference."*

Another click. *"You leave that part to me. It will be taken care of by Saturday night. Okay?"*

My heart shook in my chest as I stared with horror at the cell phone. Oh my god. No. No, no, no. The arsehole had recorded me. Not only that but he'd cut his own words out of the conversation so that the only one who was implicated was me.

This was bad. This was really, really bad.

If I'd heard that recording, not knowing what had happened, I knew I'd be certain that I was the killer.

Slowly, I twisted toward Balor, in desperate need of seeing his face. I needed him to tell me this was going to be okay. I needed him to look into my eyes and know I didn't do this. But he still faced forward, refusing to even blink.

"I didn't do this," I whispered. "You heard the clicks in the recording. He edited it."

"He may have edited it," Balor said through clenched teeth. "But no splicing in the world could have come up with what we just heard."

"Balor."

He didn't meet my eyes, jaw clenching tight.

I turned back to the vampire, my heart throbbing in my chest. Thaddeus looked far too pleased with himself. He had set this up. He was angry that I hadn't given in to his blackmail, and now he was throwing everything he could right back in my face. He must have known during his last visit that I wasn't going to go through with it. So, he'd recorded me. Specifically to set me up.

Tears burned my eyes as I stared him down, my fear and grief transforming into rage. "Where did that recording come from?"

"An anonymous tip sent it in to Thaddeus," Matteo said with a smile. "Apparently, your co-

conspirator no longer wanted to be involved in your murder."

"An anonymous tip." I let out a hollow laugh. "Don't you find it strange that the other side of that conversation has been edited out? Almost like the 'co-conspirator' as you call him knew that you'd be able to recognise his voice."

"The co-conspirator also provided some additional information when he sent over this recording," Thaddeus said smoothly, as if I hadn't said anything at all. "He said he'd been blackmailing you, as confirmed by the tape, and he thought it best to share with the world what he knew about Clark Cavanaugh. Or should I say Clark McCann?"

I felt as if I'd been punched in the gut. The world tipped sideways, every single vampire in the building blurry before me. My breath had left me, and I couldn't find more. Lungs tight, ears swarmed with bees, it almost felt like I was dying.

"McCann?" Elise's soft voice broke through the thick silence. "You mean like the McCann's who—"

"Elise," Balor growled, voice shook through with emotion.

I couldn't bear to look at him, knowing how much hatred must be swirling in his eyes. This was not how I wanted him to find out. This was wrong in so many ways. Hundreds of eyes had turned our way. Hostile eyes, who wanted nothing more than to see our Court torn apart.

"That's right. It seems that Clark is one of the McCann's. The only surviving McCann. For now," Matteo added. "Wasn't there a rumour of a daughter, one involved with the assassination mission somehow?"

"Oh, yes," Thaddeus added. "Everyone thought she'd been killed in the crossfire, but it turns out she survived. And here she is. How odd that she has insinuated herself deep within the Crimson Court. A Court I hear Nemain now has her eye on as well? Clark has clearly been sent to cause strife, to spy, to get close to the Prince."

"Enough!" Balor's voice boomed through the building, anger and pain radiating from him in waves. "Clark, look at me."

I swallowed hard, hands slick with sweat.

"Look at me!"

Our bond snapped tight between us, his dark magic curling across my skin with such ferocity that it shot pain through my head. This time, I didn't even try to fight him. Instead, I slowly turned his way and lifted my eyes to his.

"Tell me this isn't true. Tell me this is some kind of ruse Nemain has come up with, a way to get underneath my skin. You can't be a McCann. It's impossible. Isn't it, Clark?"

I could only continue to stare at him, my heart beating wildly.

"You're half-shifter," he continued. "Your father, you said, he was a shifter. Cedric McCann was fae. There's no way in hell you're his daughter."

"My real father, who I've never met, was shifter." I swallowed hard. "Cedric was…he was my step-father, Balor. I'm so sorry. This isn't how I wanted you to find out."

His eye churned with a kaleidoscope of emotions.

Pain, horror, rage. His entire body shook as he stared me down, the soft adoration disintegrating into nothing. He looked at me now like I was a stranger, a girl he'd never seen before. To him, maybe I was. I'd lied to him since the day we'd met. I could have told him, time and time again. But I couldn't bear the thought of him looking at me like this, at turning me away as if I meant nothing to him at all.

"So, it's true," he said in a rough voice. "You're her. You're a McCann."

Tears filled my eyes. "No, I'm not. I'm Clark Cavanaugh now. I had no idea what they were doing, Balor. I had no idea who they would kill. Their crimes are not my own. You have to believe me."

"You helped," he whispered. "They said you helped."

I pressed my lips together, hot tears dropping onto my cheeks. "I'm so sorry. I didn't know what I was doing."

"She's telling the truth, Balor," Moira suddenly spoke up. "That was Cedric's power. Manipulation. He got her to do his bidding. It wasn't her choice."

I opened my mouth to explain that Moira was right, but Matteo's sharp cry put a stop to any words. His eyes had narrowed even more, pale face now red as he stared me down.

"Enough of this. We're not here to listen to sob stories of murderous faeries." He whirled toward Thaddeus, who had stood watching the entire exchange with a bemused expression on his face. "Trial Master, what do you recommend we do to those who have wronged us? How shall this faerie pay for taking the life of not only one of ours but also one of theirs?"

"I have the perfect solution." A strange smile spread across Thaddeus's face. "She must face our harshest trial."

27

At Thaddeus's words, about a dozen vampires suddenly surrounded me. Chains clamped tight around my wrists and ankles. I didn't even try to fight them off. It was hopeless. Thaddeus was in charge now. Together with the recording and my horrible past, he would ensure that I would never see the fresh light of day ever again.

It had taken me a long time to forgive myself for what I'd done, to come to terms with my involvement in the assassination. If it hadn't been for my grandmother, I probably would have turned myself in, but she'd shown me the truth about Cedric's power. I should have suspected it as soon as he came into our lives. At first, my mother hadn't really liked him all that much.

Over time, he'd weaselled his way in, using his odd charm to win my mother over. I'd never truly fallen for it though. There was something odd about him, something I'd never been able to put my finger on. He could build my mother up and tear her down in a single sentence, manipulating her into slowly changing from the woman I'd grown up with to the murderer she became.

For the longest time, I'd thought that my happy memories of her were a figment of my own imagination.

They weren't.

Cedric had twisted her into something else. A tool for his own gain. Someone he could use to gain power.

What he hadn't anticipated was me.

Thaddeus grabbed the chains and dragged me toward the bank of escalators that criss-crossed through the main galley. A cluster of silent vampires trailed behind, a reminder that I had no other choice than to go along with this without a fight. As they led me to the single escalator that dove down into the basement instead of up into the glittering space above, I cast one last glance over my shoulder.

The expressions on my friends' faces were a mixture going from bad to worse. Stone cold Moira, always frank, always strong, looked like she was on the verge of tears. Elise's eyes flickered with shock and horror as she shook her head back and forth in slow motion. Duncan glared at me, and Cormac was the same. They clearly believed everything they'd seen and heard tonight. It was hard to blame them. Most of it was true.

And Balor. It almost burned my soul to look at him. No emotion played across his face at all. He was a mask of cold indifference. Ice, stone, pure steel. He was the infamous fae who I saw in his club, high above everyone else in his glass box, too apart to get close to anyone. He was the smiter.

"Enough stalling." Thaddeus yanked on the chain, and I stumbled toward the escalator. The floor almost rose up to meet my face, but I managed to get my bearings before I fell. He pulled me onto the stairs, smiling when my entire world disappeared behind me.

The subterranean cells beneath the Circle of Night's pristine London home were about what you'd expect. Dank and dark and cold. There was a strange metallic scent in the air that I didn't want to think about. Probably blood. If the stains on the dirt-packed floor were any indication, a lot of it had been spilled in this place.

I was half-afraid I'd discover scores of human prisoners down here, vessels for the vampires' animalistic hunger. After the whole black market blood thing, along with Thaddeus's cunning tricks, I was becoming less and less inclined to trust that these vamps kept their hunger at bay, no matter what they liked to present to the world.

But luckily, it was just me. Of course, that meant the next few hours, or days, or months of my life were going to be brutally lonely. When I'd been on the run, I'd gotten so used to living life on my own. I'd come to terms with it, had even started to enjoy the quiet calm of introverted life. Joining the Crimson Court had changed me. There was always someone around, no matter what. We ate together, we drank together, and we trained together.

"In here." Thaddeus unchained my bonds and shoved me into one of the cells. I stumbled forward, catching myself just in time. I whirled toward him, fists curled, ready to throw my weight behind my attack. He slammed the cell's door in my face, right as I launched myself his way.

My body slammed hard into the bars, pain lancing through me.

"Tsk, tsk." He turned toward the guards, dismissing them. Once they'd disappeared back up the escalator, he smiled. "Surprise, Clark."

"You're going to pay for this."

He let out a low chuckle. "And exactly how will I pay for this? Everyone knows the truth about you now, and you're stuck inside that cell. I'm out here, the hero for discovering the truth and delivering the true killer of Matteo's son right into his lap."

"You know, funny thing about the truth," I said, narrowing my eyes. "It always comes out. Trust me. I should know."

His glittering eyes met mine. "You know what? You're right. Unfortunately for you, as you've learned, sometimes it takes years, decades, for secrets to be revealed. You'll be dead long before then."

"So, that's it then?" I asked with a laugh. "You're going to have them kill me, all because I refused to do your bidding."

"I did warn you, Clark."

"Why?" I threw up my hands, stalking from one end of the cell to another. "You're a member of the Circle of Night. You're clearly close to Matteo. Are you trying to take over or something? You think taking out his son will mean you're next in line?"

Sighing, Thaddeus stepped up close to the bars and sneered. "You know nothing, fae."

"Then, explain it to me. If you're going to ruin my life, at least tell me why."

Maybe if I kept him talking long enough, someone else would come down the escalator and overhear his plots against me. It was the only hope I had. Sure, I was going to have some kind of trial before I was officially sentenced to death, but it wasn't like it was going to be particularly helpful for me. They'd already made up their minds. All of them. I'd been able to read the judgement in their eyes.

To them, I was already guilty. I'd conspired to get a fae Princess killed, and now, I'd done the deed myself.

"It's for the good of the Circle," he finally said. "Vampires, as a whole. Matteo has grown soft in recent years, forming alliances with the fae and the shifters. I can still remember when I fought in combat against your kind. They killed mine, and I killed theirs." He shook his head and stepped back. "I refuse to align myself with my enemies."

"That was hundreds of years ago."

"No, not hundreds." He shook his head. "Tens, maybe, but not hundreds."

"The past is the past," I said, and suddenly, Caer's words filled my ears again. What had she said? Something about accepting the past in order to survive in the future? My heart thumped hard. Had Caer seen this? She must have known that one day I would be forced to confront my past. But how could accepting my past have anything to do with my survival now? My past had gotten me into this mess.

"Vampires are vampires," Thaddeus continued. Apparently, now that I'd gotten him talking, he was pretty chatty. "It is in our nature to feed. We shouldn't be suppressing the most carnal parts of ourselves.

When Matteo realises the alliance with the fae must end, we can once again drink straight from the vein, just as we're meant to."

"If only you could hear yourself, you'd realise just how insane you sound. You actually murdered an innocent just so that you can drink human blood again."

"I'll do whatever it takes," he hissed, striding forward with flashing eyes. "And I will make sure you don't make out of this trial alive."

28

A full day passed before they came to get me again. As vampires, and arseholes, they'd totally forgotten that I needed food and water. So, when they pulled me out of my cell, I was more than a little light-headed. A part of me just wanted to curl up on the floor and never wake.

But another part of me was mad as hell.

"It's time for your trial," Thaddeus said as his lackeys fastened the chains around my wrists and ankles again. Once he was certain I couldn't break free, he grabbed ahold of the chain and yanked me toward the stairs.

The main lobby of the building had been transformed. Several tall chairs sat on either side of the Lutine Bell now, holding up vampires decked out in dark cloaks and hoods. Matteo was among them, and his glittering eyes watched me as I was dragged across the floor.

The vampires in the balconies above cheered, a sound so loud that I wished I could cover my ears.

Thaddeus left me in the center of the room. I was inside a circle that had been carved into the floor, just in front of a long line of guards that blocked the exit. Out of the corner of my eye, I sensed movement. Slowly, I twisted toward the shadows that had caught my attention. Elise was waving at me, Moira grimacing by her side. Balor stood just behind them, arms crossed over his chest, face as cold and hard as it had been the day before.

Just knowing they were there made me sigh.

Thaddeus stood in front of one of the empty chairs. "Clark McCann—"

"Cavanaugh," I cut in, my voice much clearer than I'd expected it to sound. "My name is Clark Cavanaugh. I took my father's name."

A murmur went through the vampires. Guessed they weren't used to prisoners standing up for themselves when they were on trial.

Thaddeus frowned. "Clark *McCann*—"

"Thaddeus," Matteo said with a frown. "I hate to cut in on this important occasion, but the results of the trial will not hold if you do not call the girl by her name."

Thaddeus clearly hated this. He ground his teeth together, eyes sparked with hate. He wanted to make me pay. He wanted to remind me of my past and where I'd come from in as many ways as he could. But he was shit out of luck on this one. My name was Clark Cavanaugh, and I was proud to sport my father's name.

"Clark Cavanaugh," he finally growled. "You stand accused of murder in front of the Circle of Night, who you have wronged. As we were in alliance with your Court at the time, you are also accused of treason. What do you say to these charges?"

"Innocent," I replied without a single moment's hesitation. "I didn't kill him, even though you tried blackmailing me to do it."

Bam. Truth bomb dropped. I'd been waiting all night to say those very words. I'd repeated them over and over to myself until I knew I wouldn't stumble. With my past coming out to the world last night, my mind hadn't been working properly. I hadn't told the Circle what he'd done.

Not that they'd believe me now, but I sure had to try.

Matteo furrowed his eyebrows and glanced at Thaddeus. "What is this all about?"

Thaddeus waved his hand in dismissal. "The girl is clearly trying to find any way out of this that she can. She's spouting nonsense."

"Since I'm on trial, do I get a chance to explain myself?"

"No," Thaddeus said.

Matteo's frowned deepened. "We have to follow protocol, Thaddeus. I'm as bereaved as you are. Even more so. My son is gone forever. But the magic is clear. If we do not follow protocol, we cannot enforce the outcome."

I didn't know what he was babbling on about, but it seemed to be in my favour, so I was going to go with it.

Thaddeus scowled, but he clearly couldn't argue. Matteo turned back and motioned for me to continue.

"Right. Here's what happened. All of it." I sucked in a deep breath and told my story. I started with the day Balor had dragged me, kicking and screaming, into the Court. How I'd wanted to keep my past a secret because I was afraid of how everyone would respond. Then, I skipped forward, going into Thaddeus's trip to see me, how he'd blackmailed me, and how I had hesitantly agreed.

By the time I got to the part where we were called in to meet with the Circle about finding Byron, Matteo was leaning forward in his chair.

"I'm not going to lie. I considered doing it. Thaddeus told me that Byron was dangerous. A murderer. It seemed like London would be better off without him off the streets." I sucked in a deep breath. "But then Matteo asked us to find Byron. At that point, I didn't know what the hell I was going to do. I could either save him or save myself. In the end, we came face to face in that warehouse, and I decided to save him. And that was that. Decision made. Before you forced us to come here last night, I was about thirty seconds away from fleeing London, because it meant that my secret was about to come to light. I'd packed my bag, I'd made plans on how to get out. So…that's it. I didn't do it. But I'm pretty sure that Thaddeus did."

Silence punctuated the room. Matteo's eyebrows were arched upward, his mouth widened into an O. Thaddeus had stood from his seat, fisted hands shaking by his sides. I couldn't tell what any of the others were thinking. Hell, I couldn't look their way. I was too afraid to see impassive stares, too scared the they'd just dismiss my words as nothing more than fantasy land.

Matteo slowly stood from his chair and turned toward Thaddeus. "Trial Master, is any of this true?"

"Of course it's not true," Thaddeus said, throwing his hands in the air. "Prisoners will say anything to escape. She's just trying to save her own neck by throwing mine under the blade."

"Perhaps," Matteo mused before his eyes flickered to something just behind me. "Balor, how much of this girl's story can you corroborate."

Shivers slipped down my spine when my Prince's familiar voice whispered across my skin. "Not much. She did have a bag, and she was leaving, but I did not personally witness any of her meetings with Thaddeus."

"Matteo," Thaddeus scoffed. "You cannot honestly be taking this girl's testimony seriously."

Matteo frowned. "Seriously enough that it calls her involvement into question. We will put it to vote, following protocol. How many are in favour of letting Clark Cavanaugh go, free of all charges?"

I held my breath, half hoping that hands all around the room would shoot up into the air. Before me, none of the vampires did, including Matteo. I glanced over my shoulder. None of the guards had raised their hands either. Only Elise and Moira were holding their fists high. Up above in the balconies, there was a scattering of hands. But that option clearly hadn't won.

My heart sunk.

"Now, who is in favour of finding Clark Cavanaugh guilty of all charges, sentenced to death?"

This option had a lot more activity. A few of the guards behind me raised their hands, Thaddeus obviously raised his hand, and about a quarter of the vamps on the balconies did, too.

I twisted back to Matteo. Did that mean—

"And now, who is in favour of letting magic decide Clark Cavanaugh's fate?"

A strange hope flickered in my chest. What the hell did that mean?

Matteo's hand shot into the air, along with most of the guards and the crowd above. I glanced around, eyes wide, heart hammering hard in my chest.

"It is settled then. The magic will decide. Clark will engage in a trial by combat."

29

"Trial by *what*?" My mouth dropped open, blood boiling in my ears. For a second there, I'd thought I'd kind of won. Or, at least, that Thaddeus had lost in his attempt to have me hung up and quartered.

But this did not sound better at all.

"Here's how it works," Matteo said, pacing from one end of the platform to the other. "We will have a champion of our Circle join you in the ring, and you will fight for your freedom. If you win, then you will be free to go, cleared of all charges. If you lose, then…you die."

I didn't like this. Not the least because I wasn't a terribly good fighter. Sure, I'd been training, but if the vamps had some kind of champion then he would no doubt be much stronger and faster than me. There was no way I was going to survive this. No way I would ever win this kind of fight.

"Do you understand?" Matteo said, voice echoing through the room.

"If I win," I said, glancing over my shoulder at Balor and his expressionless face, "does your alliance with the fae still stand?"

"Of course not," Thaddeus hissed, his raven hair slicing across his shoulders as he strode toward me. "The alliance is done."

Matteo cocked his head, frowning. "She has a good point, Thaddeus. If the Crimson Court has not conspired against us, then we have no reason to break the alliance."

"Well, she will not win. So, this is a moot point."

"Perhaps." Matteo's eyes lingered on Thaddeus for a long moment, a strange emotion flickering in his eyes. I couldn't help but hold my breath, hoping and praying that maybe he'd realised one of his closest compatriots had been the one to turn on him and not me. But then the emotion dimmed, and Matteo turned to the vampire guard by his side. "Ready the champion. Be certain he has his sword."

My blood iced in my veins. "Sword? You're having your champion fight me with a sword? That's not particularly fair, is it? I don't have a weapon."

Matteo inclined his head toward the back corner. "Moira, I believe you have something for your fae."

Moira strode forward out of the crowd, her long golden hair pulled back into a high ponytail that reminded me of the first day I'd met her. She wore all black and thick combat boots, two swords sheathed around her waist. I blinked, heart lifting. She had *two* swords, and the golden hilt of the one of her right side looked a hell of a lot like mine.

The guards parted to allow Moira to enter the circle. I turned to face her, and she pulled my sword from the sheath. The steel sang as it whistled through the air, a song that soothed all the fear and anxiety in my bones.

She came to a stop just in front of me and held the sword on top of two open palms. "Thought you might need this."

"Thanks, Moira." Before I reached out to take my weapon, I took one glance over Moira's shoulder toward Balor. Why hadn't he been the one to present me with my steel? Why had he let Moira do it instead of him? His single red eye met my gaze for only a second, just long enough for me to see the anger churning inside.

With a heavy heart, I turned back to Moira and grasped the sword's hilt, raising it high before me. It felt reassuring in my hands, heavy and certain and real. I might not be the best sword fighter out there, but I was better than I'd once been. This sword and I had been through a lot together.

"Kick that champion's ass," Moira whispered before giving me a wink and returning to the crowd.

"Champion," I heard Thaddeus's slippery voice ring out from behind me. Slowly, I gripped my hilt and turned back to the Trial Master and his council. Another vampire had joined them while Moira had presented me with my weapon. Just as I'd expected, they'd chosen the largest vampire I'd ever set eyes on.

The tall, burly male standing before me was unlike any vampire I'd ever seen. He was built like a tank, bigger than both Duncan and Cormac, two of the strongest fighters in the Court. His hair was cut short, buzzed down to his scalp. Ferocity flickered in his full red eyes. A jagged scar dented his skin, leading from his right ear down to his neck.

This guy was not a normal vampire. With their healing powers, they didn't have scars.

My heart beat a little faster. How could I win this fight if I didn't truly know what I was up against?

Matteo stood and clapped his hands. As everyone fell silent, he dropped his head back and began. "Clark Cavanaugh's trial by combat will now commence. There are no rules to the fighting. There are no safe words to make it end." His gaze dropped down to me. "You either win this or you die. Good luck."

My tongue felt like sandpaper, and my palms were slick. Still, I kept myself steady. Taking a deep breath, I held my ground, raising my sword before me while the champion stalked my way. He looked fierce and determined...but also, a little bored?

His sword swung lazily in his hands this way and that, like this was all some kind of grudge work job that would be over within seconds.

Balor's voice suddenly broke into my mind, so loud that it made me stumble to the side.

Remember your training. You're faster. You're smarter. I will not allow you to lose.

My heart thumped hard as his words disappeared from my mind. The champion continued to stalk toward me, and all the while I couldn't help but cheer at the fact that Balor still cared. He cared so much that he had somehow managed to infiltrate my thoughts. We'd exchanged words in our minds before, but not like this. Only when I had reached out to him.

But I couldn't think about that now. There was a

massive vampire monstrosity stomping my way. He had one job and one job only. That was to kill me.

Only seconds later, he was in front of me. With a guttural roar, he swung his massive sword at my head. I ducked down low just in time. He grunted and swung again. And again. I dodged blow after blow after blow. My heart raced as I jumped back time and time again, ducking and whirling and hurling to the side.

I got in no blows of my own. He was faster than he looked, and it was all I could do to keep up with him. If I paused for even a second, his sword would slice right into my sweat-stained skin.

"Come on, Clark!" Moira shouted from the corner, giving my rapidly-deflating hope a much-needed boost.

The vampire suddenly slowed, pausing in his unending attack against me. He narrowed his eyes, calmly sizing me up as if just now taking me as a slightly bigger challenge than a pesky fly. I took that moment to make my own move.

With a deep breath, I threw my feet forward, slicing my blade through the air. The champion growled as I hurled toward him. He raised his own sword, blocking my attack. The clash of steel echoed through the cavernous space, and the impact of the parry sent my skull reeling.

I stumbled back, shaking the clanging out of my head.

The champion rushed forward. He raised his sword high, his blade coming down toward my arm. I jumped sideways, breath puffing out. Pain lanced through my body, and the iron scent of blood peppered the air.

An audible gasp went through the crowd.

Gritting my teeth, I glanced down at my arm. I'd managed to avoid most of his attack, but the sharp blade had sliced through a chunk of my skin.

Growling, the vampire threw his sword down on the ground and stalked toward me. Eyes wide, I backed up, even though I was the only one left with a blade. I lifted my sword, swinging it wildly toward his head. He ducked, and then kicked out his foot.

His heavy boot slammed into my stomach. With an oomph, I dropped my sword, doubling over. He kicked again, this time in the side, knocking me flat onto my back. Stars danced in my eyes, and I could barely breathe around the pain. The champion stood over me, glaring down at me with a grin.

Tears in my eyes, I rolled to the side and tried knocking him off his feet with my legs, a move that Balor had taught me when I'd first joined his Court.

It did absolutely nothing. The monstrous champion didn't even move. Instead, he reached down and grabbed the back of my neck, yanking me up. He held me up before him like a rag-doll, my feet dangling helplessly above the floor. My heart roared in my chest, spikes of fearful adrenaline shooting through me.

The champion's lips twisted into a cruel smile. Despair charging through my gut, I whispered to the raven within me, begging and pleading for her to come out. But there was no sign of her at all. No shift of my eyes; no pain in my arms. The raven was far too scared to come help me now.

I was on my own in this.

"Finish her off," Thaddeus shouted from the crowd, his voice full of excitement. "*Now*, champion!"

As if on command, the monstrous creature dropped me. My legs gave out beneath me as they slammed hard into the marble surface. The champion stalked away from me, grabbing his sword from the ground. Gritting my teeth, I slowly pushed myself up to my feet, curling my hands into fists.

I wouldn't take this sitting down. I didn't care how outmatched I was, I would keep fighting until the very end.

Suddenly, the explosion of glass crashed through the hushed silence. Screams cut through the noise as shards rained down on our heads from above. I looked up. Overhead, two dozen birds had swarmed into the Circle, their brilliant black wings soaring through the air.

My heart leapt as I watched the ravens flap toward me. They circled once and then dove, their gazes focused on the slack-jawed champion standing before me. I took a step back, watching as they spun around the vampire, dropping lower and lower until they were only meters above his head.

And then they dove. Cries shot from their throats as they surrounded him. It was a swarm of feathers and beaks, black shadows engulfing the champion. His sword fell to the ground as he spun in circles. He threw out his arms, trying to block them, but the birds were relentless.

Horrible slurping sounds joined the screams. Blood soared through the air. I could only stare, hand on my hammering heart, eyes wide. The ravens had come to save me. *Again.* I didn't know how and I didn't know why, but I'd never been more grateful for anything in my life.

After several long and brutal moments, the vampire's body thumped onto the floor. The ravens lifted away from him, still swirling in circles over the fallen body. Staring hard the champion, I knelt down and grabbed my blade. A hush went through the room as I strode toward him.

I came to a stop beside his body. He was a vampire, and he would heal. The only way I could win this fight would be to take his life away from him. With a deep breath, I lifted my weapon and slammed my blade against his neck. I turned away as his head rolled across the blood-stained floor. I couldn't bear to look at it. Despite how much I'd seen and heard since joining the Court, I still didn't have the stomach for so much gore.

The ravens cawed and settled on the floor around me. A few blinked up and met my gaze, a strange intelligence flickering in their dark eyes. Another landed on my shoulder. And then another. And another, until at least a seven ravens had gathered on my arms. Slowly, I turned to face Matteo and his council. Thaddeus was on the edge of his seat, gripping the arms, and breathing fast through flared nostrils.

"That's not fair. She cheated," he croaked out.

I lifted an eyebrow and glanced at Matteo.

"I think not." Matteo stood. "Clark Cavanaugh, the ancient magic has revealed the truth for us. You are innocent, cleared of all charges." His gaze slid to Thaddeus. "But he is not."

30

I sat on the steps outside of the Crimson Court, watching Balor drag himself toward me with the moonlit river a backdrop behind his muscular frame. After the trial, I'd headed straight for home, leaving all the violence behind me. In the end, Matteo had arrested Thaddeus. He would have his own trial for the murder of Byron the Bloody, and I didn't have a single doubt in my mind that he would lose.

Unfortunately, I had my own second trial to face. And he was walking right toward me. It had taken awhile for the others to arrive back at the Court. I had a feeling Balor had been stalling.

He came to a stop as I stood, his hands slung into his pockets. "Clark."

My heart thumped hard. There was so much sadness and resignation in his voice, and a distance that I hated to hear. "I'm sorry, Balor. I'm so sorry."

Clenching his jaw, he glanced away. "Moira and I had a talk. She explained what happened with your parents, and she made me understand that what you did was not your fault."

"Really?" I took another step toward him, but he shook his head and moved back.

"I understand it, but I can't say that I find it easy to accept."

"What does that mean?"

"It means that I'm sorry you had to go through what you did at the Circle of Night. It tore me up to see you up there, fighting that thing. I wanted to intervene. I wanted to save you." He sucked in a breath, voice catching. "But that would have only made things worse. You understand that, don't you?"

"Of course." I nodded. If Balor had charged in guns blazing, Matteo would have likely lost his damn mind. I saw now that the leader of the Circle had quickly realised that Thaddeus had been behind it all, when I'd told my side of the story. He had wanted the magic of the trial to prove it.

If we'd taken that chance of justice away from him...

"And I appreciate that you made sure Matteo reinstated the alliance if you won," he said.

I could hear the unspoken word at the end of that sentence. There was a big *but* coming, and I had a horrible feeling I knew exactly what that was.

"You're going to banish me. You're going to make me leave the Court and London behind." Tears finally sprung into my eyes. I shook my head, taking a step toward him. "Balor, please."

He held up a hand and finally lifted his gaze to meet mine again. It was hard and cold and so very, very distant. "I am not going to make you leave

London. This is your home. But I do not think I can have you in my House anymore. You were manipulated into what you did to my sister, but I don't see how I can ever get past it. Seeing you every day...it will just be a reminder of what has been taken from me."

"Balor, please." I choked on the words, big, ugly tears streaming down my face. "I don't know what I will do if you're not in my life."

He took a step back, grinding his teeth together. "I'm sorry."

~

I had nowhere else to go. He would still be expecting my arrival, not knowing what had transpired that night. When I knocked on the warehouse door, Ronan had it open within seconds. He took one look at my face, went straight over the fridge, and grabbed me a beer. I'd downed the thing before he'd even closed the door behind me.

"Tough day?" he asked, crossing his arms and leaning against the wall.

"You have no idea." With a sigh, I plopped down on the sofa and stared up at the overhead beams that criss-crossed through the lofted ceiling. "So, plans have changed."

"Oh yeah? I wondered why you were so late." Cocking an eyebrow, he crossed the room and sunk onto the sofa by my side. "Don't tell me you need to hightail it on out of here without practicing your shift. That's a bad idea, Clark. You need to get control of it before you're out on your own."

"Not exactly." I flicked my eyes his way. "I know

you don't like company, but...how would you feel about having a temporary flatmate? Balor kicked me out of the House, and I don't have anywhere to stay."

He was silent for a long moment.

"It won't be forever," I quickly added. "I'll be back in the Court before you know it. I just have to prove myself to Balor, make him see that his House is where I belong."

Ronan's eyebrows winged upward. "And how the hell are you going to do that?"

"That's the part I don't know yet. I was hoping you could help me figure it out."

~

Thank you for reading *Bad Fae Rising*, the third book in The Paranormal PI Files. Curious about Clark's first meeting with Balor? You can grab the prequel story for free by signing up to my reader newsletter.

One Fae in the Grave, the fourth book in the series, launches June 12th and is available for preorder on Amazon.

ABOUT THE AUTHOR

Jenna Wolfhart is a Buffy-wannabe who lives vicariously through the kick-ass heroines in urban fantasy. After completing a PhD in Librarianship, she became a full-time author and now spends her days typing the fantastical stories in her head. When she's not writing, she loves to stargaze, binge Netflix, and drink copious amounts of coffee.

Born and raised in America, Jenna now lives in England with her husband, her dog, and her mischief of rats.

FIND ME ONLINE

Facebook Reader Group

Instagram

YouTube

Twitter

www.jennawolfhart.com

jenna@jennawolfhart.com

scroll out from inside her jacket, handing it over to me with a hard look in her umber eyes. "Look them over real careful, alright?"

I reached out with confidence and grabbed the scrolls, wondering what this girl's angle was. If she was serious … well, hell, I'd take an ally from the inside. But the chance of one of the Three actually deflecting from the coven? Highly unlikely.

"Thank you for your business," the girl said, lifting her wrist up, the moon tattoo shattering into pieces.

With that, she skirted around us, headed up the porch steps and disappeared inside.

I didn't dare open the scroll right then and there. Not when I was damn near certain one of the dozen pairs of cat eyes in those bushes belonged to the Crone's familiar.

"Let's get the hell out of here," I said with a slight shiver, handing the maps to Montgomery to slip inside his jacket.

We'd just picked magical vampire maps up from a coven of werewolf eating witches. And now, now it was time to go to school.

Once we were safely tucked back inside the metal walls of the pack's GMC Yukon, I took the maps from Monty and unrolled them on my lap. Inside, there was a small scribbled note from the Maiden.

Call me sometime and we'll talk; you have until the sun rises to rid yourself of the false map, it said, and it was signed simply, *Whitney.* It was strange, to think of the Maiden as an actual person and not just a figurehead for the coven. The Crone was so … inhuman, I guess her strangeness seemed to wear off on the other two. But if I really let myself think about it, the Maiden's life was probably much like mine, straddling normalcy and supernatural oblivion at all times, just perching on the edge of a cliff and waiting to fall.

"There's a phone number here," I said, wondering if I'd ever feel confident enough to use it. But trust the Maiden? I so did fucking not.

Looking at the two maps she'd given me, they were almost identical to one another. Both showed the continent of North America from Canada through the USA all the way down to Mexico. They were awash in constantly shifting hues of red and pink, slight variations that required the use of the key in the bottom corner.

Kingdom Ironbound was the first color I sought out, using my finger to trace across the map. With this large of an area, it was almost impossible to see the tiny pockets of territory they still had left in the state of Oregon. Good thing I had Majka's map as backup.

As I studied the maps, I handed the note over to Anubis to read aloud to the rest of the group.

"*Call me sometime and we'll talk; you have until the sun rises to rid yourself of the false map,*" he said, sitting between me and Nic in the front seat. "What the hell does that mean?"

"I have no idea," I told him as he passed the note back and let the other boys have a look. That was one of the major bonuses of getting seven mates for my Contribution —lots of eyes to look things over. "But … I think I know which one is real."

Using Majka's map, I identified a small area in the bottom corner of Oregon that wasn't owned by Kingdom Ironbound *or* Crown Aurora. The hot pink color matched to another group called *Kingdom Kindred.* It was the *only* area in the Pacific Northwest that belonged to that group. The rest of their territory—and it was *substantial*—spread across Texas, Louisiana, Mississippi, and Alabama.

Now.

That piece of territory did *not* show up on one of the maps.

"Somebody put Whitney's number in their phone. Nic, pull the car over." I turned around in the seat and held out a hand toward Silas. "Lighter, please," I said as he raised his dark brows at me.

"What's going on?" he asked as Che lazily typed the Maiden's number into his phone and handed the note back to me. When my fingers brushed his, I felt it, that snap of lust that had come over me like a storm yesterday. There was no denying it was there. *Crap.* What I *really* needed was a day off to process everything that'd happened in the last few days. Instead, I had to deal with witches' tricks.

Silas dropped the lighter in my open palm—I was almost afraid to touch him, too, just in case we sparked another surge of magic inside the tight confines of the SUV.

"Right here, Nic," I instructed as I turned back around.

"Yes, Alpha," he said as he flicked on his blinker and came to a stop in a no-parking zone near the college. I hopped out, taking the map with the missing territory and the note with me. The back door of the SUV opened, and Tidus peeked his head out.

Pausing next to a trash can, I lit first the note and then the map on fire with the lighter, watching as they burned. The note disappeared in sprinkles of gray ash, but the map … it *melted.* Oozed like goo into the can, as thick and viscous as oil. In the air above it, a series of fiery runes appeared, flickering through three separate designs before the map was dissolved.

"What. The. Fuck. Was. *That?*" Tidus hissed, standing beside me suddenly. I was so focused on burning the map, I hadn't noticed him getting out of the car.

"A spell," I said, pursing my lips and taking a step back from the strange ooze inside the can. "My guess? Something that would activate *after* my bargain of protection had expired." I exhaled sharply and took a step back, bumping into Tidus and feeling that rush of earth magic swirl around us.

Uh-oh.

It swept around me and crashed into my hands with the force of a fucking hurricane.

The lighter fell from my fingers and hit the cement as a whole different set of runes etched themselves across my knuckles, flickered, and then burned away. The sharp scent of magic mixed with the acrid reek of soot and ash.

"Is everything okay?" Nic asked, coming around the front of the SUV to stand beside Tidus and me. I exchanged a glance with the gray-eyed boy and then knelt down to pick up Silas' lighter. "Zara?"

"Everything's alright," I said, shaking out my hand and taking one, last look at the trash can. I didn't know *what* spell it was that our newfound magic had just obliterated, but it was pretty obvious we'd just narrowly avoided getting tangled in something nasty.

I glanced back at Tidus and Nic.

"But we better check the other map first; grab it for me?"

Nic did as I asked, handing me the scroll and stepping back, sliding his hands into his pockets to watch. The wind tousled the strands of his dark red hair and made him look so classically handsome that my heart literally hurt inside my chest.

'Do you mind?' I asked, projecting my wolfspeak voice so that only he could hear it.

At least he knew me well enough that I didn't have to spell it out.

'Go for it,' he said, a slight sigh escaping his lips. *'I can handle a short kiss a hell of a lot better than ... well, you know.'*

Smiling softly, I turned back to the Alpha-Son of Pack Amber Ash. I held the paper tight in my right hand, put the other on the back of Tidus' neck, and before I could question what the hell I was doing, pressed my mouth to his.

"Oh!" I heard Anubis whisper from the front seat. "Damn it, I *knew* I should've gotten out with her, too."

Tidus put his arms around me and wrapped me up tight, that sandalwood scent of his making my skin pebble with goose bumps, a cool breeze wrapping around us and teasing strands of bloodred hair across my face. I felt the easy whisper of earth magic glide along with it, touching my skin with delicate fingers, dancing down my fingertips and into the scroll.

Nothing happened. No more runes. No more black goo.

When I pulled back from him and cracked my eyes, I found a smile stretching across those lips that was hard to resist. Despite the witches and the bullshit, I smiled back. Kissing a stranger … kissing my *mate* … that was the *fun* part of the job.

"Map is all good then, I take it?" he asked, his gray eyes crinkling at the edges with humor.

"Map is great," I said, feeling the thundering pace of my own heart, matched only by the rapid gallop of his. Nic looked like he wanted to kill someone, but less so than usual. I think he might've actually *liked* Tidus. "Thanks for helping me check it."

"No, thank *you,*" he said and I heard both Nic *and* Che scoff.

Great.

Now I had *two* sarcastic a-holes to deal with.

PACK VIOLET SHADOW

Unsurprisingly, lecture was cancelled.

It was a little difficult to teach a class when you were, you know, dead. Drained of blood. Dragged from the forest by the ankle. That was the last I'd seen of Professor Heath, but there was no doubt in my mind that he really was dead.

A note was taped on the door outside the lecture hall where our wildflowers class was usually held, just a vague scribble explaining that Mr. Heath would not be in today, but that we should check back on Wednesday.

And only we knew the real reason why—our fucking professor had been drained by a daywalking vampire. The very same daywalking vampire that I was supposed to pair up with for our final project.

Nic and I exchanged a glance and stepped away from the door so our classmates could read the hastily scrawled message.

"No fair—you guys have a get out of class free card?" Faith said from behind me. I turned to look at her, a sick sense of dread twisting my stomach into knots. Not only did Monday mean facing Julian and the truth of what was happening to my pack members, it also meant that I had to look my best friend in the eye and know that her mother was dead, that her dogs were dead, and that with every second that passed between us, I was lying by omission.

It also meant I had to stare at Owen, leaning casually against the wall next to her, hands folded behind his head like he was some sort of slouchy badass or something. *God, he's such a douche.*

"Guess so," I said, trying to keep my voice light and fluffy and cheerful. Inside, I was drowning in secrets. Honestly, I'd considered not coming at all today. In fact, I'd planned on using this Monday as a rest day long before the Pairing even rolled around. I'd figured after all the pomp and circumstance of the ceremony, I'd need a moment to myself.

I'd been right.

But circumstances being what they were, I'd made the decision to carry out the plan Nic and I had come up with to follow Julian. That is, if he even showed up today. He of all people should know that Professor Heath wasn't coming to class.

Besides, Faith had stayed the night at Nic's place again and needed a ride. If I left her to her own devices, she'd probably just lay in bed with Owen all day.

"You're so lucky," she said with an exaggerated eye roll, "I have a test today and I so did not study."

I gave her a look and a raised eyebrow, just like I would have on any normal day. Although today … was anything *but* normal.

"Hey Zara," a voice said from behind me.

Nic let out a little growl that I stamped down by grasping his left hand with tight fingers. A quick look soothed his metaphorical hackles before I glanced over my shoulder with a faux smile plastered on my face.

"Julian," I said brightly, trying to keep the images I'd seen yesterday from infiltrating my mind. *Julian's sharp white teeth puncturing Mr. Heath's throat, the vampire's pale skin shining under the bright rays of the sun, the limp way my professor's body sagged in his aggressor's arms.*

I made myself turn around, wishing that I had more than just Nic for backup. But the boys and I had decided together that if a bunch of random werewolves were to show up at the university all at once, Julian might get suspicious. They were just a stone's throw away, close enough to smell trouble if there was any but far enough away that Julian wouldn't sense them there. Like I said, a werewolf's sense of smell is three times better than a vampire's.

"I was just wondering," he started as I surreptitiously sniffed the air around him. Like the Unseelie Queen had said—he must be using witch hazel. That mint, apple, and blood smell was completely gone. Instead, Julian actually smelled like a human. I wondered if that was from casual contact with other students … or the dying touch of a recent victim. Hell, as far as I knew, he could have a human chained in his basement for the sole purpose of rubbing their scent onto his clothes. It'd be a smart way to fool a werewolf. We grew up learning to trust our noses and right now, Julian smelled as unassuming as any other human in this hallway. "Since class is cancelled, did you want to hang out in the student lounge and start planning our project?"

The way he said the words … you'd never know that he

was responsible for a man's death just twenty-four hours prior.

Even though it hurt my mouth, I made myself keep smiling back.

"If it's okay with you," I said, hiking my book bag a little higher on my shoulder, "I'd rather just keep our Tuesday appointment. Nic and I are gonna go grab something to eat." I shrugged loosely. "I was running late this morning. No time for breakfast."

Julian's brown eyes stayed on mine, searching me out, studying me. He looked at me like he had insider knowledge, something I was either too stupid or naïve to figure out. Joke was on him; I knew everything.

"No problem," he said, but I could hear the disappointment in his voice. Goose bumps rose up all across my arms. *Sorry dude, but whatever you've got planned for me, I'm gonna have to cancel; there's no way in hell this wolf is becoming fuel for your next daywalking adventure.* "Tomorrow, we can even head over to my place if you want—it's within walking distance."

Julian paused and reached up to ruffle his dishwater brown hair with long, pale fingers, pretending to be the sheepish boy next door instead of the murdering monster he really was.

"Just as friends, of course," he said to Nic.

"Of course," Nic growled back, with a little more force than necessary. Julian just laughed and nodded at Faith and Owen before turning and heading toward the closest exit. Maybe it was just me, but it looked like he was walking a little faster than normal.

"You guys are going out to eat?" Faith asked, yanking on my book bag strap. "If you bring me something back, I'll love you forever."

"You'll love me forever anyway," I said with raised brows, turning my fake smile her way. Looking at my best friend, it should've been real … but then my mind filled with images of revenants and blood and it was all I could do not to throw up. "Now go to class. I'll meet you at the SUV after."

I turned away and headed after Julian before he could get too far ahead of us. When I glanced back, I saw Owen meandering toward the student lounge, checking out girls' asses as he went. Unfortunately, Faith didn't notice, slipping into her classroom and letting the door slam behind her.

"You ready?" I asked Nic as we stepped into the bright sunshine, the yellow rays reflecting off the stubborn white cling of snow on the landscape and blinding us. "This could get ugly."

"I'm counting on it," he said with a grim half-smile, shooting off a text to Anubis.

Within a minute, he was jogging into view, lifting up the fabric of his hoodie and unhooking the two badass toolkits from his waist. I hadn't wanted to bring them into the school with me for fear Julian would scent the wood and bone tools inside, but I sure as hell wasn't about to follow him to wherever without them.

"Stay right behind us," I reminded Anubis Rothburg as

he blinked red eyes at me, his blue-black hair comically spiked and standing straight up on the top of his head. He looked like an anime character with that do. "And keep your phone on."

"Yes, Alpha," he said with a slight smile, waiting while we used the cover of a tree to put our belts on and hide them with our coats. "Be careful out there, okay? If you die, I might get mated to your creepy little sister."

I flashed a grin at him before taking off in Julian's direction, following the subtle human scent he'd left in his wake. It was almost too faint; if I'd been anyone else, I might've had trouble keeping up. But there was a reason I'd gotten a reputation as the White Wolf.

Nic and I didn't talk, not even with wolfspeak. Instead, we focused on keeping as much distance as possible without losing Julian. It was a little tricky, I'll admit. The University of Oregon campus was riddled with smells—and not just from humans. Here and there I'd pick up the scent of something decidedly not human—a skin-walker, a weretiger, a fae, a witch. As we left campus, it got even worse, restaurant smells and car exhaust mixing into the medley and trying to trick my nose.

'Left?' I asked at one corner as Nic lifted his head and let his nostrils flare wide as he tried to get a read on our target.

'I think so,' he replied, but he sounded just as unsure as I felt.

We continued on anyway. If we lost the trail, it wasn't the end of the world. Tomorrow, I'd get another chance. Hell, tomorrow I'd get an invitation. But I really, really wanted to find this place today. Not only did it give me an extra twenty-four hours to figure out how to deal with Julian, but he wasn't expecting me right now. Tomorrow, he would be.

Three blocks later, down a tree-lined street with sidewalks still sprinkled with snow, I thought we were done for, Julian's faint scent melting away to join a thousand other ambient smells in the air.

'There,' Nic said, using wolfspeak as he put a hand on my arm and brought us to a stop. At the end of the block, on a corner lot taken up by an old blue and white house, there was Julian. He was leaning casually against a tree and smoking a cigarette, like the world was exactly what it looked like at face value. Normal, unassuming, everyday.

Nic and I ducked low behind a parked car and peered through the windows. Vampires might be lacking in the smell department, but their eyesight is just as good as ours —maybe even better. Still, I was banking on the fact that he wouldn't see us because he wasn't looking for us. People— even vampires—only see what they want to see.

We'd just settled down to watch when a car pulled up to the curb and a dark-haired woman got out, heading over to the passenger side door to open it. As soon as she did, a familiar scent rushed out at me, almost knocking me onto my ass.

The person that stepped out of the car, heavy and pregnant, face wrinkled with worry, was the former Omega Female of Pack Ebon Red, the woman who'd served as nanny and babysitter for most of my life.

'Fuck.'

Nic said it first, although I was thinking it.

We exchanged a quick look before turning back to the distorted view through the car's windows. Like a lamb headed to the slaughter, Selena followed the woman—presumably another daywalking vampire—over to Julian. Pleasantries were exchanged and then ... she walked right up the steps and into the house.

The sound of the door slamming behind her had an ominous ring to it. Had I been in wolf form, all of my hair would've been standing on end.

The question was: was Selena helping Kingdom Ironbound or was she another victim?

I had a feeling my time for figuring out the answer to that question was limited at best.

It was time to accept the Unseelie Queen's invitation.

“That vampire woman,” I said as I sat in the shade of a large blue spruce, a veritable feast laid out on the blanket in front of me. One of the boys—I think it was Anubis—had gathered up a bunch of leftovers from last night's banquet and made a picnic basket out of it. The venison steak I'd been too stressed to eat yesterday melted against my tongue like butter. Even cold, it was goddamn delicious. “She had the faintest scent of wolf on her—and not Selena's scent either.”

As good as the food was, it did nothing to hide the bitter taste that filled my mouth at the thought of my former babysitter. She was either a captive … or a traitor. Regardless, that didn't sit right with me.

“Anyone you recognized?” Montgomery asked, more interested in taking mental notes than eating. All the other boys—save Jaxson—were shoving their faces full while the Alpha Sons of Pack Ivory Emerald and Azure Frost watched me with tight lips and wrinkled brows.

“It was clearly *pack*, but I couldn't put a name or a face to the particular scent. It was too weak for me to even say *which* pack, although there's no doubt in my mind that that woman's been in contact with a wolf other than Selena."

Anyway, as close as the packs were, with over five hundred thousand werewolves living in North America alone, it was impossible to know everyone. Even if I *had* gotten a really good sniff, the best I could hope for was to identify the specific pack rather than the individual.

"Do you think being booted from the pack was cause enough for your omega to deflect to the Bloods?" Jax asked, repeating my worry aloud. I couldn't decide which was worse—the woman who'd practically raised me being involved in this mess or becoming a victim to it.

I sighed and leaned back, looking up at branches heavy with melting snow. A single cold drop fell onto my lips and I licked it away.

"The question is: do you think an omega would even have the gall to pull a move like that?" Che asked, and I heard Nic give a derisive snort. Maybe fucking Che Nocturne just two days after the Bonding Ritual wasn't the best idea?

I'd been driven by primal lust … but now tensions were sky-high. Sky-fucking-high.

"You don't know a damn thing about Selena," Nic groused and I swear, I could *feel* Che smirking at him.

"Then why don't you tell me, Ebon Red?" he purred in that sumptuous voice of shadows.

"Hey," I said, dropping my chin and taking a deep breath. Both Nic and Che—the only two people I'd ever had sex with—stared back at me with dark, considering eyes. I ignored them both, reaching inside the front pocket of my black hoodie and withdrawing the pair of maps. As soon as we'd arrived back at the Pairing House, the boys and I had spent hours putting little stickers on all the spots where pack members had gone missing. Hours of tense, uneasy silence.

I was done with it.

"I don't know what's happening with Selena," I said as I fingered the scrolls and let my eyes drift around the circle of alpha males. Tidus was smiling at me; Anubis was hanging on my every word. The others were more reserved: Jax and Montgomery listened intently while Nic and Che glared at each other. Silas and I locked gazes just before he pulled out a pack of cigarettes and made the rest of the boys groan. "But we can't exactly waltz in there and find out for ourselves."

If I could have, I'd have stormed the house and dragged Selena out myself—either to rescue her or interrogate her. But rushing into a house full of vampires was a bad idea on the best of days. Even if I took all the boys with me, the chances were that we'd be outnumbered. Besides, there was no way to know if an Ageless—a vampire over a hundred years old—was waiting in there, too. If so, there was always the possibility, however remote, of being rolled—i.e. hypnotized—and brought under their control.

Especially if a fight broke out first.

Yes, werewolves were resistant to ambient magic, but with enough injuries, that resistance started to break down. Before the fight was over, the eight of us could end up on our knees licking the vamp's feet, rictus grins tearing across our bloody faces.

"This is our Contribution," I continued, unrolling the new map for a brief moment. It looked like it had some kind of weird disease now, covered in all those tiny black sticker dots. It was both disheartening and invigorating, seeing the enormity of the problem but also knowing we *were* making at least some sort of progress on it. The one thing that'd become abundantly clear from this particular exercise: the pack disappearances were not exclusive to Ironbound territory.

Either they'd recently lost a lot of ground to other vampire Kingdoms—like they'd done with Crown Aurora—or else the kidnapping, draining, and *eating* of werewolf flesh was not limited to a single group of Bloods.

No.

Based on the random clusters of disappearances around the continent … it looked like more than one Kingdom was involved.

My best option at this point was to eat the queen's mushroom, visit Faerie, and see what help—and at what cost—the Unseelie were willing to offer me.

I was so not looking forward to it.

"This is our Contribution," I repeated, rolling the maps back up and tucking them into the picnic basket, "and we have a responsibility to follow every lead to its final conclusion. Clearly, the witches fed me Ebon Red flesh for a reason. They *want* me to know. That scares me, boys. Really and truly frightens me." I looked up at them all, each pair of eyes their own unique color.

My gaze landed on the matching aubergine shine of my guard's.

"Zara," Nic started, because he was pretty clearly in the *let's-not-do-this* camp. And with good reason. I wasn't arguing that this was a move without risks, just that it was a move we needed to take.

"This could be a trap," Jax added, just as calm and placid as always. He was sitting with one knee popped up, his white blonde hair appearing far more yellow than usual against the backdrop of snow. Montgomery's on the other hand practically blended into the landscape. "How do we know the Unseelie Court isn't in league with Kingdom Ironbound and Coven Triad?"

I took another deep breath and then pulled one of the faerie queen's mushrooms from the same hoodie pocket. We'd gathered up both rings worth, so there were enough for everyone, but that it didn't make it any easier for me to take the plunge. I'd never been to Faerie, but I'd heard horror stories. Majka still whispered when she spoke of the place.

I studied the purple and white mushroom between my fingers, turning it in a slow circle.

"We don't," I said, but we'd already discussed this, hashed it out as a group in the SUV on the way home. It was *all* we'd talked about since the Julian/Selena incident that afternoon. Hours of alternating debate and tense silence between me and my boys, and I knew we were split down the middle, fifty-fifty.

I had to be the tiebreaker; I had to make the decision.

I was the *Alpha.*

"But if the queen were already working with the Kingdoms, she wouldn't need to trick a small contingent of wolves into Faerie," I said with another long inhale of the cool, crisp winter air. "No, she'd already know that between the court, the coven, and the kingdom … that we were screwed."

And then before I could think twice about it, I popped the damn mushroom in my mouth. If I'd let myself mull it over for even a minute longer, I'd have probably talked myself out of it altogether.

For about three seconds, I was just sitting there chewing and wrinkling my nose at the rubbery texture of the raw mushroom.

And then … a blanket of darkness rushed up and out of my mouth, a heavy weight of black on black speckled with stars. It swept over me like a wave, crashed into my body, and dragged me under, cutting me off mid-scream.

The sound of Nic shouting my name was the last thing I remembered.

I woke up panting, surrounded by the scent of citrus and wolf.

A heavy weight lay sprawled across my chest, and when I reached up, my fingers found the thickness of a white winter pelt.

Jaxson Kidd, the Alpha Son of Pack Azure Frost, was deadweight across my chest, lying comatose across my ribs. As gently as I could, I pushed him off and he lolled to the side, hitting the rocky ground beneath us like a corpse. His lack of movement scared me so much that I had to put my ear to his chest to make sure his heart was still beating.

The warmth and movement of his body reassured me enough to sit up and take a quick look around. It was dark enough that for a second, I had to wonder if we were in a cave or tunnel of some kind. But no, after a few quick blinks, my night vision kicked in and I found myself looking up at a pair of moons the color of fresh bruises. One was lavender while the other glowed a sickly periwinkle blue.

“It's quite picturesque, isn't it?” a voice oozed from in front of me, coming from the same direction as the sound of running water. As soon as I registered the bubbling of water on rocks, I knew I was in trouble. In Faerie, nothing good lives in the river. That much I knew from Majka's random stories.

“Very,” I said as chills chased across my skin. I scooted closer to Jax, using his warmth and nearness to bolster my spirits. I'd need them, considering I was looking into the face of a grinning white horse. Or should I say, *kelpie*?

The fae creature smiled at me with big, blocky white teeth in a ghostly face. Its fur was tinted from the glow of the double moons, turning it a sickly purple-blue color in the darkness that was hard to distinguish against the rolling landscape and the river. It had a mane and tail made of slimy, dark green reeds that curled down its muscular neck and draped in twisted tangles from its rump. As soon as I made eye contact with it, I knew I was in trouble.

It was lying on its side on the rocky ground at the river's edge, like a horse taking an afternoon nap. Except … horses don't grin. And they don't have eyes so devoid of light that they're black on black, dark even in a night shrouded landscape. They also don't look at you like they're keeping dirty secrets.

"Flesh is very hard to tear with such dull teeth," the creature told me without skipping a beat. "I'd much rather have sharp fangs like your friend there. Do you think he'd mind so very much if I added them to my collection?"

Magic swirled in the air around us, acrid and metallic. The kelpie was trying to glamour us with faerie magic. But like I said before, werewolves are resistant to ambient magic. It would take more than the kelpie's natural powers of persuasion to get me to hand over Jax, let it drag him into the dark, icy depths of the river.

With a snort and a sneeze, my new mate came to with a sharp jerk of his massive, muscular body. In an instant, he was on his feet, hackles raised and teeth bared. I followed him up—and so did the kelpie, standing there on legs *just* this side of too long for a horse. If I looked askance, the faerie didn't look any different from the placid, grass eating animals I was used to. But straight on? Not even a human being would mistake the kelpie for an herbivore.

This … this was clearly a predator.

'Kelpie?' Jax asked me, and I was surprised that he recognized it, too. Most werewolves were completely ignorant when it came to the various types of fae. But I guess he'd been groomed from birth to be a leader, just as I was. Somebody in his pack must've been to Faerie because kelpie, they definitely did *not* cross the Veil.

"What's the matter?" the fae asked innocently, standing there on spindly legs and flicking its slimy green tail. "You don't want to take a swim with your friends? The water's nice and warm, I promise."

The pungent scent of rot plumed in the air with each word, tainting a landscape already riddled with unfamiliar smells. It was almost distracting enough to make me miss the hint in its words.

Friend*s*. Not friend. It wasn't just referring to Jax.

My heart leapt into my throat as I heard the sound of splashing in the distance.

"Jaxson," I said, those two syllables harsh and sudden, exploding from my lips at the same moment I took off running. The sound of paws and hooves scrambling across the rocky shore followed me all the way to the edge of the water, but I had to put some faith into Jax and hope like hell he had my back.

Mourning the loss of my favorite hoodie (growing up, most werewolves learn the hard way not to devote much love or money to clothing), I shifted mid-leap, diving into the rough waters of the river and hoping I wasn't already too late.

When it came to the fae, each individual species seemed

to be notorious for something. You know how in the feline world, cheetahs are known for their speed, lions for their manes, and tigers for their stripes? Well, faeries are kind of like that only … not. See, instead of being famous for markings or mating habits, how high they can jump or how fast they can run, most fae gain notoriety for how they kill.

Kelpie, for example, lure their prey into the water with magic, often convincing them to climb on their backs for a little ride. Once they're submerged, they hold their victims under until they breathe their last, watery breaths.

And then they eat them, wet and raw and still warm.

'Where are you?' I called out, using wolfspeak to fling my voice far and wide. At this point, I wasn't sure who I was looking for, only that one of the males I'd promised to protect was in this goddamn river, this icy, dark, awful river.

I fought against the current as best I could. My wolf form was definitely better at navigating the rough waters than my human form, but I was still a creature of the earth and it was slow going. Besides that, I could barely see through the frosty rapids, my body slamming into rocks as I swam in the direction of the frantic splashing.

'If you can hear me, I need a fucking answer!' I sent out in a frantic wave, my mind conjuring images of Nic or Silas, flailing beneath the sharp hooves of a kelpie, fighting for just one more breath.

'We're on the opposite shore,' Nic sent back, sounding groggy and disoriented. He'd probably just woken up. *'I can see Jax and I can see you,'* he said with a sudden sharp bite to his voice. *'Zara, get out of the water!'*

'I'm going under,' another voice said just a split second later, a flash of fear and pain cutting straight through me. All of a sudden, I could feel the tight hot ache of burning lungs, the rush of cold water over broken skin, the growing intensity of a life and death struggle.

Che Nocturne was in serious trouble.

'I'm coming!' I called out, hoping like hell that it wasn't already too late for the Alpha Son of Pack Violet Shadow. I could taste his fear on the back of my tongue, rancid and bitter, tainted with surprise. Che must've either fallen in the river or been dragged into the water while he was still passed out. What a way to wake up.

"Zara!" Montgomery Graves called out from the shore. He had his iron sword clutched in one hand, the other resting on the curve of his belt, fingers teasing the hilt of a matching knife. His black trench coat billowed around him in the breeze.

As I continued swimming toward the flickering beacon of Che's fear, Montgomery waded into the river and tried his best to follow along in the waist-deep water along the edge of the shore. The way his green eyes scanned the horizon did not bode well for Che. If Monty couldn't see him from where he was standing, then Che was already underwater.

'Che, can you hear me?' I asked, trying not to panic, knowing that I was going to anyway.

'Hear you ...' he replied, and even though he was speaking inside my head, the words were hard to hear. Che was fading and fast. If I didn't get to him in the next thirty seconds, I'd have six alpha males to choose from at the end

of the Pairing instead of seven.

I shifted in the water and used a nearby rock to push myself under.

It was so goddamn dark down there that had I been human, I'd have been completely blind. Even as a 'were', I was having trouble seeing. The dark current rushed against my face, chilling me to the bone. It'd been so long since I'd actually felt cold that the sensation was a bit of a shock. I guess it was true what I'd said—werewolves are *nearly* impervious to cold. Nearly. As in, an icy river in Faerie will still freeze our supernatural asses off.

Che was a blur in the darkness, part of this thrashing tangle of color about ten feet in front of me. The kelpie was wrapped around him like a snake, its spine twisted in a way that was about as far from a horse as one could get. Looking at it down there, wrapped in the arms of its watery domain, I wondered how I'd even made the comparison to begin with. It hardly looked equine like that, its mouth clamped onto my mate's shoulder, red blood blooming in the water around them.

A macabre dance of life and death waltzed through the swirling currents, just two dancers spinning across a liquid floor, destined for a watery grave.

I kicked off the submerged corpse of a long dead tree and shifted mid-dash, slamming into the kelpie's side with all the power of a werewolf. Its teeth dislodged from Che's shoulder, leaving him floating on his back in the rapids like a doll. As soon as he was separated from the kelpie's grip, Che went spinning through the blackness and slammed into a partially submerged rock.

I stopped fighting the current, hoping it would take me with him. Instead, I felt an awful scraping along my spine.

Despite what the first kelpie had told me, those blunt teeth of theirs really could do some damage. The pain was exquisite, a deep burning sensation that cut through the cold of the water. Before I could even think to react, I was being whipped against the force of the current and thrown to the mucky bottom of the river.

'Somebody grab Che!' was all I managed to get out before the kelpie was crushing me into the mud with the force of a freight train. It was as strong as any vampire, as any werewolf, and I was in its domain. Down here, this faerie clearly had the advantage.

I snapped my jaws at its flank and managed to sink my teeth in, tasting the metallic sharpness of blood as the kelpie screamed, its voice echoing strangely underwater, bubbles escaping its too wide mouth. It lunged at me then, grabbed me around the throat and clamped down hard enough to cut off my air supply. Fortunately—or unfortunately, depending on how you look at it—I was already at that point where I was so desperate for air, I'd been about to suck in two huge lungfuls of water. While the kelpie's bite hurt, it also gave me the smallest reprieve against drowning.

'Zara, where are you?' It was Silas this time, calling my name, a frantic flair in his words ricocheting through his pack connection. He was worried, desperate, pacing the bank just above me. But the kelpie and I, we were so deep now that it was doubtful that Silas could see us—wolf eyes

or no.

Using the same technique I'd tried with Nikolina in Coyote Creek, I shifted into human form.

The sudden change of shape dislodged the kelpie enough that I was able to slip out from underneath it, letting the current rip me away and toss me in Che's direction.

But holy shit.

As I was flung back from the violent force of the water, I could see the kelpie spin, still as graceful as a dancer in the midst of a ball. It turned and came right at me, rocketing through bubbles and the foamy gurgles of white rapids.

My body slammed into Che's a split second before the kelpie's slammed into mine.

An explosion rocked the water, throwing the faerie, me, and the Alpha Son up and out of the river. We landed on the bank in a wild tangle of limbs and blood.

"Heads down!" Montgomery called out, just an instant before I dropped my head and felt the cool brush of air against my wet scalp. Gripping the iron sword in both hands, Monty swung it in a wide arc and severed the kelpie's head right from its body.

Blood sprayed everywhere, violent crimson bursts spurting over my naked, wet form, drenching me in hot copper liquid. Meanwhile, my body had ideas of its own, my lungs and stomach muscles contracting painfully as I coughed up water and felt around desperately for Che.

The kelpie's legs continued to kick, nailing me in the arm, the leg, its body jumping with electrical impulses that transcended its mortal death. Jax appeared a few seconds later, white fur bloody, tongue lolling, and grabbed a mouthful of the kelpie's flesh, dragging its corpse down the beach to give Che and me some space.

"Wake up," I whispered, red hair plastered against my face. I was shaking, actually *shaking* from the cold, as I touched a hand to the side of Che's pale cheek. Water bubbled up past my lips as I continued to cough it up, desperately trying to summon some of that skittish wild magic to heal my mate. "Come on, Che," I breathed as Montgomery and Anubis knelt down on the opposite side of his body.

"I know CPR," Monty said, very matter-of-fact, already shrugging himself out of the trench coat.

"If someone …" Che whispered roughly, rolling onto his side and throwing up a massive amount of water. He shoved his arm against his mouth and took several deep, shaky breaths. "If someone's going to put their mouth against mine, I'd prefer it was Zara's."

I smiled tightly, sniffling and pushing heavy strands of dark red hair back from my face. Nic was behind and to the left of me (as usual) while Jax stood guard near the riverbank with Tidus and Silas. In the distance, I heard an echoing scream that was half-human, half-horse. Another kelpie.

I shivered and then stiffened up as I felt the pain in my back.

"It's bad, Zara," Nic whispered from behind me, but I didn't care. We were all alive, and I would heal.

"Are you alright?" I asked after Che had thrown up a

few more times, finally pushing himself into a sitting position and using his wet t-shirt to clean his mouth off.

"I'm fine," he said, his voice like liquid smoke. But even with the violet eyes, the dark hair, the rippling muscles underneath the clinging wetness of his shirt, he didn't look imposing. No, he looked scared. "What the hell was that thing?"

"Kelpie," I said, pursing my lips and wondering what the fuck the Unseelie Queen was thinking, setting us up to take our first steps in Faerie on the edge of an infested riverbank. "It's a type of fae that drowns its prey before it eats it."

"Oh?" Che said, voice still scratchy and weak from his near drowning. He lifted his head and gave me a look dripping with sarcasm. "Is that all? Just another creature that chows down on wolves? Well, shit, and here I was thinking we'd stumbled into something truly grotesque."

'Everything has a right to eat,' Jax said, limping over to stand next to Nic. With a lupine groan, he flopped down and put his large head in my lap. *'Please tell me you have a little more of that healing magic up your sleeve?'*

"I guess we'll find out," I said as I laid my hands on his neck and felt the deep, bloody gouges left by the first kelpie's mouth. My fingers dug into the wet, sticky fur and an instant later, I felt it, that cool energy leaking from my hand into Jax's throat. His skin closed up beneath my fingertips, sealed together and smoothed out until the only evidence left of his wound was the blood clotting his coat.

I breathed out a deep sigh of relief.

Without this strange, hidden magic of ours … Che and I,

we'd be dead.

"That explosion," I started, looking up and meeting Che's purple eyes. "More magic."

"More magic," he agreed, pausing and then shakily getting to his knees.

Before I could figure out what he was doing, Che was tugging his soggy wet shirt over his head and pulling me into his lap. As soon as the aching mess of my back made contact with his chest, the pain receded like an outgoing tide and my breath caught, not just from the damp smell of decaying leaves and moist earth but from the hot touch of Che's body. Being pressed against him like this, it made me remember that just yesterday, I was lying naked beneath him in the forest.

"I was wondering what you were doing out here," a voice said from my left, snapping me out of my thoughts. I scrambled to my feet just in time to come face-to-face with the sloe-eyed faerie queen.

She was standing barefoot on the slippery rocks, looking perplexed at the headless kelpie.

Today's body of choice was tall and thin with skin like crushed diamonds and long dark hair, as black and limitless as the eerie depths of the kelpies' eyes. It wasn't black the way a raven's feathers are dark, the way a cat's coat ripples like the night. It was just this void, this tumble of lightless strands that coiled on the ground like shadows.

Since the sidhe are wingless faeries, the queen had dressed herself in a loose white gown with flimsy gray wings made of wire and cloth attached to the back. Torn strands of ashy gray fabric drifted in the breeze like ghosts.

"What the *fuck* is your problem?" I snarled, naked and wet and covered in faerie blood. I must've been a sight to see because for a second there, the queen looked a bit taken aback. It didn't last long—within a few seconds, that arrogant mask was fixed firmly back in place. But I'd seen the slip-up and I would not soon forget. "If you wanted to try and kill us, I'm sure there are easier ways."

"If I wanted you dead, you would be," she said, kneeling down and reaching for the severed head. At first, I thought she was going to use her fingers to close the kelpie's eyes. Instead, she plucked them right from its head and tucked them into a pouch hanging off one hip. "This is not where I intended for you to end up."

She didn't bother to elaborate or explain what went wrong. Instead, she just stood up, smiled sharply, and wiped smears of blood onto the front of her white dress.

"If you'll follow me, you can get cleaned up and we can talk business."

The Faerie Queen of the Unseelie Court turned on her heel and headed up the gradual slope of the bank. As far as I could tell, we had two choices: follow her … or hang out here and wait for more kelpies to show up.

"Let's go," I said, starting up the hill without looking back to see if my mates were following me. I didn't have to see them to know; I could *feel* it. After the Pairing Ceremony, I could feel each one of them like seven extra heartbeats inside my chest.

But Nic and Che … their presence was ten, twenty, thirty

times stronger.

Gee. I wonder why?

I wasn't going to say anything yet, but I was pretty sure that by fucking me, Che had saved his own life. If we hadn't had sex, I don't think I'd have found him, drowning in the dark wet limbs of an icy river.

The Unseelie Court was supposed to be a glamorous gathering of nightmares, glittering monsters, and alluring fiends. There were spires made of bone and thrones of living flesh, molded and tortured into the appropriate shape. As Majka had once said, it was like a chandelier made of teeth. Pretty from afar, disturbing up close.

So when the queen took us to a crumbling manor of white stone, picked her way over the rubble that once served as a front door, and showed us to a decaying room around a natural hot spring, I started to get suspicious.

'What sort of fae queen makes a mistake as costly as that?' I said, referencing our messy entrance into the world of Faerie.

'Or lives in ruins?' Anubis asked, shifting back to human form and slipping into the steaming pool of water with a sigh. I was already there, sitting on the edge of a stone bench and looking up at the skeletons of stained glass windows above our heads. Here and there I could catch a glittering beam of moonlight on the edge of some colored glass, but for the most part, it was just an elaborate weave of

metal holding up an empty sky.

'Or offers a helping hand to the Alpha-Heir instead of the reigning Alpha?' Montgomery added, studying the warm, clear waters of the pool for several long moments before shrugging out of his clothing to join us.

“Please tell me I'm not the only one that's freezing my nuts off,” Silas said, the first person to speak aloud in the eerie quiet of the bathing room. I guess he figured the fae queen would be much less interested in hearing him complain than she would be about us speculating as to her true intentions.

“You still have nuts? You're lucky. I think mine've retreated all the way back up inside my body,” Nic said, cringing a little when I threw him a look with a raised brow.

“Please don't make me regret the decision to spend the next twelve months trapped with seven dudes,” I whispered and he gave me a weak half-smile. Maybe because my joke was funny. More likely because we both knew it wasn't *really* my decision to make.

“A wolf should always be on his best behavior while in the presence of foreign company,” Anubis said, using some of the hot water to smooth down the hair on the left side of his head. It wasn't working. Instead, his pack's signature navy dark hair was spiked up in all directions, like he'd taken a whole palmful of gel to it. “Son of a bitch,” he cursed as he caught sight of his reflection in the water, two sets of red eyes blinking as he studied the mirror image of his face.

“Son of a bitch?” Che asked with a mean smirk. “Is that

part of your best behavior vocabulary?"

Anubis snapped his gaze up and dropped his hands into his lap with a splash, meeting Che's gaze dead-on. A small dominance war played out between them before they both glanced away simultaneously. It wasn't a draw, not really, more like a *let's save this for later* sort of a thing.

"There's not a Numinous out there that isn't raised to think that werewolves are rude, crude, bestial, and base when really, we're a dignified, cultured species with a long history and—"

"Oh, for fuck's sake," Che said with a roll of his purple eyes, ducking under the water for a brief moment and slicking his dark hair back from his face. Despite the fact that he'd just nearly lost his life in a river, the water didn't seem to be bothering him. That is, that's what I thought until I saw a slight tremor run over his skin, like the brush of a ghost's icy fingers down his spine. "You sound like a textbook," he spat out, climbing from the water and standing there casually, arms crossed over his wide chest like he didn't have a care in the world. Now that I was really looking for it, I could see that he was almost desperate to get out and away from the steamy waters of the pool. "Or an Alpha-Mother lecturing a group of kids. Don't tell me you actually believe that crap."

"Are you serious?" Anubis asked, rising out of the water, droplets clinging to the tanned surface of his skin, beading on his muscles and sliding down his chest. "Do you really hate yourself that fucking much? Or is it just our people in general you don't like?"

"Hey, you got me," Che said with another mean twist of his lips. "You're right—I hate the whole world and everything in it."

"Zara," Nic said softly, the fingers of his left hand curling into a tight fist. He wanted me to put a stop to the argument and really, I should have, considering there was a nearly one hundred percent chance that we were being watched right now. But I couldn't resist the impulse to see a little deeper into the boys' personalities.

"It didn't seem like you hated Zara yesterday," Anubis snapped, and then he went completely still, his entire body stiffening. I could see his muscles locking into place beneath his skin as he glanced over at me. "Shit, shit, shit. I have such a huge fucking mouth," he growled, dropping back into the water and turning to face me. Of course, he didn't dare make eye contact. "I'm sorry Alpha," he whispered, prostrating himself as best he could in the waist-deep waters of the pool.

I stared down at Anubis, naked and submissive in front of me. If he'd had a tail at that moment, it'd have been tucked. His head was turned away, eyes downcast, back hunched. If I'd wanted to, I could've ripped him a new one and all the others would've done is sit there and watch. Instead, I smiled.

Che and I had very nearly escaped being a kelpie's midnight snack; my best friend's mother had died while trying to become a vampire, and my people were being eaten by witches. Now was not the time to pull one of my mother's moves out of the proverbial hat and put Anubis in his place.

"First you go through my underwear drawer and now this?" I asked, and I swear, the entire room took a collective breath. Anubis lifted his head slightly to look at me, brows drawn together in confusion. I so did not want to be having this conversation right now, with all of us naked and warm and shrouded in steam, but … "Yes, Che and I mated in the forest yesterday," I said, bringing up the subject everyone but Nic had so carefully stayed away from last night. And god, last night was such a mess. Nic and I had slept—slept only, mind you—in the bed while the others had sprawled out in the study, across the couches and chairs in the living room, and even (in Jax's case) the porch.

But we didn't need to be spread out and disjointed; we needed to be united.

"If there's anything you need to say, now's the time," I said, looking around at the seven men standing naked in the room with me. It was a little distracting, to be surrounded by seven good-looking guys without a single scrap of clothing between them. As a werewolf, nakedness was as natural as breathing, but so was attraction and mating and physical closeness. I was going to have to find a way to balance all of those things.

A knock at the door put a permanent pause on our conversation.

"Come in," I said, sitting up straight and waiting as the half-rotten door swung wide on creaking hinges. The Fae cared as much about nakedness as us wolves did, so the servant waiting on the other side didn't bother asking if it was okay to come in. Instead, a small crooked woman with wrinkly tree bark skin, as tattered and folded as old leather, crept into the room. Her nose was almost as big as her too-wide mouth. It stretched quite literally from one pointed ear to the other, cutting her face in half.

Without a word, she entered the room and placed a pile of clothing on one of the crumbling stone benches. Behind her, several more small withered faeries entered with more clothing, towels, a wooden tray with brushes and tiny glass bottles with metal wings on their caps.

"Brownies," Jax said, sitting on the edge of the pool in human form. His blue eyes watched them carefully as they left the items and disappeared on silent feet. "A type of lesser Fae."

"Um, the term lesser Fae isn't really used anymore. It was a derogatory label for any species of Faerie that wasn't Gentry. It's now considered politically incorrect," Anubis said, trying once more to unsuccessfully smooth his hair back.

"What are you, the fucking PC police now?" Che snapped as he dug through the piles of clothing and settled on a pair of purple linen pants with bones sewn into the side seams. And you thought werewolf fashion was weird … "Take a look around—we're not exactly in Kansas anymore, Toto. Do you think those man-eating horse monsters care about politically correct?"

"I think they'd care if you called them *lesser* Fae," Anubis said which only got him a snarl in response. "Maybe that's why you almost got eaten, did you ever think about that?"

"Boys," I said, standing up on the bench and rising to my full height. As soon as I did that, all attention was on me. "Let's just focus on getting out of here alive, shall we?"

"Um, what's a Gentry?" Tidus asked as he pushed himself out of the pool with the strong, rounded curves of his biceps bunching with the motion. The tattoo on his arm caught my attention like a beacon, drawing my eyes to the keyhole and the key lying next to it. I so badly wanted to know what it meant. According to Silas, not all tattoos had to have meaning—not all of his did—but I had a feeling there was a story lying in wait on Tidus' sun-kissed skin.

"A Gentry is a member of the Faerie nobility," I explained as I tossed the long wet rope of my hair over one shoulder and squeezed out the excess water. "The ruling class. For centuries, it's been almost entirely dominated by one species—the sidhe."

"Gotcha," Tidus said as he ruffled up his blonde hair with one hand, spattering the stone wall behind him with water. After a moment, he paused. "Wait, what's a *'shee'*?"

"Are you sure you're an Alpha-Heir?" Anubis asked as he picked through the clothing and … grabbed a pair of linen pants in crimson with bones sewn down the side seams. Hmm. Now that I was standing by the piles of clothing, I could see that all the boys had been given the same outfit in different colors. "Who was responsible for your education? The sidhe are the most magically gifted of all the Fae *and* they hold the thrones of the most powerful Faerie courts."

"Maybe he was too busy surfing to attend class?" Silas asked, his tattoos bright and shiny under the droplets of water clinging to his skin. He fished out a pack of cigarettes from his pants and grinned when he discovered they were still dry. "Thank god for small miracles," he mumbled as he tried to figure out where to store them in the faerie-bone pants. He ended up settling for tucking the pack under the waistband.

"Shit, is it a crime to want to hit the waves instead of learn about flesh-eating ponies all day? I'm not sorry," Tidus said with another one of those magnanimous grins. "At least I've got something to talk about that *doesn't* relate directly back to werewolf politics."

"Considering our lives and the lives of our people depend on werewolf politics, I don't think it's such a terrible thing to be knowledgable about," Montgomery added, putting on a pair of green pants (I was starting to see a theme here—Pack Violet Shadow in purple pants, Pack Crimson Dusk in red ones, Pack Ivory Emerald in green and so on). He tossed his sopping wet trench on over the top, along with his belt and swords. After what I'd seen today, I wasn't feeling inclined to tease him for any of it.

"Thank you," Anubis said, throwing out an arm toward Montgomery. "At least somebody here gets me."

"Yeah, the guy with the long white braid and the fucking swords," Che scoffed, leaning his back against the wall and crossing his legs at the ankle. I had to wonder, watching him like that, if he practiced that swaggering bad boy slouch in the mirror. It was textbook. "Congratulations on that."

"Do you like potatoes?" I asked Che randomly, pausing naked next to the largest pile of clothing. Apparently the entire gauzy stack was all mine. Lots of fabric, very little coverage, very Fae.

"Potatoes?" he asked, turning a look on me that was half-amused, half-terrified. He was still reeling from what'd happened at the river and doing his best to cover it up by acting like a douche-y a-hole. I could see through him almost as easily as I could see through the glittering robes the Unseelie Queen had left me. "Um, sure, why?"

"Because you seem a little down in the dirt right now," I said, and then waited with a stupid half-smile to see if I'd get any reaction out of him. After a moment, both Tidus and Anubis laughed, so I guess it wasn't *that* terrible of a joke. I just figured asking a random question about tuberous vegetables would probably go a long way towards stopping the fighting.

"If Zara's trying for puns then we're in serious trouble," Nic said with a small smile, yanking on a pair of black pants and fingering the small bones on the side. "Stop being such a *spud* and try to remember why we're here."

"I didn't know Ebon Red was famous for its comedians," Che said, but at least he was smiling. Sort of. Okay, so maybe it was a bemused smirk I was looking at, but it was better than the cruel twist of lips he'd been wearing earlier.

I pulled the flimsy silver robes over my shoulders and belted them at the waist with a gray-black belt made of leather and studded with teeth. I wasn't sure what—or more likely *who*—the teeth had come from, and had a feeling I didn't want to find out.

"Be careful what you say while we're here," I said, slicking red hair back from my face. "And if someone asks for your name, just tell them it's Wolf."

Silas opened the door for me with a tattooed hand, his chest a kaleidoscope of color that begged to be explored with fingertips and tongues and teeth. Our eyes met as I passed, and I couldn't help wondering what he thought of me and Che. After all, I'd just met the guy. Silas and I, we had a history.

I swept past him and into the hallway, the robes dragging across the debris strewn ground behind me, bare feet slapping against the old stone. The rough texture actually helped me refocus my mind on the task at hand. Romance and sex … those were luxuries I could only afford if I could keep the boys and me *alive* long enough to have those sorts of encounters.

"I can't feel the earth here," I whispered aloud, glancing over to find Tidus on my right. Nic, of course, always stayed on my left, but the guys seemed to be rotating this position amongst themselves.

"Me neither," he said, and for a moment, the expression on his face was actually serious. Since the Alpha-Son of Pack Amber Ash seemed to operate in permanent goofball mode, I knew he must be feeling the strain, too. There might be leaves and grass and trees and dirt here, but the fact was—we were a long way from the place we knew as home. I didn't know what, exactly, the Veil was and how it separated Faerie from our world, but it was clear that we didn't have the same connection to this place as we did our own.

It also confirmed something else. As the Fae queen had said, all of *that delicious earthy magic* that we'd been using lately, it really was a part of who we were. We weren't just borrowing it from the world around us. I wondered, though, if we were to stay here … how long would it last? Would it eventually drain from us after a time, without the land to replenish it?

I had no idea.

Since I had no clue where I was going, I started back toward the door we'd entered through and hoped somebody would snag us on the way.

About halfway down the hall, a brownie appeared from an adjacent hallway and crooked one, long, wrinkled finger at us. Even from here, I could see that she had three joints where in a human, there'd be two; it was an eerie sight.

'It's pretty clear the queen doesn't want anyone to know we're here,' I told the boys as we followed the brownie down the long hallway and around a corner, toward a set of doors carved with the sharp, alien faces of faerie. One was sitting properly in its frame while the other lilted sloppily to the side. *'Hardly any servants, no guards, no other members of the Court. If helping us out really does benefit the fae, then why should it matter that we're here? Why keep it a secret?'*

'Maybe it's not her *Court that she's worried about?'* Montgomery mused, making me wonder if my instincts were starting to go haywire. Had I made a mistake by

eating that mushroom, bringing my boys here? God, I hoped not. It felt like I'd been making a lot of mistakes lately, and I didn't like it. It made me feel out of control when it was more important than ever that I stay *in* it.

Once we reached the doors, we came to a stop and waited while several other brownies joined the first. Together, they used a heavy, knotted rope to drag the one good door open, the old hinges creaking and groaning like the lost souls of long dead faeries.

Inside, the Unseelie Queen sat inside a circle of bones, gesturing with a pale, glittering hand for us to join her.

"Protection against witches," she explained as we moved inside what was probably once a grand throne room. There was a dais on one end, covered with debris and the colorful remains of the shattered glass skylights from above. The floor was stone, and in places, I could see that it had once been polished to a smooth shine. Strange white trees grew from cracks in the floor and walls, twisting and curving like ghosts into the room, their leaves an ebony black that mimicked the color of my eyes. The only light in the room came from the slashes of eerie purple and blue moonlight cutting through the spaces in the dilapidated roof. "Take a seat," the queen instructed as the boys and I stepped over the bones and into the circle.

She smiled at us as we took our places, folded our legs beneath us and settled in for … well, goddess only knew what. I had no clue what the faerie had in mind—hopefully, filling us in on everything she knew was part of the plan. Were there werewolves involved in all of this, too? The thought of Selena working to round up her own pack members for the slaughter gave me this awful, empty feeling in my gut. I didn't believe that was true, not at all, but I had to do my due diligence. Rushing into this thing … nothing good would come of it.

"I thought you might like to dress your men in matching outfits," the queen said, clearly amused at the circle of werewolves in identical pants. "It's a common practice in Court to dress one's paramours in similar attire—lest anyone else get confused as to whom they belong."

"It doesn't exactly look like we're *in* Court though, now does it?" I asked, putting my hands on my knees and watching as the queen lifted her sloe-eyed gaze to mine. "Why hide us out here in these ruins if we're welcome guests?"

A frown crossed the faerie's face, as sharp as the blade of a knife. I could feel it cutting me from across the circle, those long fingers of hers twitching against the tattered white fabric of her dress. It was shredded in a very purposeful way, deshabille chic or something.

"You presume much, *Wolf,*" she hissed, her dark hair lifting in an unnatural breeze. Watching her now, I would not forget how quickly she'd moved in the forest, pinning Tidus up against a tree by the throat before I could even register that she was moving. But sitting here, in this big, empty room with a half-dozen brownies for company … I was starting to get a hunch.

"Who are you?" I asked, knowing that even if I *was* right and the faerie sitting across from me was *not* actually the

Unseelie Queen like I'd thought, she'd still be privy to glamour magic I couldn't break. Either she revealed herself to me willingly or I'd never know who I was *really* talking to.

"Are you asking for my name?" she said, her voice like the crack of dry, brittle bones. The unspoken threat inherent in her words was obvious. I didn't react, waiting calmly with four of my alpha males on one side, three on the other. Their presence gave me strength—even if some of them were virtual strangers. Alpha-Majka was right; the Pairing had been more than just a series of empty rituals. I felt a closeness to the men around me that I couldn't explain.

I totally should've taken today off like I'd planned, I thought, resisting the urge to groan. It was one thing to deal with daywalking vampires and faeries who thought teeth covered belts were the height of fashion. It was a whole other animal to try and do all those things while sorting out my feelings for the seven men I was now essentially engaged to.

"You know mine," I said, lifting my chin and breathing deep, fighting past the reek of decay that permeated the old room and pulling in the musky, wild scent of wolf instead. With so many different packs represented by the boys, when they got together, it all just sort of amalgamated into the earthy, natural scent of *werewolf.* "Zara Wolf of Ebon Red," I announced, the ritualistic nature of the words bringing a calm, soothing sort of effect washing over me. "I've accepted your invitation and brought my mates to Faerie, just as you asked. So tell me: do you actually have any authority with the Unseelie Court or are you acting on your own?"

The dark fae sitting across from me smiled, a sinuous slip of laughter crawling from lips the color of ashes.

"You're quite the quick-witted one, aren't you?" she asked, pulling a small shimmery pouch from a deep pocket on the side of her dress. At first, I thought it might be made of the same gauzy material as the robes I was wearing. On closer inspection, it looked like it might actually be made of bits of translucent *wing.* I could see the delicate webbing in the moonlight, like veins in a dragonfly's wings. Only … on this side of the Veil, it was more likely *pixie* wings that I was staring at.

The sidhe girl loosened the leather drawstring on the pouch and dumped a small pile of knucklebones onto the ground in front of her. Based on the various shapes and sizes, I had a feeling these had been collected from a variety of species. Right away, I got the whiff of *wolf* off one of them.

"Sometimes," she began, leaning close to the morbid mess on the stone floor, studying the bones and the pattern they'd made. There were also runes carved into some of them, symbols I didn't recognize that shimmered with the same, sickly silver light as the dual moons above our heads. "Those who *should* take action, don't."

She snatched the bones up and put them back in the pouch again, shaking it carefully before dumping them back out on the floor. I had no idea what she was doing—some sort of divination spell most likely—but for what purpose, I wasn't sure.

"And that means, what, exactly?" Che asked, drawing the fae's attention over to him. "Look, we don't really have time for riddles. Why don't you just tell us what you're all about so we can get the hell out of this nightmare?"

"How uppity," the girl said, teasing one of the bones with the tip of her finger. "Maybe that's how you like your lovers, but I prefer mine to be seen and not heard." She looked up at me and smiled another one of those awful smiles, letting it stretch across her face in a gruesome caricature of a grin. Her skin caught the light and shone like diamonds while strands of abyss colored hair dripped into her face. "I didn't have to tell you anything, you know? I could've left you to flounder in uncertainty, the Bloods on one side and the witches on the other. I did you a *favor* by paying you a visit."

"You must have a reason," I said as she picked up the bones once again, stuffed them in the pouch, and handed it over to me. Without hesitation, I took it, shook it up, and dumped the knucklebones on the floor. A cold chill slithered down my spine when I realized what was happening.

"Zara?" Nic asked, nudging my left knee with his own. I ignored him, picked the bones up, tried again. And again. And again.

"They're falling in the same pattern," Montgomery said, leaning close, his white braid sliding over his shoulder and into his lap. "Every single time, it's the *exact* same pattern."

"Precisely," the faerie said, leaning back on her palms

and looking up at the strange sky through the hole in the roof. "No matter how many times we ask the dead, the answer's the same."

I handed the bag over to Tidus and let him try, watching as the yellow-white bone fragments clattered against the stone floor and, against all odds, managed to land in the very same way they had for both me and the faerie girl.

"And what is it exactly that they're saying?" I asked her, feeling my heart rate pick up, my breath catch, my palms start to sweat. The girl ignored me for several moments before dropping those purple-black eyes to mine.

"I've decided," she said, sitting back up. "You can call me Aeron."

"I can *call* you Aeron, or is Aeron actually your name?" I asked. All I got was a wicked smile in response. "Are you at least going to tell me what your connection to the Unseelie Court is?"

"I'm just like you," she told me, taking back the pixie-wing bag from Tidus. "The … Alpha-Heir as you might say? I'm the queen's daughter."

Oh. Great. A literal faerie princess. One who played with bones for fun. Even better.

The faerie girl stood up and stepped backward out of the circle.

Sensing that our short meeting was about to come to an end, I stood up, too.

"I need to know if there are wolves involved, if there's more than one coven, one kingdom."

"I'll answer one question," she said, holding up a single

finger and smiling with teeth too sharp and pointed to be human. “Just one. You decide what that question will be.”

I glanced around at the boys and then looked up, meeting her dark gaze dead-on.

“What did they say?” I asked. “The bones.”

A breeze blew in through the roof, ruffling the faerie girl's dress, teasing my wet, red hair around my face. It carried with it the sweet scent of decay, making me wrinkle my nose. There was something big and dead and rotten nearby.

“The hunters have become the hunted; the monsters have become the prey.” Aeron reached out with a toe the color of shattered diamonds and rested it against the fractured remains of a human femur. “Either find a way to harness the magic inside that blood of yours, use it to fight this war … or watch it wielded against you.” Aeron's gaze met mine and in it, I swear I could see my destiny, scrawled in blood and dripping. “The fates have never been so unclear: your ascension as Alpha either harkens a new era for the wolves … or their last gasping breath.”

She kicked the bone aside, breaking the circle and sending the eight of us crashing straight through the floor.

For the longest time, I just sat outside on the porch with my knees tucked up onto the cushioned seat of the rocking chair, a blanket slung over my shoulders. Now that the ceremony was over and most of the wolves had either gone home or spread out across the sixteen thousand acre property, the Pairing House was showing just how remote it really was. From where I sat, all I could see were trees drenched in moonlight, snow dripping down the long thin points of icicles.

I didn't know exactly how long we'd been in Faerie, but we'd left in the afternoon and come back in the late evening. Across the Veil, it'd been night the entire time. I didn't know if that was because time worked differently over there, if they were on a different solar calendar than we were … or if it was simply one endless stream of night.

The screen door opened and Silas slipped out, a pair of black jeans slung low on his hips, a loose red and black striped tank hanging over his slim, muscular form. He paused for a moment and then lifted a cigarette to his lips, flicking the wheel on his lighter and coloring the lower half of his face orange with the flame.

"I thought you might want this," he said, moving over to stand next to me. I waited while he dug my phone out of his front pocket, the wolf and moon charms jangling as he passed it over into my hand. "Someone's been blowing up your notifications. It buzzed right off the coffee table and onto the goddamn floor."

I smiled as I flicked a thumb across the screen and found several texts and missed calls from Faith. Apparently, she'd snuck Owen into her room at the house and hid him in the closet when her dad had come knocking. And she'd been lecturing *me* about how I was eighteen, an adult, capable of making my own choices? Please.

But my smile faded pretty quick when I remembered the blood, the syringe sticking out of Diya's arm, the wooden sword cutting through her neck.

"Faith likes to send me disturbing updates when Owen's around," I explained, holding up the screen so Silas could read the newest text.

listen One-Kiss-No-Date, it's time u & Nic just went 4 it already! the sex 2nite was ah-ma-zing! Owen does this thing w/ his tongue that—

"Okay, that's about enough of that," Silas said, pushing my hand aside and smoking his cigarette with the other. "Please tell me she doesn't send you pictures, too."

"Usually not," I said, smiling as I tucked the phone under the blanket and watched as Silas folded his arms over the porch railing and leaned out into the night. "But once she *did* forward me a dick pic."

"Fuckin' A," he snorted, gray-white smoke rising from the cigarette clutched between his tattooed fingers. "Humans are weird as hell, aren't they?"

"As weird as a werewolf princess living in a cottage in the woods with seven men who cause magical explosions when she touches them?"

"Point taken," Silas said, glancing over his shoulder to flash a sultry smile my direction. The silver light from the moon caught on his scar, limning it in color and reminding me that we didn't just have problems of gargantuan proportions to worry about, we also had large, medium, and small ones, too.

Silas was hiding something from me.

I'd nearly forgotten.

I almost asked him about it. Almost. But then I remembered that not only had I *not* gotten any answers about Selena and Kingdom Ironbound, but I'd also managed to have an ominous fortune laid at my feet by a bone wielding faerie princess.

"What's One-Kiss-No-Date mean?" Silas asked after several quiet moments had passed between us. Most of the boys were asleep, scattered across the house like broken dolls. Sleeping on floors and couches was all fine and dandy for a night or two, but it wouldn't work for a whole year. I'd have to see about getting them all to use the custom bed in the upstairs bedroom. It shouldn't be all that weird—wolves slept in puppy piles all the time. I think it had more to do with a sense of rivalry between them than it did any sort of modesty or discomfort at physical closeness.

"Prior to … Thursday," I said carefully, referencing my first time with Nic. "I'd only had one kiss and no dates." Silas smiled a little at that, turning around to face me. Now, his bad boy lean was more … casual, less practiced looking than Che's. Che Nocturne was angry; he had a bone to pick with the life he'd been given and was supposed to lead. Silas was just … well, Silas. Tattooed, scarred, disturbingly beautiful with his gold eyes and chocolate dark hair. "I guess now you might call me Seven-Kiss-No-Date," I said with a small half-smile.

I'd only just now realized that I'd kissed seven guys, had sex with two of them … and still never been on a real date. How depressing was that? The worst part was, the only person I wanted to talk to about all of this was Faith and yet, how could I burden her with something so frivolous when I knew—I *knew*—the awful truth I was keeping from her? And besides that, how was I supposed to tell my best friend —my *human* friend at that—that I'd not only lost my virginity to Nic Hallett, but also slept with a guy I'd met on fucking Friday. Oh, and that I'd kissed all of the others at least once.

"Hey Faith, you know how I lied to you and told you my mom was trying to marry me off to another well-to-do family? And remember how disappointed and weirded out you were? Well, guess what! I've started making my rounds and I've already managed to get two of them into bed!"

Nope.

Not happening.

I was either going to have to make a werewolf friend

that I *wasn't* dating that I could tell all my gossipy secrets to or else I was going to be stuck befriending Aeron, the creepy dark fae girl who possessed other people's bodies and accidentally sent my boyfriends to die at the hands … hooves? … of flesh-eating horses.

"We could at the very least change that to Seven-Kiss-One-Date," he said, and it took me a moment to figure out what he was getting at.

"Are you asking me out?" I said, blinking up at eyes the color of a warm summer sunset. In the snow drenched dark of night, they almost seemed to glow with their own inner light.

"Why not? We're supposed to get to know each other, right? Let me take you out, make you forget about all of this shit for a little while."

"You mean like how it was just prophesied that I might bring about my peoples' last dying breath?"

"Exactly," he said, coming over to sit in the rocking chair next to mine. His natural scent—that warm cherry vanilla flavor—helped soften up the harshness of the tobacco clinging to his skin. "We could go to a concert, grab a milkshake afterward, take a relaxing stroll through the cemetery."

"You find cemeteries relaxing?" I asked, feeling the right corner of my lip curve up in a flirtatious smile. Sitting this close to Silas, looking into his eyes, watching his breath plume in the frigid air between us, I could feel that attraction bubbling up between us, nice and hot, scalding the inside of my belly, my throat, my thighs. I wanted him both the way I'd wanted Nic—as a human—and the way I'd wanted Che—as a wolf. It was almost a relief, to feel both sides in agreement like that.

"Fuck yeah," he said, leaning back in the chair and crossing his bare feet at the ankle. "The only humans that are there are dead, and the Numinous …" he trailed off with a small laugh and shook his head, referring to the non-human, non-animal species of the world with a resigned sounding sigh. "Well, they don't often give a lot of shits about humans at all—especially not dead ones."

"Just pick a day then and if we're not fighting a vampire-witch war that particular evening then … I'd love to."

"Is your boyfriend going to crap his pants over this?" Silas asked, reaching out the tattooed hand with the wolf on the back of it. He tucked some hair behind my ear, and I noticed right away that his pulse was picking up, thundering against the side of his neck. He was either very, very nervous … or very, very turned-on. Maybe a little of both.

"Nic'll be fine," I said, although *fine* was a relative term. Knowing him, he'd probably freak first and calm down later. But that was his natural personality. It was just how he was, and I loved him for it. I tried to imagine what it would be like if *I* were in his shoes, watching him kiss and fuck and flirt with six other girls.

The thought made me murderous.

"Are you sure about hanging out with this Julian guy tomorrow?" Silas asked, interrupting the mental rage I'd just conjured up. "If the vampires really are working with the witches, then he should already know that *we* know. This whole thing stinks of a setup."

"It really does," I said, thinking of Selena, sobbing and shaking and pregnant. The day my mother had kicked her out, she'd packed her bags in a haze of tears, hugged me and my siblings close, and walked out with a backwards glance that I would never—*never*—forget. For a werewolf, banishment is worse than death. It's like a severing of the soul, an excavation of the heart. I could barely even imagine what'd be like to wander this world alone. Things were hard enough and I had plenty of backup. "But I have to at least try and see what information I can get from Julian." I tapped my fingers against my leg and listened to the staccato song of the forest. A rustle of leaves here, the terrified squeak of a mouse there, the distant melancholy cry of an Ebon Red wolf on pack lands.

My own throat tickled with the need to call back, to tilt my chin to the sky and let them know that yes, yes, I was here. Pack was here. Everything was going to be okay.

Instead, I ran a palm down my face and gave Silas a brave smile.

"You want to try crawling into bed with Nic and see what happens?"

He shrugged his tattooed shoulders at me and I swear, my heart skipped several beats.

"If it means I don't have to sleep on the couch next to Jax, then sure."

I grinned, stood up and offered him my hand.

We made our way upstairs, curled up in the warm sheets next to Nic, and dropped off the edge into sweet, sweet oblivion.

The next morning, I woke up late as usual, shook Nic until he grumbled a mild curse at me and dragged myself into the small upstairs bathroom. By the time I came down the stairs, the house was rife with the smells of breakfast.

"Are those potato pancakes?" I asked when I walked into the dining room and found Nic digging into a plate of latkes smeared in ketchup. A pile of crispy bacon sat on the other side of his plate while a steaming cup of coffee was parked next to his left elbow.

"Maybe you dating a bunch of other guys isn't the worst thing that ever happened," he joked as he gestured with his chin in the direction of the kitchen.

Montgomery was standing at the stove in a black apron, his white hair hanging in a thick braid over one shoulder, a spatula in his right hand. He glanced up as I walked in, throwing a cautious smile my way. The whole scene was pretty domestic ... except, you know, for the swords hanging off his back and the white wolf with the blue eyes sitting at his feet.

"You cook?" I asked as I padded over to the breakfast bar and glanced at the four separate frying pans going all at once. Montgomery was even making use of the built-in griddle that ran down the center. This was the same, exact stove that my mother had in her house. Just more proof that werewolves like things done *just so.* Even something as simple and inconsequential as a kitchen appliance had rules, traditions, patterns to follow.

"I told you my sister, Patience, was just one in a litter of seven, right?" he asked, flipping a potato pancake onto a plate and handing it out to me. "How many do you want?"

"Three please, plus a heap of bacon."

'Toss me a slice, would you?' Jax asked, blue eyes as bright as a summer sky. He waited with his tongue lolling until Montgomery tossed a crinkled slice of bacon his direction, snapping it out of the air and downing it in a single swallow.

"I haven't had a hot breakfast before class since I graduated high school," I said, remembering the fancy omelets that Selena used to make. Both Nic and I had decided not to let her cook or clean for us anymore after senior year. I knew Nikolina and Majka found it strange, to treat the omega as anything *but* a useless tool, but I wanted to be a different kind of alpha. "Nic and I never manage to get up on time. And then usually Faith calls me at the last minute looking for a ride. Speak of the devil," I mumbled as Montgomery loaded up my plate and I mouthed a silent thank you at the same time I answered the incoming call.

"We're heading out the door right now," I said but all I got was a scoff in response.

"Are you, really? Because I stopped at both your house *and* Nic's and you weren't at either of them. According to Lana, you guys *moved in together* without fucking telling me!"

"Faith—" I started, but she wasn't done.

"Are you guys doing it now?" I hesitated for just a fraction of an instant too long. "Oh my god! You lost your virginity and you didn't *tell me*!" She was screeching now. So loudly, in fact, that if I tilted my head toward the open front door of the Pairing House, I could quite literally hear her voice echoing across the property. "I borrowed my mom's car because dad said I could until she came home and so I thought it'd be nice to surprise you guys for once with breakfast and I went to McDonald's and then I find out that you and Nic *finally* got over your weirdness and started having sex and you didn't even tell me and—"

"You're speaking in run-on sentences. I know you hate run-on sentences."

"I do!" she said, and I could just see her chewing on the end of her braid, standing outside of Nic's parents' house next to her dead mother's car. My stomach tightened and nausea rolled over me in a wave. "Where are you, Zara Castille? I'm coming over there."

I stood there for a long moment, catching Nic's bewildered expression.

'You can't tell her about the Pairing House,' he said, blinking big, dark eyes at me. His terrified expression was actually kind of cute, considering the piece of bacon he had hanging out of his mouth and all. *'Zara, don't.'*

'Your mom's the one who told her we moved out in the first place,' I countered, noticing Che slipping into the room and taking a seat at the table. There wasn't an alpha-son in

that room who wouldn't be able to tell that Nic and I were using wolfspeak to have a private conversation. But they also probably wouldn't understand why it was such a big deal either.

"Zara?" Faith asked, and I could hear this … unsure quality in her voice that I wasn't used to. "Please tell me you've just forgotten the address and are frantically searching for the lease so you can—"

"There's no address," I said, making the decision right then and there. I wasn't going to alienate my best friend just so I could avoid an awkward, probably really confusing conversation about why I was living in a relatively small house up a dirt road in the middle of nowhere with seven men. I was like, Snow fucking White or some shit. "If you take the road behind Lana's house and follow it all the way up into the trees, you'll find us."

"Um … oooookay," she said as Nic dropped the piece of bacon from his mouth to his plate and stood up, chair scraping across the old wood floors. "You're living on your mother's property?"

"Hurry or we'll be late for class," I said, ignoring her question and ending the call before she could get another out. I needed a minute to think. "Nic, I had to tell her."

"No, you didn't," he said, gesturing at Jax with an angry hand. "Can you please shift back? I don't want to explain a wolf the size of a small pony to a human this early in the morning."

Jax just grinned at him, his body flowing like water, molecules sliding past one another and rearranging themselves into a very attractive, very naked man.

"Is that better?" he asked coyly and I watched as Nic struggled to control his temper, clenching his hands into fists at his sides and gritting his teeth.

"Other than the fact that your dick is out and hard, yeah, it's a start."

"Oh? You want this covered?" Jax asked, pointing at the half-erect length of his shaft. With a bemused chuckle, he snagged an apron off a hook in the kitchen and threw the loop over his head, turning around and flashing the sculpted muscular perfection of his ass. "Hey Zara, do you think you could tie this for me?"

"You see?" Nic said, gesturing in Jax's direction again. "*This* is what Faith is going to be walking into. I hope you've got a *really* good explanation ready because I know I sure as fuck don't."

He snatched his shoes off the chair next to him and carried them into the living room.

"Would you mind putting some clothes on?" I asked with a small sigh, rubbing at a wrinkle between my eyes. Good thing werewolves aged slowly or else I'd have had quite a collection of stress wrinkles on my forehead already. "You need to get dressed anyway to head over to the university."

"Really?" Jax asked, turning back around and crossing his arms over his chest. "I was hoping you'd let me get away with just a leash and collar?" He smiled at me, flashing one, sharp canine tooth.

I found myself smiling back, shaking my head and

taking Nic's seat to wolf down—excuse the pun—my breakfast before Faith showed up. From Nic's parents' house to here, it was only about a ten minute drive.

Che tapped his fingers on the surface of the table as he watched me.

"So," he asked, drawing my gaze up and away from my plate. Those purple eyes of his were impossible to ignore; Faith would notice them right away. Then again, she'd pretty easily accepted Montgomery's shock white hair, Anubis' crimson stare, and all my own general weirdness without question. Push come to shove, we'd use the contacts lie again. "You think your friend will like me?"

"Most definitely not," I said, closing my eyes and trying not to groan with pleasure at the creamy texture of the potato pancakes. I took a bite, rubbed it around in the ketchup blob left on Nic's plate and stuffed the last piece in my mouth.

"Why not?" he asked, his voice as smooth as silk. But there was an edge there, hiding underneath his words that I couldn't miss. I wasn't sure what, exactly, it was. Maybe it was because we'd had sex and never got a chance to talk about it? Maybe it had something to do with his nearly dying yesterday? I didn't know and I didn't have time to find out—I could hear Faith's tires coming up the drive behind the house.

"While she doesn't mind dating them herself," I started as I folded a piece of bacon into my mouth and swallowed it almost as whole as Jax had. "She doesn't really like the bad boy type."

I smiled sharply and stood up, trying to calm the frantic racing of my heart. Faith hadn't met Che yet, and I'd been too preoccupied with other things to ask how Nic had introduced her to Tidus the other day. It'd been bad enough, showing up with four 'suitors' and asking her to try and understand where I was coming from. Now I not only had to tell her that Nic and I had had our first time together, but that I'd also *added* two more boys to the mix.

"Mother help me," I said, stepping onto the porch and moving down the steps to the grass, digging my toes in and trying to draw strength from Mother Earth herself. Diya's car rolled into view around the corner, creeping up the windy dirt road behind the Pairing House. Seeing it, I was struck with a massive wave of guilt. It made my throat go dry, my tongue swell. I didn't want to lie to my best friend. Fuck, I didn't want to lie to anyone. It wasn't something I wanted to make a habit of.

"Hey," I managed to choke out as Faith climbed from the car, glancing up at the log walls of the cabin with a skeptically raised brow. She was dressed in jeans and a pink tank with a strawberry on the front, a white and yellow fast-food bag tucked into her right hand.

"Zara," she started, tossing her black braid over one shoulder and slamming the door behind her. "Girl, you have a *hell* of a lot of explaining to do."

You have no idea, I thought as Faith picked her way over to me, dropping a narrowed brown gaze on me. It was ripe with accusations. If she only knew how many things I was *really* keeping from her …

Faith pushed the McDonald's bag into my hands and then crossed her own over her chest.

"Well?" she asked, catching me in a rare moment of speechlessness.

I guess even Alphas need a moment to catch their breath sometime.

"You kept telling me it was time to get my own place," I joked, cracking a somewhat melancholy smile. It felt like a bunch of bullshit, talking to Faith about boys and houses when what I really should've been doing was telling her the truth. "So I did!"

I gestured at the Pairing House with an open hand, trying to keep the mood lighthearted.

"Did you screw Nic?" was the next question she whispered, taking another step close to me. I could smell a whole host of things on her—sugar, flour, butter, cocoa. It was obvious that Faith had spent the morning baking.

I just hoped it wasn't stress baking.

Although … considering her mother was still missing, it probably was.

"Why would you think that?" I asked, trying to grin my way through this. Faith just stared at me for a moment before pushing past and raising her hand to her mouth.

"Nic!" she called out as I moved behind her and tried not to sweat so profusely.

Dealing with Faith in a mood could be twice as scary as dealing with my mother.

"Nicoli!" she shouted, heading up the porch steps … and pausing just inside the front door. "Whoa. Did I miss a party last night or something?"

"Faith," I said, moving around her and into a living room filled with furniture older than my grandmother. "You remember Anubis …"

"Hey, Faith," he said, standing there barefoot … and shirtless.

Her eyes locked right onto the firm grooves and valleys of his chest.

"And Jax … Montgomery. Silas, of course."

I looked around at the scattered assortment of boys and tried to figure out a way to explain this that didn't sound completely deranged.

Well, Faith, you see, I'm technically sort of engaged to all of these guys. More than engaged, really. We're magically bound together. For the next twelve months they'll fight beside me, sleep beside me, fuck me on forest floors surrounded by leaves.

"You met Tidus the other day …"

"Good morning!" he said cheerfully, ruffling up his blonde hair and grinning. "How's Owen doing?"

"He's … fine," Faith said suspiciously, casting a look my way. She was clearly pissed.

"And I'm Che Nocturne," Che said, appearing in the entrance to the dining room and slouching sideways against the wall. He was sin incarnate, standing like that, a swirl of smoke and shadows with violet eyes and a wicked smirk. "Zara's boyfriend."

"Zara's … boyfriend," Faith repeated, and I was just about positive that her eyes were going to topple straight out of her skull. “You're Zara's boyfriend?”

“Suitor,” I corrected quickly.

'Mate,' Che said inside my head, drawing out the vowel until it was long and sticky, clinging to the nerve endings in my brain and making it really, really hard to think properly. *Asshole*.

Faith just stood there, completely silent. When she reached up, took hold of her braid, and started tickling her lips with it, I knew I was in serious trouble.

Finally, Nic came back down the stairs, fully dressed, and parked himself in the middle of the room. We exchanged a long look.

'I warned you,' he said as Faith scanned Jax (thankfully wearing a pair of jeans although not much else), Montgomery in his apron, and Silas pulling a pack of smokes from his back pocket.

“Can I, um, talk to you outside for a moment?” Faith asked, snatching my arm and dragging me down the front steps next to the lavender bushes. “Zara Vodja Castille,” she admonished, planting her hands on her hips and going into full outrage mode. “Why are there so many shirtless men in there?”

There's no advice column on how to answer your best friend when she asks why there are so many shirtless werewolf hunks hanging out inside your house.

There should be.

“Zara, I sense Nikolina's hand in all of this,” Faith warned, standing up and focusing an accusatory stare on my face. “Why are they all here? Why the fuck is Nic okay with all of this? I thought you said you guys finally—"

"We did," I said, feeling a small flutter inside my chest.

Nic and me. *Finally.*

It was meant to be.

"You did?!" Faith shrieked, snatching me up in a huge bear hug. If I weren't a werewolf, it might've suffocated me. "Tell me *everything.* How did it happen? Here? In your room? Oh my god, at *school*? Zara, you didn't!"

I laughed and tilted my head back, studying the swaying limbs of the pine trees, the snow melting in slow, careful drips from the branches. The air smelt crisp and fresh, like each breath I took was soothing some of my anxiety.

Mother Earth was a powerful force to be reckoned with.

"I didn't," I said, dropping my chin to look at her. "It was in Nic's room, and I started it."

"You vixen!" she breathed, taking my hand and squeezing it hard. "I knew it. I knew it would be you. Holy shit, was it good?"

"Fantastic," I whispered back and then … remembered that there was a high probability that all the boys inside that house were listening to us talk. Fucking werewolf hearing.

"I say we skip school today and go out for coffee," she said, biting her lip and practically bouncing up and down. "I need to know the exact date and time—down to the *minute*—and how many times since and which boxes you've checked off the universal sexual to-do list." Faith paused and glanced over at the Pairing House as Che stepped out onto the deck. "Oh, and why the hell he's not beating the crap out of all these hangers-on."

“They live here, Faith,” I said, pulling the metaphorical bandage off and trying not to wince.

Alpha's don't wince.

“They live here?” she asked, looking completely puzzled. “Like a fraternity or something?” With another glance back at the Pairing House, I could tell she was analyzing the size. For a cabin, it was roomy. But nobody in their right mind would believe eight people could live in it together.

“They live here with me and Nic,” I continued, my mind frantically putting together a stupid but hopefully believable story. “My mom's promised that if I live here with them for a year, she'll keep paying my college tuition and living expenses through grad school.”

“Zara …” Faith began, getting ready for a lecture. I could see it brewing in her eyes like a storm. “Are you listening to yourself? Your *mom* is making you live with a bunch of strange guys for … what? … some slim chance that you'll stop being in love with your childhood friend and suddenly want one of them instead? To try and set up some sort of powerhouse rich people family legacy thing? Are you *insane*?”

“It's an investment in my future,” I argued and Faith threw up her hands.

“I can't even *believe* this. Zara, come the fuck on! I mean, I'm super excited that you screwed Nic, but there's so much wrong with this scenario that I'm having a hard time focusing on the good news.”

Che plodded down the steps, a pair of black leather

Converse in one hand. He paused next to us and smiled.

"It was nice to meet you, Faith," he purred in that deliciously decadent voice of his, winking one purple eye and then meandering over to the SUV.

"And who is that again?" Faith asked as she watched Tidus and Nic come out of the house next. We were running late and today, I needed everything to be perfect. Julian might know—via Coven Triad—that I was aware the witches had something to do with my missing pack members, but that didn't mean he was aware I was onto him, either as the witches' ally *or* as a daywalking vampire.

And I needed to get as close to Selena as I could—traitor or not.

"And Tidus?" Faith added slowly, watching the blonde surfer boy with interest.

"Tidus and Che are … they're both my suitors," I said with a small sigh, this guilty nibble taking over my tummy and making it churn. I had too many lies to contend with; I didn't want anymore.

"Hey Faith," I started, meeting her stare dead-on. It still irked me a little sometimes, how easily humans made eye contact. I fought my instincts and took a deep breath. "The other day … after I slept with Nic …" A long pregnant pause, speckled with snow and ice. "I slept with Che, too."

Faith made us so late that Nic and I missed our entire calc class. I just *barely* managed to get us there in time to meet Julian.

"Hey," I said, breathing hard, trying to put a bright smile onto my face. "Sorry, I'm late. My mom had a doctor's appointment and wanted me to watch my little brother for a while."

"No worries," Julian said, smiling back at me like he was just a normal college kid, not a daywalking bloodsucker that had murdered our teacher. "I'm just glad you're here now."

His smile twisted a little, into something that was verging on the edge of flirtatious.

Gross.

It took everything in me not to snarl.

'One day,' Nic started, his voice hot and angry inside my head, *'I'm going to rip this guy's throat out.'*

That fixed my smile, made it real again.

"Shall we?" I asked, holding out a hand for Julian to lead the way.

He hiked his bag up on his shoulder and we headed outside. Only … we didn't follow the same path as yesterday. Immediately, my guard was up.

'Fuck,' I heard Che curse inside my head. *'Now what?'*

The boys were positioned in much the same way as they'd been yesterday, set up in various random locations outside Julian's range of smell.

'Group up,' I decided, changing the plan. *'Keep close.'*

I had a bad feeling about the way this was going.

"So, where do you live? We're headed to your place, right?" I asked as we started down sidewalks gritty with salt. Already, the beautiful white blanket of snow was melted and grimy, in slushy gray piles on the sides of the road. At least back home, on Pack land, it was still beautiful and untainted by humanity.

"Actually," Julian said as we continued on, tossing a look over at me that was pure innocence. "I was hoping I could buy you lunch or something? There's this great little café a few blocks from here."

I tried not to show my disappointment. I didn't want to have lunch with this guy; I wanted to see the inside of his fucking house, get a sniff of it and find out where Selena was. *Damn it.* But I also couldn't risk him getting suspicious either.

"Sounds great," I said with another false smile. The lie rolled across my face too easily. It wasn't that I had a problem lying to a guy like Julian, but it was becoming too simple for me to do it. I didn't like that.

'Eat fast and see if you can get him out of there,' Nic told

me as we turned the corner and headed for this little hole-in-the-wall advertising hot sandwiches in the window.

"My lady," Julian said, opening the door for me.

As soon as I stepped aside, I heard the click of a lock.

Son of a bitch.

I pretended not to notice. After all, I was pretty sure a normal human would've missed the soft clicking, especially since it was buried in the sounds and smells of a working restaurant. Several people sat around, chowing down on sandwiches, sipping sodas and iced teas.

Even with the witch hazel cloaking their scents, I knew they were all vampires.

I could *feel* it.

'He locked me in,' I said, as calmly as I could. There was no sense in getting panicked. Panic would only lead to poor decision making, and I needed a clear head.

I could feel the surge of fear and fury from the pack though, this hot, scalding flash of rage that caught me and made my heart thunder. Fuck. Vampires could read a person's pulse from a mile away, by *sight* alone. I didn't need them to know that I was nervous.

'At least a dozen Bloods in here,' I added.

'Pretend you forgot your phone at school?' Anubis suggested.

But I knew it wouldn't work.

Julian had me where he wanted me and he wasn't going to let me out.

"Order whatever you want," he told me with another smile, gesturing with his chin at the chalkboard behind the register. "My treat. Basically, everything they make here is the fucking bomb."

"Smells like it," I said, picking out several distinct scents in the air: pastrami, roast beef, sliced turkey, sourdough bread, a nutty wheat bread, mayonnaise, mustard, tomatoes … Everything that I was smelling seemed legit. But I still had zero fucking intentions to eat any of it. "I'll take a half sandwich on white bread," I said, picking out something normal, unassuming, average. "Turkey with lettuce and cheddar cheese, no condiments. Oh, and a root beer please."

I stepped aside to let Julian order next.

'Zara, we're outside. You want us to break in there?' Montgomery asked.

'No, just wait,' I told them, *'but be ready.'*

I might've been an alpha, but with this many vamps in one room, even I'd be hard-pressed to defend myself. The only thing I had going for me was that I was about ninety-nine percent sure they *didn't* want to kill me.

They wanted my fucking blood.

And my flesh for the witches.

It took a serious amount of effort for me to sit down at one of those tables, unzip my backpack, and pull out my laptop.

"So," I said, feeling my skin prickle and twitch at the sight of so many vampires in the bright sunshine. My whole life, I'd been warned about the Bloods, about their physical strength, their magic, their longevity. Hell, they were literally the *only* species on the planet that defied death.

And now, their one weakness, the *one* obstacle that kept them from total domination was gone.

"According to the syllabus," I started, speaking empty words while my mind struggled to come up with the next move in a game where I didn't know all the rules. *Fuck.* "We need to come up with a project that not only demonstrates our overall knowledge of local wildflowers, but also emphasizes what we've learned in the actual class. It should have both a written and a visual component, preferably something organic …"

I smiled at the text on my laptop screen, Mr. Heath's personality written all over it.

Students should be prepared to present a visual component (Powerpoints are absolutely banned from the classroom), preferably something organic, something from Mother Earth's breast. Remember: this is *a class about plants. Don't be afraid to get dirty!*

Damn.

I was really going to miss that guy.

Then again, I bet his husband and five year old daughter would miss him more.

Fuck you, Julian, I thought as I kept my smile in place and watched him unload his own book bag. *What reason did you have to kill Mr. Heath, huh? Vampires can feed without killing their victims, so why? What was the purpose of all that?*

"I was thinking," he continued, putting his last book on the table and smiling over at me. "That we could actually dig up some invasive species—like silver-leaf nightshade—and make a small garden box filled with various species to bring in. Then we can write up reports on how each species impacts similar native varieties."

I nodded; that wasn't a bad idea.

Even if a daywalking vamp *did* suggest it.

"Excellent," I continued, putting my mouth on the straw of my drink and sucking up the liquid until it hit my tongue. There was no way in hell that I was going to swallow it though. Julian's gaze tracked the movement of the soda in the clear straw, and his eyes crinkled at the edges as he smiled.

"I'm glad you're onboard," he continued, flipping open a local guide that Mr. Heath himself had written and sold at the on campus bookstore. "Because I've already taken the time to mark some of the species I think we should go for …"

As Julian turned to dig around in his bag, I slipped my hand beneath the table, shifted my claws and made a tiny slice along my lower belly, just above the waistband of my jeans.

The second that blood perfumed the room, I could *feel* it, all of those eyes on me.

Even Julian had a hard time controlling his reaction, snapping his face over to stare at me.

"Shit," I whispered, biting my lower lip and lifting my eyes up to meet his with a meek shyness that I certainly did not feel. "I think I just started my period …"

Now, given enough time, Julian would probably be able

to tell that the blood he was smelling was not menstrual, but the shock of the scent in this room, with all these Bloods … It was enough of a surprise and a strain that he didn't seem to notice.

"Do you mind if I use the bathroom real quick?" I whispered as I dug around in my backpack looking for a tampon. Making a chagrined sort of face, I lifted up the plastic wrapped stick. I was definitely *not* on my period (wouldn't that have sucked for my first week with the boys), but this was a trick that worked every time—even on a species like a vamp that didn't have menstrual cycles (don't ask, it's complicated).

"Of course—you don't need my permission," he told me as I smiled a *thank you*, moved to get out of the booth and then paused like I'd just thought of something.

"One bite," I said with a laugh, grabbing my sandwich. "I'm *starving.*"

I took a massive bite, winked at Julian, and retreated into the bathroom. As I moved, I could feel each and every vamp in that room zoning in on me, studying me like a walking piece of filet mignon.

It was disturbing, to say the least.

'Zara, we need an update,' I heard Nic ask, clearly stressed.

'Give me five,' I told him as I slipped into a stall and spit the sandwich into my hand. It was gross, but I needed to give it a sniff and see if I could identify what was in it. Clearly, there was *something.*

I spit a few times in the toilet, to clear the strange taste from my mouth.

As I ran my tongue across my teeth, it hit me. Even though I couldn't smell—thanks to the witch hazel—I could *taste* it.

Wolfsbane.

Fucking wolfsbane.

My skin broke out in goose bumps.

'It's wolfsbane,' I told the boys, projecting the alarm I felt into my wolfspeak voice. *'Fucking wolfsbane ...'* Even though I hadn't consumed it, just barely touched it to my mouth, I felt dizzy, disoriented. Chucking the remainder of the sandwich in the bowl, I lifted the back of the toilet as quietly as I could, cupped up some of the clean water (still gross, but technically the stuff in the back is drinkable) and rinsed my mouth out.

'We're coming in.' This from Montgomery.

'Just wait,' I commanded as I carefully replaced the lid and put my back to the stall wall. *'Just fucking wait.'*

Sliding to the floor, I let out a loud groan and slumped to the side.

And then I waited.

Waited.

Waited …

The bathroom door swung in and I listened as footsteps approached my stall.

"Zara?" Julian said, his voice rife with false concern. "Are you okay?"

I waited, lying comatose on the floor, doing my best to control my breathing. As a Blood, Julian would be able to sense my heart rate; I needed to be believably passed out.

"Zara?" he asked again, knocking on the door and waiting some more. Smart guy. He didn't walk in here cackling about his plans. Somehow, I almost wished he had —it would've made this whole thing a lot less fucking terrifying.

Vampires were weak to the sun for a reason; nature is all about balance. Bloods belong in the night, not walking around in seventy degree sunshine. It just wasn't right. They didn't have a lot of weaknesses and their allergy to sun was supposed to be one of them. Without that, the scales were tipped overwhelmingly in their favor.

Between the daywalking vamps and the witches? They could take over the whole damn world.

"Zara, I'm coming in!" he continued, still pretending to be the concerned acquaintance. I kept my eyes closed, but I could hear Julian's clothing rustle as he bent down and crawled under the door toward me. The fact that I couldn't smell him had my wolf brain going crazy, but I tamped down on the feeling, focusing on my breathing. "Zara?"

Julian pulled me into his lap and rested a hand on the side of my neck.

After a few moments, he lifted his fingers up and pushed me aside, letting my head conk painfully against the tile.

"She's out!" he called, rising to his feet and unlocking the stall door. A split second later, the bathroom door was swinging open and several footsteps made their way toward me.

"You sure about that?" one of them asked, and I waited

as yet another vamp came over and tested my pulse with his fingers. They didn't need to do that; they could tell my heart rate from across a crowded room; they were being superbly vigilant. "Get the shot and we'll give her another dose, just to be sure. Allister didn't seem to think this plan would work—he said she'd taste it."

Allister.

Allister fucking Vetter.

Silas' dad ... is in on all this?!

The sense of betrayal I felt in that moment almost undid me, blew my cover completely. I just barely managed to keep it contained.

And I didn't dare tell the boys, not when I was in here. Their collective surge of emotion would screw everything up for sure. I couldn't believe how easily I could *feel* them now. Our pack bond was amplified a hundred times over. And with Nic and Che? A thousand times over.

"She's fucking out, isn't she?" Julian snapped with an angry snarl. Hmm. Guess that was his true personality coming out. He wasn't quite the nice guy he claimed to be—what a surprise. "Hell, just get the goddamn wolfsbane if you're gonna look at me like that," he snapped, and I heard the angry retreating footsteps of the vamp that'd checked my neck.

'They're going to drug me,' I told the boys, struggling to keep my heart rate down. *'I need to bust out of here* now. *Don't come in, but give me a distraction up front.'*

'Roger that,' Anubis said as I waited for the bathroom door to close.

"Jesus," Julian cursed, just a split second before I surged to my feet and slipped out of the stall.

As soon as he saw me, his eyes widened, big brown saucers in a pale, pale face. I didn't wait for him to react though; I simply hit him as hard as I could in the throat.

If I'd had time for it, I'd have killed him.

Instead, satisfied that I'd kept him from making any sounds, I retreated out the bathroom doors and ran for the front. Vamps are fast, but so are 'weres'. That, and just a split second after my feet hit the tile of the dining area in the restaurant, an SUV was coming up the sidewalk and smashing through the wall of glass in the front.

"Right here!" Tidus called, one of the back doors already hanging open. I sprinted through the room of confused Bloods, most of them slightly disoriented from the crash and the brights Nic was flashing their way, and snatched my laptop and bag off the table. The textbooks I left, but that was no big deal—I could get more. As I clambered over broken glass and past the huge, jagged shards that were all that remained of the window, I grabbed for Tidus' hand. He yanked me into the back and I sprawled into his lap, the smell of salt and sand and sea filling my nostrils. "You okay?" he asked as I struggled to sit up.

The SUV was jostling us all around as Nic put it in reverse and hauled ass out of there.

If I hadn't been so wound up, I might've enjoyed the fact that I was sitting in Tidus' lap, feeling his strong, hard arms wrap around my waist. And the curiously concerned look on his face was just too cute for words.

"Silas," I said, my voice low and panting from the sudden rush of adrenaline. He stared at me from the backseat, an unlit cigarette hanging from his lips like a pacifier. "Did you know your dad was involved with Kingdom Ironbound?"

"I—" he started, but I already knew.

Even if Silas didn't know everything, he had some idea.

I thought of that night, the evening after the Coyote Creek Challenge, and how he'd attempted to confess something to me, right before we ended up making out instead. It was partially my fault for brushing him off, but … it wasn't as if that were his only opportunity to confess.

"I didn't really," he started as Che let out a vicious snarl and grabbed him by the front of the shirt.

"You *knew* and you let Zara walk into a trap?" he snapped, shaking the other boy and dislodging the cigarette from his mouth. Silas wasn't one to take shit, though, and he slapped Che's hand away. Before I could intervene, the two of them were fighting in the back seat.

"Should we call Nikolina?" Nic asked, but I reached up between the seats and snatched his cell from him. The same logic applied: if my mother found out, she would tear Pack Obsidian Gold apart looking for traitors.

She would tear *Silas* to pieces.

"No," I said firmly, clearly speaking as the Alpha Female and not just as Zara. "Nobody will say a damn word about this." I was shaking with adrenaline, but at least I was still sitting in Tidus' lap. That was the *one* good thing about that moment. "Boys!" I shouted, and the sound was sharp enough that both Silas and Che paused in their scuffle. "Enough."

"He's a goddamn fucking traitor," Che snarled, but I didn't accept that. I didn't *believe* it.

"Silas," I said, taking a deep breath and meeting his golden eyes over the back of the seat. "We're going to go home, take a moment to regroup, and then you're going to tell us everything you know, do you understand?"

He stared at me, almost defiantly for a moment, and then swallowed hard.

"Yes, Alpha," he said, his voice grave.

It was the most serious I had ever seen him.

"Fuck," I cursed as I glanced down at the screen of Nic's phone. There were about a million texts from Faith.

Tried 2 call Zara, no answer. Need ride! Car transmission out!

"We need to pick up Faith," I said, sliding off Tidus' lap into the seat next to him.

Now all we needed to do was come up with an excuse as to why the front end of the SUV looked like a crumpled tin can.

What a fucking day this was turning out to be.

"I cannot even *believe* the nerve of that guy," Faith was saying, complaining about the nonexistent college student that had supposedly caused Nic to swerve and crumple the front of the car. “People in this town are crazy. They just walk out in front of you without paying attention to where they're going.”

Normally, I'd have played along with Faith, thrown in some good bitching and complaining about the mysterious ghostly douche jaywalker, but I didn't have it in me. Not only did my mouth have that rank, sour taste from the wolfsbane, but I was still partially in shock that *any* member of our pack would be involved with the Bloods and witches—especially in something as sinister as this.

And then there was Selena to think about. Going into that café hadn't told me a damn thing about what'd happened to her.

I took a deep breath and slicked my fingers through my hair, trying my best not to scream.

“Zara,” Silas said, his voice a hell of a lot softer than normal. Faith was sitting in the front, still going on about university students (of which she *was* one), so she couldn't hear us.

I glanced over my shoulder at the same moment Che growled from his side of the bench seat. One look from me and he turned away with a scowl, pointing his glare out the window on his right.

“I wasn't in on it; I'm not a traitor.”

“Please,” Che muttered under his breath, still scowling.

“I'm not,” Silas snapped back and for a moment there, his teeth were all wolf, razor-sharp and dripping. I glanced up at Faith and found her tugging on the sleeve of Nic's hoodie. "My dad … I knew he was planning on … I don't know, rigging the Pairing somehow. But I didn't know about the witches or the Bloods or the missing pack members. Zara, I would have *told* you."

"What were you trying to say to me in the Pairing House the night of the Challenge?" I whispered. "What did you need to tell me?"

"I …" Silas paused and took a deep breath, pinching at the front of his sweaty t-shirt. It was stuck to the hard planes of his chest like it was glued there. "I was going to tell you everything I knew about my dad, all the things he'd told me … all the things he'd *threatened.*" He stopped again and met my eyes, gold irises boring into purple-black ones. "It wasn't a lot. Just enough, Zara, but …"

"Is that why you begged me that first night?" I asked, taking a deep breath and trying to control the rush of emotions swirling around inside of me. "Begged me to pick you? It wasn't for *your* safety, was it? It was for everyone else's?"

Silas glanced away, but I could see the flicker of truth in his eyes.

"This is *fucked,*" Che breathed, sitting on the other side of Montgomery. The Alpha-Son of Pack Ivory Emerald sat stoic and unmoving, arms crossed over his chest, face forward. I think he was giving himself time to process—smart move. "Pretty convenient story, don't you think? Silas, willing to save us all by taking the Alpha Male position before we got hurt. Silas, who's *just* now mentioning that he knew about this shit, but conveniently *not* the worst parts of it. Zara, I can see right through him. Why can't you?"

"What are you guys whispering about back there?" Faith asked, drawing my attention back to the front. I tried to plaster a smile on my face, but I don't think I in any way managed to get close. The look she gave me said volumes. "Look, I still haven't forgotten what we talked about this morning."

I felt my cheeks blush slightly—and I was not a person who embarrassed easily.

"Faith …" I started as she zoned in on me with a *look.* It said *you are so full of shit, your eyes are* brown. "Can we discuss this later, please?"

"Later is great," she said, turning back toward the front of the SUV and folding her arms resolutely over her chest. "Because I'm spending the night at *your* new place tonight. Just try and stop me."

I opened my mouth to protest, but then snapped it shut just as quick. Why not? I could use some time to gossip with Faith. Even if every moment felt like a lie, like I was hiding the reality of her mother's death from her.

I was a terrible friend.

"That's fine with me," I said, refusing to meet Nic's gaze in the rearview mirror, or acknowledge the penetrating stare of Che Nocturne behind me.

The two men I'd slept with, both glaring at me at the same time.

Yep. It was definitely time for a girl's night.

Everyone needed a moment to cool down and gather their thoughts, so I steered Faith inside while several of the boys went *'for a walk'*. I wasn't sure if any of them were actually going for an evening stroll or if they all just planned on going wolf, but I didn't care. As long as they were out of the house and not fighting with each other, it was fine by me.

"This place is really cute," Faith said skeptically, giving the massive shower in the downstairs bathroom a suspicious look. She was also chewing on her braid again, so I knew I was in trouble. "Why, it looks like this bathroom might fit, say, eight people," she continued, casting a look over her shoulder and then laughing. "What was this built for anyway? An orgy?"

I laughed, but the sound was forced and Faith zeroed right in on it, coming over to stand in front of me in her orange hoodie with the pineapple on the front of it. I had no idea if there was a special meaning to it, or if it was just another random bit of Faith fashion. She certainly had her own unique way of looking at the world.

At the very least, it was food related. That part made sense.

I stared at her and the silence got way too long and awkward for my liking. Things were never awkward between me and Faith—not even when I was hiding the usual werewolf stuff from her. No, this was so much worse. *That shower,* I wanted to say, *it's big because we had to wash off all the blood, Faith. There was so much blood.*

"I'm planning on dragging all my new boyfriends in there for a mind-altering sexual experience, obviously."

Faith paused and cocked her head to one side, folding her arms over her chest.

"Zara, what the hell is going on? I mean, this cottage is cute, but it's not really big enough for eight people to live in. I know you said your mom, like, wants you to marry a rich guy, but … if they're so rich, why don't they have their own places?"

"It's complicated," I said with a dry laugh, but had bullshit like that ever worked on my best friend? She'd known me for far too long to accept empty nonsense like that. "These guys are sort of, like, royal blood. My mother wants me to work with them for a year and see who I get along with best."

"That's weird, Zara," Faith said, uncrossing her arms with a sigh and walking around me, pausing as she noticed Tidus standing in the entry to the living room area.

"You guys want pizza or something?" he asked, smiling like he didn't smell the nervous pheromones that were perfuming the air around me. I knew he could, of course, but at least he had the decency to pretend that everything was okay. “Do you think they'll deliver all the way up here in the woods?”

A slight smile stretched my lips as I thought of how nice it felt to sit in his lap, how his hands on my hips had sent this vibrant need arcing through me. Tidus was the kind of guy who lit up a room just by being in it. He didn't have to say anything, do anything; his presence was enough.

“Hawaiian *please,*” Faith whined, moving around me and continuing her exploration into the living room, running her hand along the fireplace mantle, before circling around the green velvet chair and heading past the long dining room table and into the kitchen. There was a small utility room back there, a washer and dryer, and a closet that I'd made sure one of the boys locked before Faith found it. Inside, there were iron and bone weapons, guns with silver bullets, and a few old 'were' artifacts from past alphas that'd stayed here during the Pairing. The last thing I wanted to do was explain to Faith why there was a statue of mating wolves in a closet next to large wooden claymores.

“Hawaiian,” Tidus said, raising his brows and gesturing at me with his cell. “Anything in particular you want, Zara? Pepperoni? Cheese? Combination?” He paused and snapped his fingers, his gray eyes sparkling playfully. Guess he wasn't upset about Silas' perceived betrayal.

Me, I was torn.

I wasn't sure if I was taking it too seriously—or not seriously enough.

“Let me guess … okay, you strike me as someone who

likes their pizza just outside the realm of normal."

"You think you can guess my pizza preferences just by looking at me?" I asked, feeling a small laugh working its way up from inside my belly. "Take your best shot," I said, lifting my chin up and smiling as Faith walked back into the living room and found the blonde surfer boy staring at me with a very determined facial expression, features scrunched like he was trying to figure out the answer to a really important puzzle.

"White sauce, roasted garlic, and chicken?" he asked carefully and I clapped my hands over my mouth.

"That's … kind of creepy, how did you do that?"

"I asked Nic," he said with a bright grin, spinning his phone around on the palm of his hand. God, he really was a cutie, wasn't he? Tidus wasn't like anyone I'd ever met before. He was bubbly and open with an easy smile and a carefree attitude that was infectious. I hardly knew what to make of him. Not in a bad way, but he was basically the opposite of Nic. My childhood friend was serious, inscrutable, overly sensitive at times. "Got ya, didn't I?"

I caught Faith's raised brow as my lips twitched into a smile.

"Can I get you anything else? Breadsticks? Hot wings? Soda?"

"What are you, her new manservant?" Faith said, but it wasn't meant to be mean, just a joke. She chuckled. "Hell, I guess I'll take a bunch of suitors and a little cottage if it means getting waited on hand and foot." She snapped her fingers. "Oh, can you grab me a molten lava cake?"

"At your service," Tidus said, taking a deep, exaggerated bow and standing back up, his white tank loose on his sun-kissed shoulders, that tattoo of his drawing my attention as he lifted up his phone and started plugging our order into the app. "I'll go pick it up. Maybe Nic'll stop scowling long enough to come with me?"

Tidus winked and disappeared onto the front porch, letting the screen door swing shut behind him.

"Dude, oh my god," Faith said, coming over to stare at me with wide eyes and a gaping mouth. "You were seriously eye fucking the shit out of that guy."

"Eye fucking?!" I asked, turning away and heading up the stairs. It was only after I'd gone up a few steps that I realized it … the giant bed. Faith was going to see the giant bed. I turned around abruptly and popped my hip out, all sassy like.

There were a lot of things I could explain my way around, but a massive eight person bed? That was going to be a little difficult to laugh off.

"I wasn't eye fucking him, Faith."

She gaped at me.

"You were practically panting, One-Kiss-No-Date." She pursed her lips and narrowed her brown eyes at me. "All these years, you've never once had a crush on anyone but Nic. I mean, since sixth grade it's been obvious to me that the two of you would get together and now …" She paused and took a deep breath, like she was trying to find the right words. It wasn't until that moment that I realized it—she was actually *upset* with me. "Zara, I just … you and Nic made me believe love was real."

She looked up at me with puppy dog eyes ringed in liner and caked with mascara and I suddenly had no idea *what* to say to that. My heart started pounding and my hand felt slippery on the wooden banister.

You and Nic made me believe love was real.

What was I supposed to say to that? How was I supposed to respond? I was struggling with that, too, the idea that I could actually care about a boy other than Nic.

"And before I even find out that you guys traded V-cards, you've slept with a guy I've never even *met*? Zara, I know I can be a little self-absorbed at times, but … I love you and I'm worried. Something's not right here; I can feel it."

I just stared at her for several seconds before she flipped a switch, wiping away all her genuine worry with a flick of that long braid over one shoulder. Before I could think up a response, she was darting past me and up the stairs. Yes, I could've used my superior strength and speed to stop her, but what was the point? There was no way in hell Faith would leave the entire upstairs of the cottage unexplored.

"Zara …"

I rolled my eyes to the ceiling, prayed to mother nature for strength, and started to turn.

"Why bother keeping a human pet?" Aeron asked, standing outside the screen door next to Nic.

"I found this wandering around at the edge of pack property," he said, pushing open the door. "Go ahead and go in," he added, letting the faerie princess into the cabin.

The place was spelled, wards from some long-ago werewolf that'd had magic. *Like me.* Even Aeron couldn't cross them without a wolf's permission. "What do you want me to do with her? Tidus wants to go get pizza or something."

Nic looked up at me, our eyes meeting briefly. He was pissed at Silas, maybe even at me for putting myself into that situation at the café with Julian. But, at the same time, he didn't sound entirely put out at the idea of hanging with the Alpha-Son of Pack Amber Ash.

That was progress, right?

"Just leave her here," I said as I heard Faith gasping from the bedroom doorway.

"Zara Vodja Castille," she warned, and I listened as her footsteps moved forward and into the only room on the top floor. One bed, one room, seven mates.

I huffed out a long breath.

"You sure?" Nic asked as Aeron produced a small glass bottle from the front pocket of her shimmery, see-through gown and popped the top. With a grin sharp enough to skin a hide, she downed it in a single swallow and waited, her image blurring like it'd been obscured by fog. A quick blink on my part and her new image settled in like it'd been there all along.

"I'm sure," I said as I tore my gaze from the faerie girl and looked over at Nic. His purple-black eyes were locked onto mine and through our connection, I felt his love and his pain and his frustration. "Go get pizza and make a friend, okay?"

'I love you, Zara,' he told me and I smiled softly. *'No*

matter what. After all this is over, even though I know you can't pick me ... make me your paramour. Keep me as your guard. I'll stand by while you rule with another man.' He paused as I felt my mouth start to hang open in shock. My … paramour? *'Even ... even if you choose that traitor, I'll stay.'*

Nic turned before I could think of a thing to say and let the screen door slam shut behind him.

Oh, goddess, please help me with all of these ridiculous men ...

I stood there gaping before I realized the princess was still standing there, waiting for me to acknowledge her.

“Sorry, what do you want?” I asked, squinting at her and sucking on my lower lip. Just when I thought I had *enough* things to think about, Nic threw me that curveball? But he *did* have a point. I could keep him on as a guard … although there weren't many werewolves in history who'd ever … mated beyond their, ah, mate.

Aeron stood there with her long dark hair slung over one shoulder, obscuring the white t-shirt (and lack of bra underneath). She looked casual and cool in a pair of low slung, faded blue jeans and black heels, the supernatural glimmer of her diamond-crushed skin faded to a more human butter-beige. Her sloe-eyed gaze still shone with an unnatural purple-blue, but I figured if Faith could handle the guys, she could probably deal with this.

“Zara, you are in such deep—” Faith started, stumbling around the top of the stairs and catching sight of Aeron. Immediately, I saw her guard go up. She didn't like sharing her best friend with anyone. I remembered once in eighth grade when Ali Gobbe tried to convince me to sit at her table with the popular (in their own minds anyway) girls and ended up with a plate of spaghetti on her blonde-streaked brunette head. "Who's your friend?"

"Faith, this is … Aeron," I said with a small sigh. Yet another lie to add to my ever growing list. "Our mothers are colleagues."

"Uh-huh," Faith said, coming down a few steps and crossing her arms over her orange hoodie. "Yet another Nikolina connection, huh?"

I just stood there staring at the faerie girl as she swung her sheet of glimmering ebony hair over one shoulder.

"To what do I owe the pleasure, Aeron?" I asked, coming down the steps and giving her a slight raise of my lips. She needed to know that right here, in this place, *I* was the boss. If I had to, I'd fight to the death to defend that privilege.

"I was hoping we could have a minute to talk?" she said, looking around the cabin like it was as foreign to her as Faerie had been to me.

"No," Faith said from behind me, refusing to move from her place on the stairs. "She cannot have a moment to talk. Look, I don't know you for shit, but I'm having a really hard week. My mom is on drugs and totally AWOL; she took my fucking dogs, too. My boyfriend is a complete loser and my best friend is … lying out her ass about everything."

"Faith," I stared, but she ignored me, clamping her palms over her eyes.

"No, Zara, don't. You're lying through your teeth, but that's okay. It doesn't matter. I just need someone to vent to, and I need to see what sort of crazy explanation you have for Che and this bed and just … everything." She paused in her rant and yanked on the end of her braid, staring down at Aeron with a deadly serious facial expression. "Come back tomorrow, okay? She's all yours *tomorrow.*"

"I don't have anywhere to go," Aeron said, giving me a very pointed sort of look. "My *mother* kicked me out."

I just stood there staring at the heir to the Unseelie throne, a throne of dead and rotten and ugly things, and I just started to laugh.

Pretty sure it was nervous laughter, but there it was, nonetheless.

"I'll entertain her for a while," Che said, standing just inside the screen door. I'd been too focused on Faith and Aeron to even notice that he'd come back, smelling of wolf and forest, lavender and bergamot oil. His purple eyes bored into mine. "Then you can spend some time with your friend and try to explain how the two of us ended up gettin' busy."

He tossed a long, slow heavy-lidded blink in my direction and then tucked his fingers into his front pockets. His smile … it was almost lascivious. And I *liked* it.

"Getting busy?" Faith asked with a long groan, turning right back around and heading up the stairs again. "Not in this bed though, right? Is this bed clean?"

"On the forest floor!" Che shouted, grinning at me and then turning toward the kitchen, disappearing past the archway and then calling for the faerie princess to come with him.

For that, I was seriously going to have to kick his ass later.

"The forest … floor …" Faith was saying as I finally finished climbing the stairs and paused in the doorway to the bedroom. The look she gave me over her shoulder could've curdled milk. "The *ground*? The pine needle strewn *ground*?"

This was going to be a long night, wasn't it?

After I'd convinced Faith that the gargantuan bed was clean of bodily fluids, we snuggled up together in the middle of it with breadsticks, pizza slices, and soda—courtesy of Tidus and Nic—and put on, of all things, a werewolf movie.

"God, I love werewolves," Faith said as she watched some hideous beast man in black and white grab a screaming, fainting woman off a park bench. I glanced her way. I'd think she was being ironic if I wasn't sure Faith was ignorant about the existence of the Numinous.

"Faith," I started, sitting up and pushing red hair over one shoulder. "We should probably talk …" The sight of Diya's body flashed in the back of my mind, but I knew I couldn't tell her, not without revealing everything else about the world that she didn't know. And honestly, if I let myself think too hard on it, confessing would be more for me than it would be for her.

"Probably," she said, dipping a breadstick into a plastic tub of marinara and swirling it around. When she flicked her brown eyes over to me, they were wide and accusatory. "The forest floor, Zara? Is that a joke?"

I didn't respond right away and she groaned, stuffing the breadstick into her mouth and falling back onto the pillows.

"Explain, please. I just … One-Kiss-No-Date, what *happened* to you?"

"I'm not … a sexual awakening?" I asked with a flash of teeth, trying to make a joke out of it. Faith was all about women taking control of their sexuality and all that; maybe this was a way I could get her to understand? "After Nic and I did it, I just sort of opened up …"

"I'll bet you did," Faith said as I plucked a piece of chicken off my pizza and threw it at her. "But how did you explain your sexual revolution to Nic?"

"He's okay with it," I said, looking her in the face and hoping she could tell that at least some of what I was saying was the truth. "As okay as he can be anyway. He knows what's riding on this … courtship."

"What *is* riding on this courtship, Zara? Money? You've never cared about that sort of thing before."

"It's not about money," I said, trying to keep the honesty going as long as I possibly could. "These guys, their families have political and business connections that could really make a difference in the world. Nic knows that."

"All these years, you've managed to keep your mom's

job a secret from me. I'm assuming you're still not going to tell me what she does for a living?" I gave Faith an *I wish I could smile* but shook my head.

"No."

"But you dating these guys is really important?" she asked and I nodded, watching as she sat up, reaching for another breadstick and picking at the bits of roasted garlic on the top. "Can you tell me why there's only one bed in this house?"

"It's a lesson in togetherness," I said, which was at least partially the truth. "A way to force us all to get along. To be honest though, most of the guys have been sleeping on the sofa or in the chairs downstairs."

"So …" Faith started as she rewound the werewolf movie to rewatch a particularly brutal death scene. "It's like one of those corporate picnics where they make you tie your legs together and do the sack races and stuff?"

"Yeah," I said, surprised at how well she was taking this. "It sort of is."

"Are you going to sleep with them all?" she asked me after another moment, and I shrugged.

"I don't know. Probably. I think so."

"You dirty bitch," Faith said, pulling the buffalo wing box close and flicking it open with a single finger. She stared at the sauce covered meat for a long time, ignoring the screeches of the movie heroine. "You're sure Nic is okay with all of this?" she asked again, voice soft. "Because I feel like you guys are meant to be together."

'We are meant to be together,' he said to me from

downstairs, using *wolfspeak* to drop in on the conversation. I had to resist a small smile. I wasn't sure if it would come out genuine … or tinged with a drop of sadness. *'No matter what happens with the others, it doesn't change that.'*

"I love Nic," I told Faith aloud, drawing her attention back to me, staring into her brown eyes and hoping she could tell how serious I was about that. "And nobody else."

Faith's mouth twitched in a smile and she plucked out a chicken leg, handing it over to me.

"Alright," she said, sounding a little more like herself, "but you still owe me detailed stories, dick lengths, and an explanation as to how you ended up doing it outside with this Che person."

"Deal," I said as I took a bite of my food and wondered how many of the guys were listening in on our conversation.

The sex stuff, I could get past, but the love thing … I'd said what I'd meant.

At this point, I *did* only love Nic.

But I knew at some point, my heart would swell to make room for another—for several others, actually.

Early, far before Faith would even dream of getting up, I rose from the giant bed, slipping on jeans and a t-shirt and heading downstairs to see what Che had done with Aeron last night.

I found the fae girl curled up on the sofa, her glamour still firmly in place, making her look like a sleeping teenager instead of a supernatural monster.

"She's been out all night," Che said, his voice as dark as the shadows behind him, dripping and hot, inviting me to wrap the sound around myself like a blanket. "I don't trust her for shit, but …" I glanced over my shoulder in time to see him shrug, his purple eyes shimmering as he watched me. "The other one," he continued, this time with his lips twisting into a scowl, "is outside. He slept on the porch last night."

"Thanks," I said, moving toward the door to face up to the inevitable—I had to talk to Silas. I had to know how deep his betrayal went and then figure out what to do with it. As I turned away from Che, he reached out, wrapping his fingers around my wrist. An instant thrill took over me, that wildness I'd felt during the hunt. With just a single touch, he made my heart pound like I was running in the Hunt all over again, paws padding over snow, the scent of prey driving my instincts forward.

"Che," I said as he stepped forward and looked down at me, running his tongue over his lower lip and flicking his eyes to the side for a moment like he wasn't sure what he wanted to say. But as soon as he switched them back to me? There was nothing *but* confidence in his gaze.

"I want your mouth," he told me without a stitch of hesitation. I felt an allover warming in my body, this hot flush that crept across my skin and made me suck in a sharp breath. I might not be in *love* with Che Nocturne, but physically … there was a connection between us.

"Duly noted," I said, extracting my wrist from his grip. He let me go, but his mouth twisted to the side in a bemused sort of frown. I started to turn away and then paused, reaching up and planting my palms on either side of his face. Lifting up on my toes, I breathed in the rich scent of bergamot and wolf, and then pressed my mouth to his.

He let me kiss him like that for just a few short seconds before putting his hands on my hips and deepening the moment into something darker, something sinister. And I liked it, too, each strong flick of his tongue against my own.

"Spend the night with me tonight," he said against my mouth, putting just enough space between us to say the words. I cracked my eyes open a fraction and found his purple gaze shimmering with primal lust and want and need, his wolf peeking out at me from a very handsome human face. "Or at the very least, let me into the bed." Che's mouth twitched a little as he released me and stepped back, making no move to hide the hardness inside his sweats. "Sleeping on the couch *blows.*"

I smiled back at him and stepped away, running my tongue across my lower lip. I could taste him there on my mouth and I *loved* it. Che Nocturne spoke to me at a bestial level my wolf could understand. *Attraction, warmth, pack, mate.*

Pushing open the screen door, I found Silas curled up in one of the rocking chairs on the porch with a blanket thrown over him, a small decorative throw pillow tucked under his cheek. Jax lay on the floor in wolf form, opening one blue eye and flicking a single ear in my direction when I came outside.

'He's just fallen asleep,' he told me as I paused there and looked down at Silas' face, praying that I was right about him, that he was telling the truth. For a traitor, there were only two options for pack justice: death or banishment. It was hard to say which was worse for a 'were'. *'He spent the night tossing and turning, mumbling things under his breath.'*

Jaxson stood up and then did a bow, yawning wide and flashing pink tongue as he lowered his front half to the floor and then stood back up, shaking out the thickness of his pelt.

'What exactly did he say?" I asked him, and if wolves could shrug, then that's what Jax was doing, lowering his front half slightly in another half-bow, as if to say *how the hell should I know?*

'Nonsense, mostly. Although I'd be lying if I said I didn't hear your name a couple of times in there.' Jax padded up to the edge of the porch and sat with his back rigid and his head raised, nostrils flaring as he scented the cool, crisp morning air. *'Che is already planning Silas' funeral,'* he added, casting an icy blue gaze in my direction. *'What are you going to do if you find out he really is a traitor?'*

"I don't know," I said aloud, because I needed to hear the words break the quiet peacefulness of the morning air. I *didn't* know, and I wasn't used to that. "First, I suppose we should come up with a plan to deal with Julian."

Moving down the front porch steps, I stood in a half-melted puddle of snow and closed my eyes, letting the peacefulness of the pack property wash over me. Jax joined me and shifted into human form on my left side.

Glancing over at him, I couldn't help but notice the firm contours of his muscles, the smooth white surface of his skin, the pale pink color of his lips. He was ice and frost, through and through, from his appearance to his attitude. I didn't know how to deal with him, what to make of him. Jaxson Kidd was an enigma.

"We need to arrange a meeting with the Crown Aurora Blood Queen," I said after a long moment, tearing my gaze away from Jax's naked body to stare out at the forest. "I need to understand why, when they have such an incredible trick up their sleeve, the Ironbound Bloods are losing so much territory."

"Do you think they're doing it on purpose?" Jax asked me, crossing his arms over his chest and tilting his chin up toward the sky. I followed his gaze and watched the sun peek its gold head above the horizon. "Relinquishing all that territory?"

"Why would they do that?" I asked, turning my head slightly to find that Jax was watching me now. The corner of his lip twitched slightly, like he was on the verge of almost-smiling at me.

"That's what I'd do, let them take all the territory, spread themselves thin …" He paused and then let a full smile twist across his face, one full of irony and bemusement. I wondered what Jaxson looked like when he was actually happy? Or if he ever really was. "Maybe watch them get comfortable in unfamiliar turf … then during the day, I'd kill them all."

A chill skittered down my spine, like frosted fingertips on a cold winter day.

Jax had a damn good point there.

Even more reason to get in touch with Aurora herself.

If she didn't know about the daywalkers yet, that meant I had leverage enough for a favor …

“This is so *weird,*” Faith whispered on our way to the university, sitting in the front row of the Yukon with me, pretending to glance surreptitiously over her shoulder at the boys and failing miserable. She was painfully obvious about it. I could see Nic rolling his eyes from the driver's seat. “You're dating *all* of these guys. It's like a new wave of feminism or something.”

“Faith,” I said, giving her a look as she chewed on the end of her braid again. Damn it. I was really going to have to stop throwing revelations this girl's way.

My stomach tightened and I found myself inhaling sharply.

Faith no longer had a mother, and it was all my fault. That wasn't something that was ever going to go away or get better. I had to learn to live with it.

“What? You're allowed to date seven guys, and I can't comment on it?”

I pursed my lips and forced myself to keep my gaze out the front window. Every boy in this car was a werewolf; no matter how quiet Faith was, they'd hear her. *How embarrassing.* Not to mention the fact that Aeron was in the far back, sitting seatbelt-less and nauseous from all the iron in the SUV.

Oh well.

I couldn't exactly leave her on pack property—we were *extremely* lucky her glamour also masked her *smell* or else my mother might've shown up to investigate—and I didn't have time to deal with her until later. If she wanted to talk to me, she'd just have to tag along and wait for an opportunity.

I tapped my fingers on the edge of the car door and tried to work out how to deal with Julian when I got to school—if he was even there.

It would be smarter for him not to show.

Now that he knew *I* knew, there was no point in hiding my males from him; I'd take them all to the university campus as a show of force.

"You're a good man, Nic," Faith said after a moment, and I swear, when I flicked my gaze in his direction, I saw his hands tighten on the wheel. "A real good man."

"Gee, thank you, Faith," he said sarcastically, pursing his lips as we pulled into a lucky front parking space and he stopped the car. Everyone else was silent, either replaying yesterday's fiasco at the diner or else purposely giving Silas the quiet treatment. Looking back at him, I caught his gold eyes with mine and saw pain flash there, hot and tired at the same time. He was hurting, but he was also exhausted. Whatever was going on, it was rooted in something deeper.

Silas was *my* concern now, my mate, a part of my pack

… and it was my job to find out.

"Walk a perimeter around the science building and if you see Julian," I told Montgomery once Faith was distracted calling out to a friend from her chemistry class, "you and Anubis stay on him. If he's on campus, he's yours. But no matter what, don't leave with him."

Aeron ambled up to stand beside me, her arms crossed over her stomach as she watched me hand out orders. I didn't particularly like her taking this all in, but then, she wouldn't learn anything I didn't want her to know. I'd be careful with what I said or did around the Unseelie Princess.

"Yes, Alpha," Monty said, watching as I turned my attention to Jax and Che.

"I want you two to actively search the campus for him. Silas, Nic, Tidus, you three are with me." I glanced over at Aeron. "You're welcome to stick with us," I added as her sloe-eyes blinked lazily in the sun. I imagined she'd follow along until we got a chance to talk.

I started off toward the building, ignoring Che's deep, rumbling growls as Silas passed by him. Taking Faith by the arm and bribing her to stick with us by offering free coffee, I steered her inside, my nose, ears, and eyes working at full capacity to search for any sign of the daywalking vampire.

To my surprise, he was waiting for us just inside the front door, his smell masked with witch hazel, but his distaste for me written across each line of his scowling features.

"Nic, get Faith the coffee I promised and I'll pay you

back. I gotta talk to Julian about our final project," I added when she gave me a raised eyebrow and a look.

"He's not part of the harem, is he?" she whispered, but Nic was already yanking her away and taking her down the hall toward the study lounge and snack area.

"I'm surprised you'd show your face here," I told him, tilting my head to one side and watching as his brown eyes took in Tidus on my right and Silas on my left. I had to admit, they made a very attractive set of bodyguards.

"And why is that?" Julian asked me, looking for all the world like your average college student. "Do you think I have a reason to hide? I'm not the one who has trouble keeping track of his people, now am I?" He smiled at me, and not for the first time, I felt an uneasiness around him, a sense of wrongness that I'd been picking up on from day one. "Oh, hey Silas," Julian said with a little wink, pushing off the wall and heading for our wildflower class.

The university had assigned a substitute, now that a police report had been filed by Professor Heath's husband. He was officially missing, a whisper the whole school was talking about. Had he run off with some young lover? Had he committed suicide?

I hated being one of a few who knew that he'd been murdered.

"I don't know him," Silas said, quivering beside me, his jaw clenching tight. I could see his canines peeking over the edge of his lip, his hands curling into fists. I smelt blood, wolf blood, and knew that he'd probably cut himself with his own nails. "I've never met this guy on my own,

Zara, I *swear* it."

Before I could even *react* to that statement, Silas was tearing across the hallway and grabbing Julian by the hair. He yanked him back and shoved his face into the wall with a sickening crunch. All around us, students started screaming and backing up; some pulled their phones from their pockets while others rushed forward to help.

"I've got this," Aeron said from beside me. I'd almost forgotten about the faerie princess for a second, but when she pulled a tiny bottled glamour from her pocket and tossed it onto the floor, I breathed a huge sigh of relief.

The students who were watching paused, blinked as if they they'd just woken up from a long nap, and tucked their phones in their pockets before stepping back and moving on as if nothing at all had happened here. As I rushed forward to grab Silas, I saw an overlay of the glamour of top of him and Julian, a peaceful reconciliation of friends, laughing and patting one another on the back.

Oh.

Aeron was talented. Talented. Beyond fucking *talented.*

"Silas!" I screamed, safe from prying eyes inside the bubble of fae magic. Before I could reach him, he'd shifted into wolf form and latched onto Julian's neck with his jaws, dragging the vampire away from the doors to the bathroom and throwing him against the opposite wall.

Fortunately the next round of classes had just started and there were few people in the halls. Good thing, too, because I didn't know exactly *how* powerful Aeron was. Her mother could've concocted a glamour capable of masking both sight *and* touch, but the princess? I just wasn't sure. And if Silas and Julian slammed into someone, the whole illusion could wear off.

"Silas!" I shouted again, but he was completely red-zoned, locked onto Julian with a ferocity that was almost frightening. He was fucking losing it.

Tidus was right beside me, trying to get control of our pack mate, shifting into wolf form and trying to block him from the daywalking vampire. It seemed ironic, defending a man I wanted dead. But this was not the place, not the right time.

Murdering Julian now could spark the war that I was so fucking afraid of.

Silas barreled right into Tidus, knocking him out of the way and grabbing Julian by the head. I heard the distinct sound of bone cracking before the vampire got control of himself and started to fight back.

His hands shot up and Silas yelped in pain as fingers dug into the sides of his neck, digging right through his skin and drawing blood.

Without many other options left to me, I shifted too, and snatched one of Julian's arms, squeezing down with all my strength and severing the limb from the rest of his body. The vampire howled in agony and yanked his other fingers from Silas' throat, turning on me instead.

Lunging up from the floor, he went for my throat and managed to sink his teeth into my neck, the sheer force of his bite cutting through the ruff of fur until his fangs were buried deep into me. With poisoned vampire flesh between my lips, and vamp pheromones tainting my blood, I felt my body start to list to one side.

'Zara!' Nic shouted in wolfspeak.

"Oh for Christ's fucking sake!" Che called out from behind me, right at about the same moment Tidus grabbed hold of Julian by the back of the neck and *squeezed.*

I collapsed onto my side as the vampire took his last breath, jaws releasing my neck as he sagged back onto the white linoleum floor with a macabre death rattle.

And the scariest part about all that?

He wouldn't *stay* dead.

'Start cleaning this mess up,' I told the boys, feeling Nic's wild fear through our pack connection. He'd stay with Faith, though. That boy knew how to do his job—even when it was hard for him. I knew I could trust Nic to keep Faith safe. *'Take him outside and put him in the SUV, but make sure you put a wooden knife in his heart first.'*

My vision was dancing and blurring as I shifted back, naked and hating that I'd decided to wear new jeans today. Should've known better.

"Here," Montgomery said, handing me a cool water bottle. He must've grabbed it from the vending machine down the hall. Quick thinking.

I took it from him, filled my mouth with cool water, swished and spit.

"Goddamn it," I whispered as Che hefted Julian's body up and over his shoulder, the sound of Aeron's laughter echoing around the empty building. Anubis and Jax had managed to clear the hallway of humans; it was just us in here now.

My fingers touched the side of my neck, felt the tiny punctures and the overwhelming wave of pleasure that hit me with I teased the broken flesh. Fucking vamp pheromones. They'd make you orgasm at the same time they drained the life from your body.

But their saliva … it was just as poisonous to a wolf as their blood.

"I have an antidote with me," Monty said, the tip of his white braid dragging through some of the copious blood splatter on the floor. He reached into his jacket, felt around inside a pocket, and produced a tiny brown paper packet. Tearing the edge, Montgomery opened the package and handed it over to me.

Inside, a sprinkling of black powder sat, reeking of sulfur and copper.

Demon blood.

"Where did you get this?" I whispered, but my voice was cracking, my vision blurring. I needed to stop questioning my blessings and utilize them instead. Taking the packet in shaking fingers, I sprinkled the foul tasting ash on my tongue and washed it down with the water bottle.

Anubis and Jax were on their knees scrubbing blood with huge wads of paper towels from the bathroom. Tidus was sitting against the wall naked, swishing soda around in his mouth to rid himself of the taint of vamp blood. Silas was doing the same, holding a hand to the wounds in his neck, his eyes closed as his breath whooshed out in panting gasps.

“There are duffel bags with clothes in them, in the back of the SUV,” I told Montgomery and he nodded, rising to his feet and jogging outside to grab them. “In the bathroom, boys,” I choked, still feeling shaky and weak and unsure as I found my feet and stumbled over to the unisex bathroom, pushing in the door and sagging against one of the sinks.

I turned the water on full blast and started washing the vampire blood off my hands and face.

“Clean up,” I instructed, trying to keep my voice neutral when what I really wanted to do was growl and rip into Silas for such a stupid stunt. He could've exposed us all in there. Worse even, he could've gotten himself or somebody else killed.

“I'm sorry, Alpha,” he said, leaning over the neighboring sink, espresso dark hair falling into his face, his naked body a kaleidoscope of tattoos. My wolf responded to the sight with a purr of pleasure. Even with the demon blood antidote in me, I could feel waves of lust and heat raking through me from the bite. My sex swelled and my nipples hardened and I knew both boys could *smell* me.

“Lock the door,” I told Tidus, simply because having a human walk in here would be downright catastrophic. But the way it came out? In a husky purr? I felt the air in the bathroom heat with an electric charge.

The Amber Ash Alpha-Son did what I asked before moving over to the row of sinks and rinsing himself carefully, the only sounds in that bathroom the rush of water and the harshness of our combined breathing.

“Come here,” I told Silas when we were both done

cleaning up. I turned, my bare ass cheeks pressing into the sink as I had him stand in front of me. Looking into those gorgeous gold eyes of his, I put my hands on either side of his throat, where the wounds were, and closed my eyes.

The feel of my palms against his rapidly beating pulse … it did things to me that I didn't know how to fight, especially not with the vamp pheromones doing their best to turn me into a raging nymphomaniac.

Add to that the fact that our bodies were close … so close. I could feel Silas' warmth, smell the cherry and vanilla scent of pack Obsidian Gold, even through the stink of blood and sweat and violence.

After a moment, the magic responded to my touch, filling the room with the scents of fresh rain and wet earth. That musky wildness that swept over us made my skin pebble with goose bumps. Silas closed his gold eyes, the scar on his face crinkling with the motion.

He was hard, too, his cock responding to the sense of urgency and need in the room, this bestial calling that I was finding hard to resist.

A knock on the door sounded at the edges of my concentration and Tidus scrambled to answer it.

It was Nic.

"What the fuck happened out there?" he asked, pausing on the opposite side of the bathroom and looking at me and Silas like he could sense the intensity brewing between us. Che stormed in right after him, the sleeves of his black hoodie pushed up, his arms covered in blood up to his elbows.

"You fucking son of a bitch!" he shouted, grabbing Silas by the shoulders and pulling him away from me. He lashed out with both palms, leaving red handprints on Silas' chest as the other boy stumbled back and hit the tiled bathroom wall.

But the wounds on his neck … those were gone.

"I can't even … fuck, man. The lengths you'll go to cover up what you've done." Che reached out and curled his fingers around Silas' throat, pushing him into the wall as he snarled and his skin rippled with the ebony night of wolf fur. "I ought to fucking kill you right here, right now. Only thing that's stopping me is the fact that I don't want to clean anymore blood up!"

"No," I said, and the single syllable snapped into place like a solid entity, taking up more of the room than all of us put together. I was panting and shaking, and I needed someone to lay hands on me so we could heal the Blood bite on my neck. "You won't touch him because your Alpha says so."

My voice boomed with authority as Che's violet eyes widened.

After a moment, he scowled, but released Silas as I'd asked. The Alpha-Son of Pack Obsidian Gold put a hand to his throat and scowled right back. If I let them, the two boys probably *would* rip each other's throats out.

"We don't know what Silas has done," I said quietly, and even though I was mad as hell about what had just happened in the hallway, I didn't think he was a traitor. No, I *knew* he wasn't. I could feel his pain and anxiety ricocheting between us, teasing our connection with fear and confusion. "But he's my responsibility." I licked my lips and took a deep breath. "He's my *mate.*"

"Zara," Nic said, stepping forward, a thread of warning in his voice. He knew what I was asking. I was asking … no, I was *telling* him that I wanted to mate with Silas. And Tidus. Hell, I wanted to mate with everyone in that room. But, you know, baby steps and all that. I'd only had sex three times in my life. It was a bit much to skip all the way to an orgy. "Shouldn't you at least find out what he's done first?"

"He's my mate," I repeated, my voice threaded through with steel.

I looked over at Che and found him with his face tight, his hands clenched into fists at his sides.

"Just make it quick then," Che snapped, and I swear, I almost put him on his back right then and there. "There's a dead vampire in the back of your SUV—and he won't stay that way for long."

Without another word, he spun and stormed out of the bathroom.

"Zara," Nic said again, but the tightness on his face told me he already knew this was happening. Right here, right now. It couldn't wait. The vampire bite was making me feel like I might burst out of my skin at any moment, a horny caterpillar from a cocoon. Okay, weird image, but still …

"No matter what," I told Nic, feeling the power of the bond pulsing between me and Silas, "he's mine. I don't care what he's done."

Nic made a low sound in his throat, raking his fingers through his dark red hair, aubergine eyes flashing for a moment before he, too, turned and left. A moment later, Montgomery walked in and offered up the duffel with the clothes in it.

Soundlessly, Tidus moved over, pulled on a pair of sweats and left with Monty following along behind him. I didn't have to say anything; he could feel it.

"Why are you sticking up for me?" Silas asked, raising his face to look at me, his expression a strange mix of lust and confusion. "I knew my dad was plotting against the packs. He basically told me to my face if I didn't snag the spot as alpha at the end of the year, that he'd make sure we *all* regretted your decision."

"You knew what was happening to the missing wolves?" I whispered, my voice low and dangerous.

"I didn't … I didn't *know,*" he said, looking up at me with those gold eyes I'd always found so fascinating, his scar a vibrant reminder of the horror his father had put him through. "I didn't know they were *eating* them," he whispered. "But I … I knew my father was involved somehow. I've known for a while."

I closed my eyes for a moment to gather my thoughts.

"I tried to tell you the night after Coyote Creek," he said hesitantly, reminding me of our make out session and the words he'd tried and failed to say. Mm. I remembered that. And I believed him. I could feel how earnest he was through our pack connection. "But I didn't know what to say without making you think I was a part of it. Now I've just royally fucked things up with everyone."

"You've never met Julian before?" I asked, the reality of what'd just happened in the hallway starting to sink in. This could be the tinder that set the war ablaze. I had no idea how important Julian was to Kingdom Ironbound. Or if that even mattered. Maybe they'd use him as an excuse to fight anyway?

"Never," he said, a growl chasing the syllables from his lips. Silas lifted his head to look at me, meeting my gaze dead-on. "I wouldn't betray you like that, Zara. I've been waiting for this moment for a long fucking time. The last thing I'd do is put our relationship at risk. I should've told you sooner what I knew about Allister. I'm just … he's conditioned me to be afraid of him. I hate it. I … goddamn it, I fucking *hate* it."

Silas traced a finger down his scar and came toward me, his tattoos bright under the fluorescent lights of the bathroom.

"He's abused you since you were a pup," I said carefully, aware of the tension in the room, in my own body, the hot heat between my thighs. "I don't hold it against you," I continued, stepping forward and running my fingers up the back of Silas' neck and into his hair.

"Zara," he said, letting his lids slide closed. "Don't."

"Don't, what?" I asked him, wondering what the hell Faith was going to say when she found out that One-Kiss-No-Date had screwed her high school crush in the university bathroom, butt naked and covered in vampire blood. Okay, so I'd have to leave that last part out, but still. "Do this?"

I put one hand on Silas' chest, right over a tattoo of a blackbird, and dragged it down the firm hard muscles of his body while he watched, running his tongue along the curve of his lower lip.

The need to mate was riding me *hard,* maybe even harder than the day of the Hunt.

At the last moment, I skirted Silas' cock and grabbed his left hand instead, lifting it up and placing it on the vampire bite. I'd intended to try for a little more of that healing magic, but as soon as his fingers touched my skin, I lost it.

With a snarl I leaned into him, crushing our naked bodies together, my wolf rippling beneath the surface, pacing like a caged animal. My mouth pressed up tight to Silas', stealing a kiss from him a split second before his arms wrapped around me and he was lifting me up on the edge of the sink.

His cock pressed up against the swollen wetness of my core, making me feel like I was burning up from the inside. The bite throbbed, pumping pheromones through my blood, making me feel like an animal in heat.

Silas took over the kiss, sliding his tongue against mine, working his mouth against my own with a barely suppressed frenzy that I knew had been brewing between us for *years.* There was a reason I'd decided to share my first kiss with this boy.

Mm.

With this man?

Because he'd definitely grown into a beautiful man.

Silas dragged his hand down from my neck, smearing

blood across my shoulder, down my arm. My lips parted in a gasping moan as he slid his inked fingers over my breast, kneading the pale flesh with his colorful ones.

I arched my back into him, squeezing him between my thighs, encouraging him to push forward, to fill me up with the long, hard length of his cock.

"We should probably slow down," he started, but I growled at him and he growled back. "Fuck it." Silas reached between us, curling his fingers around the base of his shaft and guiding himself into my opening.

It was like *magic* between us, the feel of him inside of me like that.

"Holy shit," Silas groaned, letting his head fall back so I could kiss the tattooed sides of his throat. It didn't escape my realization that this was his first time. A harem of virgins, that's what I'd been given at the Bonding. It was a strange thought, that, but I didn't have time to contemplate it.

"I trust you, Silas," I told him, putting my palms on either side of his face. His gold gaze fell to mine, giving me a brief glimpse into his soul, all those feelings he kept bottled up inside. "You won't keep anything from us again?"

"Never," he whispered, putting his hand on the back of my head and giving me a kiss that curled my toes and made my body clench with need. Silas groaned and then licked the side of my mouth, like a wolf.

Speaking of wolf ...

"Silas," I started, but I didn't know quite how to say it.

Putting a palm on his chest, between the two bloody prints Che had left, I pushed him back a step and he groaned, sliding out of me with a snarl playing on his lips.

"Oh, fuck, Zara," he whispered as I slid off the edge of the sink and turned around, sweeping bloodred hair over one shoulder and glancing back at him. "Like this?" he asked, sounding both shocked and *thrilled* at the same time.

"Like this," I said, my breathing coming in these frantic, angsty bursts. When this was over, I was going to be embarrassed as hell—I was sure of it. But even though my actions were motivated by the bite, my intentions were pure.

"I wish I had words to describe what I'm feeling right now," he whispered, his voice this rough, sexy growl that had my tongue playing across my lips, my nipples pebbling to hard points. Silas stepped up close to me, taking hold of my hip with one hand using the other to find my opening again, sliding into me with a relieved groan.

The sensation of him fucking me from behind was so different that I almost lost it right there, nails curling against the sides of the sink as I looked up and found my face, so very different than what I was used to seeing in the mirror.

I looked like a goddess.

A lupine moon goddess.

My pupils were big and dark, bleeding into the purple-black color of my eyes, lids heavy and drooping. My mouth was swollen and red and my pulse was dancing like a wild bird. I leaned back into Silas as he took hold of my other hip and began to move, filling me with long, easy strokes, like he'd done this plenty of times before. I knew he hadn't though. No, what I was feeling was pure instinct.

My breasts swung with the movement and my head drooped, red hair pooling in the sink as I struggled to stay standing upright. When Silas' hand came around and found my clit? I was shocked. Pleasure arced through me, a fireworks display that lit up my brain and drew these *noises* from me that I'd never expected to make, not in a million years.

"I can feel it, Zara," he snarled, but I was already there, climaxing over a bathroom sink at the University of Oregon. Wow. What a strange life I led. My body locked down on Silas' and brought him to orgasm just a few messy moments after my own.

We stood there, still locked together, trying to catch our collective breath.

"Zara Wolf," Silas said, his voice heavy and thick and full of male satisfaction. It would've annoyed me if I hadn't glanced up and found the same expression on my face, feminine satisfaction written into every inch.

"Silas Wolf," I said as he pulled away with a groan and I quickly made my way to the toilet. It wasn't pretty, but it was a fact of life. "Bring me some clothes," I told him, feeling the memory of his body against mine, warm and hard and wild.

Silas did as I asked, handing me a pair of sweats, a tank top, and even a bra and panties.

"Thank you," I told him, taking the stack and looking up into his face.

First, sex.

Now, vampires.

I just had to figure out a clever way to clean up the *rest* of Silas' mess.

Montgomery dragged the vampire's bloody body from the back of the SUV and threw him over his shoulder like a sack of flour.

"Jax, do a quick sniff and see if there are any hikers or backpackers out here," I said, putting my hands on my hips and looking around the empty parking lot. We'd taken the Yukon to a remote area on the far side of the national forest, far enough away from the edge of pack property that we *should* be able to get through this interrogation without Nikolina or any of her guards sniffing us out.

I tried to keep my back straight, head up, but I felt lazy and warm and sated. My wolf wanted to curl into a ball next to Silas and tuck her head under his chin. I was wearing sweats and a tank, my feet bare, my body *throbbing* with desire. The sex had stripped the vampire bite from my neck, but somehow, it hadn't taken the lust from my blood.

It'd only amped it up.

"How long do you think the werewolf blood sustains them?" Aeron asked from behind me. I glanced over my shoulder at her, my lips set into a frown. I didn't really *want* her around for this, but I supposed if she was claiming to be our ally, then this was as good a test as any. The fact that Julian was missing … it wasn't going to be a secret that his disappearance was our doing anyway. "Maybe we should just chain him up, leave him in the sun, and see how long it takes before his flesh starts to melt off?"

I looked at the faerie princess and raised a brow.

"Maybe," I said, reaching up and pushing bloodred strands of hair from my face. "But only after we get the information we need from him." I should've been weirded out by the rictus grin spreading across Aeron's face, but I was more concerned with the strange, tense nature of the boys around me.

They worked to get the wooden cuffs and chair out of the back of the Yukon, the ones we'd picked up from the Pairing House earlier, in complete silence. The tension was palpable enough to cut with a knife.

"Silas and I mated," I said, feeling like a broken record. *Nic and I mated; Che and I mated; Silas and I mated.* "If you need to talk about it, then just say something instead of moping around."

I think I was speaking more to Che than anyone else, but it was Anubis who turned to look at me, his blue-black hair spiked up in all sorts of random directions.

"I think we'd like to hear from Silas what, exactly, it was that he knew. In regards to his father, I mean." He paused, glanced away, and licked his lips. "Alpha," he added respectfully. It was cute, seeing him act all formal when he was dressed so casually in jeans and a tight red tank with black Japanese symbols on the front of it. "Your wisdom is unquestioned—"

"Not by you," Che said, pausing to look at me like *I* was the worst kind of traitor there was. Silas was on my right, leaning against the SUV with his arms crossed in front of him, staring at the pine needle covered pavement, spots of snow still staining the ground, even *with* the bright spring sunshine beaming down on us. "But I question it."

"Do you now?" I asked, staring him down and ignoring Aeron's chuckles behind me.

"Thank you, Darkest Deeps, for blessing me with an immunity to this nonsense," is what I *think* she said, but I had no idea what that meant so I ignored it. For now. After this was over, I'd have to have a talk with her. I couldn't have a faerie girl clinging to my fur when there was so much other shit to deal with. Besides, the glamour she was wearing was *strong,* so strong that I was damn near certain that she didn't make it.

To trick a wolf's nose?

That had to be queen's work.

"Silas, tell him what you told me," I said, staring at Che and hate, hate, hating that he was refusing to break eye contact with me. Much longer and I'd *have* to put him on his back.

"I knew my father was involved with the missing pack members. I didn't know how or why or what he was doing to them, only that *he* knew, that he was partially responsible somehow." Silas dragged a finger over his scar out of habit.

"That's it. He's threatened to kill me—and all of you—if Zara doesn't pick me at the end of the Pairing Year. Beyond that, I don't know. I don't know fucking anything."

"Yeah," Che said with a skeptical laugh, leaning his head back and digging his fingers through his dark hair. "You knew so little you had to kill a guy to keep him quiet."

"I lost it," Silas whispered, but his anger seemed to be under control. When I glanced over and met his gold gaze, sparks flickered through my body. Yes. A natural response to stress was a coupling. *In that case, I probably need a good dozen or more orgasms to even my mood out ...* "I just lost it. I saw my dad's face written all over Julian's smirk, and I flipped. I know I made a mistake, and I'm sorry."

I caught Nic's expression from across the parking lot, his beautiful, stern face silhouetted against a sea of fir trees, oaks, pines and spruces. He scowled and turned back to the task at hand, clamping Julian's pale, floppy wrist to the wooden chair he was slumped in.

Montgomery was on his other side, back stiff, shoulders tense.

"I knew my father was involved with the missing pack members."

That statement was probably getting to him, I was sure of it.

"Doesn't cut it for me," Che said, shaking his head and dropping his chin to look at me again. "Not by a long shot. I feel like I just sat around and waited for *my* alpha female to mate with a traitor."

"Your female?" Silas said, and if the sex had calmed him

down in regards to the anger issue … it'd revved him all the way up with this one. He stood up from his slouch and turned fully to face Che.

"*My* female," Che repeated, lifting his lips in a snarl.

"Enough!" I shouted, my voice echoing around the quiet, snow drenched forest. It was just us in this tiny parking lot at the end of a dirt road with nothing but an outhouse and some picnic tables for company. I let myself scream *loud.* And when I was done shouting, I curled my hands into fists, my nostrils flaring wide, and I panted with adrenaline. "We have enough enemies as it is. Why make more? We're supposed to work together."

I put a hand to my chest and closed my eyes.

I could feel Tidus ahead and to my right, Jaxson padding up behind me on quiet paws, Anubis standing next to the SUV and biting his lip. Nic and Montgomery kept on task, making sure that when we removed the wooden knife, and Julian woke up as an undead vampire, that he'd be perfectly immobile. The eight of us—and Aeron—could take him on, but it wasn't a fight I wanted to have if I could help it.

I'd had about enough action for one day.

Well, enough of *one* kind of action. I supposed I was open to some more of the other kind, the naked, sweaty, sexy kind …

"You all feel like you're *mine,*" I said with a slight curl of my lips, letting the wolf into my voice before I opened my eyes and looked around at each boy in turn. "Mine." It was a simple, animalistic concept that I knew they'd understand. Because we weren't human, we were fucking *werewolf.* "My males." I let out a long, low breath. "So if you think of me the same way, as your female, then you should know that when you fight, it hurts." I nodded and dropped my hand to my side. "It hurts me, more than it hurts either of you."

I padded between them, feet sloshing in half-melted snow, and made my way over to Julian.

The entire clearing was silent as death.

Fitting, I supposed, as I looked down at a corpse.

Reaching out to take hold of the knife's wooden hilt, I yanked it hard and spattered black blood across the front of my shirt and sweats.

The boys got up close to me, creating a circle around the vampire. Jax had shifted back to human form, his naked body pressed up almost against mine on the right side. Nic was on my left, and then it went Che, Anubis, Montgomery, Tidus, and Silas. They all stayed quiet, thank Mother fucking Earth. I guess my words had had their intended effect—they seemed chagrined.

"How much longer until he wakes up?" Tidus asked a few minutes later, his voice reverent and low, completely different than his usual bubbly tone.

"Fifteen minutes, give or take," Anubis whispered, and then we all stood and waited, attention focused on Julian and not much else. Aeron stood off to the side, leaning against a tree with her human glamour so smack-on that I kept scenting human and getting little thrills of alarm. It made me wonder how many times I'd encountered a fae in disguise in the past. Hopefully not many.

I could only guess that glamours made by a faerie queen were expensive … and the fae did not pay for things in any sort of reasonable currency. They paid in blood and bone, death and suffering, sex and favors.

"T-minus thirty seconds," Anubis said after a while, checking the phone in his pocket and then looking up at me. I took a deep breath, crossed my arms under my breasts, and waited.

When Julian did come to, it was with a gasp of startled shock, jerking awake in the chair with a scream of rage. He thrashed against his restraints, snapping at the air in front of him like an animal, yowling like a demon, his brown eyes flashing a cherry red that was probably his true color, underneath the thin glamour he'd been wearing.

"You bitch!" he screamed at me, which was not a particularly creative insult to throw at a female werewolf. "What have you done? You fucking *cunt*."

"Address my Alpha like that again and I'll have your throat," Anubis snarled, grabbing a handful of Julian's hair and yanking his head back. "Show some respect." The wood seared the back of the vampire's head and he shrieked in agony, his voice echoing through the swells and valleys of the forest.

We'd put him in a relatively shaded area, and vampires were certainly slow to burn, so it'd be a while before we got to see exactly how long-lasting werewolf blood really was.

"Julian," I said carefully, as his brown hair faded to a strange silver color, the cheap glamour flaking off like it'd never been. That wasn't the important part of his disguise.

No, the glamour was weak, possibly even made by a vampire instead of a witch. It changed his hair and eye color, sure, but it was the witch hazel and the wolf blood that really disguised him, hid him in plain sight. "How do you know Silas?" I asked, and not because I doubted my new lover's words, but because I wanted the rest of the men to hear it directly from the horse's mouth.

"Fuck!" Julian yelled out, sagging in the seat as the wood drew his strength out of him and left welts across his remaining wrist and both ankles. Only his bloody clothing kept the rest of his skin from searing against the chair. His left arm was still missing, but that didn't seem to bother him much. If he drained a human or two of blood, it'd grow right back. "Where the fuck am I?"

"How do you know Silas?" I asked again, gesturing to the Alpha-Son of Pack Obsidian Gold. "You greeted him by name this morning. I'd like to know how you two became acquainted."

"Tell him you'll cut his cock off if he doesn't answer!" Aeron called out with a disturbingly enthusiastic chuckle. She was of Faerie after all, and the fae, well … they reveled in torture. It was an art form to them.

"I don't know Silas," Julian said, looking around the group as best he could from his position in the poisonous chair. Staring down at him like this, helpless and shackled, I almost felt sorry for him. I had a feeling he really was around our age, maybe eighteen or so. If he hadn't murdered our teacher right in front of me, I'd have probably been sympathetic. "I just know his dad."

Che scowled and looked away, but he didn't say anything.

"How is Allister involved in this shit?" I asked, hoping this interrogation would go smoothly. I did *not* want to cut some kid's dick off to get answers.

"Really?" Julian asked, sniffling and glancing down at his missing arm like he'd literally *just* noticed it was gone. The arm itself was lying on the ground about three feet from where we were standing. It was morbid as hell, that was for sure. "You think I'm going to sit here and spill all my secrets? Don't be ridiculous."

Julian's tongue traced over his lips, probably searching for more of my blood. Too bad for him we'd wiped it all off ahead of time.

"It's that or we kill you," I told him with a sad side smile.

"Aren't you going to kill me anyway?" he snapped, literally *snapped* his teeth like a rabid dog. "What does it matter if I talk?"

Montgomery pulled a wooden knife from his belt, reminding me that I needed to either have a new one made or dig one up out of the Ebon Red weapon stores. There was an entire building on pack land that was filled with weapons, artifacts, old spells, and 'were' history. It was hardly used anymore, but always on twenty-four hour watch.

Werewolves didn't often need weapons; we *were* weapons.

"Actually, no," I said as Monty came around the outside

of the circle and Jax moved swiftly out of his way. "I'd prefer if you had a frank discussion with us and then took a message home to your queen."

"Puh-lease," Julian said as Montgomery knelt down in front of the chair, his black trench coat fluttering around his feet as he reached out and put one long fingered hand over the vampire's. "I'm not a fucking moron. I'm not leaving this chair alive."

"No," I said as Montgomery flicked his emerald eyes up to me. "But you might leave it as one of the undead if you cooperate." I nodded my head ever so slightly, watching as Monty's carefully crafted facade fractured into small pieces, revealing the cool, icy rage underneath.

His family was missing.

And he wanted them back.

"You cut pieces off our wolves," he said, so quiet I could barely hear him, adjusting his gaze to look up into Julian's red-eyed stare. "And you *ate* them. You tried to make *us* eat them."

The vampire didn't flinch, holding my mate's gaze with a steady, seething anger.

"So now, I'm going to cut pieces off of you. For each question you *don't* answer, I'm going to take my pound of flesh." Montgomery lifted the knife up, this short shining piece of wood that shouldn't rightfully be able to cut anything, and used it to cleanly slice off the very tip of Julian's middle finger.

I didn't know the entirety of the science behind it, but something about the raw, earthy nature of wood was anathema to a vampire. It sliced through them like a warm knife through butter, and it was the only known way to kill an undead. Even flames couldn't be counted on to completely eliminate an Ageless undead Blood—if the fire didn't sever their head, there was a chance they'd regenerate.

'I don't know if I can watch this,' Tidus said, taking in a long, deep breath. *'I can handle violence when I have to, but torture?'* He exhaled and closed his stormy gray eyes for a moment.

Julian though, he barely flinched—and neither did Montgomery.

"How is Allister involved in this?" I repeated, not wanting to give away too much of what I knew. *We* knew the vampires were daywalkers because they were drinking wolf blood, but they didn't necessarily know that we were aware of that. The witches had purposely revealed their cards with the Ebon Red flesh, but the vamps had only accidentally let a certain amount of information slip. That was what I needed to play off of.

"Allister Vetter," Julian said, watching the tip of his finger bleed black blood over the wooden arm of the chair. In a minute or less, it'd stop and heal over, just like the wound on his shoulder. But to actually grow it back, he'd need to drink blood. And lots of it. In fact, if his injuries were severe enough, only the blood of the dying would suffice. "That idiot was right, wasn't he? You smelt the wolfsbane."

"Wrong," I said, crossing my arms over my chest and looking up just in time to meet Tidus' eyes when he reopened them. “I tasted it.”

'If you want to leave, you can go,' I told him, making sure to project my voice to the rest of the alpha pack. *'I won't hold it against you.'*

Nobody moved and after a while, I realized that no matter how horrible this became, they would stay.

“Allister Vetter,” I repeated and Julian leaned back, smirking at me.

“It bothers you, doesn't it? Knowing that one of your own is the orchestrator of this whole mess? Coven Triad didn't go to him; he sought them out.” Julian grinned as he said it, and I knew this was a confession compelled out of him less by torture and more by arrogant glee. He wanted to see me react. “Not everyone's as excited about this new pack structure as you are, Ebon Red.”

I didn't engage, just stood there and watched him as the trees above us ruffled and fluttered in the afternoon breeze. Tiny spots of sunlight caught on Julian's skin and he watched them with a nervous flick of his tongue over his lips.

Too long in the sun, and he would burn nice and slow. Eventually, his neck and head would separate and he'd die, but it would be long and drawn-out and painful. I stepped aside to let a shaft of sunlight cut across his face and he flinched.

“Kingdom Ironbound,” I said, just to gauge his reaction. He was staring up and over my shoulder at the blue sky and the golden eye of the sun with a wariness that told me he wasn't quite as used to his daywalking abilities as he pretended to be. "Crown Aurora."

Julian slid his attention from the sun to my face and smirked.

"What's the connection between the two?" I continued.

"Eat shit, you arrogant bitch. You and your idiot mother really think the other packs are going to roll over and accept you as alpha? That's a fucking pipe dream."

Anubis grabbed a handful of the vampire's hair again and slammed his skull into the wood with a sickening crack that I couldn't quite identify as wood … or bone.

"Crown Aurora," I said, very carefully, putting a single hand on Montgomery's shoulder. I took zero fucking pleasure in Julian's plight, but my people were being kidnapped, drained, *eaten.* Goddamn fucking eaten. And who knew what else was happening while they were in captivity. Rape? Starvation? Torture? I'm sure what we were doing to Julian now was nowhere *near* what my people were suffering.

Montgomery's father, mother … his little sisters. Fucking *pups.*

"Tell me what their involvement in this is about? I know Ironbound has been kidnapping wolves and selling them to Coven Triad for the daywalking potion"—total lie, but I didn't want to give away all that we knew in case someone else was listening—"but what's Crown Aurora's hand in all this?"

"Hand?" he asked with a sharp, manic sounding laugh. I kept my gaze trained on his face, studying each twitch of his brows, the wrinkling of his mouth, the blinking of his eyes.

A good portion of communication is relayed through body language, and there aren't many species—Numinous or human—that are as good at reading it as a werewolf. "They don't have a hand in shit. They're *nothing.* Some piece of shit family of backwoods cousin fuckers."

I knelt down next to Montgomery and looked up into Julian's face.

"If they're nothing, then why are you so angry with them?"

The vampire moved to spit in my face, but I had superhuman speed, too, and I simply moved out of the way. With a fresh meal in his tummy, time to heal, and a little training, he could probably match me … or with enough years, kick my ass. For now, I was much faster.

"If you're looking for an ally in Crown Aurora, you're *barking* up the wrong tree, bitch. They won't work with anyone for *any* reason. A mountain of gold couldn't sway them. Go to their door and try if you want; they don't want or care about what we have. They'll slit your throats like they did to my cousins and they won't bat a damn lash."

"Cut his whole finger off," I said aloud, and then in wolfspeak added, *'don't actually do it; follow my cues.'*

Julian just flared his nostrils at me and wrinkled his lips up enough that I could see the sharpness of his canines peeking out.

"Do it," he challenged, narrowing his eyes at me, the scent of mint and apples hanging heavy and cloying in the air. Now that he was undead, that smell would slowly mature into a deeper, darker smell, like the heavy wetness of decaying leaves. "It doesn't matter anyway. I was dead the moment your boyfriend lost his shit."

Julian let his lids fall closed and leaned his head back against the wooden chair, ignoring the burn of the wood against his neck and scalp. I had to wonder as I watched him, what his purpose had been all along. To get close to me? To keep an eye on me at school? Or had he made a serious error in letting me escape yesterday?

It was a mistake that might be worth his life.

If there'd been other vampires on campus—a definite possibility with the witch hazel—then they hadn't followed us in an effort to save their colleague, hadn't jumped in when Silas had attacked him in the hall.

They'd left him for dead.

"That's enough," I said to Montgomery, moving my hand to his head and resting my palm on the crown of his shock-white hair. It was even paler, even more pure, than the piles of virgin snow dotting the shadowy forest floor. "He's not going to tell us anything else." I pursed my lips tight. *'Move slow, play along,'* I added in wolfspeak. And then … "Kill him and bury his body in the woods."

"Yes, Alpha," Montgomery said, standing up and moving behind Julian with the wooden knife.

The vampire didn't move, didn't open his eyes, but he *did* move his lips.

"Dark Goddess watch over me," he whispered, and I saw then that he really was prepared to die to protect his Kingdom's secrets. I waited, watching as Monty put the knife to the daywalker's exposed throat …

"Let's give him a message and send him on his way," I said, just as the front of the blade drew a trickle of blood from Julian's neck. A hot crimson drop slid down his skin and mixed with the red spatter from our earlier fight.

Julian cracked his eyes and smiled wickedly at me.

"Letting me go," he said as he ran his tongue over his lips. "Would be a *huge* mistake on your part."

"Would it?" I asked with a smile of my own. "Oh well. I guess it's my mistake to make then. Go home, tell your queen that I want my people back and that I'm willing to negotiate. I'll expect you to bring me her answer on Monday, in the math building's study lounge. If I don't get one, I'll assume she's more interested in a full-scale war."

I stepped back and crossed my arms over my chest.

'That's what they want, isn't it?' Jax asked as Monty sheathed his knife and Aeron watched the whole play-through with that dark, mysterious gaze of hers. *'A war? Coven Triad didn't make you eat the flesh of your own people because they wanted to* talk.*'*

'You're right,' I said as Montgomery carefully opened the wooden shackles and stepped back. The rest of the boys followed suite and we all watched as Julian fell forward with a groan and *crawled* away from us on his hands and knees, careful to avoid the bright shafts of sunshine. *'I think they want us to come after them with everything we've got, full force. Clearly there's already a plan in play here. That's why Nikolina and the alphas ... they can't find out about this.'*

I watched Julian go and I hoped the 'message' I sent

actually bought us *more* time rather than less. At any moment, Allister could tell the rest of the North American Convocation what he knew. How he'd explain *how* he knew was another story, but he could get the cavalry moving before I had a chance to stop the avalanche.

'Sending Julian with this message should buy us the rest of the week to figure this out. If they think we're already committing to war, then that should keep Allister from moving when we're not ready.'

I took a deep breath and glanced over at Montgomery.

He was shaking. It was slight, but I could see the waver in his hands and fingers. I wondered if I'd made a mistake by letting him put his knife to Julian?

“Let's go home,” I said as I backed away and turned, starting across the wet, icy pavement with my heart in my throat.

Vampires, witches, faeries … and boy trouble.

It was hard to say which of those was the worst.

We took the back road through pack property and showered off first thing when we got to the house, then scrubbed down the SUV and burned our clothes before Nikolina or Majka could come sniffing around. There was still a very good chance that they'd smell the overwhelming stink of vampire blood, but I had an excuse ready, another lie tucked into the deep recesses of my mind, ready to be wielded at a moment's notice.

I didn't want lying to become a skill of mine … but it looked like it was well on its way to being honed.

If only I could find a trustworthy witch as a contact. I would kill for some of that witch hazel in my life, I thought as I leaned back in the wooden rocking chair on the Pairing House porch and stared at the forest. I *could* call the Maiden—Whitney was her name, wasn't it?—and ask if she'd be willing to supply us some, but I couldn't figure out her angle and that bothered me. What kind of witch goes against their own coven? Considering their species seemed inclined to consume the flesh of my own, it was rather unlikely I'd find a true ally in any member of Coven Triad.

"Lucky you with all those mates," Aeron purred as she came up the porch steps and stared down at me, glamour in place, dark hair braided and hanging over one shoulder. She smiled at me with a wicked twist of lips. "Must be nice, having all those males around to slake your thirst."

"Ready to tell me what you're doing here?" I asked with a sigh.

Part of me was … well, fucking *thrilled* at what'd happened with Silas. The rest of me was a mess. Not only had my mate attacked a vampire on a campus literally *crawling* with humans, but he'd also made me and Nic miss a day of class.

That was going to be a definite hit to both our grades.

"I told you," she repeated, sitting down in the chair next to me and folding her hands neatly in her lap. "My mother kicked me out for trying to help you."

"The Unseelie Queen," I said slowly, the creak of my rocking chair a lullaby that mixed with the sweet songs of the forest. "Kicked you out … out of where?" I glanced over at her, trying not to look at the guys who'd been on SUV cleaning duty as they shuffled past me and into the house.

Somehow, I managed to snag Silas' eye and felt my breath catch.

He even paused on the deck and tucked his fingers into the pockets of the jeans he'd borrowed out of the duffel bag. They were even tighter on him than usual. I think Nic was a bit skinnier than Silas.

"That date," he said after a moment, exhaling and raking

his fingers through his espresso-brown hair. "Is the offer still open?"

I forced my lips into a smile and felt my heart beating rapidly inside my chest. *Oh, God. I just had sex in a bathroom?! Faith is going to freak all the way out.*

"You know it is," I said quietly as Che walked by and purposely used his shoulder to knock Silas out of the way. The Obsidian Gold Alpha-Son snarled at the screen door as it swung shut behind his rival, but didn't move off the porch. "Just as soon as I hear back from Aurora."

After what'd just happened at the university, a meeting with the Crown Aurora Blood Queen was absolutely vital. I'd sent Nic's mom, Lana—who was tentatively assigned as my guard, even though I didn't actually need one with the boys around—with word and hoped that she really did care more about her son and me than she did Nikolina. Her loyalty should be to the alpha, but I was technically next in line. I trusted her as much as I trusted anyone outside the circle of my mates.

Montgomery's pack had disappeared in Ironbound territory; Coven Triad didn't want us to know about Kingdom Kindred. The rest of the disappearances were scattered so randomly, it was hard to say who else might be involved. More than one Blood Kingdom sure, but if Crown Aurora wasn't in on it, it didn't seem to be a coup.

At least, I hoped not.

I had no idea what the Blood to wolf ratio was in the United States, but with the Coven on their side? The odds weren't good.

I *needed* to ensure that Crown Aurora was as against Ironbound as we were. And I had to find a way to manipulate them into helping us without revealing the fact that our blood was a magic rich elixir that allowed them to walk in the daylight.

Fuck my life.

"Pick a place," I told him, ignoring the sideways smirk on Aeron's face. "And we'll make a night of it."

Silas' nostrils flared and he nodded, giving me a look that said he was desperate to talk, but giving me the space I needed anyway.

"Juggling seven lovers," Aeron said after he went inside, her voice a liquid purr that brought to mind nightmares and freshly dug graves. Her people were, after all, stewards of the dead and dying, a home to unwashed souls and wicked hearts. "It's hard, but not impossible. My mother has ten men in her harem."

"It's not a harem," I said, leaning my head back against the wood of the rocking chair, flaring my nostrils to take in the scents of the forest.

"It's not?" Aeron asked, her laughter like rough nails raking down my spine, painful but almost … pleasurable at the same time. This girl was terrifying. "It sure seems like it is. You have seven males in your stable, ready to mate, willing to die to protect you. A harem."

"Where, exactly, have you been kicked *from*?" I repeated and felt the shift in mood, like a cold, wet fog rolling in from nowhere. I opened my eyes and looked over at the princess of the Unseelie court, her sloe-eyes downcast, ebon colored hair draped over her nearly exposed breasts. The dress she was wearing was as thin as fog, that was for sure. As soon as we'd gotten back to the house, she'd stolen a party dress Faith had bought me and that I'd never worn, and slipped into it. "Your house?"

"From Faerie," she snapped at me, flashing teeth as she turned a rictus snarl my direction. "I was banished across the Veil for trying to help you."

I blinked at her and curled my fingers around the knees of my lint covered sweats.

My body felt … like it'd come awake recently, welcomed this new phase of my life as a sexual being with open arms. I wanted *more.* Having sex with Silas hadn't quenched my thirst; it'd made it *worse.*

I'm horny, I thought, and the idea might've made me giggle if I hadn't just been told by fae royalty that she'd been banished from her own kingdom.

"Why would your mother banish you?" I asked, trying to puzzle my way through this nightmare. "If what's happening to my people is such a big deal for yours, how could she possibly ignore the threat?"

"She doesn't think it *is* a threat," Aeron told me, leaning forward, the gauzy dress drifting in the wind and sticking to her calves. "She believes you'll all kill each other, that it won't end the way I *know* it will. You saw the bones, Alpha-Heir. The dead don't lie."

I exhaled sharply and stood up from the seat, noticing that Jax was standing at the edge of the clearing, his face lifted, nostrils flaring as he took in a scent.

“Complete destruction or total salvation, right?” I said as I glanced down at Aeron.

“I have to be on your side,” she said, following my gaze over to Jax. “Because I know my skills at divination; I'm never wrong.”

“And the queen doesn't agree?” I asked, feeling myself get tense. The longer Jax stood there, listening, waiting, the more anxious I got.

'What is it?' I asked him, starting toward the steps of the porch and pausing with one hand resting against the wood column. The lavender bushes perfumed the air with a sweet scent, but when I lifted my own head up, too, I could smell it.

The metallic scent of *witch.*

“The queen is a fool,” Aeron called out as the screen door opened and Montgomery came stalking out, pulling a bone knife from his belt. “But I am *not*!”

'It's the Maiden,' Jax said as I headed down the steps and started tearing my clothes off. I ripped the t-shirt over my head, stumbled and kicked my way out of the sweats and panties. The bra was the last thing to go and let me tell you, it was quite the feat to unbuckle it while running.

Across the grass I sprinted, shifting as I went, letting the change roll over me in a warm, hot wave. My paws tore across the earth, Montgomery right behind me, Jax taking up my other side when I raced past him.

'Stay here,' I told the other boys, weaving my way through the trees toward the smell. If I didn't get there soon, my mother and her betas would. It was bad enough that we

had a fae on the property. But a witch, too?

If Nikolina found out about this, she'd kill them both.

We hit the edge of the property and found Whitney waiting, standing just outside the legal border of my mother's land, on the national park side. Technically she *wasn't* on pack property, but werewolves aren't much for technicalities.

"You never called," she said as I came to a skidding stop, kicking up mud and pine needles. I shifted right away and stood there panting, raking bloodred hair back with shaking fingers. As I watched, the Maiden pulled out a small spray bottle from her leather jacket and doused herself in witch hazel.

Within seconds, her scent was gone, scrubbed like it'd never been.

My wolf growled and shifted inside of me. She didn't like that, didn't understand it. Smell made the world real; scent was a powerful motivator. And something with no smell? She didn't know what to do with that.

"What are you doing here?" I asked her, panting and trying my best to catch my breath.

'Are you alright?' Nic asked, speaking for the rest of the boys I'd left at the house. *'Do you need us?'*

'We're okay,' I told him, putting my hand on the top of Montgomery's snow-white head. He was lighter than Jax, a stark white without a single drip of gray, black or brown. A true white wolf—unlike me with my red and black speckles.

"I'm glad you figured out the trick with the map," she said on the end of a long sigh, pulling out a pack of cigarettes and lighting one up. I wrinkled my nose and both Jax and Montgomery growled in frustration. The stink of tobacco polluted the air and blocked the sweet smells of the forest from all of us. "The Crone was not pleased."

"Why the hell are you here?" I asked her, throwing up a hand in frustration. After the day I'd had, I was just about tapped out. All I wanted to do was collapse in bed and sleep away the rest of the week. That was *never* going to happen, but I could grab an hour or two, couldn't I? "And please don't tell me you got kicked out."

"Kicked out?" she asked, her voice even, almost husky. I had to admit, she looked pretty fucking cool in her dark blue lipstick and black pointed hat, a pink sheath dress and brown boots. Her ebony skin was painted with little silver sigils that glimmered when she moved. "No, not exactly. I'm just … trying to save my people, same way you're saving yours."

She locked her eyes on mine, taking a long, slow drag on her cigarette.

I narrowed my own eyes and crossed my arms over my bare chest, not at all ashamed by my nudity, not in Whitney's presence. The boys … well, I never felt *ashamed,* but was Jaxson checking out my ass? It was a little weird, considering he was in wolf form and all.

"Save them from what?" I asked, wondering how much Ebon Red or Ivory Emerald flesh she'd consumed. Maybe a lot … or maybe none at all. Because she was the Maiden, anything that she did that could be perceived as causing harm to others put her at risk. Did eating the flesh of a kidnapped werewolf count against that? I sure as hell hoped so. "Being eaten? Oh, no, wait, that was *my* people."

"Yes, well," Whitney said, ashing her cigarette on the forest floor, little gray flakes floating like twisted snowflakes. "Seeing my people corrupted in the pursuit of power goes against everything I am, everything the Maiden represents. Harm to others extends beyond the walls of our coven. I can't sit by and watch the wolves harvested like chattel."

Whitney took a step forward and Jax let out a deep, angry snarl, warning her away from me.

"Relax, puppy," Whitney purred, glancing up as Aeron came around the trunk of a large spruce and crunched her way across snow and ice in feet as bare as my own. The way the witch girl watched the fae girl … was certainly interesting.

'They're lovers,' Montgomery said, reading their body language as easily as if the women had spoken their feelings aloud. He pressed his big white body against my leg, and I felt that pain and horror in our pack connection, the fear of knowing that each minute that ticked by, his family suffered.

I shouldn't have let him torture Julian … it'd been too much.

"Whit," Aeron said, sliding in close to the other girl and putting a single hand on her bare arm, smearing the silver sigils across the witch's skin.

'They can't be lovers,' I said, licking my lower lip. *'The Maiden is bound to a life of chastity.'*

"Aeron," Whitney responded, holding her cigarette out

to the side and leaning in toward the faerie princess. They closed the distance between their lips like they were in the middle of a sensual slow dance, heavy half-lidded eyes closing, their bodies quaking with strain and want and ardor. When they finally did touch, the kiss was closemouthed and full of quivering need, an achy brush of lips that looked like it might drive them both insane.

'Not physical lovers yet,*'* Jax corrected, sitting down next to me, pink tongue lolling from his mouth. *'But their dual involvement in our business suddenly makes a bit more sense.'*

"What's going on?" I asked aloud as the two girls broke apart and stared into one another's eyes for a long, quiet moment. When they both finally *did* turn and look at me, it was like they were drugged.

"What?" Aeron asked, pushing her glamoured black hair over one shoulder.

"How do you two know each other?" I asked, crossing my arms over my chest and hiding the hardened points of my nipples. It was *cold* out. That, and … seeing the two girls touch like that, knowing they couldn't take it any further without stripping Whitney of her position as the Maiden … it made me ache for the boys, crave their lips on mine, their hands on my skin, their cocks pushing between my thighs.

"I summoned Aeron across the Veil," Whitney said, ashing her cigarette again and taking another drag, the cherry burning bright in the quiet dark of the forest. "We made a deal for her to take me to Faerie and read the bones;

they can't be read this side of the Veil, you know? Dead don't often stick around this plane long enough to tell fortunes." She puffed on her cigarette, pulling the burn all the way down to the filter and flicking it aside. "And, well, we didn't expect to feel what we feel."

"You guys are into each other?" I asked.

Whitney flicked her gaze over to Aeron and took in a deep breath.

"More than that," she said, looking back at me. "But that's neither here nor there. I called on Aeron because I needed help. I see my coven diving into a black hole, and I don't know how to stop it. The …" She paused and closed her eyes for a moment. "The power we get from consuming the flesh of wolves is enormous. Your people have magic stored from centuries of living with the earth, coexisting against mother nature's breast."

Jax let out another growl as I dropped my hands again and touched both him and Monty, feeling our pack connection ground me to the spot. Helped keep my temper in check, that's for fucking sure.

"But it's not our magic to wield. Witchcraft is all about balance, of coexistence, of taking what the goddess gives us and being grateful for it. I've seen our destruction in Aeron's divinations. If we keep on this path, we'll suffer for it."

"So you're betraying your coven to keep them safe?" I asked and Whitney sighed.

"It's not a betrayal. You don't understand the power of the Crone," she whispered, looking straight at me; the fear in her eyes … it was very much real. I could *smell* it, even through the dousing of witch hazel. "I have to be careful about how I do this or I'll end up in her evening stew."

Montgomery shifted into human form beside me, panting slightly, his anxiety amping up all of a sudden.

Shit.

I curled my fingers through his and he squeezed my hand back hard enough that he might've broken something had I been human.

"She eats other witches?" he asked, voice quivering slightly. I looked up at his face, his white hair unbound and hanging in a sheet down his back. I wasn't really a fan of long hair on men, but on Montgomery, with that knightly persona of his … it worked. It worked really fucking well.

"What doesn't she eat?" Whitney asked, and I felt goose bumps crawl across my skin. "But yes, my statement was *literal.*"

"The wolves … my sisters …" Montgomery started, his voice an icy wind that chilled me to the bone. "Where are they? Are they dead?"

"A few wolves have died in our care," Whitney said carefully, letting Aeron curl her fingers around her upper arm. "But the Crone's been harvesting flesh and letting them heal for the most part."

"Where the fuck are they?" Montgomery growled, shaking all over by this point.

"I don't know. As the Maiden, I'm not privy to any sort of information that might compromise my standing in the Three—"

"*Fuck!*" Monty yelled, raking his fingers through his long hair. He turned away and punched a tree as hard as he could, breathing heavily through his nose. It was the first time I'd seen him break like this. True, I hadn't known him long, but in the last week we'd been through some serious shit and he'd stayed calm, composed.

Not now.

"I tried to divine their positions, but the fates could not answer," Aeron said as Whitney got out another cigarette.

"Wherever they're being held, I can promise the spellwork is top-notch, baby. Even you wouldn't be able to divine past that." Whitney put her arm around her … girlfriend's? … waist and pulled her close. "But that's not to say we're out of ideas. That's why I came here tonight. I need a way to contact you. *Call* me. I've put a spell on my phone. If you call it, all the words that leave your lips will sound like gibberish to any scrying ears."

I moved toward Montgomery and slid my arms around his waist, putting my cheek to his bare back. It was quite the intimate move for a human, but for a wolf … it was natural to touch in situations of high stress.

Monty turned in my arms and pulled me into his, giving me another hug like the one we'd shared inside Faith's shed. Only … we were naked this time and Montgomery was throbbing with adrenaline and rage. I could *feel* it.

He squeezed me as tightly as he'd squeezed my hand earlier, Jax's furry body pressing up against the backs of my calves. I decided to relax into it, despite our audience, and put my cheek to his chest, so I could look at the two girls across the snow spotted clearing.

In the shadows, both the witch and the fae girl looked like pretty nightmares.

"Call me so I have your number," Whitney repeated, reaching up to adjust her black pointed hat. "And I'll call you when I know what to do next."

"I just sent word to the Crown Aurora Blood Queen that I'd like a meeting," I said, searching Whitney's face for the truth. She could be full of shit, and so could Aeron. After finding out that a wolf—an *alpha* at that—was working for the enemy, I was feeling even less trusting than usual.

"Good idea," Whitney said, smoking her new cigarette. "When this all started, both our coven and Kingdom Ironbound sent reps over to speak with the Crowns. They killed every single witch and Blood in that entourage." She sighed like she was as tired as I was. Bone weary. That deep sense of fatigue that sneaks over and pulls you under whether you like it or not.

I listened to Montgomery's heartbeat as I watched the Coven Triad Maiden pull her girlfriend just a little bit closer. They had to walk a fine, strange line with that Maiden magic. I wasn't sure *what* exactly would break Whitney's connection to the Three, but I hoped they were being careful. Even with the restrictions placed on her by her position, being a part of the ruling coven council was far better than being a Maiden cast aside.

"Tell me about Allister," I said next and Whitney paused, dropping her face to look down at the forest floor. When she looked up at me again, I knew I was going to get it, the awful, horrible truth.

"The wolf?" she asked, but she already knew. "The Alpha Male of Pack Obsidian Gold," she said again, and I was glad that Silas wasn't here for this. I could barely handle the feelings tumbling out of Montgomery, all of that rage and sadness, that awful aching helplessness. It was taking over him, a dark wave of shadows and ice. "He was the one that brought your peoples' … *unique* abilities to our attention. The flesh … the blood … He made a contract with the Crone." Whitney paused and the edge of her blue painted mouth twitched. "Much like you did, although he didn't so effortlessly weasel out of his end."

Whitney glanced down at Aeron for a long moment, meeting the fae's eyes, and then looked up at me.

"We haven't been kidnapping 'weres', Zara Wolf. Allister Vetter and his people … they've been delivering them."

"I need to run," Montgomery told me at the bottom of the Pairing House porch steps.

Whitney was long gone, but we had an appointment to meet for coffee on Saturday. Aeron, on the other hand, was still here. Apparently, she had nowhere else to go. I'd have to figure out what to do with her later. Right now, I needed to deal with this first.

"You need to come inside and take a warm shower," I told him, putting my palms on either of his quivering biceps. Those emerald eyes of his were haunted and broken and full of rage. I hadn't realized, in all his easygoing affability, how much he was affected by everything that'd happened. He'd hid it so well, I hadn't felt it through our pack connection either.

Maybe if we'd had sex ... my mind inserted, but I wasn't sure if I was ready for that, after what'd happened between me and Silas earlier. There was so much going on, what I *really* needed was a moment in bed with a slice of yesterday's pizza, a cold beer, and a shitty background movie I wouldn't pay much attention to.

'How old are you?' I asked Che, sliding my palms down Montgomery's arms and guiding him gently toward the porch steps. He walked like a fucking zombie and that scared the hell out of me.

'Twenty-one, which is probably why you asked, right? What do you want? Vodka? Tequila? Bourbon?'

'Honestly? A cold beer would be really nice right now,' I said, and I felt him chuckle. *'There are places on Ebon Red property to grab alcohol—it's even brewed on-site—but I don't want to deal with anyone else tonight.'*

'Okay, Alpha-Red,' he said, his voice that deep, lovely purr, even in wolfspeak. And lucky me, there was only a *hint* of anger in there. *'I'll go buy your underage ass some booze.'*

'Only in the human world,' I replied coyly, because human laws were inconsequential to us. I was eighteen, far

older than necessary to enjoy a beer. There were no steadfast rules in the packs, but generally anyone over fifteen was allowed to make their own choices when it came to consuming alcohol.

Che came out of the Pairing House with Tidus and Anubis on his heels and watched as I pulled poor Montgomery up the steps to stand beside them.

"Can I get you anything at the store, man?" he asked, jiggling the SUV's keys in one hand. I wondered if he'd asked Nic before he'd grabbed them? The Yukon might've belonged to Pack Ebon Red—aka Nikolina—but since he was the only one who drove this particular one, he kind of considered it his. He wouldn't be happy to see Che Nocturne in the driver's seat.

"No, no … I just … I need to *run,*" Montgomery said again, and I felt the change ripple across his skin like wind across the surface of a pond. He stared down at me, but he wasn't really looking at me. He was too deep into the moment, letting it all catch up to him at once.

"Running helps," I told him, trying to get him to not just *look* at me, but to *see* me as well, "but not when you're trying to run *from* something you can't handle or *toward* something you can't change. Come inside, take a shower, and lie down in the big bed."

"How can I lie down when my sisters are being chopped up and put in a monster's stew? When somebody could take a knife, just like I did today, and cut my father's fingers off? How can I relax when I know they're suffering?" Montgomery licked his lower lip and made a low, soft growling sound in his throat, closing his brilliant green eyes for a long, quiet moment. "How, Zara?" he asked, and I swear, my heart broke into little pieces for him.

"Wars are not won by charging in tired, hungry, and broken." I put my hands on either side of the much taller werewolf's face and waited for him to open his eyes. When he did, they were at least clear enough that I knew he was listening to me. "Careful cunning, Monty. That's what's going to get us through this. Denying yourself basic needs won't lessen their suffering. Let's shower, eat, and rest up. By tomorrow, we should know if Aurora's accepted our request for a meeting."

"No need to wait," Nic said, coming out to join the rest of us on the porch. He tucked his hands in his pockets and gestured with his chin. I followed his gaze and saw the distant shape of an Ebon Red wolf loping toward us.

It was Lana.

"I'll go meet her so she doesn't accidentally sniff out that faerie girl," he said, running his tongue over his lower lip as he passed me by, purposefully brushing his body against mine. I still needed to address the whole *paramour* comment, but hell, I didn't know when I was supposed to find the time.

"We'll bring you some sour candy back," Anubis said carefully, like he'd really thought through his response. "That'll cheer you up, right Monty?"

"Wow, you really do take in a lot, don't you?" Montgomery said softly, smiling at Anubis for the briefest flash of a moment. "Thanks for remembering and … yeah, sour candy is good." He took my hand in his and pulled me toward the screen door, past the three boys left on the porch and inside.

"Sour candy, huh?" I asked as Montgomery guided us through the living room, into the study, and over to the large bathroom that seemed so out of place in such a small cabin. It'd been modified *specifically* for me and the boys. Now all the future generations that used the Pairing House would remember Zara Wolf and her seven mates.

"I like the way it burns," he told me as he twisted the knob for the hot water and then turned to glance over his shoulder. "But then it's sweet at the end. You know you shouldn't eat anymore because it'll hurt, but your mouth …" He looked right at mine when he said that. "It *craves* it. The saliva just … flows until everything's wet."

I stood there with my heart thundering in my chest, trying to decide if Montgomery was intentionally throwing innuendo my way, or if I were misreading him.

"I know so little about you," I told him, standing naked in the middle of a bathroom with a man I'd met only a week ago, but whose feelings and heart seemed to pound behind my rib cage in a thunderous rhythm. "How does Anubis know you like sour candy and I don't?"

"He asked," Montgomery said, turning and stepping backward into the shower until he was pressed against the tiled wall. Water ran in clear rivulets down his face, catching on his mouth, his jaw … and the hard length of his cock. He was definitely aroused. He hadn't been outside, but he was now.

"How old are you?" I asked, because I didn't even know that much about the guys, their ages. Not that it *really* mattered. Werewolves viewed time differently than humans. We lived longer, but we also matured earlier.

"Seventeen," Montgomery said, which made me blink a few times in shock.

"You're seventeen?" I asked, and he smiled. It wasn't quite a full smile, but at least it was something.

"Does that bother you? That I'm younger?"

I took a few steps closer and climbed into the shower with him, reaching for a bottle of shampoo and lathering up my hands with it. I worked the suds into my scalp as I stared the Alpha Son of Pack Ivory Emerald down, hot water spattering my legs.

"No."

"No?" he asked, tilting his head slightly to one side. He had the look of a knight, a warrior, the right hand of the queen. There was this trustworthy aura about him that I quite liked, *especially* after learning about Allister's betrayal.

I'd known since age sixteen that Silas' dad was a monster; I guess I just hadn't realized the extent he'd go to to prove that.

"Are you sure?" Montgomery asked, the sweet smell of cut grass and roses cutting through the light fragrance of my shampoo. As I stepped into the hot water, he reached out and curled his fingers around my wrists, pulling my hands away from my scalp. Without even touching my face, he somehow managed to get me to lift my chin up to his.

"Human law says we shouldn't touch until I turn eighteen."

"It's your body," I told him as he held my hands in place above my head and then gently but firmly pushed them into the wall behind me, pinning me there. "What do you think?"

"You talked about basic needs on the porch," he said, and I could see where this was going. He wanted to mate to forget, to release his tension and his rage. I was okay with that … just not yet. Not yet. With Montgomery, I wanted our first time to be something earned, something he *craved,* and not just something he gave into. I wanted him slow and rhythmic and attentive. "Was this what you meant?"

He leaned down and pressed our mouths together, the hot slick of water between our lips adding an extra layer of sensation that thrilled me from my head down to my toes. I hadn't realized I was so cold before this moment—and not from the weather, surely, but the awful revelation that one of our own, a *leader* amongst our people, was at the root of their disappearances.

Montgomery's kiss was deep and long, a single sweep of tongue that seemed to last forever. He pressed in close to me, our bodies brushing so lightly together that it was almost torture. I wanted to tear my arms from his grip and throw them around his neck, let him pick me up and mate me against this wall … but I also wasn't going to let that happen, not like this.

"I won't let you fuck away the pain," I whispered when our mouths parted just the smallest fraction of an inch. "It wouldn't be fair to either of us, not for our first time together."

He stared at me for a long moment and then carefully released my arms from above my head, running his fingers through the soapy wet strands of red hair and helping me rinse myself clean.

"Then what can I do?" he whispered as his fingers massaged my scalp in a strong, easy, rhythm that had my eyes sliding closed with pleasure. "I feel like … like I want to grab my weapons and storm Coven Triad, fight my way through as many of them as I can until I drop to my knees in a pool of blood."

"No," I said as I laid my palm on the flat expanse of Monty's lower belly. His muscles contracted as he sucked in a sharp breath, and I couldn't help but notice the hot water slicking down the length of his cock. "I won't let you do that either."

"Why?" he asked, but I was already dropping my hand and curling my fingers around the base of his shaft. Montgomery exhaled sharply and dropped his own hands from my scalp to my shoulders, squeezing my muscles with those long fingers of his.

'Nic,' I called out, because I'd made a promise and I intended to keep it. *'I'm with Monty in the shower ...'*

'You don't have to keep doing this,' he told me, his wolfspeak voice an even keel that ran through my head like a winter wind through pine boughs. I knew then that he was in wolf form, standing outside in the forest alone. I could almost smell him in that moment, the sweet honeysuckle and pine kiss of Ebon Red. *'You don't owe me this, Zara.'*

'Love does not demand debt, but it thrives on respect. I love and respect you, Nic.'

That felt like a weird thing to say, my fingers curled around the base of Montgomery's cock, but … it was true. No matter what else I was doing, that wouldn't change. And besides, if I wanted this to work, I'd have to rethink I everything I thought I knew about relationships.

'Zara,' he said, and then I heard a howl from outside the cabin, a melancholy song that made my skin prickle with goose bumps. *'Thank you.'*

I felt Nic take off on four strong paws, his muscles rippling as he let himself go completely, darting through the woods of pack property. At least I knew he was safe out there, even by himself. I was more worried about Che, Anubis, and Tidus at the grocery store.

"Why?" I repeated, focusing back on Monty, on eyes so green they put the forest to shame. "Because … you belong to me now."

It wasn't a question.

The Bonding Ritual, the whole Pairing Ceremony … I had a feeling there was something to all those 'empty rituals'. I could *feel* it, zinging through my blood, hot and wild. One-Kiss-No-Date was my nickname, remember? And yet … I couldn't seem to stop myself as I slid my hand up the length of Montgomery's cock and shivered with pleasure at the sound that slipped past his lips.

Or maybe *couldn't* wasn't the right word. I *could* do anything I wanted. And yet, this was what I wanted to do. I felt like magic was rippling through me in waves, that same earthy quality that had popped up the night Nic and I had lost our virginities to one another. It swirled through the room like a cool breeze, one that smelled of fresh spring leaves and flowers.

Montgomery squeezed his hands on my shoulders again, kneading the tender flesh and making me groan. It wasn't exactly a sexual touch, but it felt that way.

"Zara …" he said, as I worked my hand up and down his body, feeling the tension melt out of him with each stroke. His long hair was plastered to the sides of his face, taking that knightly look of his and making it just a little wilder, a little more *animal.* He was a gorgeous man, Montgomery Graves.

Leaning in close, I put my lips to his neck and kissed the wild flicker of his pulse, loving the taste of his skin. My eyes closed of their own accord and I breathed in the deep musky scent of wolf, the floral whisper of roses, and the grassy scent of the earth.

"This is better than a run, isn't it?" I whispered as I worked his body with my hand, tilting my head up to meet his mouth when he turned to face me. Our lips slanted together, hot water speckling our skin as our tongues tangled and I kept up a strong, steady motion with my hand.

"So much better," he murmured, but the words came out in a half-growl, and I felt Monty's wolf shift and rub against me, calling to the wild nature inside of me, to *pack.* In that moment it most definitely did not feel like he was Ivory Emerald and I was Ebon Red; we felt like we belonged together.

The whisper of magic in the back of my mind promised that yes, this was true, that I should embrace it. Old magic was awake and alive in my blood, just in time to herald our species' greatest comeback … or our final downfall.

I didn't know why … but I was going to do my best to find out.

"Oh, Zara," Monty moaned as our kiss deepened and he pushed my body fully against the wall with his own, trapping his shaft between us, making it harder for me to move. It didn't matter. We fumbled our way through it, my fingers stroking a climax from his body, spilling his seed all over me. "Zara …"

"Let's go upstairs," I whispered, my own body shaking as I grabbed Monty's wrists and moved his hands from my shoulders to my hips. "Well, clean up first … and then go upstairs."

"Yes," he said, exhaling sharply, a small smile returning to his lips. "Let's do that."

I told u jizz turns 2 glue in the shower! is what Faith texted me after Monty fell asleep in the big bed. He was lying beside me, his long hair bound in a tight braid and curled down the length of his back. He slept on his tummy with a deep, easy breathing that told me was seriously out.

Good thing, too, because I soooo did not want him to see

this text message.

U never said that b4, I texted back, leaning into the pillows and closing my eyes against the chilly breeze sneaking through the open window. The nice thing about being a werewolf was that we could have the windows open year-round, since the only place we seemed to actually get cold was in the hellish depths of Faerie rivers …

Have so, she sent back and then, *and I cannot BELIEVE u jacked that Monty dude off same day u did Silas.*

I groaned and put my phone against my forehead.

I could barely believe it myself. I blamed it on the magic, but maybe … it was because I was a teenager who'd just been hooked up to seven *really* hot guys who all wanted to have sex as much as I did? I mean, was I thinking too much like a human in being worried about this? Or too much like a wolf in that *mate them all* was my primary objective?

U said u wouldn't judge, I sent back. I'd originally texted just to check up on her—I had two Ebon Red guards with her whenever I couldn't be—and somehow it'd turned into a graphic storytelling session. Such was Faith's way.

Not judging, just ... half jealous & half shocked is all, she replied.

Setting my phone aside, I ran both hands down my face and sucked in a long breath, grabbing a piece of leftover pizza from the box and biting the end off of it.

Faeries. Witches. Vampires. Boyfriends.

Oh my.

"Knock, knock," Anubis said from the bedroom door,

cautiously moving into view and bowing his head respectfully in my direction. “We come bearing gifts.”

He lifted up a case of beer in one hand and a reusable grocery bag in the other.

“Thank the goddess,” I said with a smile, gesturing him into the room. I noticed that when Anubis climbed into the bed with me, he kept a decent amount of space between us. He liked rules and boundaries; he wouldn't approach me unless I approached him, not in this capacity anyway. I couldn't help but smile when I thought about the way he'd defended me from Avita during the Challenge. “How're Silas and Jax faring with Aeron?” I asked as I took a bottle of beer from him and was excited to see that it was already cold. Anubis handed over a bottle opener and put a huge smile on my face. He always seemed to be prepared.

“Does sitting in silence on opposite ends of the couch while Aeron sleeps in a chair count as faring well?” he asked, reaching up and touching the spiked navy tips of his hair. Anubis looked at me with crimson eyes and then smiled. “Mind if I have a slice?”

“Go for it,” I told him, dragging the pizza box close and letting him snag a piece of Hawaiian. As I watched, he plucked a few extra pineapples from the box and layered them on top of his slice.

After I was done eating, I was seriously going downstairs and rounding up the rest of the boys. Even if they didn't want to touch each other, this bed was plenty big enough for all of us. Leaving Aeron alone downstairs *was* a bit of a risk, but with the werewolf wards on the cabin, she shouldn't be able to cause us much harm while *inside* the Pairing House. There were tales of a long-ago alpha who'd invited a rival into the house to talk. When the foreign wolf pulled out a gun and tried to shoot a silver bullet, the weapon had turned on her and fired directly into her forehead instead.

Whether that was true or not, I didn't think the eight of us staying together would affect our chances of defending ourselves against the fae girl if needed. If anything, it would only help.

"Does it bother you that we were supposed to be mates?" I asked randomly, picking up the remote and thumbing through shows until I landed on some lighthearted fluff that I could fall asleep to. Because that's what I was going to do, recline into these pillows, stuff my face with leftovers and try to get some sleep.

I'd need it to get through tomorrow.

Meetings with vampire queens.

Unruly faerie visitors.

Mysterious witchy double agents.

"Aren't we still mates, though?" Anubis asked as he leaned back into the pillows, scooting just a few inches closer to me and tossing a glance my way. He was dressed for bed in black shorts and a loose t-shirt, his stance casual, his smell intoxicating.

I pretended not to notice.

Four guys in a single week?

And after my record was zero for eighteen years?

It was a tad overwhelming, especially since all I was

doing was acting organically. It's not like I had a checklist for these guys or anything, some game of sexual conquest I was trying to win.

"But if you mean, am I disappointed that I'm not the guaranteed alpha?"

I glanced at him and noticed Anubis was staring rather intently at the piece of pizza in his hand.

"No." He took another bite and focused his gaze on my face. "I can't imagine working this Contribution alone."

"The Contribution wouldn't be so all-encompassing if there weren't so many of us," I added, but Anubis was already shrugging his shoulders.

"It's a good thing you were assigned to deal with this. The way you're handling it, with careful maneuvers instead of all-out war? That's a good thing. Our people are lucky." He chewed his pizza for a moment before continuing. "And the magic," he said, "it's waking up. There has to be a reason for that."

Trailing his fingertips across the bed, Anubis touched my knuckles and a cool breeze filtered into the room. Not the cool crisp bite of outside air, but something different. That sweet, sad song of nature that was both uplifting and somber at the same time. I closed my eyes and breathed it in for a moment before looking down at the Crimson Dusk Alpha-Son's brown fingers atop my so very pale ones. We made a pretty picture like that, tangling our fingers together ever so slightly.

I won't deny that I was fucking thrilled.

Pulling my knees up close, I took another bite of my

pizza and glanced at the screen, looking at the romantic scene playing out on the movie but not really *seeing* it.

"Have you thought about talking to your Alpha-Mother about it?" he asked as I listened to Monty's breathing, and let the dual scents of magic and wolf swirl through me. Anubis' gardenia and jasmine smell made my toes curl into the sheets. I liked it *that* much.

"Majka," I said, and it hit me like a ton of bricks. She hadn't offered, but then again, I was the Alpha-Heir; I wasn't going to be handed solutions. I had to come up with them on my own.

No, no …

As Nikolina often said, *It's always* us *and* we, *Zara*, *not* me *and* I. Us and we. The boys.

"I could seriously kiss you right now," I said, sitting up on my knees and keeping hold of his hand. Anubis looked back at me from crimson eyes decorated in long, thick lashes, and his mouth popped open of its own accord.

"Oh, shit," he said as I tossed the rest of my pizza in the box, set my now empty beer bottle on the floor, and took his other hand.

"She might not know a lot, but she *can* control what little magic she does have. I can't even *believe* I didn't think to ask her." Anubis smiled at me, and it was this perfect mix of cocky and sweet; I had no idea how he managed to pull it off.

"Glad I could be of service, Alpha," he said and then grinned mischievously. "Especially if it makes you want to kiss me." Leaning in close, I brushed my lips against his and then planted a big one on the smooth skin of his cheek. The shudder that passed through his body was unmistakable.

"If you hadn't gone through my panty drawer," I joked as I leaned back, "then the kiss would've been on the lips."

"Oh, god," Anubis groaned, letting go of my hands and falling back into the pillows. "Doesn't the witch hazel buy me back any points?" He dropped his palms to the mattress and looked up at me with a single raised brow.

"It buys you a lot of points," I said, lying down on my stomach and folding my arms under my cheek. He turned toward me and we just stared at each other for a few minutes until the bedroom door opened.

I knew without even having to look that it was Nic.

"Have a good run?" I asked him as he rustled around near the closet and then climbed onto the bed, inserting himself on my left side, between me and Monty. He cuddled up close and put his mouth near the back of my neck, making me shiver.

"It was perfect," he said, putting an arm around my stomach. It was cold from the outside air—not cold enough to bother me—but I liked the feeling of his body warming up against the heat of mine. Anubis just watched us both with an eager sort of expression, like he'd crawl into my arms if I invited him. Hell, maybe I should? "By the way, Lana brought news from the Crown Aurora Blood Queen. Tomorrow night, she'll meet with us—at her Kingdom Seat."

I saw Anubis frown at the same moment my face

scrunched up.

The Kingdom Seat was basically like the vampire's version of the White House. It was where their ruling members spent their nights, dealing in Blood business. I couldn't decide if I should be glad she'd invited us there … or terrified by the prospect.

Because a vampire queen or king would only invite guests there if they *really* wanted to talk … or if they wanted to kill the people they'd just invited in.

"We're supposed to meet them at the old library," Nic continued, his body vibrating with either adrenaline from the run … or something else, I wasn't sure. It wasn't like we'd had time to talk after the Silas thing. And now with Montgomery? I'm sure Nic wasn't happy. "I'm not sure why we can't just meet them *at* the Kingdom Seat, considering everyone and their Alpha-Mother know where it is."

"They want to get a look at us first," I said with a long sigh, weighing my options. They all felt so heavy right now, those choices. Maybe sleep would help some? *If* I could force myself to relax enough to doze off, that is. "Make sure we're alone, probably."

"Not like we couldn't bring the cavalry in anyway," Nic grumbled, but the logic made sense to me. It was an exercise in trust. The Crowns wanted us to meet them at a specific location, alone, and *then* they would escort us where we needed to go. I wondered if maybe they were more concerned with making sure that nobody knew we were on our way to see them. Kingdom Ironbound for example?

I sat up and untangled myself from Nic's arms, leaning forward and tugging the grocery bag close, snatching another beer, and climbing off the bed.

"Where are you going?" Nic asked, his dark hair ruffled up and threaded through with pine needles and small twigs. It was an adorable look for him.

"To grab the others," I said with a raised brow, tipping the beer to my lips and setting the grocery bag of snacks on the dresser. "I can't sleep knowing Jax is probably on the porch again, and Silas …" I was sure Jaxson had already told Silas the news about his dad. I needed to at least *see* him before I could fall asleep.

"Okay," Nic said, as Anubis gave me a thumbs-up and Monty continued to sleep peacefully. "Just be quick; I want to hold you tonight."

The way he looked at me in that moment … it set all my nerves alight.

"Deal," I said with a smile, tipping back the rest of the beer and heading downstairs.

I found Silas asleep on the couch, Aeron asleep on a chair, and Tidus, Che, and Jaxson shooting the shit out on the porch.

They all went silent as I came out and I knew they were smelling Monty all over me. Showering off the proof of our time together did *not* entirely eliminate the smell for a werewolf. Not even close.

"Lucky bastard," Che said, one foot tucked up in the rocking chair, the other on the boards of the wood deck. He looked like a dream of sex and nightmares in his sweats and black tank, a beer in one hand, and a look of dark desire on his face.

"I'd like you all to sleep upstairs tonight," I said, ignoring his comment and glancing over at Jax, surprisingly still in his human form and sitting on the edge of the porch railing, legs dangling. He gave me that cool, frosty glare of his and took another sip of his drink.

"Thank god," Tidus groaned, standing up from the second rocking chair and stretching his arms above his head. He put his hands together in a prayer position, a bunch of wooden bangles on his arm that I hadn't noticed before. They clinked together in a pleasant way as he shook his clasped hands in my direction. "I thought you'd never ask," he added with a bright, easy grin.

"That eager to jump into bed with a bunch of dudes?" Che said, and I gave him a look that he returned with a dark smile. "I guess even if the traitor's up there, it's better than sleeping on the couch."

"He's not a traitor," I said, my voice darkening a shade. Che barely looked like he noticed and not for the first time, I wondered if I was going to have to actually challenge him and put him on his back. I knew I could do it. I didn't *want* to, but I could.

As I glared at him, I noticed the skeleton hoodie he was wearing and raised a brow.

"Did your things come in today?" I asked, and Jax breathed out a long sigh, almost in relief. I looked over at him and realized he was wearing a robe I hadn't seen before, his blonde hair wet from the shower. As tradition dictated, all the packs had arrived to the Pairing on foot, traveling weeks or even months to get here.

But all their clothes and personal effects? Those had to be shipped. Oddly enough, Montgomery's had arrived just a few days before he had. It'd been a morbid thing, seeing those big crates of clothing, weapons, books, and pictures and wondering if the boy they'd belonged to was dead. Thinking about it now and knowing Monty personally … it broke my fucking heart.

I was pretty sure *his* crates were still in the storage room at the Hall. Obviously, he'd grabbed his weapons and some clothes from them, but the rest of his stuff needed to be moved over here. Hell, so did mine and Nic's. I think it hadn't quite hit me yet that this place was supposed to be a home. A year was both long and short at the same time, but I knew that with the amount of pressure on us, we wouldn't survive if we didn't get comfortable here.

We both needed *and* deserved a place to decompress.

"I think everyone's stuff is here finally," Jax said, glancing over his shoulder at the waning gibbous moon in the sky. Long ago, our people were connected to the moon as closely as the tides; we ebbed and flowed with it. Now, moonlight enhanced or strength, increased our healing powers, but it wasn't the force it once was.

I wondered if at some point, we'd just lost our fucking way as a species. Maybe that's what the magic was all about? One last chance to reconnect with who we were, with the earth, the moon, the stars above …

"I'll send word to Lana tomorrow to have everything brought over," I said, putting my hands on my hips and looking at the three boys around me. I knew little to nothing about them, really, but I wanted to know more. That was a good start for all of us, right?

They're all mine, a little thought in the back of my head whispered. I tried to ignore it, but it was persistent. As soon as the Bonding Ritual had ended, I'd felt it. Like we were fated by Mother Earth herself to be together.

I was supposed to choose a mate at the end of the year. But why choose? The packs might adjust more easily to a uniform leadership if I *kept* all seven men as my mates. Then again, maybe I was the only person in that group who wanted it this way?

"Sit down and have a beer with us?" Che asked, handing an unopened one in my direction. "Just one," he added when I hesitated for a second. Tidus sat back down in the rocking chair and invited me with a single hand to sit in his lap.

I took it—and the beer—happily, settling in against his warmth, his sandalwood, amber, and sunshine scent surrounding me in a pleasant sort of way.

Sitting there in the peaceful quiet of night, I had to wonder if this wasn't exactly what we were all fighting so hard for.

When I woke up in the morning, the first thing I noticed was that the boys had forgotten their vows to stick to their own portions of the bed and were literally sprawled in an adorable mess of arms and legs.

As wolves, the urge to create little puppy piles was strong, and in sleep, human inhibitions were stripped away. It did take me about fifteen minutes of careful maneuvering to find my phone though.

The wolf and moon charms jangled as I extracted it from underneath one of Silas' ridiculously firm butt cheeks and carefully let myself out of the room, grabbing one of Majka's favorite dresses from my closet first.

I was going to shower, slip into the outfit, and then see if I couldn't get her to agree to train me in whatever she knew about magic. She might not have a lot herself, but my grandmother had been born in a time when alphas could wield plants as weapons, bring lightning crashing from the sky, and stir up storms. Big magic. Old magic. Magic that had gone missing without anyone knowing why.

"Good morning," I said when I came downstairs and

found Aeron at the table, shoveling food into her mouth like a starving animal.

"I would possibly consider having males in my harem, if they were to cook me things like this," she said, pausing and tossing a dark ebony wave of hair over one shoulder. She pointed at her plate of corned beef hash, eggs, and toast like it was a five-star meal in a fine restaurant, something to be revered.

"Good to know," I said as I moved past her and found Montgomery in an apron again, cooking at the stove. He met my eyes from across the breakfast bar and something passed between us, this hot spark of carnal knowledge, the sweet memory of my lips on his neck, my hand on his cock.

"Good morning," he said, Anubis and Tidus leaning against the kitchen counters behind him. They watched our interaction carefully. "Are you hungry?"

"Starving," I said, and I realized my voice was coming out in a purring growl that I so was not going for. If I'd been the type to blush, I'd have probably gone full pink in the face. "I need to shower and see if I can find Alpha-Majka at either the Hall or the big house."

"You're going to talk to her about the magic?" Anubis said, probably more for Tidus' and Montgomery's benefit than my own. I nodded and took a seat on one of the bar stools, trying to keep myself from getting too much inside my own head. Left to my own devices, I'd probably go hang out with Faith all day and let myself mull over each sexual interaction I'd had with the guys.

As things stood, Faith had left me a text saying she was

going to sit at home and study all day for her test on Monday, and *I* had to deal with my seven boyfriends' moving boxes, my grandma aka the last werewolf to ever wield magic, and a bunch of overdue anthropology homework for the online course Nic and I were both enrolled in that'd gotten pushed to the back burner.

Even if it was like putting lipstick on a pig, I wanted to try to make the life I was leading as normal and enjoyable as possible. Even if the alpha generally didn't work, I wanted an education and a degree I could be proud of. I wanted to be able to sit outside and drink beers with the boys and look at the moonlight. Those really were the moments life was made to live, so I'd take them where I could get them.

“She can control her magic enough to direct it to close doors, throw unruly wolves across a room, delicately stir her tea with a small spoon. She has something to teach me, at the very least. I just hope she's not difficult about it.”

Tidus came around the corner and took up the seat next to me, the sound of Aeron's fork scraping across her plate muted by the soft sounds of jazz coming from the iPhone dock in the corner.

“Whose music is this?” I asked and I knew right away when Montgomery grinned that it was his. “You listen to jazz?”

“Either jazz or metal,” he said, shaking his head and lifting a pair of perfectly fried eggs out of a pan and onto a plate. As Alpha, I was automatically handed the food first. It was expected that I'd eat before all the boys. I thought about refusing, but then I realized that the three alpha-sons with me in that kitchen probably wouldn't feel comfortable eating until I did.

I took the plate from Monty, a fork from Anubis' outstretched hand, and cut into the soft round surface of the egg, spilling yellow goo across the white porcelain. Monty plopped a nice fried bit of corned beef hash on the side and then shook his head slightly.

"I don't know why," he said, continuing our conversation about music. "I know jazz and metal are at opposite ends of the spectrum, but I feel like I need them both. When I need to stay calm, it's soft jazz. When I need to amp up, heavy metal."

"I can listen to anything," Tidus said, ruffling up his sandy hair and leaning back on the stool. "Doesn't matter. Rock, pop, rap. I'm down for all of it." He glanced over at me and winked, a big theatrical wink that made me grin.

"I like angry classical music," I admitted, "lots of screaming violins, heavy hands on piano keys, wordless noise that stirs the blood."

"That's the true alpha in you," Anubis said, grabbing the pieces of toast from the toaster and passing them over to me. "That need to get stirred up. My mother likes her music angry, too." He referenced the Alpha Female of Pack Crimson Dusk with a small smile.

"What do you like?" I asked him and found those crimson eyes lifting to mine. He met my gaze, but only for a brief second before glancing away. It wasn't that I got the air of submission off him either. No, I didn't think Anubis Rothburg had a submissive bone in his body. But he *was* respectful, and he knew how to play politics better than anyone. If I had to choose one of the seven to take with me to a meeting, it'd be him. Whereas I felt like Silas and Che had the ability to ruffle feathers, it seemed Anubis might have the skills to smooth them.

"Me?" he asked and leaned back with his butt against the edge of the copper apron sink. "Shit, I don't know. I like visual-kei, basically Japanese rock 'n' roll with all the theatrics. Oh, and anything old-school boy band. Backstreet Boys or *NSYNC, like I can get down with that."

I laughed and tried not to choke on my eggs.

"You're into Japanese rock and boy bands?" I repeated, because if Monty thought his mix of jazz and metal was eclectic, we now had a new winner.

"Basically, yeah," Anubis said with a slight smile, picking up a sketchbook from the counter next to him and pulling a pencil from behind his ear. He started sketching like he didn't even realize he was doing it. "My hair won't stay flat, no matter what I do. I figure my options are either shave it off, or let it grow out and join a visual-kei band myself." He paused in his sketching and gestured at the navy blue of his hair. "And then I guess boy bands just remind me that there's fucking frivolity left in the world, you know? That luxury of liking something silly just because you can."

"That was way better than my answer," Tidus said with a laugh and I grinned.

"Very poetic," I said, and I wasn't teasing—I meant it.

Anubis just smiled and kept his eyes on his sketchbook. "What are you drawing?" I asked and was surprised when he handed it right over to me.

A half-finished sketch of a woman looked back at me, her curves generous, her face fierce. Her hair blew in the wind in a wild wave, a fan of tendrils framing her in her glorious nudity, nothing but a thin silver belt wrapped around her hips. The chain was made of interlocking moon shapes, similar to the Coven Triad symbol, but with each phase of the moon represented. It crossed over her right hip with two loose pieces hanging down and blowing in the drawing's silent wind.

"This is beautiful," I said as Tidus leaned over to take a quick look and whistled under his breath. I looked up to find Anubis staring at me, hands tucked in the pockets of his jeans, his mouth twisted to the side in that interesting mix of sweet and sexy.

"It's you," he told me, and when I looked back down at the woman … I realized he was right. *Holy shit, is that what I look like?!* It'd been a while since I'd really *seen* myself. Either Anubis was greatly exaggerating my looks, or I needed to pause and take a good, long look in a mirror.

"If this is how you see me, then thank you," I said, glancing back down at the image.

"That's not just how he sees you," Tidus said, stealing a bit of corned beef hash from the edge of my plate. Normally, a move like that would set an alpha off. I'd seen my mother pin people on their backs for less. But with Tidus? It felt natural to share food with him. Even my wolf side agreed with that. "That's just how you look."

My lips twitched as I heard Aeron's chair scrape across the floor.

I glanced over my shoulder and found her watching me carefully.

"I'd like an escort to take me off pack property for the day. There are some fae living Low-Side that I'd like to speak with. But I'll need to be picked up again as well." Low-Side was fae speak for this side of the Veil. Sometimes they even called Faerie High-Side. I didn't know where the terms had come from, but I wouldn't have been surprised to learn that *Low*-Side was intended to be disparaging.

"I'll take her," Silas said from the living room, rubbing at his forehead with the heel of his hand. His dark brown hair was combed smooth and those gold eyes, they were all for me.

"Take Nic," I said, nodding with my chin toward the key hooks near the front door. "And when you're down there, stop by Lana's and ask her to get the pack to move your shipping boxes over here. We also need someone to clean out mine and Nic's rooms back at the main house."

"I'll do that," Nic said, coming down the stairs and giving Silas a *look.* I knew the last thing they wanted was to spend a single moment together—especially after yesterday. But they were going to have to learn to work it out. "We have enough time before the meeting to get it all done, I think."

"Nobody goes through my panty drawer this time," I

said with a small grin. "Just close your eyes and dump the whole damn thing into a box."

"You might be alpha, but don't expect miracles," Nic said, a rare glint of humor in his voice. Usually that was reserved specifically for our private time together. Since time away from the other alpha-sons was going to be in short supply for the next year, I was glad he was letting loose, even if just a little.

"Don't think I won't notice a missing pair," I said, ignoring the way Aeron's face twisted up in slight disgust.

"Never mind," she whispered, sweeping her dark hair back from her face. "I do *not* want any males in my harem."

"I sure as fuck wouldn't either," Che said, appearing from upstairs with no shirt on and padding past his two archnemeses with barely a sideways glance. "I woke up with Jaxson's erect dick stabbing me in the leg. How gross is that?"

"It wasn't stabbing you," Jax purred, coming down the stairs next—completely nude, mind you—and turning up a cold, mean smile in Che's direction. "It was *caressing.*"

"Save that shit for Zara," he said as he walked by and gave me a dark look, one that was *dripping* innuendo. "If she even wants it, that is."

"Somebody give Aeron their phone," I said, ignoring their banter. It was playful enough that I actually found it comforting; Jax and Che were getting along. "You do know how to use a cell phone, right?" I asked as Anubis dutifully handed over his.

"No lock screen," he said with a smile, watching as I passed the phone—with its Japanese anime cover—over to Aeron.

"I might be sidhe, but I'm still from the twenty-first century. I'm no older than you are," she said, looking at me from eyes that definitely did *not* feel like they belonged to a girl my age. I remembered how quickly she'd moved, how she'd shoved Tidus up against a tree before I could finish blinking. She might not be the Unseelie Queen, but Aeron was still a force to be reckoned with.

She took the phone and slipped it into the pocket of the jeans she was wearing, jeans that looked suspiciously like mine. Whatever. Like I said, werewolves know better than to get too attached to clothing.

"My number's plugged into that. Just call us when you're ready to be picked up." *Words I'd never expected to hear leave my lips.* Ready to be picked up? I couldn't even believe we were carting around a faerie princess.

"Thank you," she said, nodding briefly and moving away before pausing suddenly, like she'd just thought of something. "Make sure you have plenty of time set aside tomorrow. I might not be able to read the bones this side of the Veil, but I *can* perform *haruspicy.* I'll need a doe."

Aeron moved away, passing between Nic and Silas and heading out the front door.

Haruspicy, huh?

The reading of an animal's entrails for prophetic purposes.

I was both disturbed and intrigued.

"Take your time," I told Silas and Nic, still holding Anubis' sketchbook against my chest. "I'm going to go visit Majka and see if she can help me with our newfound magic." I smiled because it was the first time I'd really thought of it properly—*our* magic. Not mine. Fucking *ours.* "Just be back in time for the meeting."

"Gotcha," Nic said, glancing over at Silas warily. "I think I'll stop by the Hall and trade out the SUV, too." Poor Nic. He really did love the Yukon. On the plus side, he'd be trading it out for an identical, maybe even slightly newer version. *'I love you, babe.'*

'I love you, too,' I told him in our private little wolfspeak channel. With a small wave, he went for the front door. Silas waited a moment, his eyes still firmly focused on my face, and then he, too, turned to go.

'Let's find some time to talk, okay?' I blurted, stopping Silas with his palm pressed flat to the screen door.

He glanced over at me, the scar on his face catching the light.

'As long as it's not about Allister. Zara, I'm not as shocked by this news as everyone else is. The Alpha Male of Pack Obsidian Gold, he hasn't really been my dad since he nearly took my eye out.' Silas smiled sharply and pushed his way out of the Pairing House. *'Fucking you from behind yesterday,'* he added after he was out of view, *'now that shocked the shit out of me in the best way possible.'*

'You dickhead,' I said, but I was relieved as hell to hear that he was in an okay mood.

"Anubis," I said as I glanced back at him and something

just *clicked* inside of me. "Will you draw up designs for our alpha silver?"

"Me?" he asked with a loose, easy chuckle, standing up from his spot against the sink and shaking out the front of his sleeveless shirt. It had the letters *XOXO* in white across the front with a big red lipstick kiss behind them. I wasn't sure what to make of it. "Really?" He sounded surprised, but also … flattered?

"We're supposed to have a consultation with the Jeweler at some point, but if we had your drawings, it would make it that much simpler."

"Yeah, and I can't design or draw for shit," Che said, holding one of the glass milk bottles in one hand and leaning his back against the fridge. "You'd be doing me a serious solid." He tipped the glass back and downed half of it in one go. I'd be lying if I said I didn't watch his throat move. Something about watching Che swallow turned me on …

"I mean, we can ask if anyone wants to design their own, but otherwise … I say go for it?" I handed him back the sketchbook as Jax took up the stool on my other side, his fluffy white wolf tail and ears shifted, but the rest of him human.

It … well, that was a huge turn-on, too.

I had the strongest urge to reach out and rub one of his fuzzy ears between my fingers.

"I don't need to design my own silver," Jax said, wagging his tail and giving me a bored, stupid sort of a look. "Take it and run with it, Crimson Dusk."

"Agreed," Montgomery said, serving up another plate of food to Tidus. "It would be a relief for me. One less thing to worry about."

Anubis took the sketchbook and tapped his pencil against the paper, chewing on his lower lip as he contemplated. Based on the expression on his face, he seemed pretty happy about it.

"It would be an honor, Alpha," he told me with a short nod and a big grin. He'd look goofy if it weren't for the big muscles in his biceps and that sinful face of his.

"*An honor, Alpha,*" Tidus repeated, chucking a piece of toast at him. Watching them together, it was easy to imagine them playing as pups. Anubis let the bread bounce right off him and waggled his pencil.

"Be careful: if I'm designing your silver then I'm probably the last person you want to piss off, huh, Amber Ash?"

"Eat shit," Tidus said, but he was laughing and had a piece of toast hanging from his mouth at the same time. It was actually pretty goddamn cute.

"Guess it's time to go talk to Grams, huh?" Che asked, watching me carefully.

"Guess so," I said as I finished off my last bite of egg and smiled at the boys. "Wish me luck."

When it came to dealing with the former alpha of Pack Ebon Red … I was going to need all the luck I could get.

Alpha-Majka was sitting on the back deck with a cup of tea, a plate stacked high with flaky meat pies, and an old tome that looked like it was liable to break into pieces at any moment.

I approached her like an alpha would, head high, chin up, eyes forward. When she lifted her head to look at me, our gazes locked and I saw the corner of her lip twist up in a snarl.

"What is it you want, Alpha-Heir?" she asked, closing the tome and looking up at me from eyes the color of a velvet sky. "It's been three days since the Pairing and already you come to me?"

"This isn't about the Pairing," I told her, pulling out one of the other chairs at the table and sitting down. My rank in the pack right now was a strange one, exalted but feared, worshipped but watched with narrowed eyes. I *was* the next alpha, but it was a position I'd truly earn over the next twelve months, not one that would be handed to me.

Technically, I was *slightly* above Majka in the dominance ranking, but it was not something I was eager to enforce. With a flick of her hand, she could send me crashing through the deck's wood railing and onto the grass. Physically, she might be getting up there in years, but her mind was as sharp as a knife.

Her tongue, apparently, was even sharper.

"Then what do you want, pup? I'm busy." She tapped her long fingers on the cover of the book. As soon as I became alpha and was given access to the vast resources at Ebon Red's disposal, I was going to have all the old works scanned and uploaded to the cloud. A single fire, a spilled cup of coffee, an earthquake … we could lose the collective knowledge of decades.

I wasn't going to let that happen.

Just watching Majka hold the tome like it was a regular paperback book made me nervous.

"You're the only wolf alive with magic," I told her, paused, licked my lower lip. "Well, except for me and the boys …"

Majka's dark eyes narrowed and she swung her gaze out toward the tree line, studying the dripping crystals of water clinging to the branches, tapping out an ancient symphony on the forest floor.

"I need to learn how to control it," I told her, trying to get her to look at me, to acknowledge me for once instead of belittle me. I was used to it, the blatant disregard both my mother and grandmother showed me. But I wasn't going to put up with it any longer. "I had my future read by the heir to the Unseelie Throne," I told her, watching as her face tightened up, the wrinkles rearranging themselves as her expression changed. "My presence either signals a bright future for our people … or their complete destruction. Majka, I need to learn how to control this magic."

For a long moment, she was silent, but then, as I sat

there and watched, my grandmother waved her hand and the small field of grass between us and the forest bloomed with pink, purple, and white flowers, their fragrant scent wafting in the wind and surrounding us.

"I don't know how much help I can really be," she said, her voice softening slightly. I felt myself relax, just a little. When it came to Nikolina and Majka, I'd always felt closer to my grandmother than my mother. "I was born in a different time, at the end of a great wave of prosperity for Ebon Red." She sighed and touched a shaking hand to the bloodred strands of her hair, her eyes distant and far away as she stared at the field of wildflowers, so much more beautiful for the icy snow that dotted the edges of the field.

"I was considered weak when I was born, you know. A disappointment. But then other litters were born and they were … much worse. The magic of the earth abandoned our people, Zara Wolf."

"I don't know if it abandoned us," I began, lifting my eyes up to the gray-blue patch of sky above the forest, "or if we abandoned it."

"That's true, I suppose," Majka said, handing over the tome in stick thin arms that still held a surprising amount of strength. "Whatever the case … we've been given a second chance." She waited as I took the book and held it on my lap, flipping it open and blinking in surprise when I found an illustration of the alpha in the silver boots and helmet, her seven lovers fanned out around her in a semi-circle.

I couldn't read the language, but I could follow the story as I flipped through and found more inked illustrations of big magic and great conquests.

What had gone wrong in the time in between her birth and mine? And why was I both a harbinger of doom and a symbol of power at the same time? It was less of a *why me* thought and more a simple academic question. How the fuck did I save my people? How the hell did I make sure there was a place in the ever changing world for us?

"I'll teach you what I know, but I imagine you'll be learning a lot on your own as well," she said, reaching out for her cup of tea. I noticed that this time, her fingers were shaking. "I know you're busy with the Contribution," she grudgingly admitted, giving my red dress a look that told me I'd made the right decision in wearing it. Reaching out a gnarled finger, she traced the edge of the fur lining on my shoulder. "But make time for our lessons. If I'm going to spend what could very well be the last year of my life teaching you, it'd better be worth it. Come see me on Sunday, Alpha-Ki. And be careful of the fae," she added just before I stood up to leave. "You only think the faeries are tales until one bites you in the ass."

"Thank you, Alpha-Majka."

I grinned and took off, taking the book with me.

I might not be able to read it … but Majka had given me the tome for a reason.

I was determined to figure it out.

Meeting with the Crown Aurora Blood Queen was a huge risk, but one that I had to take. It was a calculated risk, like everything else I did nowadays.

It was now or never.

"I hate these outfits," Nic said, which made my lips twitch in amusement. "I thought these were sacred outfits to be worn *only* at the Challenge."

That was a reach and he knew it, but nice try.

"Nothing in Pack Law says they can't be worn outside the ritual," I told him, sitting between Silas and Che in the center row of the SUV. I felt like they needed a physical barrier between them, even if their tempers had cooled off since yesterday. "So expect to be wearing these a whole hell of a lot more. Like, say, to the grocery store to buy bananas?"

"That would go over well," he grumbled, weaving the new, undamaged Yukon through icy side streets toward our rendezvous point with Kingdom Crown Aurora. "Me in chains and leather pants at the natural grocers, buying organic cucumbers and twenty pounds of raw steak."

"Whoa, what are the cucumbers for?" Tidus asked with a chuckle, ruffling up his sandy blonde hair in the front seat and reaching out to punch Nic playfully in the shoulder. Nic stiffened up, but didn't react which was a *huge* thing for him. Aw, Nicoli Hallett was making a friend.

"Trust me," I told him, crossing my legs at the knee, the fur trimmed folds of my dress falling aside and flashing the long, white lines of my my thighs, "I don't need any extra cucumbers."

Anubis and Tidus both burst out laughing, but the rest of the boys stayed quiet.

The dynamic in this car was definitely not optimal. If we had any chance of succeeding in this, we'd have to do it together. If the boys were at each other's throats, we were all destined for failure. We had enough opposition as it was.

"I like the outfits," I said instead, reaching out to finger the fur cloak hanging off Silas' tattooed shoulders. He turned his gold eyes to look at me, the intimate knowledge of our joined bodies traveling between us. I could feel him, the same way I'd felt Che when he was lost under the dark depths of a raging faerie river. "Good thing, huh? Considering I designed them."

"They're beautiful, Alpha," Anubis said from behind me, making me smile. "Although I *am* having trouble keeping my … male parts from sticking together. Is anyone else having that problem?"

"Are you fucking kidding me?" Che asked, turning around and looking at Anubis with raised brows. "This is real leather. It gets sweaty in there. It's just something you have to deal with."

"Would it be rude to reach in and separate?" Anubis asked as I clamped a hand over my mouth and tried not to laugh. "I'm sorry if that's rude, Zara Wolf."

"It's not rude," I said with a sharp, wolfy grin, glancing over my shoulder and finding Anubis with his hand literally stuck down his pants. When he caught me looking, he cringed like he was embarrassed and withdrew his fingers. It was hard for me to forget, even looking at him chagrined and blushing, about lying together with our heads on the same pillow, facing each other. "It's just funny as hell."

"Zara," Nic said a moment later, just before the smell hit me.

Mint and apples, *blood.*

Vampires.

We pulled the Yukon into a parking space in the lot outside the old library building.

An entourage of vampires was waiting for us.

"Stay in the car," I said to the boys as we watched the vampires—all undead and Ageless, I was sure—circle the SUV and then return back to their own vehicle, a sleek black limo that I was pretty sure belonged to the queen. Although if I were a betting woman, I'd guess she was most definitely *not* in it tonight.

They flashed their lights at us, turned, and left the lot.

We followed right along behind them.

A butcher shop.

How was I not surprised?

"Do you think we could waltz in there and order a pound of 'were' meat?" Che snarled and I felt rather than saw Montgomery tense up from the back seat. "I mean, it doesn't bode well that *this* is where they've brought us for the meeting, does it?"

"This is the Kingdom Crown Aurora Seat," I said as I licked my lips and gestured for Che to open the side door. "This is the one stronghold they want *everyone* to know about."

Che climbed out ahead of me as Nic and Tidus slipped out the front doors, the boys a glorious sweep of sin in their tight, leather pants and long, black fur cloaks. Thin decorative chains crisscrossed over their chests, but the silver moons in the center had been replaced with wooden ones, carved of ash and polished to a shine.

As silver is to werewolves, iron is to fae, and wood is to vampires. Doesn't matter what kind. Something about the inherent power of earth just didn't sit right with creatures of the night.

The butcher shop was called *Sweet Bread Meat and Fish Market,* and it was famous for being the only place in town to grab rare and exotic meats. Hell, it was the only place in the *state* to grab certain delicacies. Techie bigwigs from Portland ordered rare caviar, slabs of wild caught venison steak, and Kobe beef from Japan.

It was a good business, prestigious enough to please the Kingdom, profitable enough to launder money through, but just unpalatable enough to ward off too much attention.

"This way, please," a blonde woman in a suit said, gesturing for us to follow her inside.

The butcher shop was pressed up close to the sidewalk, smack dab in the middle of the gentrifying area of downtown Springfield, Eugene's smaller sister city. It was six blocks down from the high school I'd attended with Faith and Nic, and right across the street from the brick majesty of a newly remodeled building.

There was no doubt in my mind that Kingdom Crown Aurora owned that, too.

"May I take the lead, Alpha?" Montgomery asked, looking ridiculously fierce in his boots, painted on pants, and hooded cloak. He still had his knives and swords, but I doubted we'd be allowed to keep them for long.

"Go ahead," I told him, trying not to get lost in the majesty of those emerald eyes, his shock white hair hanging down his back in a long braid. He really did look like a character from a fantasy novel or a video game, some hero from a distant land. Instead … he was mine. I wouldn't soon forget the feel of his cock in my hand.

I just wasn't sure that I knew quite what to do with him.

Montgomery took point, leading us into the front of the shop, strings of small white bulbs giving the closed store a peaceful, sleepy feel. As soon as we walked in though, I could smell it—blood and death and viscera, meat and bone and gristle.

I almost choked on it.

To a human, I doubt they'd smell much beyond the sweet potpourri scent floating around the showroom floor, jars of jam and tins of locally sourced chocolate adding to the ambiance. It was quite cozy in there, the little café counter in the corner with its chalkboard of special sweetbreads and glasses of local wine for sale. A hipster's paradise.

The blonde vampire in the suit took us through a door behind the counter, down a hallway and into a white and silver kitchen, polished and gleaming. It smelt like bleach on the surface, but to a werewolf's sensitive nose, it *reeked* of meat.

Although I was happy to discover, no wolf flesh.

On the other hand, I caught distinct whiffs of other Numinous and felt my stomach twist into knots.

'It smells like ... mer-flesh,' Anubis choked as the salty-sweet scent of mermaid teased my nose. The fish-legged beauties of the sea were a favorite of several different land-dwelling species including their own dark cousins, the sirens, as well as various races of demon. *'It's a fucking slaughterhouse in here.'*

'It's connected to the back of the shop,' I said, thinking of all the things Nikolina and her betas had taught me about the local scene, all the tidbits of information gleaned from Majka's rantings. *'The actual slaughterhouse, that is. This area technically isn't zoned for it, but since when does a*

vampire ever need the permission of a human? They just roll the inspectors and continue to do their killing here.'

'If we end up drawn and quartered,' Jax drawled, his claws extended, clearly fighting the urge to shift into wolf form. *'Then make sure they know Azure Frost meat is worth at least twice that of Violet Shadow.'*

'You're a macabre son of a bitch,' Che told him, sauntering forward on my right side, looking like a veritable badass with his dark hair and violet gaze, his eyes rimmed with thick, black kohl.

Our vampire host paused and unlocked another door, stepping back and indicating that we should head down the curving steps into the lower level, the *underground* level.

That's where the queen would be waiting.

"We can keep our weapons?" Montgomery asked, his back stiff as he addressed the living vampire on his left. Now that the door to downstairs was open, I could smell the undead lurking, waiting. Their scent was even sweeter than that of their living counterparts, an even brighter, crisper bite of fruit on the back of the tongue.

"You may keep your weapons," she said, blinking dark eyes and waiting for us to descend below. "If you feel need to use them, you'll soon be dead anyway."

She smirked at us as Monty narrowed his eyes and turned away, leading us down a set of stone steps lit with beautiful wall sconces—electric lights, of course, not candles. Even vampires enjoyed modern day conveniences.

"Pompous bastards," Montgomery said aloud, his voice echoing in the enclosed space as we followed after him, my long skirts sweeping the stone floor, pooling around my ankles in swathes of red fabric, leather, and fur. "If they think I'd have trouble beheading one or more of them before my time ran out, they've got another thing coming."

"Let's hope it doesn't come to that then," a woman said as we rounded the last curve of the staircase and paused in front of the pale-eyed, blonde haired queen of the Crown Aurora vampires. Her smile flashed two sharp points of fang as she stood in the center of the small room, her generous curves swathed in layers of red velvet, her pale neck exposed and bleeding.

"Zara Wolf of Ebon Red," I said, lifting my chin and pausing as the boys fanned out around me. They were good at that, creating a circle of protection around their alpha. Half of me was thrilled with that sense of security and protection, but the other half of me … wanted to be the one doing the protecting.

"Welcome," Aurora said, not bothering to introduce herself again. I guess werewolves were more stuck on formality than Bloods. Didn't surprise me much. "Follow me and we'll get comfortable," she said, not at all concerned with the fact that she was *alone* in a room with eight werewolves.

I thought immediately of the Challenge, of the lesson I was supposed to learn by getting my ass kicked … and how very accurate a lesson it really was. My humility was at an all-time high, my arrogance in check. I was on my way to becoming a powerful Alpha Female, but I was *not* a true Alpha Female just yet.

Aurora turned in a swirl of red velvet trumpet skirts and took off down another hallway, the stone walls fading to wallpaper and wood moldings that cost a pretty penny. But I knew it was for more than just show—that wood molding was designed to keep *other* vampires out.

'Are you guys getting déjà vu?' Anubis asked, putting a hand on my shoulder and peeking his head between me and Nic. *'Dark, underground, filled with monsters who want to eat us? This is just like the witches' lair.'*

'Please don't say that,' Nic said, glancing over at me like he thought I might be upset.

But I didn't scare that easy.

'I'm better prepared this time,' I assured the boys, catching Nic's concerned stare and forcing a smile. *'I've got this.'*

'And we've got your back,' Silas said from behind me, making my skin prickle with remembered passion, hot and burning, wild and fierce. God. I wanted *more.* These guys were going to be the death of me.

"Take a seat," the queen said as the doors at the end of the hall swept open, and she sauntered through, gesturing at the various chaises, couches, and chairs around the room before sweeping herself into a throne made entirely of human bone. I knew it was human because I could *smell* it.

The boys and I paused in the center of the room, a thick cloud of cigarette smoke making our nostrils twitch and our throats burn. Half the seats in this room were already occupied. And the activities taking place on said seats? Sex and violence was everywhere.

Humans bled while members of Crown Aurora sucked their necks, their cocks, took blood from the femoral arteries in their thighs. The room was ripe with the coppery scent of blood and the warm, unmistakeable reek of sex.

I had to breathe through my mouth to maintain my composure.

"Now," Aurora said as a human girl draped her head in the queen's lap, her red hair falling down the pale lines of her naked back. "What can I help you with? You know, it's been … *fuck,* well, almost a century since I had an official visit from Pack Ebon Red."

I filed that information away for later.

A century? Majka's map? Interesting.

"Kingdom Ironbound," I began, cutting to the chase as werewolf protocol dictated. But these were vampires and where we enjoyed pomp and circumstance with little chatter, they liked lazy sensuality and sin with lots of it.

"Please," she said, and I felt her power roll over me like a wave. If I hadn't been the Alpha-Heir, hadn't been with my boys, she might actually have been able to roll me completely. Holy shit. "Have a seat. I can't carry on a casual conversation if my guests are uncomfortable." The queen paused and spoke to a nearby vamp in a thick, eastern European tongue that I recognized right away was Croatian.

Like Majka.

Wow.

I was going to have to look my grandmother in the eye and ask her outright what the fuck was going on here.

'Let's find somewhere to sit that isn't drenched in blood

and other ... uh ... bodily fluids,' I told my men as I took a look around the room and tried not to stare at undulating bodies and thrusting hips, red blood against white, brown, and black skin, flashing teeth, bare breasts. *'This should do it, I think,'* I said as I moved forward and took a seat in a large chair near the corner, a spot that I hoped would give us the advantage in case things went sour.

We were near the door, against the wall, as far away from the queen as we could get.

I took the seat, folding the voluminous skirts of my Challenge dress under my thighs and waiting as my mates took up various positions around me. Nic and Montgomery went the serious route, taking up positions behind my chair with their arms crossed, gazes taking in the other people in the room like they were all threats. And let's be honest—they probably were.

Tidus and Anubis sat on the seat with me, Anubis stiff and formal and Tidus … looking around the room like he'd never seen anything this strange in his whole damn life. Couldn't blame him on that front either. This … bacchanalian affair was unlike anything I'd ever been a part of.

Yes, there *were* occasions when mates would pair off and well, *mate,* during certain pack functions, but it wasn't like this, this desperate, quiet greed.

'I may never have sex again,' Silas said as he leaned against the wall and took up a characteristic bad boy slouch, arms crossed over his tattooed chest as he watched Jax crouch near the door, his face shuttered and unreadable.

'The only person that would hurt would be me,' I joked back, trying to lighten the mood. Silas gave me a sorry half-smile, but that was about it. I was also careful to project my words to the *entire* group, trying to make sure everyone felt inclusive in our new pack within a pack.

Juggling these men, I thought as the vampire queen pulled the redheaded girl into her lap, tilted her head to the side and sunk her teeth into the woman's pale skin, *is going to be the hardest part of the whole damn year.*

Seven alpha males. One alpha female. Love would be my greatest weapon.

'Sorry, Zara,' Che said as he unfurled his body across the floor in front of my feet, propping his head on his hand, *'but I might be in agreement with the traitor on this one—the smell in here is fucking awful.'*

'Call me traitor again,' Silas growled, his entire body going tense, *'I dare you.'*

"Traitor," Che whispered aloud, and I had to raise a hand to keep Silas from going after him. My fingers curled around Silas' wrist and dragged him over to the chair. Using the force of my grip on his arm, I made him sit in front of me.

'Enough,' I told them before their fighting could escalate. *'If you want our people to go extinct then keep at it. You can rip each other apart before or after the witches and the vampires have their turn, take your own pound of flesh.'*

The two boys still sat stiff and angry, but at least they refocused their attention back to the matter at hand.

We were literally sitting inside the Blood Queen's lair.

Surrounded by blood and sex and *vampires.*

Aurora smacked her wet, red lips and smiled at me.

"Much better," she said, as my stomach roiled and I tried not to react to the overwhelming number of smells in the room. Mint and apples, copper, sweat. "Go ahead, Wolf. I'm listening. You walk into my home and speak the word *Ironbound.* I hope you have a good story to go with it."

"Kingdom Ironbound," I began, projecting my voice into the small, dark room. The walls and ceiling were covered in wooden panels; a chandelier dripping dark crystals gave off little light. The entire place was decorated in rich, dark colors like aubergine and crimson, black and charcoal gray. "Has found a way to daywalk."

The entire room went still, so utterly still that I had to blink a few times to make sure I was really seeing it, that eerie stillness of the dead. Because in this room, there were no living vampires, just the Ageless undead.

"Daywalk?" the Blood Queen said, throwing the redheaded girl to the ground in front of her throne of bones. "They walk in the sun?"

"Unscarred and free," I told her, keeping my hands in my lap, my body language neutral and easy. She was getting angry and *fast.* I had to make sure none of that rage was directed toward me. "They've made a pact with Coven Triad, and drench themselves in witch hazel."

"Why are you telling me this?" the queen purred, standing up, her hair moving like a live thing, the skirts of her dress rustling in an unnatural breeze. I could see the dark pits of her pupils dilating, shrouding her pale eyes with darkness. "How do you know these things?"

"They've been kidnapping and killing members of my pack," I told her, paused, rephrased. "*Our* packs. I don't know why and I don't care. I just want it to stop."

I took a long, deep breath.

"Ironbound is purposely seceding territory to your Kingdom *and* they've introduced a new Kingdom into Oregon, the Kindred."

The Crown Aurora Blood Queen moved across the room like sensuality perfected, a curvy hourglass figure with generous hips and bosom, a face carved of alabaster, and she paused two feet in front of Che Nocturne.

"Kingdom Kindred," she said, tilting her head at me like she expected I'd give away all my secrets. "What about them?"

"For whatever reason," I began, trying to keep my breathing even and my gaze level with hers. It wasn't easy, looking into eyes as black as pitch, no white to be seen, just bottomless darkness that stretched into forever. "Coven Triad doesn't want anyone to know about them."

"Coven Triad," the queen repeated, and with each crumb of information I fed her, I saw her rage amplify into a terrible, palpable thing. I could taste it on the back of my tongue, the inhuman violence, the fury of the dead.

The way she looked down at me, it was like *I* was responsible for it all.

I made sure to clarify.

"I decided to bring this matter before you in lieu of taking action. Blood business is only *my* business when it involves the packs. As the reigning queen of this region, it's your job to police the area. A new Kingdom, new magic. I'd hate to see you burned in your sleep."

With low, easy breaths, I fought to keep my heart rate from picking up speed and giving away my anxiety. Sitting trapped in this room with an angry vampire queen, her closest confidantes, and their food? Not my idea of a good time.

"Daywalking ..." Aurora said, her voice trailing off as she turned and snapped her fingers. "Bring me Harlem," she said as she turned and moved away from me, splashing through a puddle of blood that was draining across the floor.

The bright wet scent of blood was making my stomach roil, but I couldn't show my disgust, not here. I stared across the room at the human whose blood it was, a young girl that was probably around my age. She bled from the thigh and didn't seem to give a shit that her pallor was poor, her head resting in the lap of a male vamp with long dark hair. He stroked her short blonde waves with his fingers, his lips set in a permanent frown, and glared daggers at me.

Most of the humans here were probably eternity chasers, people who wanted to become vampires. In exchange for willingly offering themselves up for both sex and blood, they were promised that true immortality lay in their futures.

It wasn't always a lie.

Every once in a while, the vamps might find a human they liked enough to turn.

Usually, though, the humans just hung around until one day, they bled a little too much and never woke up. It was sad, but it was the way things were. I couldn't change any of that in a single meeting.

If I wanted to make a difference in the world, I had to become Alpha first.

If I took care of my people, made sure we were whole and happy and well, the rest would follow suit.

Aurora disappeared out the door we came in, one of the other female vampires following along behind her. They left us there to watch them fuck and feed and frown, cigarette smoke dancing like fog in the still, warm air.

'I don't know how much more of this I can take,' Tidus said, and I felt his gag reflex through our pack connection it was so strong. *'The smells in here ... it smells like death, blood, and sex. I can't take it much longer.'*

'Hold strong,' I told him, reaching out to take his hand, curling my fingers through his. *'We need this meeting to go well; Crown Aurora is the* only *vampire Kingdom we can count on to wipe out the daywalkers instead of join them.'*

In that regard, Julian had been *extremely* helpful, confirmed that this risk—trusting what I knew to Aurora—was worth it. If she'd slaughtered an entourage of witches and Ironbound Bloods, she wasn't likely to join them. Besides, I'd seen Julian's true fury toward Crown Aurora mirrored in his body language.

'Harlem,' Anubis said after another few moments of silence, *'isn't that the name of the Blood Princess?'*

Not ten seconds later, the doors reopened and a blonde girl stood staring at us, her eyes the same color as the queen's, her hair the same white-blonde. The *only* biological child of Queen Aurora stood staring at us from the entrance to the room. She *looked* eighteen, but I had no idea when the queen had gone from a living vamp … to an undead one. This girl could be as old as my mother for all I knew.

“We're well aware of the fact that werewolf blood gives us the ability to daywalk,” she blurted, and the entire room went still and silent. I rose to my feet and Silas rose with me.

“Come again?” I said, my voice an icy chill that even Nikolina would be proud of.

“We know,” the girl—presumably Harlem, the Blood Princess—said carefully, her white-blue eyes boring into mine. Now that I really looked at her, I could see the dancing of her pulse beneath pale, pale skin. She was *alive,* so perhaps she really was the age she looked? And the Crown Aurora Blood Queen, she can't have been dead all that long.

I wondered who might've killed her.

“We don't drain wolves,” she said after a long moment, lifting one arm up and using a steel knife from inside the folds of her cloak to slice a nice, long gash down her wrist. “Come and see for yourself.”

'Careful, Alpha,' Anubis warned, and I felt the other boys tense as I made my way toward her and paused, lifting her wrist to my nose. As soon as I got close enough, I smelled it.

Wolf.

The smell of wolf deep inside this girl.

My eyes flicked up in surprise.

She didn't smell like *pack,* not exactly, but there was a hint of werewolf in there, something old and deep and ancient.

“My mother has a werewolf as an ancestor, and it's her blood that fuels our kingdom, her power that runs through our veins. Ever since my mother formed this kingdom, we've had the power to daywalk.”

My mind reeled as I stared at her.

I wasn't sure which part was more surprising … the fact that there'd been daywalking vampires all along … or the fact that a werewolf and a vampire could have fertile offspring together. In living history, that'd never happened.

I supposed the princess was proof it could. I could *smell* the wolf in this girl's veins, pure and clean, organic. It was a *part* of her. Faint, but apparently even a faint kiss of our earthly magic was enough to provide protection from the sun.

I could see now why they'd kill to protect their secret.

“We've heard rumors of strange attacks on kingdoms in the South, near Kindred territory,” the girl said, withdrawing her arm and lifting it to her lips. She ran her tongue along the wound, nice and slow, maintaining eye contact with me the entire time. “We suspected demons, but with the information you've just given us, we have a better idea now. The type of attacks that were launched … they spoke to an intimate nature.”

“And the queen?” I asked, wondering where she'd gone and why she'd sent her daughter in her place.

"We can fight Ironbound, but if they have witch support, we'll need backup."

Ah, *now* I could see where this was going.

"I will go with you and help coordinate a daylight attack on Kingdom Ironbound," the girl said, throwing a glance in the direction of my boys. Her blue-white eyes opened in surprise and appreciation, lashes batting as she took them all in, their leather pants and furred cloaks presenting quite the pretty picture.

A low growl escaped my throat and brought the vampire princess' gaze back to my own.

"Mine," I told her, nice and low and quiet. But everyone in that room was a Numinous; they could all hear me.

"I will go with you as a liaison," the girl continued, ignoring me and throwing the hood of her white and silver cloak up over her hair. "I'll also serve as collateral to ensure there is no confusion of loyalty."

Her smile made my chest feel tight.

"The queen asks that you do the same: leave one of your males here for the time being." The girl stared at me with that smirk frozen in place, her eyes the shape of sideways teardrops, her nose tiny and pert. She was gorgeous, flawless, like a porcelain doll made of bone and blood and death.

"No," I said and I felt the room ripple around me. "My mates are not collateral. A wolf is only as strong as their pack; I won't leave a male here."

"Then you'll give us blood," the vampire girl said, looking me hard in the face. She knew what could be done with just a drop of blood, let alone a pint or two. “From you and each one of your males.”

“Blood is a big gift—especially to a vampire. *Especially* when we know some of the local vampire kingdoms are working with witches.” I crossed my arms over my chest, glad to be wearing the dress with my grandmother's black bear fur trimming the edges. It made me feel powerful, in control. I needed that here, the strong scent and feel of pack.

“A living daughter is a big gift—especially to a sea of revenge hungry wolves,” the girl said, licking her lips. There was something else dancing in her eyes, a want, a need, a secret barely kept. “We don't do binding agreements like the witches or fools' bargains like the fae. If that's what you're looking for, you'll be sorely disappointed. We need you and your mates to fight with us against Kingdom Ironbound.”

“What sort of support are you looking for?” I asked, studying the delicate features of her face. Harlem was a girl made of bone and shadows, too pretty to be real, too dangerous to be trusted. “I don't want the Convocation to know about any of this.”

“You will do, Zara Wolf. You and your seven mates.” Harlem smiled at me, the skin around her small nose crinkling slightly. “But be prepared to wield that big magic of yours.”

'How does she know about that?' Nic asked, a thread of alarm in his voice.

Good question.

"The wolves have been without magic for decades. I'm sure you're well aware of that," I said as Harlem stepped around me, her long cloak dragging across the bloody floor. She didn't seem to mind that she was soaking it up as she went.

I turned around, following her with my eyes.

"You know why, right?" Harlem asked me, glancing over her shoulder. Her eyes glimmered like chips of ice in her pale, pale face.

"Why?" I asked, and I was glad that vampires had better hearing than humans. I was speaking so quietly, if Harlem hadn't been one of the Numinous, there was no way she'd have heard me.

"The witches," she said, letting her mouth curve into a purposeful smile, flashing fang. "What do you think all that alpha silver is intended to protect you from? They've been siphoning magic off of your people for close to a century now, long before they ever started eating your flesh. Find a way to stop the slow drain *suck* of a spell they've cast … and you'll change the world."

After our conversation with Harlem, I was shaking.

Witches, witches, witches.

I could hardly fathom a conspiracy as big as the one she was alluding to, but she wouldn't talk until we'd given our blood. Once again, I was forced with making a split-second decision that could cost us everything.

I decided to go for it.

"What about the alpha silver?" I asked her, after we'd been escorted to another, smaller room. This one far more sterile than the other. In fact, it looked like a doctor's office—if you ignored the stone walls that is. Sterile instruments, reclining chairs that looked much the same as the ones at blood donation centers, and the reek of iodine and bleach.

Despite the boys' protests, I was the first to sit in one of the chairs and let the vampire woman in the suit swab my arm with iodine and stick me with a needle. Red, red blood slid up the inside of the tube and the room filled with the honeysuckle and pine scent of Pack Ebon Red.

"The alpha silver is the only thing that's prevented you from losing everything," Harlem said, leaning against the wall, her cloak leaving little red drips of human blood on the floor beneath her feet. "The alphas are both the conduit and the channel for the magic of their entire pack, correct?"

"I suppose so," I said as I watched the blood drain from my arm. "Figuratively anyway."

"No, literally," Harlem said and I watched as Jax curled his lips back in a growl. I didn't much like a vampire trying to dictate my own people's rules and customs either, but if I was here, I was going to at least listen. "The Pairing Ceremony starts the shift from one alpha to the next. That's why it lasts a year, so the transfer of power is complete. Zara, as the Alpha-Heir, you can draw on the magic of your *entire* pack. You bathed in the blood of the current alphas, correct?"

I thought for a moment about that fountain, the one in the old dining room, where I'd stopped and smeared blood across my face, dipped my hair … I'd thought it was only my mother's blood in there, but maybe the other alphas had contributed? I hadn't thought to ask. Either way …

Was I now being told it wasn't quite the empty ritual that it seemed?

"How do you know all of this?" Nic asked, scooting a bit closer to me. He put his hand on my bare ankle, and I felt an instant relaxation wash over me. "Seems a bit strange to me that a vampire would be so interested in wolf history."

"Part vampire," she whispered, her eyes shining, her jaw clenching tight. "I'm a quarter *wolf*."

"How is that even possible?" Montgomery asked, giving her a look that would've scared me had it been directed my way. Clearly, he didn't have a fondness for vampires. "Wolves and vampires can't create viable offspring."

"Well, someone figured out that little puzzle at some point, didn't they?" Harlem asked, slicing her palm with the thumbnail of her other hand and lifting up a bloodied palm for Monty to sniff.

He turned his face away sharply.

He didn't need to get close to smell the wolf in her blood; it was obvious enough in this small room, even with the myriad of competing scents.

"So you're obsessed with werewolf culture then?" Anubis asked, looking at her with his head cocked slightly to one side. "Can you shift?"

The energy in the room shifted suddenly. Harlem's pupils bled black into the pale blue of her irises and I watched as her body went completely still … as still as *death.* I stiffened up, too, prepared to rip the IV from my arm and charge her if she went for one of my boys.

But she didn't move from her spot against the wall.

"You can't shift," I told her, and my skin rippled with disgust. I couldn't … god, I couldn't imagine being trapped in a single form. My body felt fluid, liquid, ready to melt into my wolf at a moment's notice. To feel those urges and be denied the change? It was tantamount to torture. "That's why you know so much about wolves. That's why you want to help us."

"I need to change," Harlem said, her pupils snapping back to their normal size, movement returning to her body as she started to breathe normally again. She pushed herself away from the wall in a flutter of that white and silver cloak.

Montgomery stepped between us, his hand on the wooden knife in his belt, and the vampire girl stopped herself short.

"You don't understand," she said, shoving the hood of her cloak back. "I *ache* inside. Every full moon, I feel like I'd rather split my own skin open than deal with this feeling another fucking goddamn day. So yes, I've studied and I've researched … and maybe I do have an ulterior motive."

Harlem took a step back from Montgomery and narrowed her eyes on him.

"Relax, *knight,* I'm not going to kill the one woman on

this planet who might be able to help me."

"You think I can help you?" I asked as the blonde vampire woman removed the IV and put a small bit of gauze over the wound. It'd heal in a few minutes or less, so she didn't bother to bandage me up.

I scooted off the edge of the chair and Nic dutifully took his place.

"You're the only one that can," Harlem said with a sigh, turning and looking at herself in the mirror over the small sink. That whole myth about vampires not being able to see their reflections? Well, that only applies to the undead, and Harlem Blood, she was very much alive. "You're the next alpha, and you're here so that means you're at least *speaking* to me. The current Ebon Red Alpha refused to meet with me."

Ah. That sounded like Nikolina.

"If you stop this slow bleed, Zara," she said as Montgomery stepped aside so I could stand next to him, "and you restore the magic, our connection to the earth will return and then maybe …"

She paused, but I didn't miss that word. *Our.* Harlem felt like she was Pack. I didn't know how the fuck I felt about her yet, but I did sympathize with her situation.

"Tell me more about this," I said as I crossed my arms over my chest. "Alpha silver, can you explain, please."

"The silver prevents the witches' energy drain spell from pulling magic out of the reigning alpha. Even wearing it a few times a year seriously fucks with their ability to siphon magic."

As I stared at her, I thought of Nikolina and Majka and how silly and stubborn they were compared to the other alphas. They didn't just wear their jewelry sometimes … they wore it *all* of the time.

Could that be why I had all of this magic when nobody else did?

"How could there be a permanent spell on my people that nobody knows about? It's not just one pack or even one Convocation of wolves that's suffered from the loss of magic—it's all of us."

"You know better than I do that all 'weres' are connected, whether or not they're from the same pack or even the same continent. A werewolf is an extension of the earth herself, and you're all tied to it. Drain *one* wolf and you drain them all," Harlem said with a low growl in her voice that made me raise an eyebrow.

"Still doesn't explain how this spell was cast in the first place," Jaxson said, looking like a Nordic king in his black furred coat and boots. The leather pants gave the outfit a modern edge that pushed all my buttons. Frankly, I was surprised Harlem wasn't checking the boys out at all anymore. Either she wasn't interested—like Aeron—or she was doing her best to be respectful. All I knew was that if I were trapped in a small room with all these men, I'd have a hard time not appreciating the view.

"I'm a talented researcher, but I'm not all-knowing," Harlem scoffed, her long white-blonde hair hanging over one shoulder. It was just a shade lighter than Jax's, with just a bit more color than Monty's. Looking at her, the blue of her eyes, the color of her hair … I was betting on a pack Azure Frost ancestor. She could very well be a distant relative of Jaxson's. There was a slight citrusy smell about her, underneath the reek of mint and apples … and blood of course. Always with the blood.

There was a reason the vampires called *themselves* Bloods.

“I have no idea. How does one culture ever get duped by another? A Trojan Horse perhaps?” Harlem glanced over and watched as Nic's blood slid up the tube, a crimson snake feeding into a plastic bag. Giving these vampires our blood … it may well have been an incident like this that allowed the witches to cast such an impossible spell in the first place.

But looking at Harlem, seeing the pain in her face … I didn't think that was her aim. Her aim was to help us to help herself. That motive, I could understand.

“What are you planning to do with all this blood anyway?” Montgomery asked after the vampire in the suit pulled out Nic's IV and he switched places with Anubis.

“First, we're going to use it as collateral to ensure *you* don't intend to pull a Trojan Horse out of your furry wolf asses.” She flashed a grin, complete with two perfect pointed canines. “And then we're going to use it as bait to get Kingdom Ironbound to come out of hiding.”

“How?” Montgomery demanded, one hand still on the wooden knife at his belt. His face was all hard angles and deadly seriousness. I didn't for one minute doubt that he could take out a few Bloods before *they* got *him*. Even if we were in their territory. No, Montgomery's righteous rage would take him far.

"Alpha blood," Harlem said, leaning back against the sink again and showing a remarkable amount of control for a vampire her age. She barely looked at the blood draining from Anubis' arm. Veritable proof that she was the queen's daughter. Most other Bloods her age would be in a near frenzy at the sight and smell of so much red. "It's … like a drug to most Bloods."

"Most Bloods?" Che scoffed, leaning against the other wall with a semi-permanent scowl etched onto his features. "And what makes you all any different?"

"You know that a Blood Kingdom shares the lineage of their queen or king, right? Well, my mother is half-wolf. That means everyone that pledges their loyalty to her, takes her blood. That makes *them* part wolf. And werewolf blood does nothing for other werewolves, if I'm not mistaken. It doesn't bolster us the way it does other Bloods."

"So, you need all of this for a trap?" Che said, sounding skeptical as hell.

"We'll offer them a little drop of blood from each of you, just to whet their appetites, but they'll need more incentive than a drip to come out of hiding. The Kingdom Ironbound Queen hasn't been seen in *years.* If we have a pint of blood from the Alpha-Heir and her seven mates, she'll come slinking from her hole like a little lizard." Harlem lifted her eyes to the ceiling, the corner of her lip curling up in disgust.

"What exactly does alpha blood do for them?" I asked,

moving over to stand between Silas and Tidus. My arms brushed both of theirs, one on either side, and I swear, I felt my breath catch. Harlem noticed, her eyes locking onto the throbbing beat of my pulse, and her lips twisted into an evil grin.

"God, you are one lucky wolf," she said, and I felt my own lip curl up in a small growl. Harlem just laughed and folded her hands together behind her head. "Relax. I'm not stupid enough to try and poach a male from the next alpha. I have *some* sense about me."

"Alpha blood," I repeated, raising a red brow. "What does it do for vampires?"

"Besides giving an undead Ageless the ability to daywalk, you mean?" Harlem stood up and pushed her cloak aside, cupping her hands together, palms up, like she was trying to catch raindrops. Her eyes narrowed and her nostrils flared. When she lifted her hands up to the ceiling, the nest of tree roots crawling through the stone shifted and wiggled like a cluster of snakes. "It's not much," she said, dropping her hands as Tidus raised an eyebrow and put a hand up to his mouth to stifle a laugh.

Harlem gave him a *look.*

"That was … magic?" he asked as she folded her arms across her chest and glared daggers at him.

"I said it wasn't much. *But* my point was, Bloods can wield magic, too. *Particularly* if they're pumped full of alpha blood."

"You're sure that's not just because you're part wolf?" Silas asked, leaning toward me slightly, pushing our shoulders together.

"I'm sure," Harlem said, looking up at the roots with narrowed eyes, like she would curse them if she could, send them away to wither and die. She dropped her attention to me as I pulled the gauze from my arm and found a perfect, unbroken bit of skin. Not even a little of that shiny pink, newly healed flesh. My inner elbow was *flawless.* "Give a Blood Queen some alpha blood? She can move mountains."

"So the silver …" I continued, leaning my head back against the stone wall. "It protects?"

"To an extent," Harlem said, putting her hands in the pockets of her short black dress. It almost looked out of place with the big, bulky cloak around her shoulders, this little black dress that looked more like it belonged in a nightclub than underneath a fantasy shroud. But somehow, the vampire girl made it work. "The more silver you wear, the better protected you'll be. I'm not exactly sure *why* that is, but my theory is that since werewolves are allergic to silver, the body refocuses its magic stores on dealing with the poison instead of slipping into the … you know, ether or whatever you want to call it that the witches have designed."

'Please tell me we don't have to wear that stuff on a daily basis?' Jax asked, wrinkling his nose up and growling at the vampire woman when it was his turn to get jabbed. I just hoped the boys took note of how tiresome it was to get poked by *one* needle; I had seven to deal with.

'I think I'm starting to regret making the warrior's choice on all the silver,' I said, breathing out a long deep

sigh. If I'd known wearing it was so damn important … I'd have gone with eight bangles instead.

'She stinks crazy bad; we're never going to sneak her past Nikolina,' Nic said, wrinkling his nose up as all eight sets of wolf eyes—and eight noses—turned Harlem's way.

'Not without witch hazel,' I said and then it clicked in my mind.

I did have the Maiden's phone number in my contacts, after all …

Hiding the Unseelie Princess from Nikolina was hard enough. And now I had to deal with this vampire girl? The Pairing House simply wasn't going to fucking work.

'Mother Earth's tits, she really does reek,' Jax said from his spot beside me in the front row seat. Nic was driving again. I don't know why. Maybe out of habit? He didn't have to do that anymore—we could all take turns driving. Or hell, maybe he just liked it? *'How the hell are we going to keep the alphas from finding out about her? Most of them are still staying at the Pairing House.'*

'We make a phone call,' I said, dialing up Whitney's cell.

She answered on the first ring.

"Wolf," she purred, "what can I do you for?"

"We need witch hazel," I told her, "lots of it and *quick.* Can you help us out?" Even as I was talking, I was trying to figure out if there was a place the girls could stay that *wasn't* going to put them on top of me and the boys. We had enough to worry about with our new relationships; we didn't need guests. *'Do you guys have an idea on where we should house Harlem and Aeron? If they stay at the Pairing*

House, it's just a matter of time until Nikolina or someone else stumbles on them.'

"I can help, but I won't be able to get it to you until tomorrow," Whitney said, adding yet another layer to this puzzle that needed solving. "Make sure you're on time, Miss Zara Wolf. We got a *lot* to cover and not much time to do it in. I gotta go, alright? But you stay safe tonight."

She hung up the phone before I even had a chance to say goodbye.

"She can't help us until tomorrow," I said aloud, and glanced back to find Harlem watching me with a very curious look on her face. It took me a minute, but then …

'Are you projecting openly?' I asked Jax, because when it came to wolfspeak, there were lots of ways to go about it. I could project to a single person or a specific group of people … or openly, so that any werewolf in the immediate vicinity would hear me. It was common enough to just send thoughts openly when we knew nobody else was around to hear us.

'Openly,' Jax said, following my gaze around to Harlem's face. *'Oh.'*

"This is the first time …" she said, tears forming at the corners of her eyes. She dashed them away angrily and lifted her chin. "I've never heard wolfspeak before, not once."

"Do you know how to project?" I asked her, and she huffed out a long sigh.

"I've studied and studied and studied, but I can't for the life of me figure it out. All the books I've read have been so

… vague. I think it's a difficult topic to describe on paper, no?" She continued talking before I could even respond. "But that's my hope, that by going with you, I'll somehow … I don't know, find a way to pick your brains."

"Aren't you supposed to be collateral?" Nic said, rolling his eyes. I was glad to see his usual cynicism and skepticism focused on an outside individual rather than on one of the other guys. That was progress, right? "Really though, you're here because you want to wolf out?"

Tidus chuckled from his spot next to the vampire princess and tucked his legs up onto the seat.

"Seems like a worthy cause to me, right? Help during wartimes in exchange for changing their princess into a werewolf. I'm down, seems like a fair trade."

"Glad you think so," Harlem said, looking over at the blonde surfer boy with a cold disinterest. I was about ninety-nine percent sure it was a facade. In reality, I think she was obsessed with him, with all of us. After all, we represented the one thing she didn't have—*pack*. And although I'd never met anyone who *wasn't* fully werewolf in their blood, I knew our instinctual urges were beyond strong. Harlem felt that itch in her skin, the want to meld into the ground with all four paws running. "Maybe you could teach me a thing or two?"

"Or maybe not," Jax said, his voice just as cold as hers. His was a facade, too, just of a different sort. Out of all the boys, Jaxson was the most connected to his wolf side. Not that there was anything wrong with that, but … I felt like his balance was off, just a tad. "Why would we give all our secrets to a vampire? You might be part wolf, but it's obvious where your priorities lie."

"Is it?" Harlem hissed, leaning forward, so close that her nose was almost touching Jax's. It was a Blood thing. When threatened, their first response was to get close to the neck. Both Jaxson and I growled at her, a clear warning to back the hell off. She leaned back and crossed her arms over her chest. "My mother sent her only heir in a SUV full of werewolf royalty. Why? Because she knows how much this means to me, enough to wage full war on Kingdom Ironbound for the privilege. You have no idea what my priorities are."

The car went silent for a few minutes, the distant sound of pop music trailing from the speakers.

I reached out and turned it up, just for Anubis' sake. It was some light, fluffy nineties stuff.

I felt his pleasure ripple through our pack bond and grinned.

"Hey," Nic said, glancing over at me and drawing my attention his way. "What if we took her to my parents' place? It's still on pack property, but it's farther away from the Hall and the big house than the Pairing House is."

I snapped my fingers at him.

"That's a good idea, especially if we have her shower right away and put her in some clothing that stinks like wolf. Get Lana to keep all the windows closed ..." I glanced over my shoulder at Harlem again and she wrinkled her face. "We're taking a big risk here."

"And so am I," she said and I sighed.

She was right; she was.

"Let's just get through tonight," I said, "and then we can all breathe easier tomorrow."

If I'd realized at the time how very untrue that statement was, I wouldn't have had a wink of sleep that night.

As things stood, I didn't end up getting much sleep to begin with …

Lana and Leslie Hallett lived in an adorable two bedroom house at the edge of pack property, so close to the border that the long, curving gravel of their driveway actually came directly off the street.

The porch light was on, the windows aglow with warm, buttery light.

On the way over, we'd swung by and picked Aeron up at some random street corner. Now she and Harlem were glaring at each other across the surface of poor Tidus' lap while Jaxson sat in the far back cargo area.

Nic and I were both slightly wary of leaving the Numinous princesses at his parents' house, but my instincts and logic both told me it'd be okay, at least for one night. Killing Nic's parents would not do much for either girl, regardless of their motives; if they were going to kill someone, it would be me or one of my boys.

"Mom," Nic said after he parked and climbed out of the

SUV, wrinkling up his face as Lana grabbed him, one palm on either cheek, and pressed a light, chaste kiss to his lips. "*Mom.*" The second time was a little puppyish and I found myself smiling.

"Oh, I miss the days when you used to lick me all over the muzzle," she said, and his face wrinkled up even more. Tidus and Anubis were chuckling, but trying to be surreptitious about it … and failing. "At least your little brothers still love me," she continued as Nic crossed his arms over his chest and his mother studied his leather pants, fur cloak, and chains. I wondered what she thought, seeing her little boy turn into a man?

Glancing at Nic, seeing the smooth muscles in his chest and belly, the natural bulge in the front of his too-tight leather pants, I felt myself go warm allover. He looked my way and hooked just the slightest tease of a smile, his dark red hair almost black in the dim outdoor lighting.

Aeron and Harlem stood off to the side, the faerie girl looking ridiculously uncomfortable and slightly irritated while the vampire girl … stared at the wolf guardswoman with rapt attention.

"Your father's inside making steaks," Lana said as one of the upstairs windows opened and Nic's brother, Levi, poked his head out. He looked remarkably like Nic—aubergine eyes, brick red hair, straight ridged nose, and high sculpted cheeks. They were the exact same age, Nic and his brother, born into the same litter of four. The other two brothers had already found mates and shared a house up the road, them and their two young wives.

"Hey dickhead," Levi said, smiling big. "Thanks for deigning to pay us a visit."

Nic ignored him completely. Since he'd started living with me so young, I knew he felt a bit like an outsider in his own family.

"We should get Harlem inside before someone sniffs out a vamp on pack property," I said, looking up at the night sky and listening carefully. A howl echoed but it was from miles and miles away. We'd timed our arrival to make sure we were here when the perimeter guards were on the opposite side of the property.

"Come on in," Lana said, her dark red hair braided and hanging over one shoulder. "All of you," she added with a little wink, gesturing us up the front porch steps and inside. "Leslie, our Alpha-Son is home!"

"Mom," Nic said again, trying to ignore Che's smirking little smile. "Can you please stop?"

"I'm just so proud of you, honey, that's all," she said as his dad came around the corner, red hair ruffled, a puppy under each arm. Lana and Leslie had what they called their 'holy crap' litter just last year. Another puppy was underfoot, his red brown tail wagging happily as he approached my feet and sniffed my bare toes. Seeing Nic's kid brothers … really made me miss mine. I was going to have to make a point to go home and snuggle Hugo sometime soon. Without me, he was all alone with my bloodthirsty siblings.

"Aren't you proud, Leslie?" Lana continued as the boys and I moved down the hall and into the gorgeous two-story living room. The second story overlooked it, facing the towering stone fireplace on one side, the flames crackling cheerfully. God, I loved it here.

"So very proud of my boy," Leslie said as one of the pups flicked a wet pink tongue across the lens of his glasses. He, too, tried to give Nic a kiss but the pups took over and ended up leaping into their older brother's arms instead.

"I have clothes waiting in here," Lana said, gesturing for Harlem to follow her through a door off the living room, into the master bedroom, and the waiting bathroom. "If you could," I heard her say as the vampire princess swept by in her glittering cloak and short black dress, "shower once, dry off, and then shower again. When you get out, use the lotions, hair oil, and toothpaste on the counter. That should mask your scent enough to get us through the night."

"Thank you," I heard Harlem reply, her voice cautious and cold, but also strangely optimistic. She *wanted* this, to feel the warmth and earthiness of *pack.* That was why I was okay with this, leaving her here. She wanted to be *wolf* more than she cared to kill two random guardsmen and their children.

The door closed behind Harlem and Lana reappeared in the living room, looking the faerie girl over in her glamour, even leaning close for a sniff.

"Wow," she said as she stepped back and studied the girl with the dark hair and blue-black eyes, "she smells like a human. Looks like a human. That's an impressive glamour."

"I would hope," Aeron said, tilting her head to one side,

black hair cascading in a wave over her shoulder. “It was a gift from the Unseelie Queen.”

'At least that answers that question,' Anubis said, standing respectfully off to one side while both Che and Tidus flopped onto the sofa. It was an interesting snapshot of their personalities—one of them cocky and arrogant, and the other friendly and outgoing.

“Well,” Lana, running her hands down the front of her red t-shirt. She was wearing matching flannel pj bottoms, surprisingly relaxed at the idea of a vampire and a faerie inside her home. It spoke to the confidence she had in me, in her son, in the new little pack I found myself a part of. A pack of alphas. “I hope you like steaks because that's on the menu for tonight. Zara, are you and the boys staying?”

I caught a glimpse of the barbecue outside and knew instinctually that there were probably enough steaks for us all cooking inside of it. *Oh, Lana, you sweetheart.*

'Mom wants us to stay for dinner,' Nic said, and the way Monty, Jax, and Silas glanced in his direction, I knew he'd spoken to all the boys. He was making a serious effort to adjust to our new situation. And knowing how much he hated it … I felt a swelling of love inside my chest, intense enough to make my breath catch.

'Then let's stay,' I told him. And in the back of my mind, I tried not to think thoughts like *what if this is the last time Lana ever gets to see Nic?* Because in reality, we could die any day. Taking a moment to have dinner with his parents was not something I'd ever regret.

My mind whirled with thoughts of Selena, Allister, the

missing pack members … but it was late, and we were all hungry, and tomorrow … there was always the rare chance those divinations would tell us something useful. We needed to be ready.

'I think we should stay, too,' Montgomery said, heaving a low, tired breath, looking like a fucking warrior king with his long, white braid, fur cloak, and leather pants. He carefully removed his badass tool kit and swords, and then sat down heavily on Lana's sofa, right between Che and Tidus.

"We'd love to stay," I said, looking at Lana's bemused expression. The buzz in the air told her we were communicating in wolfspeak, even if she couldn't hear it.

"Good," she said, nodding her chin and glancing over at Leslie as he struggled to get all three pups into a little playpen near the archway to the kitchen. "It's hard enough making day-to-day decisions with just one other person's feelings to contend with. I don't envy you guys, having eight peoples' bullshit to deal with." I smiled back as she clapped her hands together and let her eyes trail over the sea of alpha males crowding her living room. "So. Which one of you handsome young men is going to help me set the table?"

Opening the door to an empty house was nice. As I walked

inside and turned on one of the floor lamps, I felt like I could actually breathe for the first time in days.

They've been siphoning magic off of your people for close to a century now.

Harlem's words about the witches rang in my head like the chiming of bells, an answer to a mystery that had been haunting my people for a long fucking time. Too long. But how, why … those were questions I'd have to fight long and hard to get the answers to.

"Finally, some privacy," Che said as he walked in and immediately unhooked the clasp on his cloak, swinging the fur over the back of the couch and sighing in relief. He pulled the wooden moon to the side and the chains fell off, sloughing to the floor in a messy, metallic heap. "I'm getting in bed before the rest of you assholes climb in and crowd me out."

He bent down and picked up the chains, flicking his violet eyes in my direction as he stood back up.

"You want to join me, Alpha-Red?" he said, turning and walking backward toward the stairs. Che paused and reached down, flicking open the button on his leather pants, our gazes locked across the shadowy living room.

"Look at you," Tidus said, moving up next to him and smacking the other man in the abs with his sun-kissed fingers. "Laying it on thick. Typical romance novel cliché, right?"

"That's what I was going for," Che said, his voice as smooth as silk. "The bad boy with a heart of gold." He patted his smooth chest with a palm. "Oh, wait? I don't even have a heart. That blows. I've fucked it up already."

Both Tidus and I laughed as Che tossed a wink in my direction and headed up the stairs to the bedroom, pushing his leather pants over his ass *just* before he turned the corner and disappeared from sight. I did not miss the scrumptious flash of butt cheeks.

Asshole.

"Are you staying up for a while?" Tidus asked as I stood in the living room and watched Monty, Anubis, and Jax come through the screen door. Nic and Silas stayed outside, and I smelled the faint whiff of cloves and tobacco from one of Silas' cigarettes. Their voices were low, but if I focused hard enough, I could make out the words.

"Do you mind if I bum a cigarette?"

This from Nicoli Hallett, a man who'd never smoked a day in his life.

"I think so," I said to the Alpha-Son of Pack Amber Ash, glancing over at his gray eyes and wondering what sort of person was hiding under all of that happy-go-lucky. Or if that really was his true personality. We definitely needed to spend some more time together. "Would you take me surfing one day?" I asked him, licking my lower lip. "I've never been."

"Never?" he asked, and I swear his smile lit up the entire room. "I'd love to take your surfing virginity," he said, the fur cloak and leather pants an interesting contrast to his tanned skin and blonde hair. Somehow though, he made it work. He didn't look awkward or uncomfortable, but rather like he was just going with the flow. I was pretty sure Tidus

Hahn did *not* expect me to pick him at the end of the Pairing.

"As I long as I take yours first?" I offered and he laughed again, the sound a bright light in all of the darkness we'd been having to deal with lately.

"Um, absolutely! It's a deal. This," he said, gesturing at his body with a loose wave of his hand, "it's yours whenever you want it. I've been saving it for you all these years anyway. And I'm not gonna lie, I'm like *super* curious about sex. I mean, I've seen a lot of porn, but uh … pretty empty on the experience end of things."

"How very blatant of you," Anubis said, pausing next to him and tilting his head slightly to one side, "telling the Alpha about your extensive porn collection."

"What can I say? Curiosity got the werewolf," Tidus said with an easy shrug of his shoulders and a self-deprecating little grin that crinkled up the skin around his eyes. "Surf's up, babe!" He tossed me a wink and a little *shaka*—you know, the hang loose thing—sign with his hand before heading up the stairs after Che.

Montgomery had already headed for the shower while Jax had disappeared into the kitchen, opening the fridge and grabbing a soda, a beam of light cutting across the floor before he shut the door.

"I don't know, man, I'm trying," I heard Nic say outside and felt my interest pique.

"Did you want to try working with the silver tonight?" Anubis asked, pulling off his cloak and draping it over one arm. I thought about the witches and Harlem's words and

… ended up just sucking in a sharp breath. Yes, I did need to practice with the silver, but right now? I just wanted to go outside and see what Silas and Nic were talking about. The fact that they were talking at all was a win for me.

"No, not tonight," I said. If the witches really *had* been slow draining my people for a hundred fucking years, one more night was not going to kill us, right? "Tomorrow," I said when Anubis raised his brows and smiled at me.

"Tired?" he asked as Jax moved up to stand beside him, also watching me. Only, Anubis was staring at me like I was his goddess and Jax was … sort of looking at me like he couldn't care less. I wanted to crack that hard shell of his and see what was underneath. The few little tidbits of his personality I *had* seen—such as his cheeky little attitude when he asked me to tie the apron on his naked body—were adorable.

"Exhausted," I admitted with a small smile, one that got just a little bit bigger when Jax handed a second can of soda out to me. I took it from him, my fingertips brushing his palm, and felt my skin ripple with excitement.

"Well, I'll be upstairs if you want me," he said, without a hint of emotion or even a smile. My turn to raise my eyebrows as he turned away and disappeared up into the room with the rest of the boys. Now that the idea of sharing the bed had been breached, the alpha-sons seemed willing to embrace the idea. If they were anywhere near as tired as I was, I could see why there'd been basically zero resistance to the idea.

"I'll be down here for a little while," I told Anubis,

lifting up the soda and then moving toward the door. At the last minute, I paused, walked over to him and pressed a soft kiss to the side of his mouth, right at the corner.

Goddess, he tastes good, I thought as I leaned back, smiled, and watched the expression on his face shift slightly. A little less scholarly … a little more lascivious.

"Have you ever had a girlfriend before?" I asked and he bit his lower lip.

"A few," he admitted, holding up a single palm in a placating gesture. "But I never did anything with them beyond a little hand holding. I've known from birth that I was destined to be your mate."

"Am I disappointing?" I asked him in a rare moment of weakness. I just felt it hit me like a truck, everything that'd happened in the last few days. I'd failed Faith and Diya, failed poor Notch and Mila … I'd uncovered secrets and betrayal, taken the boys to places I didn't know we'd make it out of. I was hiding this whole operation from my mother and the other alphas, leaving the Convocation in the dark when I *knew* for a fact that they'd storm both Julian's house and the Triad historical society with all their might. Was it worth that, that risk and sacrifice to save our missing members? Or was *my* slow and steady approach the right way?

"Disappointing?" Anubis asked, tossing his cloak onto the back of the couch and putting his hands on my shoulders. His skin was warm and beautiful, such a rich shade that looked so gorgeous against my own cream colored flesh. I lifted my hands and put them atop his.

"Not at all. Zara, you're everything I imagined you'd be: smart, strong, clearheaded and …" Anubis licked his lips and I couldn't tell if he was being a submissive wolf … or a flirtatious human. "Beautiful. In human and wolf form," he added, his mouth making that sinful little slash across his face that'd I'd noticed when I'd first met him. "Just … stunning."

He leaned in and pressed a kiss to the corner of my mouth, just the same as I'd done to his. Except … as he was kissing me, I turned my mouth and let our lips connect. For a split second, we were mouth to mouth, frozen in place.

I opened my lips first and flicked my tongue against Anubis' mouth. He parted his own lips and we worked our way into an easy, natural sort of kiss. You'd never know it was only our second kiss *ever* together.

His hands slid down my arms, fingers curling loosely around my hips, bracing himself for our kisses but leaving any further steps to me …

I pulled back a minute later and laid a palm on his chest, those crimson eyes even prettier up close than they were from far away. Face to face like this, I could see darker striations of purple and a gradation of red in his irises. Like two little planets, each a world in their own right, drawing me deeper and deeper into that gaze …

Outside, a rash of raucous coughing ensued follow by low, sensuous laughter.

Nic and Silas.

"You head up to bed," I told the Alpha-Son of Pack Crimson Dusk. "And I'll be up in a bit."

I turned away in a swish of bloodred skirts and black fur trim, and headed outside into the waning moonlight to find both Silas and Nic on their backs in the grass, looking up at the blanket of night and all her little silver stars, tucked away beneath her navy folds, twinkling pretty in their eternal slumber.

"Since when did you start smoking?" I asked, putting my hands on my hips and looking down at Nic, sprawled across his fur cloak, a cigarette in one hand and a disgusted facial expression on his handsome features.

"Since never," he said, stabbing the cherry out in the wet grass and passing it over to Silas as he coughed and hacked, rolling onto his side as I reached out and unhooked the clasps on the front of my dress. The thick heavy fabric fell away as it was intended to—to make it easier to shift—and I was left standing pale and nude in the moonlight.

I threw the dress down to make a little bed and laid between the boys on my back, so I could look up at the sky and the waning moon, too.

Normally, being nude like this wouldn't mean a damn thing …

Right now, it felt like it meant a whole lot of things. I knew my nipples were hard, peaked into sharp points, and my sex … it was swollen and warm and wet from kissing Anubis. The boys could smell my arousal, I knew.

"I seriously don't know how you manage to choke those things down," Nic said, pretending not to notice the sexual tension that had stretched nice and taut between the three of us. I wondered if this hyper-sexuality we were all feeling would lessen over time? I hoped so. Or … not. I mean, I liked it but it was distracting as hell.

"When my dad first caught me smoking," Silas said, blowing the sweet smell of cloves and tobacco into the night sky, one tattooed arm tucked behind his head, the other lying by his side. "He broke my arm, and then he told me I'd either learn to smoke them properly or he'd break it again. Basically, he *forced* me to learn to take it. I think he figured no werewolf in their right mind would be able to do it, but fuck him, I proved him wrong."

Silas stopped talking and the world went quiet for a few moments, the only sounds the rustling of the tree limbs and the distant night sounds of the forest.

"That guy is such a piece of shit," Nic said, and I knew we were all thinking of Allister and his involvement in this witch-vamp war of ours.

"*We haven't been kidnapping 'weres', Zara Wolf. Allister Vetter and his people ... they've been delivering them.*"

Whitney's words were loud in my mind, almost a scream. Of *course* a wolf was helping facilitate this. My people were strong; it'd be quite the challenge to round them up like chattel and carry them off. But if someone they trusted were to call a meeting? Invite them to a rendezvous point? Hell, he was the alpha male of Pack Obsidian Gold. He could simply … command wolves of lower rank to go where he wanted and do what he wanted …

"I'm sorry I didn't tell you sooner," Silas whispered, his gold eyes focused on the endless ceiling of navy and stars above us. I looked over at him, my head pillowed in a sea of red hair, and then I reached out with my right hand and touched my fingers to the bare skin of his hip, just above the waistband of those deliciously tight leather pants of his. "I should have. I … he's always inside my head, smiling and baring his teeth. He's … he invades my every waking moment. I feel like I'm walking on eggshells still, even though I know I'm technically out of his reach now …"

"Now you're mine," I told him and Silas visibly shuddered, rolling away from me and curling into a fetal ball. I watched him go, and then I scooted close enough to spoon him, curling one arm around his stomach and pressing my face to his back. He smelled like cherries and vanilla, like tobacco and cloves. I was starting to really fucking like that smell.

When I closed my eyes, I could feel his body pushing inside of mine, his hips hitting my ass as he fucked me over the bathroom sink. And I wouldn't soon forget the look on his face in that mirror … or the one on mine.

"I've been waiting a long time to be mated," Silas said with a tired sigh, letting his cigarette fall from his fingers to fizzle out in the wet grass. "Just so I could get the fuck away from him, and yet … he found a way to infiltrate everything. *Everything.* He's literally putting the future of every werewolf on this fucking planet at risk with his bullshit."

"We're going to fix this," I promised, because the White Wolf … never broke her promises. I'd have to hold myself to the words falling from my lips, my voice a husky whisper as fragile as the icy drops of dew that clung to the grass. I'd been completing my tasks lately with less than stellar results … finding Faith's mom … but finding her dead. Or discovering the fate of our missing pack mates … but spending days slogging through politics and bullshit as I tried to find a way to rescue them.

Silas turned back toward me and I scooted a few inches so he could lie on his back again, flicking his gold eyes to the side to watch me. In the distance, a branch cracked from the weight of the still melting snow. In a few days, it would be gone completely and spring would finally get a change to blossom and bloom, turning the pack's property into a fragrant garden of scents and smells, plentiful with prey.

"Nic and I were just discussing his uh, *feelings*," Silas said, obviously desperate to change the subject. He sat up and looked back at me, his scar barely visible in the light. As a wolf, it should've healed. We rarely scarred. And yet … whatever his father had done had left a permanent mark. One day I'd ask, but now was not the time. "Tell her what you told me," he said, pushing up to his feet. "And then come join us in the house, okay? Like, you're a fucking annoying little asshole, but you need to speak your damn mind."

Silas grabbed his cloak and the discarded cigarette, and headed toward the front porch, leaving me and Nic alone.

Alone.

For the first time in days.

"Your feelings?" I asked, because I'd heard just enough of their conversation to wonder.

"Zara," Nic said, and his voice sounded broken. I turned

toward him and found his aubergine eyes locked on the moon, refusing to look at me. "I … I'm not all that good with words, you know that."

"I know that," I said, a slight smile blooming on my face. "But I don't care. I can read you like a book, Nicoli Hallett."

"You probably think of me as a possessive asshole …" he started, but I was already sitting up and crawling over to him, straddling his leather covered pelvis with my hot, warm heat. The motion made us both catch our breaths. Sitting up there, with the stars above my head and the wet grass and snowy forest around us, the air perfumed wth the homey smell of honeysuckle and pine, of Pack Ebon Red, I felt my arousal like a weight inside my tummy. I *needed* to sate it.

But first, I would talk. Because Nic needed to talk. And he deserved it. He'd loved me his entire life, wanted me for years, and yet he'd known for a long time that he could never have me. Even now, even after managing to sneak him into the Pairing, he didn't believe he was going to be with me at the end of it. No, as far as he was aware, one of these cocky assholes, like Che or Jax or Silas, these boys who waltzed in here with bad attitudes, was going to be my mate forever.

We lived in a society of monogamous pairs, pairs that mated for *life.* And although Nic and I had mated, he wasn't guaranteed the same security that any other werewolf would've gotten. No, he was left sitting here, watching me fuck men I barely knew when he'd been waiting *years.* And no, that didn't entitle him to anything, but he had a right to be upset. In fact, I was surprised he wasn't *more* upset. To the other alpha sons, he might've been a bitchy little asshole that needed to be put in his place, but to me, he was my childhood friend and the man … no, the *person* that I loved.

"If I close my eyes," I told him, looking down at his beautiful face, that arrogant haughty little face that hid the most loyal and the most loving man I'd ever met in my life. "And imagine that *you* were the alpha-heir, that we'd just had our first time together and then all these … these beautiful, sexy girls waltzed into your life and got to kiss and touch and fuck you when I'd been waiting forever … Nic, I'd probably challenge and kill them."

"Zara," he started, but I wasn't done.

I leaned down and put my cheek against his, his hands sliding up my back.

"If it were you, and I told you how upset I was and you just told me to fuck off, that it was none of my business and you could mate with whoever you wanted … that would kill me."

His hands tightened on my hips and he sucked in a sharp breath. I could feel him hard and ready and wanting inside his leather pants, so I sat back up and scooted down, just far enough to reach his button and zipper.

"It's not like I think I own you or anything," he whispered, but he was preaching to the choir. I knew. I knew and I understood and I honestly didn't give a flying *fuck* if somebody else was too ignorant or too broken or too unwilling to understand it, too. "I just … you get one mate,

Zara. One. And all of these guys, these … fucking strangers have a better chance than I do. It's not like you can choose us all," he said, his voice strangled and far away.

But as I sat there and looked down at him, I wondered about that. Why choose? That was the thought I'd been entertaining for a few days. It was just a seed of a thought, and I had no idea how the packs would react to it, how these men would react to it, but it was worth exploring, wasn't it?

Because as I sat there and looked down at my childhood friend, I *knew* that I couldn't pick him. And yet I knew that I wouldn't give him up either.

"You said you'd be my paramour?" I asked and he nodded, a sharp sudden movement that told me so much. He would and he'd feel grateful to sit in the shadows and watch me rule with another man.

"Or just your guard. Zara, if you don't pick me … and you don't want me, then please, for the love of Mother Earth, don't mate me to another female. You're it for me, Zara. It's just you. There might be a million stars in this sky, but there's only one moon. I think … I could see it being possible for you to love like the night loves stars, but not me. I only get one great love in my life. I'd rather castrate myself and be your guard than take another lover." He paused and closed his eyes. "Whatever decision you make, I'll support it."

I popped the button on his pants and then curled my claws—because I'd somehow shifted claws without even meaning to—and yanked the ridiculously tight leather of his pants down and over his erection. The thick hard length of his shaft bounced out, excited to be free, and I grinned.

"I won't let you go," I told him because … at the end of this year, I'd be the Alpha Female of all the packs. Me. I'd be the boss. And I wouldn't have to let Nic go. My word … it'd be fucking law. "I promise, Nic. I promise."

"Fuck, Zara," he said, but it was hard to read the emotion in his voice because I was lifting myself up and positioning him at my opening, sliding down the warm length of his velvety cock as I tossed my head back and sighed with pleasure. "*Fuck, Zara,*" he said again as I moved my hips, rocking nice and slow, wanting to drag this out as long as I could.

Nic looked like a fucking king, lying beneath me on a black fur cloak with red silk lining, his dark red hair fanned around his head, his eyes the same inky purple color as my own. He slid his hands over the swell of my hips to my waist, and then palmed my breasts, kneading the tender flesh with strong, sure fingers.

I bit my lip and moaned at the same time he teased the hardened points of my nipples with his thumbs. I was so wrapped up in the moment that I didn't realize my tail and ears were peeking out until Nic's mouth curved to the side in a smile.

"Oh, Zara, so cute," he murmured, grabbing a handful of my long red hair in his hand and gently tugging my face toward his. He kissed me at the same time as he stroked the soft fur of my wolf ear, kneaded it between thumb and forefinger and making me groan. I could feel my tail wagging in response. "So fucking cute," he said again as our tongues danced to the ancient rhythm of our bodies, the beautiful sonata of a forest night.

Long, slow movements slicked my wet heat along Nic's shaft, working his body with the tight clamp of my muscles. The first two times we'd had sex, I'd felt more human than wolf. This time, I felt like a nice, even mixture of both. I loved Nic, cherished him as a friend, but my wild side also responded to him the way a female responds to a male when she's ready to mate … I wanted him in so many ways right then, so many, many ways.

I sat back up, pressed my body to Nic's and made sure I was holding every inch of him inside of me. Bloodred hair cascaded over my shoulders, strands of it hanging over my breasts as I put my palms flat on Nic's chest and rode him like a queen rides her king, like an alpha female rides her alpha male.

Nic belonged to me.

The rules of the Pairing … didn't change that. After all, we once had a great heroine who had seven husbands, didn't we? And there were no rules *against* me having more than one mate. Of course, it all depended on what the other alpha males wanted. I guess we'd ride out the year and see what happened at the end of it?

Nic and I locked gazes, his hands finally settling on my hips as I rocked, rocked, rocked my body just right, my clit rubbing against his pelvis. The way he looked at me then, I really did feel like the moon, shining with silver love and light from an endless sky.

The natural rhythm of muscles squeezing his cock,

fluttering against his shaft, drew an orgasm from him that arched his back up off the ground and spilled his seed in me. I paused then, but I didn't try to finish myself.

Instead, I climbed off of him and sat with my butt in the wet grass. I could feel that it was cold—my body registered the temperature—but it didn't *make* me cold. I loved being a fucking werewolf.

Nic rolled onto his side and looked up at me.

"I don't know how you plan to keep me *and* keep the peace at the end of the year, but … if that's what you say you're going to do, I believe you."

"I promise," I told him again as he sat up and we locked gazes. It was hard to say in words how good it felt to fuck him after wanting for so, so, so long. It was … like the planets in my own personal solar system were *finally* in orbit. Finally. Finally. Fucking *finally.*

"That's more than good enough for me," Nic said, and rather than tuck his wet cock back into his leather pants, he just kicked off his boots and peeled the pants off, sitting as naked as I was in what was essentially our front yard.

Good thing we were on pack property, huh?

"You didn't climax?" he asked, raising his dark red brows. I glanced over at him and smiled sharply.

"Not yet," I said, and then I stood up and offered him my hand. He took it, and we went into the Pairing House together, our skin bathed in starlight and sweat.

It was another of those rare moments of happiness, those distant twinkling stars we were always chasing after … I took hold of the memory, stuffed it in a mental pocket, and promised I'd keep it safe. Even if I lived as long as my Alpha-Majka, I wouldn't forget.

Not ever.

After a quick stop in the downstairs bathroom (sex was messier than I'd ever anticipated as a virgin), Nic and I headed upstairs to find most of the alpha males were already asleep … Most of them.

"Montgomery," I said, pausing near the foot of the bed, my eyes focused on the Ivory Emerald Alpha-Heir, sitting pretty in the window seat on the far side of the room. His braid was hanging down the front of his muscular chest, and he was still wearing his leather pants and boots, even though his cloak was gone. "Are you okay?"

I knew *okay* was a relative term, considering the fact that his family was still missing, but … I hoped he knew what I meant.

"I'm just thinking," he said, and as I watched him, his forehead tight with worry, I saw the shadows of my own worry flitting across his face. *God, we really are similar, aren't we?* Monty was the Ivory Emerald version of me.

"About?" I asked as I moved over to the opposite side of the bed, sitting on the edge, my knees just inches from Montgomery's. This room had never been intended to hold an eight person size bed. It fit, but just barely.

Nic crawled onto the bed behind me, giving Che a decent amount of space. I wasn't sure if he was asleep or not; it was hard to tell with the sounds of so many people breathing, shifting, muttering softly while they danced through dreamland.

Moonlight struck Montgomery's face in a silver wave, highlighting those knightly features of his. He had a warrior's face, strong and stern, but with a slightly soft edge that gave him the appearance of a just man. The perfect face for a king. Well, in this case, an alpha male. But really, they were one in the same.

Looking at him like this, I could not fucking *believe* that he was only seventeen. Wait till Faith found out about *that* part of the equation. She wasn't going to let me live this one down …

"Everything," he said, reaching up to push the feathery white bangs from his forehead, his green eyes as bright as new spring leaves. "This … supposed witch spell that's draining our people dry. And the level of greed that it must've taken for the witches to want *more.* It wasn't good enough to watch the werewolves suffer a slow, uneasy decline. Now they're *eating* us. Now, they want fucking war." He went to brush his bangs back again and ended up shoving his fingers through his hair.

"The waiting's the hardest part," I said, but he just turned his gaze and stared out the open window, toward the dark woods just behind the Pairing House. The dirt road that connected this building to the rest of the property snaked down and to the right, disappearing into the trees. "The fighting is easy. The fighting means something is getting done. It's in moments like these that you really feel helpless."

"Time is a cruel mistress," Monty said, looking back at me with a desperate plea in his face. "These divinations tomorrow, how are they going to help us? Aeron said she couldn't read the bones this side of the Veil."

"Not the bones, no, but both she and Whitney seemed to think either the tarot cards or the *haruspex* would help. They didn't say how, but it's worth a shot. And anyway, I wouldn't mind more time just to talk to the Maiden. I'm sure she hasn't told us everything she knows."

Montgomery stood up, a slow easy unfolding of his tall, lean form, and then he walked over and knelt before me, just like the knight I saw him as. He leaned forward and pressed his head into my belly; my right hand automatically touched on the top of his head, his hair as white as snow, glossy and full and soft. I dug my fingers into it as he put his hands on my hips and pulled comfort from our touch, from the closeness of wolf and pack. Of male and female … of *mates.*

"I think I could get addicted to this hugging thing," he whispered, his words feathering against my lower abs. My muscles tightened out of reflex as Montgomery dragged his right hand down my side and along the pale length of my thigh.

'Nic,' I started, because I felt that charge all of a sudden. My aching body still tender and wet with need, my nipples still hard. I could mate again, no fucking problem. Sitting

here like this, I felt as if I could mate *all night.* In my mind, an image flickered of me lying in this bed, taking one alpha male after another … taking all seven of them in a row.

Goddess, I fucking *wanted* that. I wanted to mate with each of these males, mark them all at once, make them mine. I knew they wanted it, too, and that's what made it so irresistible. Not tonight, but … soon. I would do that before the year was out.

Oh, shit. Who was I kidding? I'd probably do that before the *month* was out.

'You don't have to tell me anymore,' Nic said, and I felt the bed adjust as he scooted closer to me, putting his lips up against my spine. *'In an ideal situation, I'd have you all to myself. But ... you're a queen. You may as well have knights. In this, I'd rather not share, but I have to admit that it's nice to have all that extra backup when we're dealing with vampire bullies and carnivorous witches.'*

'You're sure?' I asked, as Montgomery lifted his head and raised his green eyes to mine.

'I'm sure, Zara. I'm not going to lie and say I won't get upset or jealous or cranky sometimes, but ... it's okay. This is our life now, and it's okay.'

"I thought," Montgomery said, not privy to my private wolfspeak conservation with Nic, but also not completely ignorant to it either, "that since you used your hand last night …"

He trailed off and slid his fingers along my inner thigh until he found the red curls between my legs, slicking a single finger along the folds and shivering at the amount of slick wetness on his fingertips. I'd showered off real quick before coming up here and already, I was wet again.

"You smell like the forest," he murmured as he teased me, one of those long fingers stroking up from my opening to my clit, using my natural lubricant to tease the hardened nub of flesh. It was so sensitive, I could've sworn my body felt each ring of his fingerprints, like they were branding themselves into my flesh. "Like the trees and the wind …"

Monty leaned in close and pressed his lips to my knee, making me shiver.

I leaned back, my naked skin pressing against Nic's taut, hard belly. As soon as I did that, touched him and Monty both at the same time, it was like all my feelings, all those good sensations, were amplified a hundred times over.

If two of my males makes me feel this good, I wondered, reaching out my right hand and curling my finger's through Nic's, *then what would it be like if I had all seven of them? If they put their hands and mouths and cocks on my body ...*

I could only imagine, but even just the fantasy in my mind … was explosive.

"Oh, Zara," Nic said, sitting up and positioning himself behind me. He let go of my hand and slid his palms around my rib cage, sliding them up and palming the heavy weight of my breasts. In the moonlight, they were full and pale and covered in silver moonlight.

"I bet you taste like honeysuckle …" Montgomery murmured, his voice low and sleepy with sex. Using his hands, he pried my knees apart and continued kissing along the length of my thigh, pausing with his warm breath feathering against my wet heat. “May I, my alpha?” he asked.

It was too much of a chore to get my voice to work properly so instead I just groaned and put my hand on the back of his head, pushing his face to the heat of my cunt. When Montgomery flicked his tongue against my folds, I almost lost it completely. A growl escaped from my throat and I found myself pushing him harder against me, using my palm on the back of his head to guide him where I wanted him to go.

Nic's hands kept my upper half entertained … more than entertained … romanced, worshipped and warm. He squeezed my breasts with slow, easy motions, taking his time to give them the proper treatment they deserved. And his breath against my ear? That was intoxicating.

“I love you, Zara Wolf,” he whispered to me as Monty made the same rounds with his tongue that he'd done with his fingers, licking the entire length of me and then focusing his attention on my clit.

My body trembled under their ministrations, shook with wild need, by back arching, my left arm sliding back and finding Nic's head, pushing his lips against my neck. He growled and scooted closer to me; I could feel the thick, hard length of his shaft against my spine as he let go of my right breast and took hold of himself in his hand, working his dick with quick, violent strokes.

“What's all this?” I heard Che say, his voice a thick curl of darkness that snaked around me and drew my chin toward his big, muscular form, standing at the end of the bed, naked and wearing nothing but a smirk for clothing.

"Come here," I told him, but all he did was turn that smirk into a grin, padding a few steps closer but staying frustratingly out of reach. I pushed Monty in deeper and gave a ragged moan when he managed to sneak two fingers inside of me at the same time he was licking me with a hot, wet tongue. "Now, Che," I said, and I felt like I might snap if he didn't show at least a *drop* of submission toward me.

Whether that's what he was doing or not, he finally closed the distance between us and knelt on the edge of the bed, putting the velvet hardness of his shaft within my grasp.

"Oh, fuck," he snarled, sitting down beside me, thigh to thigh. We turned toward each other, and as I began to work his cock, he reached out with his right hand and pulled my arm down, destroying the barrier between us.

Without another word, he turned my chin more fully toward him and kissed my mouth like a beast who's just discovered the perfect prey. He could hunt me every night, slay me with passion and pleasure, *eat* me like Montgomery was doing. And then he could start all over again the next day.

I was a strong, powerful person and I did not submit to others, but with Che's tongue taking over my mouth, borrowing control for a brief moment, I wondered what it'd be like to play along, let him fuck me like *he* was in charge.

It wasn't something that sounded appealing on a frequent basis, but every once in a while? Wouldn't it be nice to just relax and let someone else take control for just a second?

Oh yes. I knew then that Che and I … we'd be experimenting with things I never even dreamed I'd want to try.

Montgomery slid his fingers in and out of me, swirling his tongue in circles around my clit, bringing my body to this state of ecstasy where all I could see behind my lids were showers of golden sparks, pleasure arching through me, up from my pussy and into my spine, out my mouth in a shout of pleasure.

I collapsed back into Nic as Montgomery withdrew, and my hand spasmed on Che's cock, making him snarl with pleasure.

"I want to mount you," the Pack Violet Shadow Alpha-Son said, looking me straight in the face with this violet eyes, his words bits of darkness plucked from between the stars and thrown right at me when I was at my most vulnerable.

Because … I don't think I'd ever *been* vulnerable before. Never. Except … maybe that night in the shed, when Monty and I first hugged.

"You *do* taste like honeysuckle," Montgomery said, sitting back and watching me, like he was waiting to hear how I'd respond to Che. Nic had paused his kneading of my breast to listen, but he didn't stop working his cock. No, he kept a nice, even steady rhythm, and I wondered if he was thinking about my body on top of his, starlight falling in white-silver beams around us.

"Fuck me," I told Che, because the magic of our pack connection was riding me hard … and I wanted Che to ride *me* hard. I could feel the lust of all three men rippling through our bond, turning me into a wild wolf of a woman. "From behind."

I'm enjoyed it so much in the bathroom with Silas … I wanted to do it again.

Nic scooted back, giving me room to get into position, and I caught the ebon beauty of his gaze. He looked like an animal, too, in that moment, awaiting his female's needs, killing time until he, too, was able to breed with her.

It was so primal … I knew that later I'd be talking to Faith about it, and I'd probably feel like a completely crazy person, but I didn't want to fight the feelings taking over me. They were fun and different, and as long as my logical brain checked in and was okay with what I was doing, there was nothing wrong with letting my animal side out to play.

Che crawled up behind me, his masculine scent making my sex clench tight, wishing he were inside me already. When his hands found my hips and gripped me tight, I relaxed into his touch, pushing my pelvis back so he'd have an easier time finding my opening. He smelt like bergamot oil and vanilla, the sweet kiss of lavender and the musky bite of fresh sweat underneath it all.

For a moment, he just sat there, on his knees behind me. Nic was on my right, leaning against the headboard and looking down at me, my bloodred hair making a mess of tendrils all over the place, pooling on the white pillow beneath my hands.

Montgomery climbed up on the other side, and he, too, took his shaft in his hand, using the juices he'd teased out of me for lube as he stroked himself. The sight of it reminded me of the warm beauty of our shower, the closeness I'd felt toward him.

"Che, now," I said, and he slapped me hard on the ass.

I whipped my gaze around to snarl at him the same moment he used his hand to guide his bare cock to my swollen folds.

We both grunted as he filled me up, my back arching, lids falling closed. Red hair slid over my shoulders as I lifted my head up and tilted it back, enjoying the feeling of being stretched, of being full, of having Che's balls slap my clit when he moved.

Oh, it was nice.

Beyond nice.

He growled and snarled under his breath as he moved, a fucking animal in his own right, a man I'd been irresistibly attracted to from moment one. I had a feeling we might have disagreements about his level of dominance down the line, but with our bodies melded together into one like this? I couldn't imagine wanting a man more. Oh, god, I didn't want to give Che up at the end of the Pairing Year, not when he made me feel like this.

Nic and Montgomery continued to stroke themselves, giving me a beautiful view of their hands wrapped around the glorious lengths of their penises. I wanted them both, too. I wanted to make Che come inside me, watch him collapse in a sweaty heap, and then do the same to the other two.

The rest of the men slept peacefully on the other half of

the bed, their breath an even rhythm that couldn't quite keep pace with the frantic thrusts of Che's muscular body against my ass. I could feel his shaft burrowing into me, the ridged folds of my cunt stroking and pleasing him, working him up to a sweaty frenzy.

"Oh my fuck," Che finally said, the first words he'd been able to grind out this whole time, his voice nothing but a sweet, sinful series of growls and purrs and incoherent murmurs. "Zara," he groaned, reaching out and tangling his fingers in the silken red strands of my hair. There was a slight pain in my scalp when he pulled, but I let him do it as he came, messy and snarling, filling me up with his wild seed.

Seed that belonged completely and solely to *me.* No other woman had had it.

No other woman would.

I would make sure of that.

I would fight off any challenger that came our way with teeth and claws and cunning.

Che … Monty … Nic … all of them were *mine.*

Che Nocturne grunted again and collapsed forward, covering me with the comforting weight of his muscular body.

"Zara," he whispered again, adjusting himself and falling to the side, near Nic. The Ebon Red guard didn't seem to mind, letting the other man press up against his leg.

I stayed on my hands and knees as Che lifted his head up and licked the edges of my lips, playfully and sweetly submitting to me. I growled at him and he pulled away, lying on his back with an arm flung across his eyes.

"I can't believe I waited my whole life for this. Sex is the *bomb,* man." Che paused, lifted his arm from his violet eyes, and looked at me. "But I have a feeling it's only this bomb with you, Zara Wolf. My female."

"My male," I said, sitting back on my knees and smacking him in his hard abs with the back of my hand. "Mine." I raised both red brows and Che just laughed, covering his eyes again as I turned around and looked over at Montgomery, my knight.

My bodyguard, my challenger, my knight.

Three different men, all with something to offer.

"Come here, Montgomery," I told him then, because he looked so calm and in control, so kingly in that moment that I just couldn't call him Monty.

Sliding down the pillows, I spread my knees and grabbed Montgomery by the end of his braid. He stopped stroking his shaft and looked down at me with those gorgeous eyes of his, their emerald color far from the most impressive part about him. And frankly, it *was* impressive as fuck. But the openness in his expression? The bare truth, and the strength, the resolve and dedication … that's what really got me.

"Alpha …" he started, his lids heavy, his mouth shiny from the orgasm he'd given me.

Montgomery didn't argue, sitting up and moving between my thighs, leaning over me and putting a palm on either side of my head. His white braid hung down and mixed with the long red strands of my hair.

He stared down, directly into my eyes, and I looked up into his.

"You're the most beautiful wolf I've ever seen," he told me, and I could tell it was more than a line. That was truth, pure and simple. I had a feeling that put in my position, a place where I was forced to tell lie after lie after lie … that Montgomery Graves might fail. And I liked him all the more for that. A truth teller without a silver tongue. "I came here for one reason, but I'm starting to think I'll want to stay for an entirely different one."

Montgomery leaned down and kissed me on the mouth, tasting of honeysuckle and the sweetness between my thighs. He used his right hand to touch the side of my head, kneading his fingers in my hair, pulling my face just a few millimeters closer so he could kiss me with everything he had inside.

I understood the Pack Ivory Emerald Alpha-Heir more in that single moment than I had the entire week we'd been together.

Untangling his fingers from my hair, Monty reached down and took hold of his shaft, positioning the head of his cock between my folds. That sweet, slow, aching that I wanted for our first lovemaking session … it was already starting.

Our eyes locked, he pushed his hips forward and gave me his cock inch by careful inch, watching my face as he filled me up, as he felt the warm embrace of a woman's body for the first time in his life.

Montgomery's body shuddered as I wrapped my legs

around his waist and slid my hands behind his neck, keeping our gazes locked together. Watching his expression change from surprise to pleasure to heavy-lidded ecstasy was a reward in and of itself. And then looking up at this kingly man with fire in his eyes and fight in his veins, and knowing that he was mine … priceless.

The feel of him sliding in and out of me, achingly sweet and slow, was so vastly different from Che's wild, violent thrusts. It made *both* acts seem more pleasurable, contrasted beautifully against one another, like rain and sunshine. The earth needed both to stay green and fragrant and beautiful.

"Oh," I murmured, no longer locked in place by feral, primal desire. No, this was that sweet, slow lovemaking. I wasn't sure that I'd done enough to earn it, but … in Monty's eyes, it looked like I had. It looked like he actually cared about what I felt, what I wanted, if I was hurting or scared or overwhelmed.

His body moved in these deep, undulating thrusts, filling me up completely, moving so deeply inside, the pleasure was almost transcendent. I could feel him in places I wasn't sure anyone else had touched before. Granted, my experience was limited, but Montgomery was long and thick, and he fit my body just right—like we were made for each other.

He nuzzled my neck and kissed my ear, working his way down my throat and then along my jaw until he found my lips. His kisses were featherlight at first, at odds with the slow but powerful movements of his hips. As I teased my fingertips down his back, I could feel his muscles moving to pleasure me, working to bring my body to another glorious orgasm.

After a while, I don't know how long, I felt Che sit up beside us. When I flicked my eyes toward him, I saw his face dark and shadowed and hungry for me. I had a feeling we could lock ourselves in a room and rut for days without tiring of it.

Nic sat beside him, watching us, his expression confused but … excited, too. Like he was enjoying himself, even if he didn't want to. His hand moved up and down his shaft, faster and faster, like he was timing his own strokes with Montgomery's movements inside of me.

Relaxing my head back into the pillows, I let Monty kiss and suck on my neck, his right hand moving to cup my breast, his body shuddering when he felt the heavy softness of it.

"Alpha," he groaned, and then he used his left hand to push my right thigh back, sliding just a bit deeper inside, grinding my clit with his pelvis. He moved us both to the verge of tears and then with a throaty groan, he released his come inside of me, shaking and shuttering. Surprisingly, he managed to keep moving for just a few seconds longer, long enough that my body began to flutter and pulse. "Zara Castille," he murmured at the same moment he collapsed.

I saw Nic's entire body go stiff, his hips bucking up toward the ceiling, his hand sliding down his shaft. He came hard as Che watched and Monty fell to the side, lying next to me and quivering, smelling like roses and earth.

Outside the window, the wind swirled with the raw, natural sweetness of our magic, cracking the branches of trees, and starting up a cacophony of avian sounds.

"Quick," I said, and I didn't know who to go to. "I'm about to come."

Montgomery scooted close, put one of his legs over mine and dropped his fingers between my thighs, using his and Che's seed as lube to fuck me over the edge, bring me whimpering and growling and calling all their names … all of them.

Every single one.

And the three boys I'd *just* fucked? Well, they didn't look as surprised as I thought they'd be.

Afterward, the four of us lay there, sweaty and smelling like wolf and sex, like our various packs, of shampoo and soap. We fell into dreamless, easy sleep, bodies intertwined, our wolves pleased with the sense of pack.

Pack.

My pack.

Zara Wolf and her seven mates.

In the morning, I got up and mixed myself some of the buttercup birth control formula that Nikolina had taught me about. The little yellow flowers smiled up at me, their petals shiny and bright, like sunshine. I felt almost bad about crushing them up with the mortar and pestle in the kitchen.

"No pups until I'm at least fifty," I said to myself, a statement that would probably weird a lot of humans out. Fifty was when some humans were becoming grandparents, not *considering* their first litter ... er, child. But with our extended lifespans, werewolves were different. My mother hadn't had her first litter until she was fifty-six years old; Majka had been sixty-three when Nikolina and my aunts were born.

I finished crushing the delicate little flowers and then transferred them to another bowl, one made of silver. It made my hands bleed when I touched it, but just the *slight* bit of silver that got into the mixture while stirring it up was enough that I didn't need to add more. A pinch of seeds from a jar marked *Queen Anne's Lace*—a white flower also known as *wild carrot*—and some of the water on the stove that I'd boiled with pennyroyal rounded out the mixture. Personally, I added honey to help with the taste but that part was optional.

"We're all taking it, too, you know," Jax said, surprising me. I hadn't heard him come down the stairs or even walk through the living room. I was too relaxed in this house. The old wards and our spot in the middle of pack land were making me lazy. I couldn't afford that.

"The buttercup?" I asked as I picked up the silver bowl and carefully poured the hot liquid into a mug. Blood droplets sprinkled across the counter, but I didn't mind. If silver protected my magic from the witches, I'd have to get as comfortable with it as Nikolina and Majka were.

"Did you know," Jax began, padding toward the counter in bare feet and skirting the edge of the breakfast bar, "that if you hold a buttercup up to your chin and there's a yellow reflection, it means you like butter. No reflection and you're not a fan."

"I didn't know that," I said, putting the silver bowl aside and washing my hands in the sink, my lips curving into a smile as I noticed Jax's white ears, and the furred fluff of his tail. Partial shifting wasn't *un*common, but it wasn't necessarily something I'd seen much of. Generally, it was saved for comfortable, familial situations. As the daughter of an alpha, I hadn't had many of those. But these boys … they both made *me* want to do a partial shift, and they also couldn't seem to resist doing it themselves. "And the buttercup?"

"That was a *yes,*" Jax purred, wearing a pair of blue plaid pajama pants that matched his glorious eyes. Even with the pungent smell of my birth control drink tainting the air, I could still smell the bright citrusy scent of Azure Frost. It made my mouth water, but I wasn't sure if that was because I *really* wanted a fucking orange … or because I really wanted Jax. "Except maybe your Ebon Red bodyguard. The rest of us have been taking buttercup once every other week for months."

"Good to know," I said, cringing a little as I lifted the mug to my lips and drank. The honey *barely* masked the acrid taste of the buttercups. To humans, this drink would be poison. To a werewolf, it was just downright fucking gross.

My phone buzzed across the countertop and I grabbed it, the wolf and moon charms jangling as I looked at a text from Faith.

soo, didn't hear from u yesterday. 2 busy w/ all those boyz? please rescue me. Owen is going out of town again & i'm scared he's gonna rob another store. have 2 work at the bookstore 2day but free later?

Poor Faith.

There was no way in hell I was going to get time to hang out today, not with the amount of shit on my to-do list. There was so much, I was starting to feel overwhelmed. And I wasn't like that, not me, Zara the White Wolf. I could do anything. But this Contribution? Even with seven mates, it was a bit much. I wondered how the Convocation was faring on their end?

I shot off a quick text, telling her that we'd for sure hang out next week but that I was too busy today. I'd barely hit send when I got a reply.

y can't we do a girls' day out on Monday?

"How do you tell your best friend you can't hang out on Monday because you'll be too busy trying to avoid a vampire-witch war from breaking out with your werewolf pack?"

"I don't befriend humans," Jax said, watching me drink the hot liquid with a crinkled expression on his face. "I only recently got a phone and only because my alphas wanted me to be competitive with the other heirs." He paused and his tail wagged, a cautious little twitch that meant he was curious to see how I'd react. His right ear flicked back and he yawned, stretching his arms above his head and flashing me that gloriously muscular body of his.

I was still sore from last night, but I couldn't stop myself from appreciating the view.

Staring at Jax over the top of my mug, I sipped slowly and let our gazes connect with a small spark of electricity.

"I do like my phone though," he said, sliding it from his pajama pants pocket and tossing it onto the counter. "It's like a portal to another world."

"Do you really not mingle with humans at all?" I asked him carefully, remembering our previous conversation.

"How often do you come in contact with humans and pay them little to no attention? Everyday at school? Every time you stop at a grocery store? Go to a movie?"

"Who says I ever do any of those things?"

He'd *implied* a certain distance from humanity, and Pack Azure Frost was known for being a little … behind the times so to speak, but it never hurt to ask.

"Not much. That's not to say I've *never* been around humans, but it's a rare and special occasion. I don't care for wolves either, actually. It's just werewolves that I like." He looked at me with that cold, quiet facial expression of his, and I just suddenly wanted to break it in half. I wanted to tear that mask to bits and see what was hiding underneath it, and I didn't want to wait.

"Like?" I asked as I finished off the buttercup drink and put the mug aside. If I asked, my mother would have one of my sisters come and clean the house for us, but I wasn't at all sure that I wanted them in my space. Not that *I* actually had the time to clean …

"Okay, like might've been a strong word. Tolerate? I tolerate werewolves. I don't like humans *or* wolves. Or any other Numinous for that matter. Cats, though, I can say with confidence that I *do* like a soft pussy every now and again."

"If that was your attempt at innuendo," I said, moving over to stand next to him, "then you suck at it. There was no subtlety there at all."

"Sorry, did you think I was trying to be subtle? I wasn't particularly interested in fucking … until now. Now, I'm intrigued." Jax flashed a grin at me that was remarkably similar to the original ink drawing of the Cheshire Cat from *Alice's Adventures in Wonderland.* "Last night, you put on quite the show. I think you woke up all my basic instincts."

"Is that so?" I asked, still standing strangely close to him. If I'd been in wolf form, I would've put my head over the back of his neck, a subtle display of dominance. As a human, that move was a little tricky … Still, I found myself leaning into him, mimicking the gesture as best I could. All it really did was put his lips at the side of my neck. "You seemed so anathema to kissing me during the Bonding Ritual …"

"Mm, that was a public display. All of this private quiet and hot heat, the scent of mating … it makes me curious. It makes me wonder, what would it feel like if she invited me to mate? Would I like it? Would I make those same sounds as Montgomery? As Che and Nic? I could *feel* their pleasure rippling through the pack connection."

"So you *do* want an invitation?" I asked, closing my eyes as Jax put his lips to the side of my neck and kissed my throat. Slowly, so slowly that for a few seconds there, I really felt like I might be dreaming, he kissed his way up my throat and along my jaw to my lips. And then he kissed around them with slow, sensual flicks of his tongue, a gesture that was half-sexual and half-submissive. Human and wolf. Both. Neither. Werewolf.

We have so much to do today, my mind warned me. *We have to get Aeron and Harlem from Lana's house, take them to coffee with us, deal with the witch, hunt a deer, prepare for Monday.* Because on Monday, Julian's response to my message was going to come in some form or another. Whether it was a non-answer that screamed *war* in all its echoing silence or something more sinister, it *would* come.

And I'd have to figure out what to do with it.

And yet … Jax smelled so good. That lemon-lime sweetness on his skin mixed with the distinct earthy scent of wolf. As I laid my hands on his tummy, I remembered last night and the crazy swirl of magic that had swept through the trees outside, all the cracking branches, the terrified scream of an owl. It'd been on and off, our newfound magic. Touching the boys *could* spark our power … or it might not. I just needed to be careful until I found a way to control it. I didn't want another explosion like the one that'd happened in Nic's bedroom that first night. The one in the river had been a blessing, but I didn't exactly want the two of us catapulted out the kitchen window right now …

"An invitation," Jax growled, and I swear, there was little to no human in that sound. "Yes."

Stepping back slightly, I ran my tongue over my lower lip.

Jax watched me with eyes too blue to be human, too blue to be wolf. Werewolf eyes. The eyes of an Azure Frost prince.

Slowly, I dropped to my knees and reached my fingers up, curling them under the waistband of his pajama pants. He just stood there, breathing hard, staring down at me with his lips slightly parted. I could see wolf teeth from here, gleaming sharp canines in the weak yellow sunshine. It lit the kitchen with beams of watery light as I pulled his pants down and out of my way.

Last night, I'd been worshipped.

This morning, I would experiment …

Jaxson was already hard, the head of his shaft damp with pre-ejac. I started there, even though I knew it would kill him, rubbing my thumb ever so slightly against the head. He gasped and fell back into the counter, leaning on it for support.

A snarl tore from his throat, but it wasn't an aggressive sound—that was *his* invitation to *me.*

Sliding my thumb down the length of his shaft, I tickled his pelvis with my fingers and enjoyed the sharp inhale of breath, the way all those muscles contracted and expanded. With my other hand, I cupped his balls, teased the surprisingly soft skin, and let them sit on my palm.

Jax didn't say a damn word. Maybe he was beyond words?

I leaned in and put my lips to Jaxson's lower belly, kissing everything *but* his cock and balls, teasing him with my tongue and drawing little circles on his taut flesh. His breathing was so rhythmic and beautiful, the sound of sex in soliloquy. I could listen to it on repeat.

He braced his hands on the cabinets behind him and just looked at me, watched me with dilated pupils and parted lips as I got closer and closer and closer …

Sitting back, I wrapped the fingers of my right hand around his dick and squeezed just enough to make his hips buck toward my face. He couldn't help it; the movements were instinctual.

I licked my lips to wet them and then slowly, slowly, slowly put my mouth over the head of his shaft.

Jax snarled, a violent, wild sound—much like Che had

the previous night. But unlike Che, he seemed to have more control over himself, tilting his head back and focusing his eyes on the ceiling above us. What he *couldn't* control were the claws that exploded from his fingertips or the way he dug them into the countertop, panting heavily as I slid forward, taking more and more of him into my mouth.

'I don't know if I can do this,' he warned me, unable to speak with human words and instead using the strange, mysterious magic that was wolfspeak. It wasn't English, not quite, just … sounds and feelings and ideas that somehow translated into meaning. I knew that no matter how hard I tried, I'd never be able to explain it to a stranger. It wasn't something that needed explaining; you either understood wolfspeak or you didn't.

Wolf or non-wolf.

'Zara,' he ground out, and even though his lips weren't moving, his jaw and neck were tight and his lips were pulled back from his teeth.

I pushed forward, taking the entirety of his shaft into my throat. As a werewolf, I had a good gag reflex. *All the better to eat you with, my dear.* And in this case, that was a *good* thing for Jax. He whimpered, his tone changing from a wild, bestial mating sound to a plea.

My lips slid back, freeing his wet shaft to the cool morning air. He tasted like he smelled, like citrus and earth, Pack Azure Frost and werewolf. My left hand teased his balls while my right stayed curled around the base of his cock, squeezing and pumping gently.

'I can't do it,' he told me, panting and shaking all over. *'I*

need to stop.'

“Why?” I asked aloud, looking up and meeting eyes the color of a winter sky, so beautifully irresistible, so wild and untamed. See, Che Nocturne came across as a beast made of shadows and darkness, of teeth and claws. Jaxson Kidd was wild and feral, a beast that belonged to no one and nothing, a wanderer.

Until now.

I wanted to be the one to tame him.

“Because you're about to come?”

“Because I'm about to grab you, push you down, and fuck you against the kitchen floor,” he said, stepping back from me, his shaft wet and erect, a bead of pre-cum pooling at the tip.

“Who says that's a bad thing?” I asked, my heart thundering wildly. I needed this man between my thighs, needed to feel his wild pumping and know that the only harness he had on his free spirit … was my body, warm and hot and wrapping him completely.

I sat back and pushed my pajama pants off, kicking them aside and spreading my legs, lifting my hands up for Jax's.

He stared at me for a moment, nostrils flaring, but I knew he couldn't resist. The sight of me, the sweet smell of my arousal. *God, I need to take a break from werewolves and hang out with Faith for a while after this ... just to reclaim some of my humanity.* I felt so wild in that moment, just as wild as Jaxson Kidd of Pack Azure Frost.

Tail and ears and claws still visible, Jaxson knelt down and covered my body with his. Our lips met in a wild frenzy, the salty taste of him still teasing my mouth and tongue. My right hand found his tail and stroked it while the other teased his furry white and gray ear, rubbing it the way I'd been fantasizing about for a while.

With a single thrust, he filled me and started fucking, taking some of that unexplained anger out, pounding my ass into the floor. He kept his eyes open, blue and feral and fierce, kissing me and nicking my lips with his sharp canines, mating me right there on the kitchen floor of the Pairing House.

It didn't last long, but that's not what I expected from this. I just needed to lay my claim, and let him lay his, too. Sneaking a hand between us, I found my clit and worked myself hard and fast, bringing my body to a quivering, sweaty climax. I clamped down on Jax's cock, grabbed hold, and tore an orgasm from him.

He was so wrapped up in the pleasure of the moment that he bit me *hard* on the shoulder, teeth sinking deep, drawing blood, the pain mixing with the pleasure and amplifying into this violent explosion inside my brain.

Jax came too, buried deep inside of me, still biting and holding on while his body was wracked with the unfamiliar sensations of a woman's cunt.

Afterward, he didn't move. He just lay on top of me, his lips resting next to the small pool of blood on my shoulder from his bite. When he lapped out with his tongue to clean the wound, tail wagging slightly, a gust of wind burst through the open kitchen window, violent and reeking of wet earth and evergreen trees.

It crashed into the decorative shelves near the ceiling and knocked down stacks of dishes, a cookie jar, a porcelain wolf statue.

Jax covered me with his body, tucking my head against his neck and holding me close until the wind slowed and the items stopped falling; he sat back and looked down at me with a brilliant ruby red cut on his forehead.

My hands came up and touched either side of his face.

"Zara," he said, as I flicked my own tongue out and cleaned his wound, the sweet scent of earth settling over as the magic soothed and calmed. "Zara," he said again, and this time, despite the feral angry fuck we'd just had, he sounded almost … affectionate.

"Jaxson," I said, kissing the side of his neck and nuzzling into him.

Even though we were scheduled for coffee with a witch … and a prophetic reading of animal entrails, I was happy.

And I would fight like hell to keep myself, my mates, and my pack that way.

No matter *what* I had to do or what sacrifices I had to make.

The coffee shop Whitney chose was on the far side of town, closer to the university than to the Pack Ebon Red property. And it was right next door to a magic shop—a Wicca/new age shop rather than a place for actual witches. Being a witch was *not* a profession. Witches were a species, not a religion or an aspiration or devil spawn.

Well, at least I didn't *think* they were devil spawn until they started eating my people. Now I wasn't sure if their entire species was corrupt or if it was just this one coven. But goddamn, Coven Triad was making a pretty good case against their own kind.

"Glad you could make it," Whitney purred, leaning back in her chair and smiling at Aeron as she breezed past the rest of us and into the coffee shop. She bent low and let her lips hover over her girlfriend's for several long seconds before she moved her mouth to the side and kissed her cheek instead. "Take a seat," the Maiden continued, waving her hand at us and then reaching down to the floor to grab a small leather satchel. "Witch hazel," she told me with a curt nod. "As much as I could get without arousing suspicion."

I flipped open the leather flap on the bag and peeked inside to find six glass bottles of the clear liquid, little plastic spray caps on the top, ready to use and smelling like … nothing at all. So unremarkable they were, in fact, remarkable. Nothing in nature lacked smell like this. It disturbed my wolf side a whole hell of a fucking lot.

"Thank you," I said, and I hoped she couldn't read the cautious optimism in my voice. I didn't trust her for shit. Not even a little. Sorry, but that was the name of the game. I couldn't trust anyone … but my new mates. I wasn't sure how, exactly, the sex tied us together or why, but there were now five men blinking twice as brightly on my internal radar. Anubis and Tidus … they were still dim.

We'd have to fix that.

"No problem. And who's this?" Whitney asked, tilting her head back, her pointed black hat shifting slightly on her head as she stared the vampire princess up and down. The Maiden was dressed in that cool, urban vibe with dark purple lipstick with gold sparkles, matching eyeshadow, and skinny jeans. Her shirt was a crop top with the Coven Triad symbol on the front, and she had a million little items pinned to it or braided into her hair. Spells, again. All of them. She could probably blow up this entire city block with one tiny pin off her shirt.

"Harlem Blood of Crown Aurora," Harlem said, letting Numinous formalities slip over our meeting. She didn't bother to hold out her hand, choosing instead to stand off to the side, near the exposed brick wall on my left.

"Our reason for the witch hazel," I said as I took a seat across from Whitney and the boys fanned out to the nearby tables.

"I'll order coffee," Nic said, putting his hands on my shoulders and looking over at Whitney and Aeron, sitting close enough that their thighs touched, the sexual tension so thick between them it could be cut with a knife. "Do you want anything to eat?"

"Yes," I said—I was fucking starving—"just pick me out something that looks good."

Nic gave my shoulders a squeeze and moved up to the counter, taking Tidus and Anubis with him. Montgomery sat on my right while Che, Silas, and Jax occupied the next table over. *A whole table of assholes,* I thought with a slight smile. *A whole table of men that I've been intimate with ...* One-Kiss-No-Date was no more.

Okay, so I still hadn't gone on a date … but as soon as Silas got the opportunity, I hoped he'd still ask.

"Harlem, can you sit down, please?" I asked. "You're making us all nervous."

With a sigh, she adjusted the hood on her sweatshirt, taking a seat at the table with Che, Silas, and Jax but focusing her attention on me and Whitney. Seeing a vampire waltzing around in the sun never got old, but unlike Julian, Whitney was a tad sensitive to the light. She had on sunglasses and a long-sleeved sweatshirt, her face buried inside the hood. Paired with leggings and Ugg boots, she was pretty much your typical suburban American girl. You know, except she had fangs and would rise from the dead at some point … But that was neither here nor there.

"You want to tell me why you've got vampire royalty following your furry butts around on errands?" Whitney asked, leaning back in her chair, her coffee mug between her hands. I couldn't help but notice she had little charms pierced through the tips of her nails, more spells to protect against the world. How clever.

"It's complicated," I said as Whitney raised her brown eyes to mine, her purple and white feather eyelashes fluttering against her forehead as she blinked at me.

"Complicated …" she began, and Montgomery let out an involuntary little growl, putting his hand on my knee for comfort.

"Yes, complicated. As complicated as your people kidnapping puppies and eating them," he snapped, closing his eyes for a long moment before he flicked them back open, his face calm once more. I didn't want to give myself *too* much credit, but I think the sex helped him with his temper. I think the sex helped *a lot.* Hell, it sure as fuck calmed me down. "So excuse us if we're not interested in divulging every little detail."

"Whoa there, down boy," Aeron said, her eyes locked onto Monty's, *her* hand on her girlfriend's, a perfect mirror image to me and my mate. "Relax. I risked fucking *everything* to help you out. *Whitney* is risking everything to help you out. Cut us some *slack.*" She snapped the last word off her tongue like a whip, and I felt the stirring of fae magic in the coffee shop.

The Sightless—the humans—sat around us completely oblivious to what was happening right in front of them. Any one of us sitting there in that coffee shop could've killed them all before they had a change to even register they were in danger. I wasn't sure if I felt sorry for them or if I were envious of their ignorance.

No.

No, I felt sorry for them.

Humans were like pawns on the Numinous' chessboard. The only thing they had on us was sheer numbers. Their weaponry was impressive, but then again, a lot of Numinous worked in military or government positions and had access to all of the same technology *plus* their own natural powers. Really, humans were like … an aside to the goings-on of their Numinous counterparts. Keeping our existence secret was less for them and more because we were all so busy trying to hide from *each other.*

Besides, you don't let the sheep *know* that they're in a pen, do you?

"Harlem is an emissary from Kingdom Crown Aurora," I said carefully, leaning back in my chair and flicking my eyes towards the boys. Jax, Silas, and Che lounged in their seats like they were bored, but to my eyes, their muscles were taut, their pulses just a little too fast. They were nervous, as they should be.

"Ah, so the meeting went well then?" Whitney asked, sipping her drink and looking at me over the rim of the cup. The movement reminded me of this morning, sipping my own drink and watching Jax. God, the taste and feel of him on my lips … Subconsciously, I found myself lifting a finger up to touch my tingling mouth.

"It did," I said, still being cautious, still not sure who the real bad guy was in this scenario. I tapped my fingers on the table and wished I could set aside a day to go get my nails done with Faith. Not for me, but for her. I didn't really care *what* my nails looked like. And honestly, first time I shifted, the paint would flake off, but I knew how much Faith would appreciate the outing. "And I'm inclined at this point to believe that you're telling the truth, that Kingdom Ironbound and Crown Aurora are not connected."

"Not even fucking close," Harlem snapped, and I saw the flash of fangs in her mouth. She paused as Tidus approached and handed me a steaming hot mocha—Nic knew all my favorite things—and then passed over an identical drink to the vampire girl.

"Coffee?" he asked, his voice the color of sunshine and bright things. If I still believed in the lupine and lunar gods of old, I'd have thought they sent Tidus here for a reason: to keep my spirits up, to keep my mates' spirits up.

"Oh," Harlem said, her cheeks blushing a ridiculously bright red color, "thank you."

I resisted the urge to growl at her, but I definitely found my fingers digging into the back of Montgomery's hand. I believed her when she said she was too smart to hit on my men. But I could also tell she was ridiculously attracted to werewolf boys. Her reaction to Levi during dinner last night was more than proof of that—she hadn't been able to take her eyes off of him.

Tidus retreated back to the counter as Nic came over and placed a pair of cheese danishes in front of me and Monty.

"Breakfast is served, Alpha," he said with a slight smile, the smell of honeysuckle and pine wafting around, competing with Montgomery's fresh grass and rose scent. They were both beautiful, those smells. If I could bottle them, I would. I bet they'd sell like hotcakes.

He disappeared again and I waited as Tidus and Anubis passed out the rest of the coffees and Nic came back with the danishes—we all basically got the same thing, probably for ease of convenience. But I thought it was sweet how they ordered for both Harlem *and* Aeron. Whitney already had a plate stacked high with ginger molasses cookies. I knew what they were based on smell alone.

"Well," Whitney said, clearing her throat, the charms on her nails clinking against her mug. "I asked you here, so I'll get this meeting started." She sat forward and put her drink aside, leaning down to pull another leather satchel up from the floor. This, too, was covered in charms and trinkets, bits of bone and tiny glass vials. Good thing we lived in such an … open and accepting town. The Pacific Northwest was one of the few places in the world a girl with a witch hat and a sea of silver stars painted across her forehead could relax in public without being stared at. Go Eugene! Yay Oregon!

I sipped my mocha and let the chocolate and coffee taste linger on the back of my tongue, cutting through the salty sweet memory of Jax's seed …

'Don't even,' he sent to me as I glanced over and our eyes locked. His smile was tight, but his eyes were shimmering. *'I can ... feel you feeling me, Alpha. My cock is already hard enough as it is.'* He looked me up and down in my tight black American Giant tank and sweats like I was wearing a glittering party dress, and I smiled.

Whitney pulled a purple suede wrapped item from her bag and set it on the table, untangling the leather tie and revealing a stack of tarot cards.

Ah.

Right.

Tarot and then … *haruspicy,* the ancient Roman technique of reading an animal's entrails. Surprisingly, the magic really worked. I had no idea *who* had actually invented it, probably a Numinous of some sort …

Some unsuspecting deer was going down today, but at

least we'd eat the meat, so it wasn't a waste of life. My heart quickened at the idea of a hunt, and I couldn't stop a barrage of memories from my first time with Che flooding my brain, naked and wild underneath his thrusting hips …

Mm.

"I hate being the fucking Maiden," Whitney said as she shuffled the cards in her hands, looking at me from across the table. "It was a position forced on me. It's based on skill and power." She handed the cards to me and nodded with her chin. "Shuffle those for me, would ya?" I did as she asked, feeling magic whisper across my skin as the cards—these ridiculously ancient things made of vellum—brushed against my fingers. My wolf shifted and growled, recognizing the kiss of foreign magic. "And as the Maiden, I'm there to observe and keep peace, to cast spells of protection, fortune, love … but they don't tell me shit."

I tried to hand the cards back, but she shook her head.

"Give 'em to your boys," she told me and I passed them to Montgomery next.

"Go on," I said, picking my coffee back up as Monty shuffled the deck and then handed it over to Che. "So basically you don't have any information to give us?"

"Nothing new," the Maiden said with a long sigh, reaching up and adjusting the pointed black hat on her head. "But I know the Crone is planning something big. That little undead vampire brat you sent scurrying back to Kingdom Ironbound told his Queen you threatened war. War is what they want. I assume you figured that out already?"

"We did," I said as I switched my drink out for my danish and Che passed the cards to Jax. "But why?"

Whitney took a sharp, long inhale and looked around the room. After a moment, she paused and snapped off a tiny dangling crystal from one nail, kissing it and whispering some strange words under her breath in a language I didn't recognize. She put the jewel on her tongue and swallowed it.

"Checking for scrying eyes," she added when I cocked a brow and wondered if *she* might be able to teach me just as much or more than Majka? But our magic was inherently different—even I could feel that. "Okay, listen," she said as Jax passed the cards to Nic next. "There's a big spell on this part of town, one that stretches several blocks and encompasses both the Kingdom Ironbound Seat *and* the Triad Historical Society. It can be activated at anytime by either the Crone or the Mother. Once they do, it'll put every single werewolf inside of it to sleep. And when I say sleep, I mean you ain't wakin' up until the circle that's been drawn around the neighborhood is broken."

'Holy motherfucking shit,' Che said in wolfspeak, and the way Harlem jumped, I could tell he was projecting wide. At least I appreciated that he hid his surprise from the witch herself.

"A spell," I said, as I thought about Nikolina storming the door of the Triad Historical Society with an entire pack of Ebon Red warriors. And with all the alphas in town for the Pairing? They'd be with her for sure, all those alphas … all that alpha blood … all that *magic.*

My skin pebbled with goose bumps and I felt my hands start to shake, putting them in my lap to try to deal with my adrenaline rush privately.

'I've got you,' Montgomery said, putting his hand over mine. *'You're not alone, Zara. You're not alone.'*

"Yep," Whitney said, putting the heel of her hand to her forehead and smearing the silver stars slightly. "Because the spell causes no harm, I was asked to help set it up. I declined, on the grounds that we didn't know for certain that it wouldn't break my Maidenhood." And yes, it was exactly like it sounded; when a Maiden committed harm against others, her hymen would break and bleed red down her thighs, a sign that she was no longer a maiden but a woman. "But they still had enough power to cast it successfully. Right now, we're *just* outside the border. If I were you, I wouldn't wander around in a ten block radius of our building."

"And the map?" I asked. "The one that turned into black goo in my hands?"

"It was a locator spell. It would've quietly bound itself to you, so the Crone could watch your movements." The Maiden sighed. "They asked me to cast it, and I did. But weakly, so you could break it with ambient magic."

I looked across the table at her face, her ethereally beautiful face and I hated that all I felt was suspicion when she talked. It wasn't a healthy way to live. I *hated* it. I wanted to handle this Contribution, rescue my people … and live the rest of this year happily ever after.

Hah.

I had a feeling that was a bit of a pipe dream …

"What about this …" I paused, searching for the terms Harlem had used last night. "This slow drain spell that's been eating away at my people for centuries?"

Whitney's face paled, and she glanced toward Aeron for a moment, meeting the fae girl's glamoured eyes before she looked back at me.

"How do you know about that?" she asked, and Harlem raised a hand.

"I've known about it for some time," she said, lifting up her sunglasses and staring the witch down with eyes the color of ice, pale, almost colorless. "What was happening to the wolves, it made no sense to me. I dug through old documents," she added vaguely, almost like she was cutting herself off from saying something more.

'Don't think we missed that omission, your majesty,' Anubis said, leaning back in his chair and looking cute as fuck in a red sweatshirt and black skinny jeans. He'd just look sexy instead of cute if he hadn't thrown on a pair of fuzzy black wolf paw slippers.

Harlem narrowed her eyes and dropped her sunglasses back into place.

"What about that?" I asked and Whitney shook her head, lifting up her palms.

"I don't drink from the cauldron. My power is all my own. It *has* to be for me to keep my position, but the others … especially the Crone …" Whitney stopped as the tarot cards finally finished their round. Tidus tried to hand them to Aeron, but she lifted her hands up.

“I can't touch them,” she said as Whitney snatched them back, breathing hard and shaking slightly.

“I can't talk about that spell,” she whispered as she started tossing cards on the table in a pattern I'd never seen before, a seven pointed star called a *heptagram* with one extra card in the center. “I'm sorry, but … let's deal with one thing at a time, okay?”

“You want us to just … let our people have their magic siphoned off?” Silas snapped, slamming his palm on the tabletop. “Does Allister know about this?”

“Are you kidding?” Whitney said, flicking a sharp glance Harlem's way. “*Nobody* knows about this. He thinks that by sacrificing his people to be eaten alive, that he'll get some magic from the Crone *as well as* the alpha seat that's supposed to belong to Zara.”

“Of course he does,” Silas snarled, clenching his teeth and glancing away, running his tattooed fingers through his hair. “Then why does he care so much about Zara choosing me at the end of the year?”

“Look,” Whitney said as she studied the cards for a moment, nostrils flaring like she was frustrated with something. This tarot set didn't seem at all similar to the kind I'd seen before, sold in Wicca shops and printed with designs from famous artists. No, I recognized the Major Arcana—like the Fool and the Empress—in the deck, but the art stunk of blood, and it was violent, horrifically violent. I was surprised the Maiden was even able to handle it without losing her position. “Allister has a very specific plan in mind, but I don't know the half of it, okay? I'm not privy to negotiations, and even though he's working with us, he clearly doesn't like either the coven or the kingdom."

She sighed again and tapped a single finger on the center card.

"The cards are … well, they're not particularly helpful today," Whitney said, pausing and looking around at my boys before turning her attention back to me, "unless you're like, über-curious about your love life?"

"Love life?" I heard Nic say, his voice rising an octave.

"Oh, we're mighty curious," Che said with a nod of his head, looking at the other guys like he was seeking consensus. "Aren't we, boys?"

"What do they say?" I asked, because even though I knew I had way more important shit to worry about, I was curious as fuck about that spread. About my love life. I truly believed that divinations, that prophecies, could be changed. After all, each person's destiny was their own … but I was beyond interested in hearing Whitney's predictions. I was still an eighteen year old in her first serious relationship…*s*, wasn't I?

"You see this right here," she said, tapping the center card again, the *Strength* card. "This represents feminine power as well as physical and mundane urges or desires, courage, zeal, and overcoming hardships. And these?" She swirled her finger around the circle of seven cards. "These are the Minor Arcana, destined to serve, fated to fall for the Strength card."

"And that means what, exactly?" Che asked, his bad boy attitude making me cringe … and turning me on at the same time. Oh dear. Faith would be so pissed, little hypocrite that she was.

"It means," Whitney said, blinking her feathered eyelashes and fixing her pointed hat once more, "that the eight of you … are destined to see the fate's prediction out *together.* You'll thrive … or you'll fail as one. So glance around, my lupine friends, and take a good look at the people sitting beside you. You just found yourself your soul mates."

Glistening pink entrails splattered to the ground in front of my white paws, staining them red with blood. The smell was intoxicating, that copper stink that my wolf brain liked so much. It said food; it said survival; it said *success.*

I sat back on my haunches and panted, my muzzle stained with red from the kill. I didn't know quite what to make of the fact that instead of a regular black-tailed deer like I'd expected … the first scent we'd picked up had been that of a *white* stag.

A white one.

It was a sign from Mother Earth, I was sure of it.

Aeron knelt down beside the carcass in the gossamer robes I'd brought home from faerie and buried in a cedar chest in the closet to hide the smell. I should've burned them, but for some reason, I'd kept them. I was glad now because Aeron was wearing them instead of stealing another one of the party dresses Faith had bought me. One day she was going to go through my closet and see the *one* that was missing and get upset. Better I didn't have two or three missing … I didn't just *not* wear them because they weren't my style, but also because I was afraid I'd end up having to shift on the fly and would end up destroying them, a sea of glitter and beads and sparkles exploding to make room for fangs and claws and fur.

'Is it just me or do faeries smell like honey and ash?' Tidus asked, wagging his gold-gray tail and sniffing the impressive rack of antler's on the stag's head. I think I was still in shock that we'd even *seen* one of these things, let alone hunted it down. It was *possible* although rare for a white stag to occur in nature.

This … felt more like fate.

'It's not fae that smell like that,' Anubis corrected, circling around the carcass on quiet paws, his ashy black coat thick and lush, striking against the snow speckled backdrop of the forest. *'It's sidhe specifically, that charred bone and sugar smell.'*

'I can't decide if I like it or if it grosses me out,' Tidus said, moving over to sit beside me, pressing his larger body against mine, melding our warmth. And as strange as it might sound to a human, my wolf side found him attractive. His chest was wide and muscular, his eyes a gorgeous gray that mimicked the sky above the forest canopy. His fur was ashy with warm caramel and gold tones around his eyes and ears, along his spine and tail. My wolf wanted to mate with

him *now.* It wasn't uncommon for werewolves to mate in *both* forms, something that even in fiction made humans shudder and shy away. But both forms were Tidus; both forms were *me.*

'I hate it,' Che said said, his wolf form a perfect, unblemished black with nothing but a pair of purple eyes, pink tongue, and white teeth to distinguish him from the shadows. *'It makes me think of old rotted corpses and tombs.'*

'Agreed,' Nic said, sitting on my left side, his muzzle stained with red, just like mine. We'd taken down this stag as a pack, unlike last time. The kill belonged to us all, but … it was surprisingly easy. Too easy. Like the stag *wanted* us to catch him.

Magic shifted in the air with the breeze, teasing Montgomery's white-on-white fur and Jax's gold-white pelt, shifting Silas' gray and brown coat.

'She smells like death,' Nic added as we watched the faerie girl, in her true form, skin like crushed diamonds, her hair a void, completely bereft of light. It was so black, I had a hard time making out individual strands, like her head was bathed in shadows.

"Tell me what you need to say, sweet stag," she said as she dropped to her knees in the red snow, the steaming carcass melting what little there was left of the white powder and turning the ground into a muddy, bloody mess. "Whisper to me, gentle spirit."

Whitney was waiting for us in the back of the SUV, drenched in witch hazel, as far from the violence she could get. Killing anything—even a deer—was enough to lose her her position in the coven. But since our tarot reading had told us an admittedly *intriguing* tale of love instead of anything at all about our missing pack mates or the impending war, she wanted to stick around and see the results of Aeron's divination. And Harlem? She'd wanted to come, but with her strong desire to shift and join the pack run, she was more of a distraction than a help; we'd left her in the Yukon, too.

"Speak, speak, speak," the fae girl hissed, running her finger along the pink wetness of an intestine, closing her eyes against the sight of all that blood and gore. "I'm listening, little dead thing."

'Do you think our magic called this stag?' Anubis asked, shaking his coat out as he stood next to Che. It was interesting, to see the two black alpha males standing side by side. Comparing them directly like that, there was no mistaking one for the other. Che was devoid of light, almost as dark as the Unseelie princess' hair. He didn't have even a hint of color on him. Anubis on the other hand, he was actually closer to *navy* than black, an unnatural color most definitely not found in nature. It was as if a mystic hand had taken a bit of powdered sugar mixed with ash and shaken it all down his back, marring his blue-black coat. *'If you study 'were' history, you often find that when Nature's Children are in the most need, she provides. Is that what this is? A gift?'*

'Nature's Children?' Che scoffed as he shook his head and snorted, his breath fogging into the cold air. *'That's an*

archaic fucking term. Nature doesn't care *whether we live or die. It's not a person or an entity. There's nobody out there looking out for us* but *us. Sorry to tell you, Crimson Dusk, but the world isn't quite as magical as you make it out to be.'*

'Well, Violet Shadow,*'* Anubis snapped, lifting the edge of his lip in a snarl, *'I respectfully disagree with your opinion.'*

'Disagree all you want,' Che said as he lifted his nose up and sniffed the air carefully. We weren't on Ebon Red land, so the risk of Aeron being discovered by a patrol were slim, but still … we needed to be careful. If my mother found us here like this, I'd have a lot of explaining to do. And I felt like we were close to a breakthrough. So, so fucking close. *'This is probably just an albino deer or a deer with leucism or something. There's no magic here.'*

'I'm sad for you, if that's what you really think,' I told him as Aeron picked through entrails and muttered under her breath, like a mad seer.

Che stood up, stretched with his front half dipping low, his ass up in the air. He trotted over nearer to me, sniffed my ear and then licked me. As soon as he did that, a gust of wind blew into the clearing, stirring the smell of fresh meat and blood with the crisp bite of snow and the earthy musk of decaying leaves.

A green vine sprouted from the ground and curled around the stag's antlers, a black rose and a red rose blooming with thick satiny petals at its end.

'If that's not a sign,' I said, standing up and moving

around the stag's head, my strange white, red, and black form reflected back in the dark glossy depths of the creature's sightless eyes. *'Then I don't know what is.'*

Leaning down, I sniffed the roses, their smells fragrant and fresh, but with a musky undertone of wolf magic. I was starting to recognize that earthy smell. It was uniquely our own, unlike any other Numinous.

"Bring me an item," Aeron said suddenly, her head snapping up sharply, flashing pointed teeth. Not just a few, like a vampire or a werewolf, but a whole fucking mouth of pointed teeth. I don't know what her future plans were with Whitney, but … I would not let that girl put her mouth anywhere near my sensitive parts.

Shifting back into human form, I cupped the delicate black blossom and glanced over at the fae girl.

"An item? What kind of item?"

"From the *missing,*" Aeron hissed, shaking her hand at me. "And we don't have a lot of time. Normally, an animal spirit flees this plane of existence within a nanosecond of death. This one stuck around, but it won't stay for long. If you want to know where to find the missing wolves, I need an item."

'An item,' Montgomery whispered in wolfspeak, and then he was off like a shot, a streak of white, like a ghost sprinting through the shadows of the forest, heading in the direction of the Pairing House with the frantic bunching of muscles. I could feel his hope surge right alongside his fear. *'Don't follow, just wait,'* he called back as I released the black rose from my grip, listening to Monty's frantic

heartbeat through the strength of our new connection.

Che shifted back into human form, too, and stared down at the black rose like he was afraid. Of what, I wasn't sure, but now wasn't the time to ask.

"He needs to hurry," Aeron said, reaching out and stroking her hand down the bloodied side of the deer. "We have a minute, maybe less."

'Got it,' Montgomery called out, and I could feel how tired he was, how fast he'd run. Closing my eyes, I reached out to him with magic at the same moment I put my hand on Nic's hand, begging the earth for her help. She'd given us the stag; she wouldn't let him die in vain.

An ethereal wind picked up, black and red petals dancing in the air that I could not place. There were no black and red flowers around here save the ebony and crimson roses in front of me. But it didn't matter. They chased the breeze, found Monty, and teased the small little trinket from between his teeth.

It danced through the wind, this tiny crocheted band that found its way into my fingers. For a split second, I looked down at it, and saw the adorably messy work of small hands. It was a hair tie of some kind? But I didn't have time to ask or analyze it. I was sure Monty would tell me later.

"Here," I tossed the little rainbow treasure over to Aeron and she caught it in long, glittering fingers, cupping it between her hands and placing it reverently on the stag's side, her eyes closed, mouth muttering words in the lilting symphony of the sidhe language.

Montgomery stumbled into the clearing in wolf form, slaver dripping from his jaws as he licked his lips and struggled to catch his breath, collapsing onto his side and panting heavily. But those green eyes of his remained locked on Aeron.

The faerie girl coughed, putting her hand to her lips as blood speckled her mouth and palm. I had no idea what the hell was going on, but at least *something* was happening. Aeron coughed again, this time leaning over and throwing up blood on the forest floor.

Her blue-black eyes glimmered as she studied the pattern and then glanced up, rising carefully to her feet.

When I walked around the stag's massive corpse to look … I found a map … made entirely of fae blood.

The world had never seemed weirder.

Montgomery swept his arm across the dining room table and sent the dishes crashing to the floor as I carefully unrolled both vampire maps. Meanwhile, Anubis pulled up a geographical map on his iPad and tossed it down on the table beside them.

"Let's see the picture," I told Nic as he carefully lined his phone up with the maps. The picture of the bloody spatter at Aeron's feet was easily recognizable as Fern Ridge Lake —the shape was far too distinctive to be anything else. Not too far from that, a square that had to have been the airport. Yes. Blood, in a perfect square. It was eerie.

"If this is the airport," I said, running my finger across Majka's map, "and this is the lake …" I found a very tiny spot of crimson Kingdom Ironbound territory buried in the pink wash of Crown Aurora. "Then this is where they are."

The area I was pointing to was so small, it was almost impossible to see without leaning close and squinting, even with a werewolf's eyesight. I found a spot near Green Hill Road and Royal Avenue, where a tiny curve of water—also visible in the fae girl's blood spatter—mimicked the shape of the Amazon Creek Diversion Channel.

A tiny black and red rose had sprouted from the earth, right fucking there.

"The corner of Green Hill and Royal," I said at the same moment Tidus flashed his phone's screen for the rest of us to see.

"Looking at Google maps," he said, "it seems like there's an old barn on the road. I don't know when these pictures were last taken, but the property is overgrown and it looks pretty shoddy. Definitely a place you could hide people and get away with it."

"What's the address?" Monty asked, still panting, his long white hair unbound and hanging down his back. He was nude—we all were—with the witch, vampire, and fae girl waiting outside on the porch for us. They'd have no trouble hearing us, but at least it gave us some semblance of privacy. Although I could practically feel Harlem shaking with the need to *run,* to shift, to be wolf. Poor girl, trapped inside her own skin. Maybe once all this was over, I could find some way to help her?

"We need to go into this the right way," I told Montgomery, and even though his hands clenched into fists and his nostrils flared, I knew he would wait … at least for a little while. "We need weapons," I began, and then paused as the screen door squeaked open.

"And backup?" Harlem asked, coming into the house and removing her sunglasses. We'd invited her past the wards earlier, so she was able to actually get inside. I didn't want to see what all that old wolf magic would do to a trespassing vampire. Even if she was part wolf, if she tried to harm me or any of my mates, she'd probably end up dead from the backlash of magic. "Because I'm willing to help. And nobody knows how to kill a Blood better than another Blood."

"We accept," I said, making a snap decision and grabbing the maps up off the table. "Montgomery, get the weapons. Anubis, get the clothes. Nic, you get the SUV ready and let your mother know where we're going. If she doesn't hear from us in … an hour and a half, have her get Nikolina and meet us there."

A series of repeated *'Yes, Alpha'* followed in the wake of my words and the three men scattered to do what I'd asked. Che, Tidus, Jax, and Silas stayed with me as I headed out to the porch to see Aeron and Whitney.

"What are you planning on doing?" I asked them, feeling my heartbeat pick up speed, my pulse race. Harlem zoned right in on it and her pupils dilated slightly, but only a little.

"I can't fight," Whitney said with a long sigh, "but if Aeron's going, then I'll follow along and sit in the car. If it comes down to losing my Maidenhood or defending my woman, I'll tell you exactly how that's gonna go down."

She put her hands on her hips and glanced over at the faerie girl, sitting in one of the rocking chairs with blood still staining her lips. She was doused in witch hazel, so at least she didn't smell. But having all three girls standing on my porch? That was risky as fuck. I was just waiting for Avita or Morel to come streaking by, spying on me and the boys. I had yet to speak with my sister about her humiliating defeat in Coyote Creek, but I intended to. I wasn't going to let her walk around, hating me and lusting after Anubis.

Nope.

Not happening.

"If Zara fails, the Veil will fall," Aeron said, untucking her legs from the chair and rising to her feet, her dark hair swishing in a shadowed wave behind her. God, she really did smell like honey and ash, sweetness mixed with old decay. "Of course, I'm coming. I didn't get kicked out of my own kingdom to dick around."

"You never *dick* around," Whitney said with a sultry purr, and I saw the corner of Aeron's mouth lift up in a lascivious smile. When they finally had sex, it was going to be explosive; I could *feel* it.

"Flirting aside," Che said, drawing my attention over to him and his gloriously naked body. I could smell that bergamot oil, lavender, and vanilla scent of his, sexy and sweet all at once. *Inviting.* "We need some sort of plan, don't we?" He raked his fingers through his pitch dark hair and glanced away, almost like he was nervous. In fact, I could detect just the slightest hint of a tremor in his voice, the same as when he'd almost died in Faerie. "I mean, charging in there guns a-blazing isn't exactly going to work if the Ironbound Bloods really do have our people held prisoner. I mean, talk about the perfect hostages."

"I've got one of my mother's AoE glamours left," Aeron said, and I wasn't the only whose eyebrows shot up to their hairline.

"AoE?" Tidus asked with a bright grin. "Like, meaning *area of effect,* like straight-up video game slang?"

"I don't cross the Veil to play Parcheesi," Aeron said with a slight lift of her lip. "I already *told* you: I'm from the twenty-first century, too. And yes, I've played my fair share of video games, thank you, *sir.*" She sneered at him, but Tidus just laughed and shook his head, rubbing one palm over the tattoo on his bicep.

"That's great," he chuckled. "So, you mean one of those glamours that masks an entire area, right?"

"Exactly that," Aeron said, running her hands down the front of the gossamer robes. They did nothing to hide the curvy body underneath. At least none of my boys were checking her out; I appreciated that. "We call them ground glamours back home. I have *one* left." She touched the sea of necklaces hanging from her throat, a cluster of tiny glass bottles with different colored liquids inside. "I can use it to mask our approach, give us a chance to look around. It'll even disguise any attempts to break in for a short period of time."

"What if someone touches us?" I asked, wondering what would've happened back at the U of O when Silas went batshit on Julian.

"They'll ghost right through for about …" Aeron looked up at the roof of the porch. "Ten minutes at most." She dropped her chin and looked me dead in the face, her eyes like the holes that led to Faerie, bottomless and alien and terrifying. "My mother has to cut her own ribs out to make these glamours. It takes her weeks to heal."

"I suppose when she finds out you've managed to stir up goodwill with the largest single pack on the face of this earth, she'll let you back into Faerie and you can thank her for us." I smiled and took a breath as Anubis appeared and started passing out clothes.

"You want me to wear these again?" Silas asked, the corner of his mouth twitching as he fingered the leather pants in his hand. "Do you really think leather helps kick ass or do you just want to see my ass in these?" He looked at me first and then over at Anubis.

"They're designed for easy shifting," Anubis said with a shrug. "The seams on the side come right apart. What else were you planning on wearing? Those pants you stole from the teenage girls' section of the department store?"

"Why the hell not?" Silas said, but he was already sliding into the pants while both Whitney and Aeron wrinkled their noses and Harlem looked pointedly away.

When … if … no, *when* things calmed down around

here, I was setting her up on a date with Levi. She was very clearly desperate to get to know a werewolf boy … And I couldn't help but wonder if she could actually have pups with one? Or would it be a Blood baby? I had no idea. Technically, she *was* pack so if she wanted to be mated, she could.

At least, in the Pack Ebon Red that I was going to build.

I had no idea how Nikolina would react.

"Let's drive over to the humane society," I said, looking at the darkening sky. "It'll be closed, but we can park the SUV next to the gate and walk to this property, come at it from the back. Whitney can wait for us there, and then we'll thrown down the glamour as soon as we cross the fence."

"Stealth to the fence, glamour, *penetrate,*" Jax said, putting an awful lot of emphasis on that last word. His icy blue eyes met mine and we both licked our lips. "I want to penetrate."

"I'll bet you do," I said, skirting his sexual innuendo to keep us focused. I wanted nothing more than to laze around and get to know the alpha-sons better. And maybe … experiment more sexually? Claim the last two men for myself.

But saving our people? That was infinitely more important.

"Do we have any wooden arrows or do I need to send someone to the armory?" I said as Montgomery appeared in his leather pants, trench coat, and nothing else. *Holy fuck.* With that long, white hair—once again carefully braided and tied off with his little sister's hair tie—and the look of quiet, righteous rage on his face … I thought he might very well be the most beautiful man I'd ever seen in my life.

"We have them," Monty said, turning around so I could see the crossed swords on his back. One was made of aspen and the other, bone. One weapon for vampires, and the other for witches. In the center was a crossbow over a quiver of wooden and bone tipped arrows. "There's more in that utility closet than you might think."

Montgomery turned back to me and nodded his head at the screen door.

"Let's go inside," he told me, green eyes locking on mine. In them, I could feel the weight of his determination and it stirred that fire raging in my belly to a roaring flame. "And I'll get you suited up."

We stood outside the SUV, dressed in leather and combat boots, covered in weapons. Well, everyone except for Jaxson. He felt more comfortable in wolf form, and so wolf form he started in.

I dropped my hand and rubbed his fuzzy triangular ears between my fingers, my gaze focused on the long stretch of overgrown field between us and the dilapidated fence that marked the edge of the property. If that wasn't where our people were, then I didn't know where else to look. A spattered map made of faerie blood and a black and red rose to mark the spot? I wasn't sure what other conclusion to come to.

'There's a distinct lack of smell coming from that property,' Jax said and I translated aloud for the benefit of Aeron and Whitney.

"Agreed. I'd expect to smell … something. Rotten wood, rats, cows, feral cats, people … but there's nothing. Nothing at all." I put my hand on my badass tool kit and the new wooden knife Monty had chosen for me from the utility closet. He was right. I guess I hadn't taken the proper time to explore the Pairing House because there was a veritable treasure trove of weapons in there, plenty to choose from. I wasn't sure if it had been used as overflow from the armory, or if it'd been purposely stocked for me and the boys.

"Then we've found the right place, I guess," Nic said, his voice tight, the world around us so dark that his eyes looked black. That's how we'd gotten our name, *Ebon Red.* Crimson hair and aubergine eyes that looked black in the shadows of night.

"Don't take unnecessary risks," I said, glancing back at Whitney. "If we're not back in an hour, you should just get out of the SUV and start walking. If my mother comes and finds you in the Yukon, she'll probably kill first and ask questions later."

"Don't worry about me," Whitney said, looking at her girlfriend for a moment and climbing out to give her this achingly beautiful kiss, all lips and no tongue. She smeared purple and gold sparkle lipstick all over Aeron's ashy gray lips before stepping back and hopping into the SUV. "Stay safe, my love." She produced a small crystal ball from her leather satchel and held it out in one hand. After a few seconds, it began to glow and an image of Aeron appeared in the glass. "I'll be watching. And if you need me, I'll be there."

"I didn't doubt it for a moment," Aeron said, turning away and looking ridiculously underprepared in her flimsy robes and bare feet. But I knew better. Aeron was an Unseelie princess for fuck's sake.

"I can't wait any longer," Montgomery said, glancing

over at me. "Alpha?"

"Lead the way," I told him, and he smiled. It was brief, so fleeting that if I'd blinked then, I'd have missed it, but it was there.

Montgomery took us around the opposite side of the animal shelter, leading us away from our target property and cutting behind it to give us better cover. We used the few scattered trees to get close before sinking to our bellies and crawling the rest of the way.

'I feel like wolf form would've made this a lot easier,' Tidus said, crawling between me and the vampire princess, her gaze flicking over to him when he spoke. *'Next time, I'm going with Jax's lead.'*

'Woof,' Jax deadpanned, and even though the situation was deadly fucking serious, I felt a tiny sliver of relief that he could still joke, that Tidus was making conversation. It meant they had hope. If they thought we were going to die here tonight, they'd have probably been silent, right?

About ten yards from the fence, we found our first Blood patrol.

There were only two of them. I doubted they expected much action out here. After all, how the hell would we have found this place without the help of an Unseelie sidhe? It would've been the equivalent of looking for a needle in a haystack.

'They don't expect trouble, do they?' Silas asked.

'Nope,' I said, just before I tilted my head toward the vamps. *'Monty, Jax.'*

The two men exploded from the long grass—our scents

hidden with some of Whitney's witch hazel. Jax went for the first vamp's throat, tearing into his living flesh before he could even scream. Montgomery put a wooden arrow through the throat of the second vamp, a female with periwinkle hair and pink eyes that reminded me of a rabbit. As soon as they were both down, he put stakes through their hearts and we moved on. Removing their heads would take too long. As long as the wood punctured their chests, they wouldn't wake up. If we had time later, we'd kill them. But that wasn't what was important. We didn't come here to kill—we came here to save fucking lives.

At that point, we just stood up and climbed over the fence, a task that was made easy by the dilapidated, rotting wood. It sagged down to the ground and was as easy to step over as a pile of soggy towels.

I was wearing a pair of boots similar to the ones I'd had designed for the boys, big leather monsters that crushed everything underfoot. At least I didn't have to wear leather pants—I had leggings on instead, for ease of movement. A black tank and zip-up hoodie rounded out my ensemble. I didn't need armor; I needed clothes that were easy to move in and easy to shed.

Aeron moved up alongside me, passed through the small cluster of trees, and reappeared in the open area of grass between the fence and the barn. With a quick flick of the wrist, she tossed the glamour down on the ground and the glass shattered.

"Ten minutes at most," she reminded us—not that we needed it.

Montgomery was out in front, running full speed for the barn door and touching a hand to the chains wrapped through the metal handles. He hissed and drew his hand back, bleeding from his fingertips.

"Silver," I said as I came up behind him and started circling the barn, the other boys spreading out across the property. Harlem stuck with me, and Aeron … started climbing the side of the barn, literally scaling it like a mountain climber. She was eerie, like an undead character from a Japanese horror film, her long dark hair billowing out behind her as she ascended to the roof and stood up, cutting an impressive figure against the night sky.

As I surveyed the property, I noticed a long metal building against the back side of the fence, buried in brush and blackberries, surprisingly obscured by the bramble. It was a huge white warehouse, but it was almost impossible to see through all the greenery, much longer than it was tall, almost like a tunnel of some sort.

Our pack mates could be in there … or in the barn behind me.

"You keep trying to find a way in here," I told Monty, glancing over my shoulder and finding his emerald green eyes locked on mine. He nodded briefly, and I took off jogging for the metal building, weaving my way through the thick brush and discovering that Tidus, Anubis, and Harlem had already beat me there. The Alpha-Son of Pack Crimson Dusk was running his hand along the length of the warehouse, searching for a way in. I followed along behind him as Tidus went around the opposite side with Harlem tagging along.

We met up on the other side.

"There was no door on our end," Anubis said, and I could already tell from Tidus' face what he was going to say before he opened those sexy lips of his.

"None on ours either," he said and we all exchanged confused looks.

"No doors?" Harlem said, blinking her pale white-blue eyes at me. "That's awfully suspicious, don't you think?"

"So we do as dogs do," Tidus said with a bright grin. "We dig."

"That could take a while," I said, glancing back at the building. "But at the same time, it might be our only choice. Start here," I told him, looking around and noticing another Blood patrol in the distance. They couldn't see us through the glamour, but it wouldn't last forever. We were already running out of time. "Go as fast as you can, both of you. I'll take Harlem and we'll look again, see if we can find a hidden panel or something. Clearly the Bloods aren't digging their way in and out each time …"

"Not on their own," Harlem said, but she had a good point. A witch could easily create a spell to get in the building without the need for a door. And there were any number of Numinous that could move earth and put it back like it was nothing if they wanted to open and then close a tunnel entrance—an earth elemental for example.

"Let's take a look anyway," I said, feeling my spirits sink. But no, no. I couldn't dive into negativity, not in this situation. I had to stay positive. "Look for loose panels, irregular bumps in the metal …"

We worked our way around to the other side of the building again and found Nic and Silas jogging over to us.

"We just got inside the barn," Nic said as Jax loped over and stood with his tail and ears perked up, closing his mouth to stop himself from panting as he scanned the horizon. "Montgomery and Che are in there now, looking around, but as far as we can tell, it's basically a garage. There are about a half-dozen different vehicles inside and check this—they're plated with silver on the inside."

"Plated with silver?" I asked, blinking at him. "What do you mean?"

"Zara," Silas said, looking uneasy, sweat beading on his forehead and running along the side of his scar. "We peeked inside the windows of the cars and there's fucking silver everywhere. The interior walls, the undersides of the roofs, the steering wheels … it's all plated in fucking silver."

I just stared at them both for several seconds before I shook my head and managed to pull myself together.

"Werewolf transport," I said, putting a hand to my forehead and breathing in deep. I looked up just in time to see Aeron climbing down the side of the barn. She made her way over to us and paused, going so still I was almost positive she'd stopped breathing.

"Do you feel that?" she asked, but all I felt was the distant buzz in the air from the glamour. Aeron moved past me and padded over to the metal building, putting her hands up against the wall. "There's a glamour here." She glanced over her shoulder. "One as strong as my mother's."

The words coming from her mouth were normal enough, but the tone behind them … was laced with wild fear.

"What does that mean?" I asked, turning all the way around to look at her.

"It means," she said, as she pushed against the wall … and pushed in a door that I couldn't see, sliding through the metal like she was a ghost. I knew it was all just a complicated illusion, but my wolf brain didn't like it, not at all. "The Seelie Court is involved …"

Aeron disappeared into the building and I rushed to follow after, sliding in behind her …

And finding myself face-to-face with the truth behind the mystery of the missing werewolves.

Dozens of people lay sprawled on the dirt floor, chained with silver and unmoving. Now that we'd broken through the glamour, all I could smell was blood.

Blood, blood, blood.

Ivory Emerald blood, Ebon Red blood, Crimson Dusk blood … Azure Frost, Amber Ash, Obsidian Gold, Violet Shadow … even the blood of lesser known packs like Silver Scarlet and Sapphire Rose, packs so small they fell under the umbrella leadership of one of the larger groups.

About half the people in that room were in human form, the other half in wolf form.

Several of the boys climbed in behind me, Harlem amongst them … and they, too, froze in horror at the sight.

The tunnel was dark, but for a few shafts of moonlight that seeped through cracks in the metal panelling that made up the roof. It was all I needed to take in the entire scene, sweeping my gaze from one end to the other, my mind desperate to make sense of it all—and fast. It wasn't like we had much time left … if any.

On one end of the tunnel, several Bloods sat at a table, measuring vials of red out and putting them in coolers on the floor. It didn't take them long to notice us. In fact, they started moving *before* we did.

Our fucking glamour was gone.

"Who the hell are they?" one of them called out as another picked up a pistol from the table and aimed it right at me. The vampire holding the gun pulled the trigger before I even had a moment to register what was happening.

The silver bullet pierced me in the shoulder, digging into my flesh with a hot, searing ache that blinded me with white stars and mind-numbing pain that threatened to drop me to my knees.

"Zara!" Nic screamed at the same moment Silas threw me to the dirt floor and just *barely* managed to keep me from taking a second shot to the chest.

Blood oozed out, hot and sticky over my hand as I struggled to sit up, my flickering vision clearing just enough to see Montgomery as he whipped out his crossbow and fired off a single wood tipped arrow into the chest of one of the vamps. Jax was the perfect backup, darting along the floor at supernatural speed and slamming into one of the others before they could pick up a weapon of their own.

Unfortunately, vampires were deadly enough in their own right.

I both *heard* and *felt* Jax's pain as the Blood yanked him off and then slammed him against the hard packed dirt floor, dropping down and biting into the wolf's throat without mercy. He intended to rip it right out.

It was the vampire's own greed that both got him killed … and saved the Azure Frost Alpha-Son's life.

"This is an alpha," the Blood said, pulling back, his mouth smeared with red as he looked down at Jax's comatose form with a glimmer in his eyes. "A fucking alpha."

Montgomery was too busy trying *not* to get shot to fire his crossbow at the vampire lording over Jaxson … but Harlem wasn't. The vampire princess moved with a fluidity that would've been scary if I hadn't been a *werewolf* princess myself. Neither of us were as fast as Aeron, but we could outrun most any other member in our Kingdom and Pack, respectively.

Except for the queens.

Harlem grabbed the Ironbound vampire off the ground with a handful of hair and threw him as hard as she could into the metal, denting it and cracking several bones in the process. Before he could even think to get up, she was on him, tearing his throat out with *her* teeth. Blood spattered everywhere as she reared back and slammed one of the wooden stakes from her belt through his heart.

She almost made the whole thing look easy.

"There's an Ageless undead in here," I tried to say as blood bubbled up and over my lips. I'd been hit in the lung, probably. "Silas ..." I had to stop and swallow several times past the liquid in my throat.

"Shh, Zara, it's okay," he said as I realized Nic, Tidus, Che and Anubis were missing. Silas tried to pull me into his lap, but I pushed away from him and stumbled to my feet, using the metal wall on my right to stay up. Facing the opposite direction, I squinted across the sea of prisoners who, even now in all this raucous weren't waking up.

There was another fight going on.

With one last glance over my shoulder, I saw that Aeron had joined in the fray and that Jax was actually struggling to his feet. He was alive; he was okay. But the commotion and the sounds from the opposite end of the building?

I started to run with Silas beside me, blood soaking my hoodie, dripping to the floor as I ran past silver chains and half-dead werewolves. I couldn't look at any of them right now. There'd be time for that later if we survived this.

If.

If, if, if.

Pain rippled through me, but I couldn't tell if it was mine ... or one of my men.

'Zara, don't,' I heard Nic croak out in wolfspeak, but I was close enough now to see through the haze, to see Nic sliding down the metal wall, blood pooling underneath him at an alarming rate.

Too much blood, way too much blood.

Werewolves could heal a lot of things, but we weren't immortal. There was no such thing in this universe as far as I knew.

'Get the fuck out of here,' Nic gasped, his wolfspeak voice so weak it barely registered. He was literally dying, right in front of me, bleeding out on in the dirt while I just *stood* there and did nothing. *'Run. Get Nikolina and come back later. Go, please. Silas, get her out of here.'*

Something hit the ground near my feet, but I didn't bother to look at it. The only thing I could see in that moment was Nic.

"The next alphas of Ebon Red?" a voice asked, and I turned to see a Blood woman in a white dress standing near another table. "More like a bunch of unruly pups, no?" She flicked her hand out and blood spattered the ground, drops of red that I could tell by smell alone belonged to Nicoli Hallett. That scent, the honeysuckle and pine of my pack meant home to me; it meant family.

The vampire woman moved forward on quiet, bare feet, her white dress nearly the same color as her pale skin. Her hair was pale too, a blonde so light it may as well have been white. And her eyes? I had no idea what'd happened to her before she died, but she had no irises, just pale, colorless orbs, as if she might be blind. The only color on her was the red from fingertips to wrist.

She lifted something up and twirled it around in a weak shaft of moonlight. Vampires had better night vision than wolves anyway—but this woman, I had a feeling she didn't need to see at all to know what she was doing.

Bone glinted, a piece of rib most likely. A piece of *Nic's* rib.

A sound escaped my throat as the moment registered in my brain, a slice of forever that I would not soon forget.

'That table,' Silas said, and I could feel him trembling beside me. Whether it was with rage or fear or just pure adrenaline, I wasn't sure. *'There's meat all over at that table.'*

Dozens of smells competed for supremacy in my sensitive nostrils, but as soon as he said that, I registered the stink of meat. Of *'were'* meat.

“What a joke,” the Ageless undead said, turning her sightless eyes in my direction. Before I could even really register her words, I was moving and so was she.

“Zara!” Silas screamed out, but it was too late. I wasn't a person anymore, just an animal. And I would fight to the death to protect my mates.

'Don't ... Zara ...' Nic tried to say, but he was fading and fading fast. All I was thinking in that moment was that I had to get through this vampire to get to Nic, that's it. She wasn't an enemy, just an obstacle, just a tribulation that needed to be overcome.

My body plowed into hers, still in human form, and the wooden knife was just suddenly in my hand, slashing away at her exposed flesh, cutting into her arms as she laughed. Someone was screaming, but it took me several seconds to register that it was me.

The vampire woman threw me off, right into Silas, and sent us both rolling across the floor and into the silver chains. I heard a whimper and realized we'd landed right on top of another werewolf.

I lifted my gaze up and found myself face-to-face with emerald eyes and shock white hair—one of Montgomery's missing family members. He looked to be about the same age as me, and I realized with surprise that he was probably a same-age brother from Monty's litter.

'Hang tight and we'll get you out of here,' I said, but I was already rising to my feet and yanking Silas up with me.

"Go find the others!" I screamed, because I could hear fighting happening in other parts of the building. But it was so dark in there, so fucking dark, even for a werewolf …

I took off running before Silas could stop me and found myself being flung against the back wall before I even registered the vampire woman moving toward me again. She climbed on top of me and pinned my wrists above my head, stinking of mint and apples, smelling like blood.

"Pup you might be," she said with a wild grin, "but you've still got that beautiful blood running through your veins, don't you?" The undead nightmare leaned in and slid her tongue up the side of my racing pulse before pausing and sighing deeply. "I never get tired of that earthy smell," she whispered, and then she was opening her mouth and carefully, seductively sinking her fangs into my skin.

I struggled underneath her, bucking and thrashing, fighting through the bright white rush of happy pheromones from her saliva, using all the strength I had to try and get her off of me. But she was old and she was undead and she was right—I was only eighteen. I wasn't Nikolina, an experienced powerhouse with all the strength of a pack behind me. I was just one werewolf. Just one person.

A gold-gray wolf appeared in my field of vision, just as I felt Nic starting to slip, violent panic arcing through me, making me sick inside. Nic was about to die. He had a minute at best. Seconds at most. I could feel him slipping away …

Tidus latched onto the vampire's left arm and wrenched hard enough to dislodge her grip, giving me just enough time to grab another wooden knife from my belt and stab it into her side. It wasn't a killing blow or even one strong enough to stop her, but it gave Tidus the opening he needed to grab her shoulder in his muzzle and rip her back and off of me, throwing her aside.

My neck screamed with pleasure from the bite, but I knew the skin was probably torn and ragged.

'Zara, I'm scared ...' Nic gasped as I scrambled across the dirt floor and into the pool of blood around him, hot and wet and sticky. *'I'm not ... I don't ... I don't want to say goodbye to you yet ...'*

"Nic," I sobbed, looking down at the hole in his shirt, at the gaping wound with the bits of broken rib showing. Even from here, I could see that the vampire had punctured his heart and left a silver pin in the side of it. Carefully, oh so carefully, I put my hand to his chest and reached *inside* of him to pull it out. "I love you, baby," I whispered, shaking, knowing that even if I took the pin out, I was going to lose him.

This was it.

This was my last moment with Nicoli Hallett.

"I've always loved you," I told him, tears streaming down my face as I slowly moved to take the pin. I didn't know why I was even trying at that point, knowing that he was destined to die, that this was our last moment together. "Being with you … it's made everything okay, no matter how bad it got. It was still okay because you were there."

'I love …' he started to say, but his eyes were dimming and his wolfspeak voice was little more than a distant howl, an echo of the strong, proud Ebon Red male that I'd just promised my life to.

No.

No.

No.

My fingers closed around the silver pin and tugged it free, tossing it aside just as Nic's heart beat one, last time. One last pump. And then it stopped. Everything stopped, except for the slow careful touch of my bloody hands to his face, the slow press of my lips against his.

That was it.

Our last kiss.

The only one I'd get for the rest of forever.

My lips touched his quiet, still ones as I leaned my body into his …

And then … an explosion rocked the metal warehouse, blowing out the wall behind Nic's body, throwing us both across the yard and sending us tumbling in the grass as the pungent scent of earth and growing things surrounded us, husky and sweet and eternal.

I scrambled up and over to Nic, even though I knew he was dead. I knew it. I knew it.

My hands touched his face again as I held my breath and hoped and prayed for a miracle, a kiss of that old werewolf magic that'd been hiding in our veins for so long, crouching beneath silver and spells and waiting to be unleashed on the world. Wasn't it enough? Wasn't it?!

"NIC!" I screamed, because his heart still wasn't beating, and his eyes were looking up at the stars, glassy and unseeing. "NIC!" My voice echoed around the property and then went silent, as if I'd been cut off by a mystic hand, shushing me, silencing me.

I raised my head and found myself staring into the eyes of a white stag.

He looked at me for the longest moment, standing with his head down, near the entrance to the barn. I swear, when I met his gaze, I felt the infinite beauty of the universe wash over me, a peacefulness I'd never experienced before in my life.

It said that everything was going to be okay, that even death played a beautiful, high note in life's symphony. Nic might be gone, but a new pup would be born to take his place, and the spirit I'd known as Nicoli Hallett would find a home somewhere else, be reborn and start a new life.

"Please don't take him from me," I begged, my whispered words the only sound in the world. There was nothing else. No more fighting, no more night whispers from crickets or owls, not even the squeak of a field mouse.

The stag moved over to us and touched his nose to my

cheek, wiping away blood and tears with his snow-white nose. When he walked, he made no sound.

"Please," I said again, knowing that I would do *anything* to save Nic, even if it meant giving my life to … the spirit of the forest? The horned god? Mother Earth's consort? I had no idea who or what this creature was, but I recognized the echo of his heart.

Mother Earth's Children, that archaic nickname for my people. It made sense to me all of a sudden.

With tears streaming down my face, I lifted a palm and the stag nudged it with his head. As I watched in silent disbelief, vines curled up from the base of his antlers and around them, twining around my wrist.

'Hush, my sweet child,' the forest spirit said, and then the vines fell away and a mark appeared on the underside of my wrist, a black rose that shimmered a rich, velvety emerald in the moonlight. *'Hush and don't cry.'*

The stag moved his head over to Nic's still, quiet face, pushed his nostrils close to the boy's mouth … and exhaled with a long, slow, sweet sigh. His breath plumed in the cool air and Nic's body convulsed, a gasp tearing from his throat that was ragged and broken and disjointed.

With a groan and a bellow, the stag collapsed onto its side, dead.

"Nic?" I asked, trembling as I laid my fingers on his shoulders and he started to breath again, choking and coughing, bleeding everywhere. There was still a hole in his chest and a piece of rib missing, but as I watched, his flesh started to repair itself.

That's when it clicked.

The thing that had fallen at my feet … the silver bullet I'd been shot with. And my own wounds? They were gone —even the vampire bite was a rough, ragged patch of scar tissue when I put my hand to it.

"Nic," I said again, laying my body against his, fat tears streaming down my face. When his strong arms curled around me … I knew I'd never regret a single other moment in my life, so long as he was with me. Just as long as he was here. "Oh, Nic, Nic, Nic," I whispered, kissing his cheeks, his mouth, his forehead.

"Zara, what the fuck just happened to me?" he asked, his voice quivering with fear as he sat up, shaking all over, his face as white as a ghost. "I could *see* you and this … this …" We both looked over to find the stag's body covered in vines, blooming with black and red roses, and as we watched, it decayed into the ground with the sweet smell of rot. As quick as they'd come, the vines and flowers withered away until there was nothing there but a pile of dried and dead bramble. "I could see it all, everything."

"You were dead, Nic," I said, but all of a sudden, sound came crashing back to us and I heard a scream, a ripple of fear and pain.

My other mates.

I had seven men to protect.

"Zara," Nic said, grabbing my arm, his flesh knitted mostly back together, enough to stop him from bleeding. But he still cringed when he tried to get up.

"Love of my life," I told him, licking blood from my

lips, and putting my hands on either side of his face. "As your alpha female, I *order* you to stay put. Do you understand me? Unless it's life or death, you don't move from this spot."

I released him and took off running, back through the hole in the metal building, and into a much brighter den of shadows and pain. The meat table was overturned, chunks of werewolf flesh scattered across the floor, some of it wrapped in plastic, other parts sitting raw and dirty in the middle of a horrific fight scene.

I knew right away where the pain and fear was coming from.

Anubis was on his side in wolf form, the undead vampire on top of him, her teeth sunk deep into a bloody wound on the side of his neck. There was no fur left there, no skin either. She was sucking blood from the muscles in his neck.

Chucking my badass tool kit aside, I shifted, shedding my clothes as I threw myself at her. Just before my body made contact, she lifted up her left hand and a wave of heat and electricity hit me like a freight train.

My body flew backward and slammed into the wall, bones breaking as I crumpled to the floor.

Magic.

I'd just been tossed aside by a *vampire* using the magic of my own people.

I guess Harlem had been right about an alpha's blood …

With a groan of pain, I forced myself to my feet and found the undead woman staring at me with her sightless white eyes. She gave me a bloody grin and then lunged, leaving Anubis' comatose form to come after me.

She didn't get a chance at me a second time.

Silas' gray and brown form exploded between us, knocking her off course and into the sea of chained wolves in the center of the room. Che was right behind him, locking his jaws on her throat and cracking her neck with a violent shake of his shadowed head. In the darkness, he was nothing but a pair of violet eyes and bloodied teeth.

Montgomery finished the vampire off with a single swing of his wooden sword, severing her head and preventing her from ever getting up again.

'Tell me he's okay?' I asked as Tidus nuzzled his bloody pack mate … and magic bloomed between them, fragrant and musky, leaves swirling into the room and settling around the ashy blue-black wolf. Even as I was stumbling over to them, I felt it, my bones knitting together inside of me.

'He's okay,' Tidus said, sounding as shocked as I felt. Well, okay, maybe not *that* shocked. I'd just seen the love of my life come back from the dead. I don't think there was anyone in the world as shocked as me in that moment—except for maybe Nic himself. *'Dude, get up.'*

'Trying,' Anubis groaned as he struggled to stand, blood dripping down his fur, his crimson eyes looking up at me. *'Alpha.'*

“What the hell happened out there?” Montgomery asked, panting as he knelt down and used a key to unlock the silver chains around his brother's—I just assumed that was his brother—ankles. “I felt … I felt a death in the pack.”

“Nic was dead,” Che said, shifting back into human form and shoving over another vampire corpse, searching his pockets. I assumed he was checking for more keys. “I saw it; I felt it. He was fucking dead.”

“I'll explain later,” I said, shifting too, and stumbling over to the hole in the wall. “Nic!” I called out and found him rising to his feet, looking stiff and sore and uneasy. He ambled over to me and joined us inside the building, his face a mask of concentration but his hands trembling. But I knew Nicoli Hallett—he'd get the job done first and freak out later. “Is everyone okay?”

Okay was a relative term for our situation, but my mates knew what I meant as we stood there naked and quivering with adrenaline and pain, fear and relief, anger and disgust.

'We're all still alive if that's what you're asking,' Silas said, moving over to stand beside me and sitting at my feet.

“And we have keys.”

I heard Harlem's voice as she jogged through the shadows toward us.

But the faerie princess … was nowhere to be seen.

“Where's Aeron?” I asked as Harlem handed the keys to me and I knelt down, unlocking ankles and wrists and necks. I could barely look at the bloodied, quiet bodies they belonged to. My people were going to need a long time to heal from this, their flesh marked with bite wounds, pockmarked with missing chunks of flesh.

A long, *long* time.

Just laying my hands on their flesh didn't heal them the

way it healed my boys. I didn't know if was because of the magic of the Bonding Ritual—because clearly there had been magic in it—or because I'd used it all up. I just didn't know. I was hoping Majka might be able to tell me more tomorrow.

"I don't know," Harlem said as I glanced over my shoulder at Silas. "Nic, take Silas and go get the SUV. Bring it over here to so we can start loading people up. And call Lana, let her know the situation here, and have your parents bring over the delivery van. Have her alert Nikolina, but no one else. *Nobody* else."

"Yes, Alpha," Silas said, but Nic was strangely quiet. I didn't blame him. He'd died and come back to life today. He'd done the impossible and neither of us knew a goddamn thing about how or why.

"Zara!" Montgomery called out as I handed the keys off to Jax, his body melting into human form with a fluidity that found Harlem gazing with rapturous need. I ignored it all, my fingers brushing against the palm of the Azure Frost Alpha-Son, giving me a much needed boost of comfort.

I found Monty in the corner with a small girl clutched in his arms, his keys now in Tidus' hands as the Amber Ash Alpha-Son struggled to unchain the other wolves. If I had to guess, I'd say there were about thirty of them in the room with us.

Thirty.

Out of hundreds of missing.

This wasn't the only holding location.

There were more places like this, maybe even worse

than this.

I didn't have time to think about that, not right now.

"She's dying, Zara," Monty said as I stumbled over and found a little girl, the same age as Patience, one of the pups from the litter of seven that he'd told me about before. "Her pulse, I can barely hear it."

"Let's get her outside," I said, because I couldn't imagine this little wolf with her cute green eyes and her white fur dying in Montgomery's arms with the smell of meat and death all around her.

We carried the little girl out into the moonlight and laid her next to the stag's brambles. I doubted I'd get two miracles in one day, but it was worth a try. Putting one hand on her, and another on Monty's bare chest, I tried to summon some of that magic from before.

But all I felt was … empty. Barren. Drained.

"We need demon blood," Montgomery said, his voice strained, choking on his own words. "But I used the last …"

He'd used his last antidote … on me.

"I can get you demon blood," a husky voice said, and I lifted my head to find Whitney … her thighs stained with blood, Aeron held in her arms, a look of tense determination on her face. She walked forward and set the fae girl down, both of them just … covered in blood. And oh goddess, it was just everywhere.

"You …" I started as Whitney—who was clearly no longer the Maiden—walked over to us, her pelvis soaked in red. She'd given it up to protect Aeron. And now, we had nobody on the inside of Coven Triad to help us.

Everything was just fucked.

But I had Nic.

I had Nic, but I couldn't lose Monty by letting him watch his sister die.

"I can summon a demon," she said as Aeron sat breathing heavily on the ground, her hand to her throat, the marks of a vampire bite clearly visible even from here. She'd lost a good portion of her neck. If she'd been human, she'd be dead right now.

"What's the price?" I asked, because I knew that I wouldn't allow anyone else to pay it.

A moment later, the Yukon came backing up onto the property, right over part of the dilapidated fence, bypassing the locked chain-link gate completely. Nic and Silas got out and started toward us, but I waved them away.

"Start loading people in, as many as you can get. We don't know how long we have here before Bloods and witches start showing up in hordes."

"We won't know the price until we summon them," Whitney said, flipping open the top of the leather satchel strapped across her body. She acted like she didn't give a fuck about her Maidenhood, kneeling down beside us in jeans that looked like they'd seen a really bad period. But I could tell from her body language that all she really wanted to do right now was break something—or someone. Hell, she'd probably broken at least one vampire someone in there based on the state of Aeron's bloody clothes. No way all of that was hers, her gossamer robes wet and dripping. "But you can always say no so long as you can give them a night to walk free."

"Do it," I said as Monty opened his mouth to protest and then squeezed it shut again. He looked down at his little sister in her wolf form, her white fur patchy and stained with red, her skin pale underneath and littered with bites. There were so many, I couldn't count them if I tried. Hundreds, at least. And on a child, too. I felt sick to my stomach.

Whitney pulled a tiny book from her bag, something old and brittle and brimming with magic. She flipped through several pages and then lifted her hand up, waving it dismissively in the direction of the tome. The pages fluttered on their own and stopped at a diagram of a circle.

As I watched, she reached down, unbuttoned her jeans and dipped her fingers inside, wetting her fingers with a good amount of virgin blood. As Monty and I watched, and the other boys loaded sick and dying werewolves into the SUV, Whitney drew a circle around herself in blood, chanted in the language of the witches and stood up. She stepped back and then bit a charm off the end of another fingernail, putting it on her tongue and swallowing.

And then she spit in the circle and magic swirled like a living thing, hot and violent and reeking of sulphur.

"*Sutannoc,*" she shouted, her voice like thunder, her eyes flickering with a storm of power. I could *feel* it in my bones and it was a mighty, mighty thing. "*Eanimeg.*"

Two names, two demons.

I sucked in a sharp breath and hoped like hell that

Whitney knew what she was doing. To summon a demon, all you *really* needed was their true name, but a little magic never hurt. If whoever was calling them was powerful enough, the demon had no choice but to come to the summons. That was dangerous work though, liable to get the caster killed. Demons were dangerous as fuck, not a species that should be messed with.

The circle of blood lit up a strange gold color, and I watched as Whitney drew several different runes in the air with a bloody finger. They flickered like fireworks as she snatched a vial from her bag and drew a pentagram over the circle of blood.

Contrary to the unfortunate ignorance of some, pentagrams were *not* evil. They were simply markers of protection. Could they be used by a person with darkness in their heart? Sure. But what in this world couldn't turn deadly in the wrong hands?

Montgomery found my hand and squeezed it tight, the comfort of our pack connection racing through us as two bodies rose from the ground, bent low, leathery bat wings wrapped around them like cocoons.

"The Twins," Whitney said, her black pointed hat lilting to one side as she sagged to the ground and dropped her book onto the dusty earth.

Montgomery scooped his little sister up in his arms and stood up alongside me, waiting as *The Twins* unfurled their black and red wings and turned to face us, turning their heads together, so they were both looking over a different shoulder, their cheeks almost close enough to touch.

"Werewolves," they said in unison, spreading their wings and turning around to face us together. "Summoned by a witch, but in the company of wolves."

"We need your blood," I said, getting straight down to business. After all, they were right: I *was* indeed a werewolf. Ritual and tradition we could do, but we didn't do speeches, especially not when the life of a puppy was hanging in the balance.

"What a coincidence," the boy on the left said, his red hair spiked up in a mohawk, his dual colored eyes boring into mine, "because we could use some of yours."

I had to admit, that threw me off.

About ninety-nine percent of the time, demons asked for unfettered time in our world. What they did with it, I wasn't exactly sure. There weren't a lot of books written on the subject. Demons existed in a realm separate from Earth, separate from Faerie even. As far as I knew, there wasn't even a *name* for it that we could pronounce correctly in English.

"My blood?" I asked and the brother on the right laughed, stretching his wings to their full width. It was an impressive move, I must admit. They must've been at least six feet … *each.*

"What the fuck are those?!" I heard Tidus shout from behind me, and I glanced over my shoulder just in time to see him stumble back and fall on his bare ass in the dirt. "What the … fuck …"

"Demons," Anubis said, pausing beside him and glancing over at us warily, "more specifically, *muinomeads.*"

"What an astute little puppy," the first brother said, his right wing black and his other red. The two demons—sorry *muinomeads*—must've been fraternal rather than maternal twins because they were most definitely *not* identical. The other boy had a red wing on the right side and a black on the left. He also had one side of his head shaved to stubble, the other half long and hanging past his shoulders. His brother had a fully spiked Mohawk, his red hair standing up in violent points down the center of his head.

They were both tattooed, ripped, and wearing … leather pants suspiciously similar to the ones I'd designed for my males.

"Blood for blood, seems fair to me. Don't you think so, Noc?" Mohawk Boy said.

"Sounds more than fair considering we were woken up from a dead sleep, Nim." They both stared at me, their eyes mirror images of their wings—one red and one black for each boy. "A pint for a pint, plus two weeks to wander, and a pound of flesh."

"You want flesh *and* blood?" I asked, glancing down at the little wolf in Monty's arms and laying my hand on her side. Through the strong connection of pack, I could feel her fading away. We didn't have a lot of time here.

"Enough to cure her ten times over," I said, just in case we came across another werewolf in as bad a shape as Monty's litter sister. "And we'll match it with our blood. Plus one week to wander and an ounce of flesh."

"Enough to cure her ten times over," the Mohawk boy—

Nim—repeated, "plus two weeks and eight ounces of flesh."

"Agreed and agreed … but four ounces of flesh," I blurted as the little girl's pulse flickered dangerously under my palm. I didn't have time to stand here and get a good deal out of these assholes. I had a fucking life to save.

"Deal," Noc said, reaching out and grabbing Monty's arm. I just *barely* managed to catch his sister before she fell. A silver knife flashed in the demon's hand and I watched in horror as he shoved up the black sleeve of my mate's trench coat and cut a chunk from his arm.

I'd intended for that to be me, but Montgomery stood there, stoic and unmoving, a warrior fighting to save what he believed in most … I almost loved him right then, fell head over heels. Hell, maybe I did? I fell so thoroughly in love with him later that when I recalled the memory, it was hard to say when I started feeling what I was feeling.

"And the blood …" Nim, the brother with the half and half hair, said, "we'll collect at the end of our two weeks." He stepped out of the circle and his twin did the same. But the circle itself? It didn't disappear. No, it burned into the ground with the rancid stink of sulphur and ash, the proof of our bargain.

If the boys and I failed in any way to deliver on the promise … the twins would be given free reign to roam this world for as long as they pleased. As long as the circle was on the ground, we were also safe from them. If we reneged and it disappeared? I'd never sleep another wink without wondering if they were coming for me.

Noc gestured vaguely in my direction, shirtless and

beautiful and alien with his dual colored eyes and whip of a smile. I didn't personally find him attractive—I liked my boys with a little *wolf* in them—but when I glanced over and found Harlem watching us, I could tell that she, in fact, did.

So she liked werewolf *and* demon boys, huh?

"Where do you want me to bleed myself, Wolf?" Noc asked, crossing his arms over his bare chest. He was literally covered in tattoos, both arms as well as the top part of his chest. As far as I could tell, he and his brother were at least identical in that right.

"I'll get a bowl from the car," I said, handing the little girl back to her brother and moving over to the Yukon's open front door. The back seats were already down and filled with unconscious wolves from the warehouse; it smelled like rot and blood and death in there. It was awful. I ignored it for the time being and opened one of the compartments on the ceiling, withdrawing one of the plastic bowls we kept in here for when we were wolfing out—werewolves got thirsty, too, you know.

When I jogged back and handed it to Noc, he grinned like a serial killer about to take down his one hundredth victim. He looked *that* excited about it.

"A plastic bowl?" he asked and looked up at his brother. "It's a plastic bowl."

"So it is," Nim said, eyeing Harlem as she helped carry a large male wolf to the SUV. Her gaze kept flicking in his direction, too. It wouldn't surprise me if they found each other later for sex … "How … unconventional."

"Fucking ridiculous," Noc grumbled, setting the plastic on the ground and reaching out a hand toward Monty. "Ivory knife, please?"

Montgomery turned so I could pull the knife from his belt, passing it to the demon and watching as he slit his wrist from the base of his hand all the way down to his elbow. When demon blood was fresh, it only took a small amount to counteract the poisons in vampire blood. But later, if we dried it into a powder like the one Monty had given me at the school, we'd need a hell of a lot more.

As soon as the blood hit the bowl, Montgomery laid his sister down on the ground, smeared his fingers in the red-violet liquid and rubbed it along her tongue.

"Please, Virtue, please," he whispered, and if the situation hadn't been so dire, I'd have thought that her name was cute—Patience and Virtue from the same litter. "Come on, honey," he whispered, tears falling down his cheeks. He dashed them away with an angry arm, blood dropping down his hand from the demon's wound.

I knelt beside him and reached out, putting a comforting hand on the back of his neck. As soon as I did that, magic swirled between us in a gust of fresh air, bringing leaves and bits of the dried stag's bramble along with it.

Montgomery continued to transfer blood from the bowl to his sister's lips. I watched Noc carefully until he pulled his arm away and closed his fingers around the bleeding wound, his black and red nails long and pointed.

"All done," he said as he stood up and moved back a few feet from us.

"A tenth, Monty," I said, taking the full bowl in my hands. "I asked for ten times what we needed. She's going to need a fuck of a lot more than I thought."

My mate hefted his sister's little body in a better position, her head up, wolf muzzle open as far as we could get it. I poured the warm blood into her throat as fast as I could without choking her, pausing and letting Monty pet her throat, encouraging her to swallow.

"Come on, Virtue," he whispered, his eyes wide, his skin pallid but sallow. He looked physically ill, sitting there with his dying sister in his lap. More blood, more petting. And again. I judged about a tenth of the liquid and then added some extra, just in case. Too much and we'd make her sick; too little and she'd *died.*

"We have as many people in the Yukon as will fit," Nic said from behind me, his voice strained and distant. "You want Silas to drive them to the Hall."

"Not to the Hall," I said, knowing that as long as Allister was on pack property, they weren't safe there.

"Why not?"

I heard my mother's voice before I even registered her presence.

Chills broke out all over my skin as I glanced back and found her there, naked and dressed in silver, a fur coat hanging half off her shoulders. Her face was an impenetrable mask, beautiful and terrifying all at once.

She looked like a goddess.

A goddess whose dark eyes flicked over to the dead brambles with a start of recognition before she managed to school her expression, turning her attention back to me.

My head whipped around when the little wolf coughed, shuddered, and then came to with a yowl of unhappiness.

It was the most beautiful sound I'd ever heard in my life.

Monty and I locked eyes before I leaned forward and pressed my lips to his, kissing him as fully and deeply as I could before I pulled away and stood up, turning to face my mother.

"The Hall isn't safe," I said as she moved closer and stared down at me like I was … less than an alpha … but more than a pup. It was an improvement, that's for sure. "Alpha, there's a traitor in the Convocation."

Back at the Pairing House, I leaned against the tiled wall of the shower and slapped the faucet onto the hottest possible setting. Obviously, as a werewolf I wasn't cold … not physically. But on the inside, I was a twisted, tangled mess of emotions.

Some of which here happy … some sad … and then there was this righteous anger inside of me that burned so hot that it felt cold.

All those werewolves, bleeding and chained, covered in bite marks, hunks of flesh missing, leaving nothing but glistening white bone and the pink-red of muscle tissue.

Putting my hands over my face, I dragged them down

and watched as the boys filed in beside me. Some of them started to shower right away … while others just sat in the hot water like me, staring at each other … or over at Montgomery.

Frankly, I was surprised that he was still here.

"You sure you wouldn't rather be with your family?" I asked as he stripped off his bloody clothes—he was the only one of us who hadn't shifted to wolf form during the fight.

Poor Monty … Although he'd gotten his sisters back, there'd been no sign of his parents.

Clearly, Kingdom Ironbound and Coven Triad were keeping the alphas elsewhere.

"I am with my family," Monty said, his voice husky and thick as he moved over to me and put his big hands on either side of my face. His green eyes locked onto mine and for several moments, we just looked at each other. After a moment, his white hair wet and plastered to the sides of his face, he leaned in close and kissed my mouth, soft but firm, like a confirmation of our bond.

He pulled away and turned to grab some soap, lathering up the bloody spot on his arm where Nim and Noc had carved their bit of flesh. The wound was healed now, but the dried rust brown flakes of blood remained.

Turning my head to the side, I found Nicoli Hallett, my childhood friend, my bodyguard, my lover … He was looking at me with a very curious expression on his face.

"We should tell them," he said, and I nodded, pushing up off the wall and making my way toward him, toward the shuttered darkness in his eyes. He'd *died* today, literally died. He'd passed away right in front of me and yet … here he was? I kept having to pinch myself to make certain I wasn't fucking dreaming.

"We will," I said as Anubis squirted shampoo on his hands and looked at me inquisitively. I nodded and he came up behind me, lathering my hair from roots to tips with sweet smelling soap. "Just not now."

My right hand slide down Nic's chest as Tidus picked up a loofah and offered it up to his Ebon Red pack mate.

"Thanks, man," Nic said, taking the soapy sponge and lifting it up to what was left of his wound, the skin shiny and pink, but closed up … *healed.* A mortal wound, erased like it'd never been. Nic stared at it for a moment before reaching a hand down and prodding at the wound. He didn't flinch or cry out … my guess was that his missing rib bone was healed, too.

"Why later?" Che choked out, standing in the water with raven dark strands of hair dripping across his violet eyes. "He died Zara Wolf, and he came back to life. I … I fucking … how is that possible?"

"Anything is possible," I said, remembering the quiet, peaceful stare of the giant stag. "Some things are just … improbable."

"But necromancy?" Jax asked, and I flicked my gaze to his, even as I was taking the loofah from Nic and scrubbing my guard's chest and belly for him.

There were a lot of penises in that shower and not a one of them was erect. The mood was somber and sad, and I understood that Nic had just gone through something …

something *transcendent.* But this wasn't a cause for mourning or fear, this was triumphant. We had gone in, rescued those wolves, saved a pup's life ... and we were all still here to talk about it.

By the hair on our chiny-chin-chin, I thought, but I didn't say that aloud. I'd had a huge dose of reality shoved down my throat tonight, and I would not soon forget it.

"It wasn't necromancy," I said, looking over at Silas and catching his golden gaze. "It was ... of the earth, as wild and natural as any of us." I bit my lower lip as I thought of the demons I'd just unleashed on the world ... The price I'd paid for Virtue's life had been high. I had no idea what those two were going to do with a whole week to wander our world. But my choices had been limited and given the same set of options again, I'd have done it all over again.

"The Earth Mother is speaking to us again," Anubis said, and this time, nobody dared make fun of him. How could they? Even if they hadn't seen exactly what Nic and I had gone through, they'd felt it through our bond, that was for sure. "Mother Nature," Anubis repeated softly.

"That's right," I said as I put the loofah aside and rinsed Nic off with a removable showerhead at the same time Anubis rinsed my hair for me. "That's why this isn't a somber occasion. We accomplished something today, something ... miraculous." I huffed out a long breath and my eyes caught on the strange green-black rose tattoo on my wrist. When I lifted it up to examine it, Nic lifted his own wrist and I saw that he had a matching symbol etched into his skin that I hadn't noticed before.

“This isn't a sober occasion,” I repeated, even as I stared at Nic and tried to puzzle out what the hell had just happened. “So let's clean off and climb into bed. In the morning, we'll figure out what to do next.”

Now that Nikolina was involved, things would be a little different. But I knew she'd trust my words about the traitor. I was her Alpha-Heir and she'd trained me well. She might not treat me the way other mothers treated their daughters, but she knew she could trust me. Right now, Nikolina and her betas as well as Lana and Leslie, would be hiding the rescued wolves in a safe location, a spot th/tat none of us even knew about.

And somewhere out there, there was a witch who was no longer the Maiden, returning bloody and tired to her coven, stripped of her title but twice as powerful as she'd been before. There was a faerie girl sharing a hotel room with a vampire princess … and there was a girl named Zara Wolf, standing in a hot shower with her seven mates.

“That sounds like a good idea,” Silas said softly, and we finished our shower in quiet companionship, the mood lifting … just a little.

Afterwards, Anubis and Tidus grabbed snacks and beers from the kitchen and met the rest of us upstairs. I put on a movie, and we all snuggled up close together, one big puppy pile of pack that didn't care that we were naked, that sex was now a part of our relationship, that there were tensions between the boys.

For that one night, we slept together in peace and harmony, cleaned of blood, our dreams taking us to a world where our wolves ran wild and free through the forest, where our souls were emptied of pain.

Tomorrow, we'd pick up our swords, our knives, shift our claws, and we'd see what Majka could teach me, what Julian would say, if there was war in our future.

But for now, we slept, and we held each other, and we dreamed like werewolves.

Not human, not wolf, neither and both.

Werewolf.

To Be Continued . . .

Pack Obsidian Gold

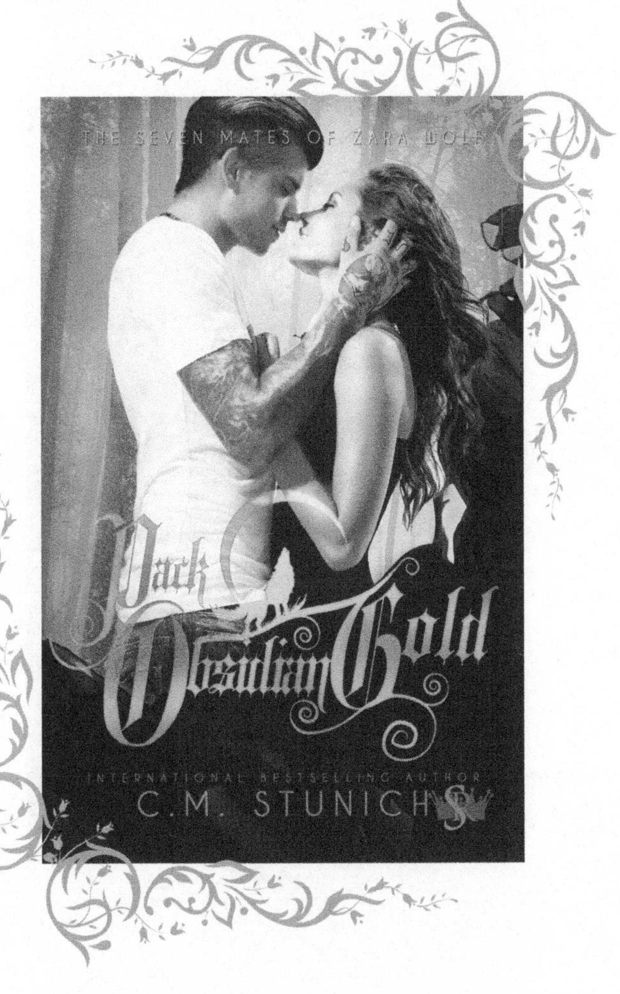

The Seven Mates of Zara Wolf Series
Book Three

Allison's Adventures in Underland

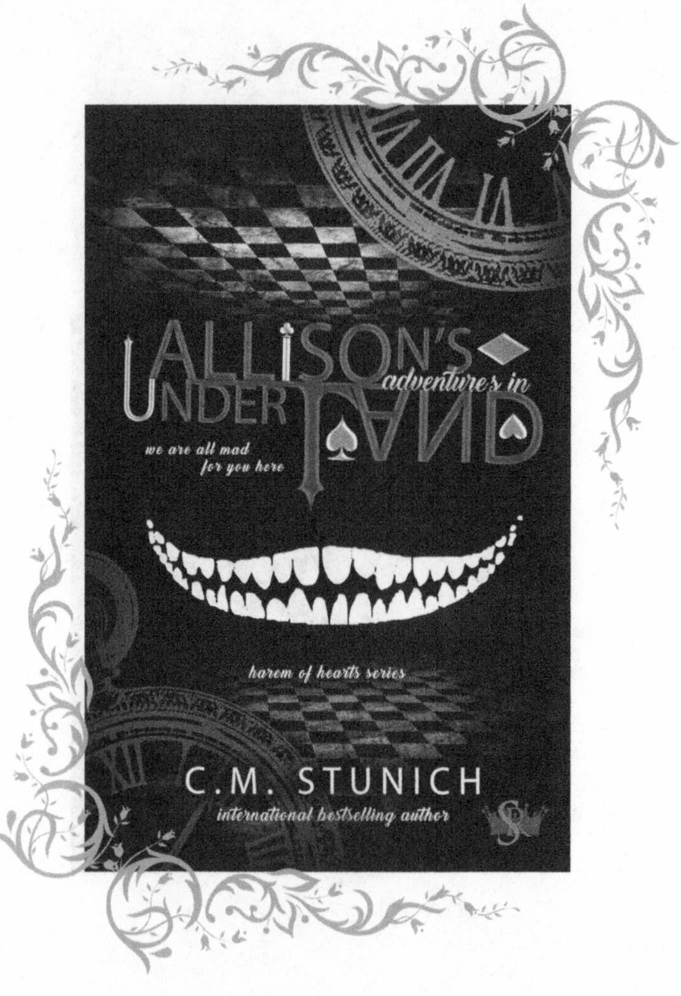

We are all mad for you here.

The Nine

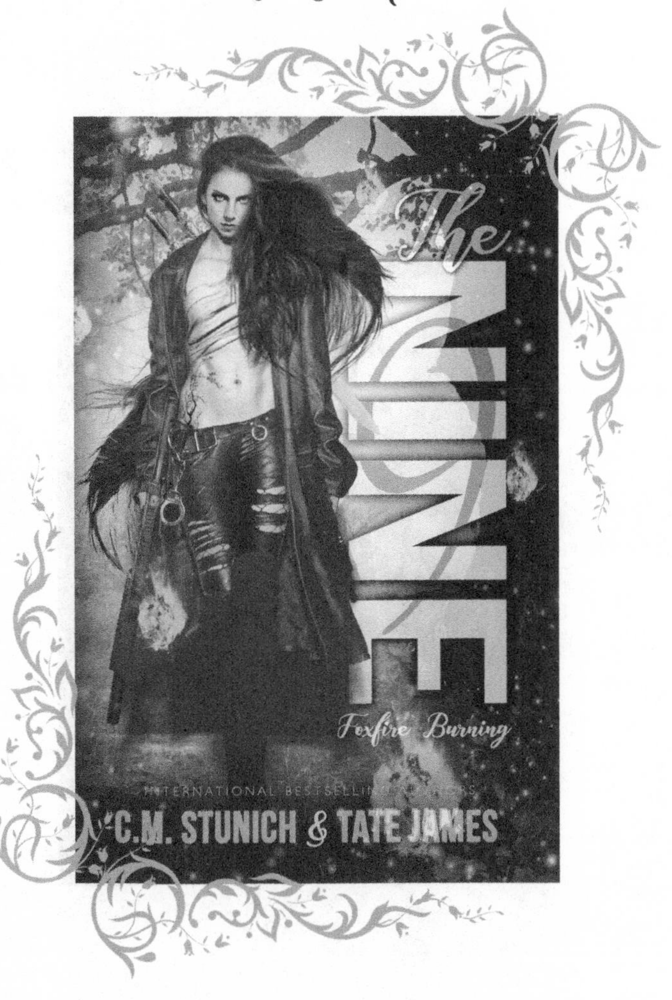

Epic Kitsune Urban Fantasy.

I Was Born Ruined

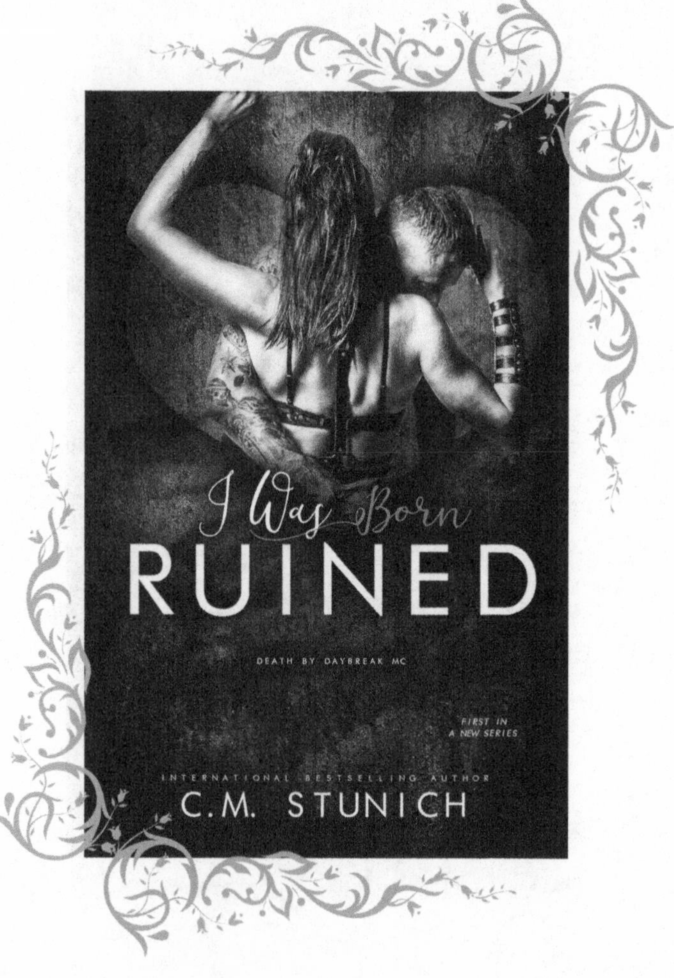

Four dangerous motorcycle club men, all hers.

Spirited

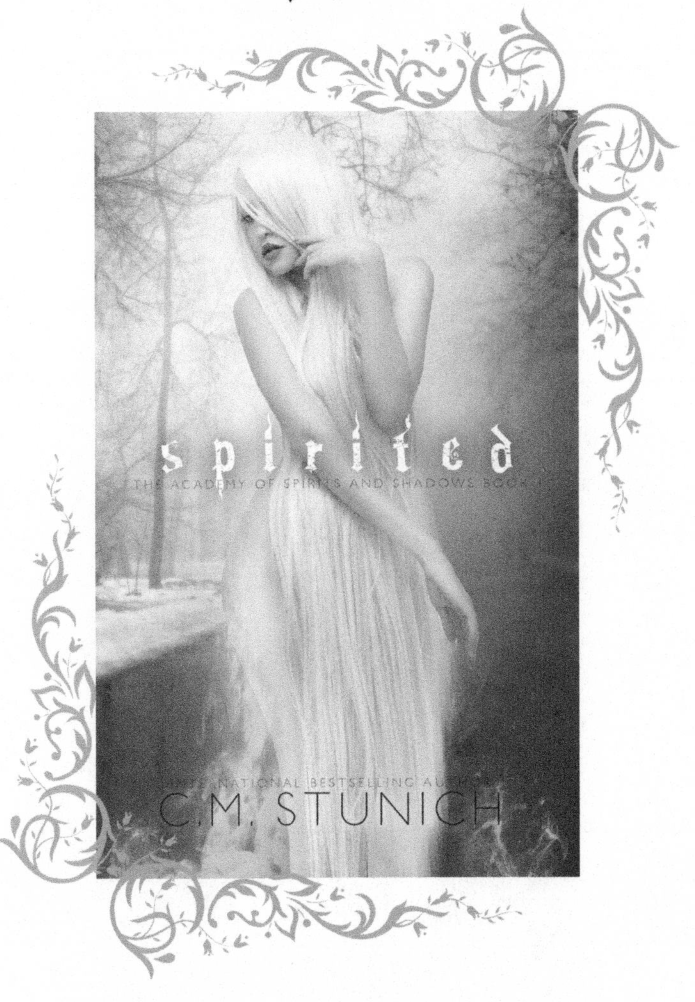

An academy dedicated to magic; a girl with six ghostly lovers.

Turn the page for an excerpt of chapter one.

Excerpt from Spirited

CHAPTER ONE
Brynn

The instrument of my own destruction loomed above me, casting a long shadow in the bloodred rays of a dying sun. Its crumbling facade was decorated with a morbid metaphor of a face—soulless eyes, a gaping mouth, tangled green locks. Okay, so I was exaggerating the broken windows, the front entrance with its missing doors, and the cluster of wild blackberries that had morphed into a monster of their own making, but come on: the former Grandberg Manor was bust.

"This is the place?" I asked, hoisting my equipment up on one shoulder and eyeing the crumbling old house with a raised brow. "It looks half-ready to collapse. You know me —if there's an even the slightest opportunity that I might trip, I will. Just be honest: am I going to fall straight through the floor?"

"Probably," Jasinda said, moving around me and over the twisted, rusted remains of the front gate. Once upon a time, this place was crawling with nobility from around the world, and its gardens … even the drawings were enough to make my mother's green thumb well, green with envy. "Air and I have a bet going on whether or not you'll make it out of here alive."

She thew a smirk over her shoulder at me and I pursed my lips.

Jasinda and Air were always making bets about me despite the fact that Air was the flubbing prince and shouldn't be making bets with anyone, let alone my handler. I had to admit though: if there was anyone around that was worth betting on, it was me.

First off, I was a half-angel which meant I could see spirits. And second, I was a half-human which meant those spirits actually deigned to communicate with me. A full-blooded angel was too haughty and highbrow to give any ghost the time of day, and a full-blooded human couldn't see one if they tried.

This special ability of mine did end up getting me into heaps of trouble. For example, there was that one time I followed a ghost straight into the queen's chambers and found her, um, indisposed with the head of the royal guard who, you know, also just happened to be my mother.

Then of course, there was the fact that I had the small, slight frame of my mother's desert dwelling ancestors but the wide, heavy span of wings from my father's side. Let's just be frank and say I toppled over a lot. Oh, and I ended up having long, in-depth conversations with people who weren't really people but were, in fact, very tricky ghosts. Even my first kiss had been with a spirit.

I took a deep breath of the cool, lavender scented air and followed after Jas, tripping and cursing in my own made up language.

"Go flub yourself," I growled at a thick tangle of blackberry that had gotten wrapped around my ankle. "You bleeding blatherer."

"Are you making words up again?" Jas said, parking her hands on her hips and sighing at me. "Can't you just say you bleeding bastard like everyone else? And don't even get me started on you using the work flub instead of fuc—"

"Hey!" I snapped, putting my palm over her lips with one hand and pointing at myself with the other. "Half-angel over here. Just hearing somebody use a word with an extreme negative connotation makes me lose a feather."

"Oh, please," Jas said, pushing my hand away from her full red lips and smirking at me as I tried to rub her makeup off on my breeches. "That's a myth and you know it. Air told me that when you were kids, he used to chase you around the castle saying damn and bastard and the like, just to see if you'd lose any feathers—you didn't."

I narrowed my eyes on her as she turned and headed up what was once an impressive flight of marble steps, now cracked and chipped like an old beggar's teeth. I shivered and followed after her, examining the red stain on my palm that stunk like copperberries. A lot of women painted their mouths with the stuff, but to me that fragrant floral scent was tinged with a metallic sting, like copper. Like blood. Thus, the name—copperberries.

As I hurried up the steps, I kept my eyes on the decaying black facade of the manor, all its intricate moldings and details stripped away by time and rain, the harsh winds that curled across this part of the kingdom in summer.

"Let's do a quick walkthrough and see if you can't sense any residual energies," Jas suggested as I set my black leather satchel on the floor and knelt beside it. The ground around me was littered with debris—leaves, twigs, bits of crumbling plaster, a dead mouse.

"Oh, that's flubbing sick," I whispered as I caught sight of the creature's spirit hovering nearby, its furred sides almost completely translucent as it took long, heaving breaths. Of course, the mouse didn't need to breathe anymore, but it didn't know that.

I pulled a dagger from the sheath on my belt—please Goddess, don't actually ask me to use this thing in combat—and prodded at the mouse's body with the jeweled hilt.

Fresh blood stained the white leather pommel and made me shiver.

"Jas," I started, because a long dead carcass was one thing, but a fresh one? Hell's bells—since Hell was an actual place it didn't count as a curse word so no lost feathers for me—but I hoped it was just a cat that had taken the rodent's life and not … something else.

"Brynn, you need to see this!" Jas shouted and I sighed, wiping the mouse's blood on the already dirty leg of my breeches and tucking it away. Before I stood up, I clasped the silver star hanging around my neck with one hand and reached out to touch the mouse's spirt with the other. The poor thing was too scared to even shy away, its soul becoming briefly corporeal as my fingers made contact with its fur.

"Goddess-speed and happy endings," I whispered as the

image of the mouse morphed and shivered, turning as silver as a beam of moonlight and fading away until there was nothing there but the warped and rotted boards of the old floor.

I stood up, leaving my satchel where it was on the ground and rubbing my shoulder as I followed the sound of Jasinda's voice. The road up to the manor was riddled with broken cobblestones, weeds, and the skeletons of long abandoned carriages. It was too rough for any sort of pack animal to make the trek, so we'd had to carry ourselves on foot, lugging all the equipment that a spirit whisperer—that's me—might need to exorcise a ghost or two or ten.

"Jassy?" I asked as I moved past the formal foyer with its double staircases, and down a long receiving hall that would've been used by servants in times past. The wallpaper was peeling like old skin, leaving behind water stained walls and flaky plaster. At some point, thieves had come in and stripped the old place of its wood moldings, sconces and chandeliers; they'd left nothing but a skeleton behind.

"In here!" she called out, drawing me through an empty archway where a swinging door might've once stood and into the kitchen. As I moved, I was conscious of keeping my wings tucked tightly against my back. My clumsiness was not limited to my feet. I was notorious among the castle staff for breaking things with the feathered black wings that graced my back. As a kid, they used to call me Pigeon Girl because I caused ten times as much damage to the royal halls as the flying rats that plagued the old stone building.

"What is it?" I asked as I leaned against the wall outside

a small servant's room—a tiny square that would've belonged to the head cook. "Jas, there was a mouse—"

"Flub mice," she said, only she didn't actually say flub but I wouldn't lose a feather even thinking about the F-word that famously rhymes with duck. As a half-angel, my powers were bound to the light goddess and she was a serious stickler for avoiding words with negative connotations. I supposed I couldn't blame her; the very words I spoke held power. The more positivity and light I imbued those words with, the more powerful I was. "Look at this, Brynn. There's a distinct spiritual signature written all over this room."

The room itself was so small that with the collapsed remains of a small bed and a sagging dresser, there wasn't space for us both. I waited for Jas to step out, pushing her long dark hair over her shoulder, sapphire blue eyes sparkling with a scholar's excitement.

"Brynn, this could be it," she said as I took a deep breath and stepped into the room. "Our big break."

Jas was always looking for that one case, that one unique spirit that we could exorcise that would prove our worth to the scholars at the Royal College. In just two weeks, I'd be turning twenty-one and that'd be it; that was the cut off date for acceptance into the prestigious training facility. It wasn't that Jas cared about the status of being a student there, or the potential for a high-ranking position after graduation, it was the library. Only students of the Royal College were permitted to use the vast, twisting hallways of the catacombs. There were books there that couldn't be found anywhere else—not to mention ancient artifacts, exemplary professors, and vast resources that could be used for research.

It was Jasinda's dream, even if it wasn't mine. I hoped she was right; I hoped this was it.

I stepped over a small hole in the floor and into the tiny windowless room.

As soon as I did, it hit me, the pressure of an angry spirit, bearing down on me with the cold burn of something long dead and waiting. Waves of icy winter chill tore across my skin like knives, despite the warm evening air that permeated the rest of the building. Whatever this was, it was powerful.

I grasped the silver star at my throat and closed my eyes.

"Haversey," I whispered, invoking the name of the light goddess.

If I were Jas, I knew what I'd be seeing: a girl shrouded in silver moonlight, her tanned skin pearlescent and shimmering, her hair as white as snow lifted in an unnatural breeze.

I opened my eyes slowly and bit back a gasp.

Every inch of the walls was covered in the word Hellim, the name of the dark god. What I had originally thought were decorative splotches on the wallpaper were actually his name, written in blood a thousand times over. It had been impossible to see in the dim half-light, but now that I had my second sight open, the letters glowed with a strong, angry spiritual signature.

I started to take a step back when my foot went through

the hole in the floor, and the rotting boards around me creaked and toppled into a black pit below.

"Brynn!"

Jas screamed my name as I fell through cold shadow and frost, hitting the soggy wet earth with a grunt and a crack of pain in my shoulder that almost immediately went numb. That was bad, really bad. Pain was one thing, but numbness meant that what'd just happened to me could be really serious.

I tried to stand up, but my arm gave out and I found myself lying in a mound of decaying wet leaves and dirt, the scent of rot thick and cloying in the air.

As I blinked to try and orient myself to the darkness, I felt a cold hand on my shoulder and a gust of icy breath at my ear.

When I turned, I found myself looking into the face of a handsome—and very angry—spirit.

His lips curved up in a smile meant to disarm me.

"Boo," he whispered as he reached out and pushed my dislocated shoulder back into place.

White-hot pain crashed over my vision and I passed out.

SIGN UP FOR A C.M. STUNICH

Sign up for an exclusive first look at the hottest new releases, contests, and exclusives from bestselling author C.M. Stunich and get *three free* eBooks as a thank you!

www.cmstunich.com

JOIN MY BOOK CLUB

Want to discuss what you've just read? Get exclusive teasers or meet special guest authors? Join my online book club on Facebook!

www.facebook.com/groups/thebookishbatcave

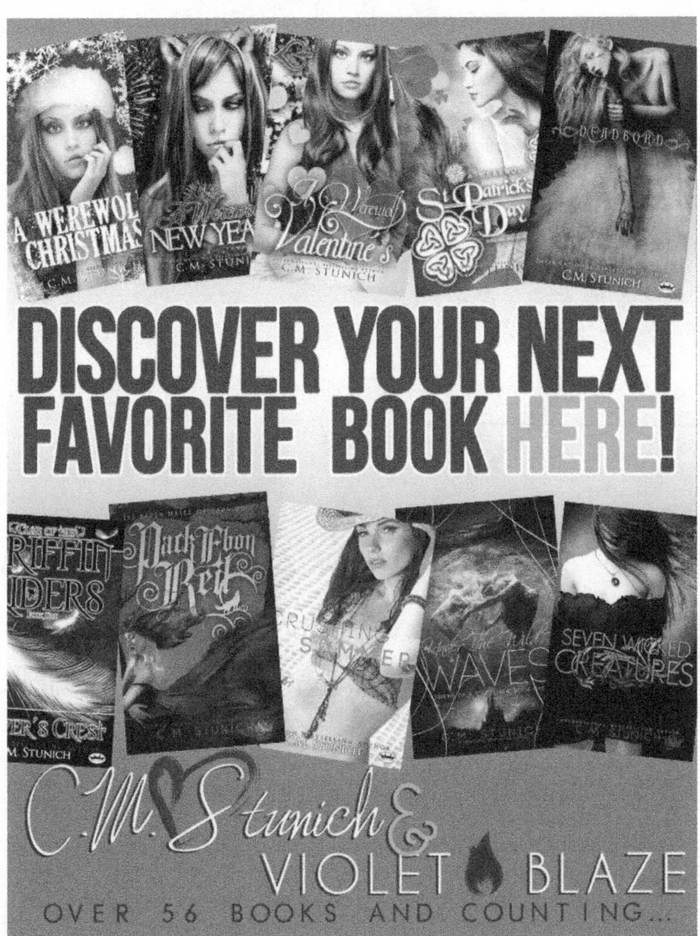

Discover your next five star read

in C.M. Stunich's (aka Violet Blaze's) collection and discover more kick-ass heroines, smoking hot heroes, and stories filled with wit, humor, and heart.

JOIN THE C.M. STUNICH NEWSLETTER – Get three free books just for signing up http://eepurl.com/DEsEf

TWEET ME ON TWITTER, BABE – Come sing the social media song with me https://twitter.com/CMStunich

SNAPCHAT WITH ME – Get exclusive behind the scenes looks at covers, blurbs, book signings and more http://www.snapchat.com/add/cmstunich

LISTEN TO MY BOOK PLAYLISTS – Share your fave music with me and I'll give you my playlists (I'm super active on here!) https://open.spotify.com/user/12101321503

FRIEND ME ON FACEBOOK – Okay, I'm actually at the 5,000 friend limit, but if you click the "follow" button on my profile page, you'll see way more of my killer posts https://facebook.com/cmstunich

LIKE ME ON FACEBOOK – Pretty please? I'll love you forever if you do! ;) https://facebook.com/cmstunichauthor & https://facebook.com/violetblazeauthor

CHECK OUT THE NEW SITE – (under construction) but it looks kick-a$$ so far, right? You can order signed books here! http://www.cmstunich.com

READ VIOLET BLAZE – Read the books from my hot as hellfire pen name, Violet Blaze http://www.violetblazebooks.com

SUBSCRIBE TO MY RSS FEED – Press that little orange button in the corner and copy that RSS feed so you can get all the latest updates http://www.cmstunich.com/blog

AMAZON, BABY – If you click the follow button here, you'll get an email each time I put out a new book. Pretty sweet, huh? http://amazon.com/author/cmstunich http://amazon.com/author/violetblaze

PINTEREST – Lots of hot half-naked men. Oh, and half-naked men. Plus, tattooed guys holding babies (who are half-naked) http://pinterest.com/cmstunich

INSTAGRAM – Cute cat pictures. And half-naked guys. Yep, that again. http://instagram.com/cmstunich

P.S. I heart the f*ck out of you! Thanks for reading! I love your faces.

<3 C.M. Stunich aka Violet Blaze